About

Fiona Brand lives in Zealand. Now that b continues to love writ life-changing time in which she met Christ, she has undertaken study for a Bachelor of Theology and has become a member of The Order of St. Luke, Christ's healing ministry.

USA Today bestselling author, **Trish Morey**, just loves happy endings. Now that her four daughters are (mostly) grown and off her hands having left the nest, Trish is rapidly working out that a real happy ending is when you downsize, end up alone with the guy you married and realise you still love him. There's a happy ever after right there. Or a happy new beginning! Trish loves to hear from her readers – you can email her at trish@trishmorey.com

Louise Fuller was a tomboy who hated pink and always wanted to be the prince. Not the princess! Now she enjoys creating heroines who aren't pretty pushovers but strong, believable women. Before writing for Mills & Boon, she studied literature and philosophy at university and then worked as a reporter on her local newspaper. She lives in Tunbridge Wells with her impossibly handsome husband, Patrick and their six children.

Australian Nights

December 2020
Longing for Summer

January 2021
Her Outback Fling

February 2021
Heat of the Night

March 2021
The Marriage Conquest

April 2021
Sun, Sea, Seduction

May 2021
Waves of Desire

Australian Nights: The Marriage Conquest

FIONA BRAND

TRISH MOREY

LOUISE FULLER

MILLS & BOON

All rights reserved including the right of reproduction in whole or in part in any form. This edition is published by arrangement with Harlequin Books S.A.

This is a work of fiction. Names, characters, places, locations and incidents are purely fictional and bear no relationship to any real life individuals, living or dead, or to any actual places, business establishments, locations, events or incidents. Any resemblance is entirely coincidental.

This book is sold subject to the condition that it shall not, by way of trade or otherwise, be lent, resold, hired out or otherwise circulated without the prior consent of the publisher in any form of binding or cover other than that in which it is published and without a similar condition including this condition being imposed on the subsequent purchaser.

® and TM are trademarks owned and used by the trademark owner and/or its licensee. Trademarks marked with ® are registered with the United Kingdom Patent Office and/or the Office for Harmonisation in the Internal Market and in other countries.

First Published in Great Britain 2021
by Mills & Boon, an imprint of HarperCollins*Publishers* Ltd,
1 London Bridge Street, London, SE1 9GF

www.harpercollins.co.uk

HarperCollins*Publishers*
1st Floor, Watermarque Building,
Ringsend Road, Dublin 4, Ireland

AUSTRALIAN NIGHTS: THE MARRIAGE CONQUEST
© 2021 Harlequin Books S.A.

A Perfect Husband © 2012 Fiona Gillibrand
Shackled to the Sheikh © 2015 Trish Morey
Kidnapped for the Tycoon's Baby © 2017 Louise Fuller

ISBN: 978-0-263-29946-5

MIX
Paper from
responsible sources
FSC™ C007454

This book is produced from independently certified FSC™ paper to ensure responsible forest management.

For more information visit: www.harpercollins.co.uk/green

Printed and bound in Spain
by CPI, Barcelona

A PERFECT HUSBAND

FIONA BRAND

For the Lord. Thank you.

"...each of the gates is a single pearl, and the street of the city is pure gold, transparent as glass."

Revelation 21:21

One

Dark hair twisted in a sleek, classic knot... Exotic eyes the shifting colors of the sea... A delicate curvy body that made him burn from the inside out...

A sharp rapping on the door of his Sydney hotel suite jerked Zane Atraeus out of a restless, dream-tossed sleep. Shielding his eyes from the glare of the morning sun, he shoved free of the huge silk-draped confection of a bed he'd collapsed into some time short of four that morning.

Pulling on the jeans he'd tossed over a chair, he dragged jet-lagged fingers through his tangled hair and padded to the door.

Memory punched back. An email Zane had found confirming that his half brother Lucas had purchased an engagement ring for a woman Zane could have sworn Lucas barely knew. *Lilah Cole: the woman Zane had secretly wanted for two years and had denied himself.*

His temper, which had been running on a short fuse ever since he had learned that not only was Lucas dating Lilah, he was planning on *marrying* her, ignited as he took in glittering chandeliers and turquoise-and-gold furnishings.

The overstuffed opulence was a far cry from the exotic but spare Mediterranean decor of his island home, Medinos. Instead of soothing him, the antiques and heavily swagged drapes only served to remind him that he had not been born to any of this. He would have to have a word with his new personal assistant, who clearly had a romantic streak.

Halfway across the sitting room the unmistakable sound of the front door lock disengaging made him stiffen.

Lucas Atraeus stepped into the room. Zane let out a self-deprecating breath.

Ten years ago, in L.A., it would have been someone breaking in, but this was Australia and his father's company, the mega wealthy Atraeus Group, owned the hotel so, of course, Lucas had gotten a key. "Ever heard of a phone?"

Closing the door behind him, Lucas tossed a key card down on the hall table. "I phoned, you didn't answer. Remember Lilah?"

The reason Zane was in Sydney instead of in Florida doing his job as the company "fixer" and closing a crucial land deal that had balanced on a knife's edge for the past week? "Your new fiancée." The tantalizing beauty who had almost snared him into a reckless night of passion two years ago. "Yeah, I remember."

Lucas looked annoyed. "I haven't asked her yet. How did you find out?"

Zane's jaw tightened at the confirmation. "My new P.A. was your old P.A., remember?" Which was why Zane had chanced across the internet receipt for Lucas's latest purchase. Apparently Elena was still performing the role of personal shopper for his brother in her spare time.

"Ahh. Elena." He glanced around the room. Comprehension gleamed in his eyes.

Now definitely in a bad mood, Zane turned on his heel and strolled in the direction of the suite's kitchenette. A large ornately gilded mirror threw his reflection back at him—darkly tanned skin, broad shoulders and a lean, muscled torso bisected by a tracery of scars. Three silver studs, the reminder of a misspent youth, glinted in one ear.

In the lavish elegance of the suite, he looked uncivilized, barbaric and faintly sinister, as different from his two classically handsome half brothers as the proverbial chalk was from cheese. Not something he had ever been able to help with the genes he'd inherited from the rough Salvatore side of his family, and the inner scars he had developed as a homeless kid roaming the streets of L.A.

He found a glass, filled it with water from the dispenser in the fridge door and drank in long, smooth swallows. The cold water failed to douse the intense, unreasoning jealousy that seared him every time he thought of Lucas and Lilah, the picture-perfect couple.

An engagement.

His reaction to the idea was as fierce and surprising as it had been when he had discovered Elena admiring a picture of the engagement ring.

The empty glass hit the kitchen counter with a controlled click. "I didn't think Lilah was your type."

As gorgeous and ladylike as Ambrosi Pearls's head jewelry designer was, in Zane's opinion, Lilah was too efficiently, calculatingly focused on hunting for a well-heeled husband.

Two years ago, when they had first met at the annual ball of a charity for homeless children—of which he was the patron—he had witnessed the smooth way Lilah had targeted her escort's wealthy boss. Even armored by the formidable depth of betrayal in his past, Zane had been oddly entranced by the businesslike gleam in her eyes. He had not been able to resist the temptation to rescue the hapless older man and spoil her pitch.

Unfortunately, things had gotten out of hand when he and Lilah had ended up alone in a private reception room and he had given into temptation and kissed her. One kiss had led to another, sparking a conflagration that had threatened to engulf them both. Given that he had been irritated by Lilah's agenda, that she was not the kind of woman he was usually attracted to, his loss of control still perplexed him. If his previous personal assistant hadn't found them at a critical moment, he would have made a very big mistake.

Lucas, who had followed him into the kitchen, scribbled a number on the back of a business card and left it on the counter. "Lilah has agreed to be my date at Constantine's wedding. I'm leaving for Medinos in a couple of hours. I was going to arrange for her to fly in the day before the wedding, but since you're here—" Lucas frowned. "By the way, why are you here? I thought you were locked into negotiations."

"I'm taking a couple of days." A muscle pulsed along Zane's jaw.

Lucas shrugged and opened the fridge door.

The shelves were packed with an array of fresh fruit, cheeses, pâtés and juices. Absently, Zane noted his assistant had also stocked the fridge with chocolate-dipped strawberries.

"Good move." Lucas examined a bottle of very expensive French champagne then replaced it. "Nothing like making the vendor think we're cooling off to fast-track a sale. Mind if I have something to eat? I missed breakfast."

Probably too busy shuttling between women to think about food. The last Zane had heard Lucas had also been having a wild "secret" affair with Carla Ambrosi, the public relations officer for Ambrosi and the sister of the woman their brother, Constantine, was marrying.

"Oysters." Lucas lifted a brow. "Having someone in?"

Zane stared grimly at the platter of oysters on the half shell, complete with rock salt and lemon wedges. "Not as far as I know."

Unless his new assistant had made some arrangement.

If she was helping Lucas with his engagement during her

lunch breaks, anything was possible. "Help yourself to the food, the juice…"

My girl.

The thought welled up out of the murk of his subconscious and slipped neatly past all of the reasons that commitment could never work for him. Especially, with a woman like Lilah.

Since the age of nine, relationships had been a difficult area.

After being abandoned by his extravagant, debt-ridden mother on a number of occasions while she had flitted from marriage to marriage, he had definite trust issues with women, especially those on the hunt for wealthy husbands.

Marriage was out.

Lucas took out the bowl of strawberries and surveyed the tempting fruit.

"It doesn't bother you that Lilah's on the hunt for a husband?"

An odd expression flitted across Lucas's face. "Actually, I respect her straightforward approach. It's refreshing."

Despite every attempt to relax, Zane's fingers curled into fists. *So Lucas had fallen under her spell, too.*

Try as he might, now that Zane had acknowledged that Lilah was his, he could not dismiss the thought. With every second that passed, the concept became more and more stubbornly real.

It was a fact that for the two years following the incendiary passion that had almost ended in lovemaking, he had been tormented by the knowledge that Lilah could have been his.

He had controlled the desire to have a reckless fling with Lilah. He had controlled himself.

Lucas selected the largest, plumpest strawberry. "Lilah has a fear of flying. I was hoping, since you're piloting the company jet that you could take her with you to Medinos when you leave."

Zane's jaw tightened. Everything in him rejected Lucas's

easy assertion that Zane would tamely fall into place and hand-deliver Lilah to his bed.

He fixed on the first part of Lucas's statement. In all the time he had known Lilah she had never told *him* she had a fear of flying. Somehow that fact was profoundly irritating. "Just out of curiosity, how long have you known Lilah?" Lucas did spend time in Sydney, but not as much as Zane. He had never heard Lilah so much as mention Lucas's name.

"A week, give or take."

Zane went still inside. He knew his brother's schedule. They had all had to adjust their plans when Roberto Ambrosi, a member of a once-powerful and wealthy Medinian family, had died. The Atraeus Group had been forced to protect its interests by moving on the almost bankrupted Ambrosi Pearls. A hostile takeover to recover huge debts racked up by Roberto had been averted when Constantine had stunned them all by resurrecting his engagement to Sienna Ambrosi. The impending marriage had gone a long way toward healing the acrimonious rift that had developed between the two families when Roberto had leveraged money on the basis of the first engagement.

He knew that, apart from a couple of flying visits in the last couple of weeks—one to attend Roberto's funeral—that Lucas had been committed offshore. He had only arrived in Sydney the previous day.

Zane had spent most of the previous week in Sydney in order to attend the annual general meeting of the charity. As usual, Lilah, who helped out with the art auctions, had been polite, reserved, the tantalizing, high-priced sensuality that was clearly reserved for the future Mr. Cole on ice. She had not mentioned Lucas. "Why not take Lilah with *you*?"

Lucas seemed inordinately interested in selecting a second strawberry. "It's a gray area."

Realization dawned. Lilah had not been subtle about her quest of finding a husband. He had just never seen Lucas as a candidate for an arranged marriage. "This is a first date."

A trace of emotion flickered in Lucas's gaze. "I needed someone on short notice. As it happens, after running a background check, I think Lilah is perfect for me. She's talented, attractive, she's got a good business head on her shoulders, she's even a—"

"What about Carla?"

Lucas dropped the ripe berry as if it had seared his fingertips.

The final piece of the puzzle fell into place. Zane realized what the odd look in Lucas's eyes had been just moments ago: desperation. Hot outrage surged through him. "You're still involved with Carla."

"How did you know? No, don't tell me. Elena." Lucas put the bowl of strawberries back in the fridge and closed the door. "Carla and I are over."

But only just.

Suddenly the instant relationship with Lilah made sense. When Sienna married Constantine, Carla would practically be family. If it came out that Lucas had been sleeping with Carla, intense pressure would be applied. Under the tough exterior, when it came to women, Lucas was vulnerable.

He was using Lilah as a buffer, insurance that Carla, who had a reputation for flamboyant scenes, would not try to publicly force him to formalize their secret affair with a marriage proposal.

That meant that love did not come into the equation.

If Lucas genuinely wanted Lilah, Zane would walk away, however that was not the case. Lucas, who had once been in the untenable position of having a girlfriend die in a car crash after they had argued about the secret abortion she'd had, was using her to avert an unpleasant situation. As calculating as Lilah was with relationships, she did not deserve to be caught in the middle of a showdown between Lucas and Carla.

Relief eased some of his fierce tension. He didn't think Lilah had had time to sleep with Lucas yet. Somehow that fact was very important. "Okay. I'll do it."

Lucas looked relieved. "You won't regret it."

Zane wasn't so sure.

He wondered if Lucas had any inkling that he had just placed a temptation Zane had doggedly resisted for over two years directly in his path.

Two

Heart pounding at the step she was taking, her first bona fide risk in twelve years of carefully managed, featureless and fruitless dating, Lilah Cole boarded the sleek private jet that belonged to Ambrosi Pearls's new owner, The Atraeus Group.

The nervy anticipation that had buoyed her as she had made her way through passport control ebbed as the pretty blonde stewardess, Jasmine, seated her.

Placing the soft white leather tote bag that went with her white jeans and comfy, oversized white shirt on the floor, Lilah dug out the discreet, white leather-bound folder she had bought with her. She had been braced for another stress-filled encounter with the dark and edgily dangerous Zane Atraeus, the youngest and wildest of the Atraeus brothers, but she was the sole occupant of the luxurious cabin.

Fifteen minutes later, with the noise from the jet engines reaching a crescendo and a curtain of gray rain blotting out much of the view from her tiny window, Lilah was still the only passenger.

She squashed the ridiculous idea that she was in any way disappointed as she fastened her seat belt with fingers that were not entirely steady.

Flying was not her favorite pastime; she was not a natural risk taker. Like her approach to relationships, she preferred to keep her feet on the ground. A stubborn part of her brain couldn't ignore the concept of all that space between the aircraft and the earth's surface. To compound the problem, the weather forecast was for violent thunder and lightning.

As the jet taxied through the sweeping rain, Lilah ignored the in-flight safety video and concentrated on the one thing she *could* control. Flipping open the folder, she studied the profiles she had compiled.

Cole women had a notorious record for falling victim to the *coup de foudre*—the clap of thunder—for falling passionately and disastrously for the wrong man then literally being left holding the baby. Aware that she possessed the same creative, passionate streak that ran through both her artistic and bohemian mother and grandmother, Lilah had developed a system for avoiding The Mistake.

It was a blueprint for long-term happiness, a wedding plan. She had found that writing down the steps she needed to take to achieve the relationship she wanted somehow demystified the whole process, making it seem not such a leap in the dark.

When she did eventually give herself to a man, she was confident it would be in a committed relationship, not some wild fling. She wanted marriage, babies, the stable, controlled environment she had craved as a child.

She was determined that any children she had would have two loving parents, not one stressed and strained beyond her limits.

Over the last three years, despite interviewing an exhaustive number of candidates, she had not managed to find a man who met her marriage criteria and appealed to her on the all-important physical level. Scent in particular had proved to be a formidable barrier to identifying someone with whom she could have an intimate relationship. It was not that the men she had interviewed had smelled bad, just that in some subtle way they had not smelled *right*. However, things were finally taking a positive turn.

Lilah studied the notes she had made on her new boss, Lucas Atraeus, and a small number of other men, and the points system she had developed based on a matchmaking website's recommendations. She spent an enjoyable few minutes reviewing Lucas's good points.

On paper he was the most perfect man she had ever met. He was electrifyingly good-looking and used a light cologne that she didn't mind. He possessed the kind of dark, dangerous features that had proved to be an unfortunate weakness of hers and yet, in terms of a future husband, he ticked every box of her list.

For the first time she had found a man who was her type and yet he was safe, steady, reliable. The situation was a definite win-win.

She should be thrilled that he had asked her to a family wedding. This date, despite its risky nature, was the most positive she'd had in years and, at the age of twenty-nine, her biological clock was ticking.

She didn't know Lucas well. They had only met in the context of work over the past few days, with a "business" lunch at a nearby cafe tossed in, during which he had told her that not only did he need an escort for his brother's wedding, but that he was looking for a relationship with a view to marriage.

Like her, she didn't think Lucas had succumbed to any kind of intense physical attraction. He preferred to take a more measured approach.

If it were possible to control her emotions and fall in love with Lucas, she had already decided she would do it.

She checked her watch and frowned. They were leaving a little earlier than scheduled. If the pilot had only waited a few more minutes, Zane might have made it.

She squashed another whisper of disappointment and

snapped the window shutter closed. Witnessing the small jet launching itself into the dark, turbulent center of the storm was something she did not need to see.

The liftoff was bumpy. During the steep ascent, wind buffeted the jet and lightning flickered through the other windows of the cabin. When they finally leveled out, Lilah's nerves were stretched taut. She had taken a sedative before she had left her apartment, but so far it had failed to have any effect.

The stewardess, who had retreated to a separate compartment, reappeared and offered her a drink. With the cabin to herself, sleeping seemed the best option, so Lilah took another sedative. According to her doctor, one should have worked; two would definitely knock her out.

She was rereading Lucas's compatibility quotient, which was extremely high, her lids drooping, when a heavy crack of thunder shook the small jet. Lightning flashed. In that instant the door to the cockpit popped open. Zane Atraeus, tall, sleekly broad-shouldered and dressed in somber black, was framed in the searing flicker of light.

The jet lurched; the folder flew off her lap. The clasp sprang open as it hit the floor, scattering loose sheets. Lilah barely noticed. As always, her artist's eye was riveted. Zane's golden skin and chiseled face—which she had shamelessly, secretly, painted for the past two years—could have been lifted straight out of a Dalmasio oil. Even the imperfections, the subversive glint of the studs in his lobe, the faint disruption to the line of his nose, as if it had once been broken, were somehow... perfect.

She blinked as Zane strolled toward her. Her vision readjusted to the warm glow of the cabin lights. Until Zane had moved, she had not been entirely convinced that he was real. She thought she could have been caught up in one of the vivid, unsettling dreams that had disturbed her sleep ever since The Regrettable Episode two years ago.

Unlike the temporary effect of the lightning flash on her

vision, the events of that night had been indelibly seared into her consciousness. "I thought you missed the flight."

His steady dark gaze made her stomach tighten. "I never miss when I'm the pilot."

Aware that the contents of the folder had spilled into the aisle, and that the topmost sheet which held the glaringly large title, *The Wedding Plan,* was clearly visible, Lilah lunged forward in an attempt to regather the incriminating sheets. Her seat belt held her pinned. By the time she had the buckle unfastened, Zane had collected both the folder and the loose sheets.

Her cheeks burned as he straightened. She was certain he had read some of the contents, enough to get the gist of what they were about. She took the sheets and stuffed them back into the folder. "I didn't know you could fly."

"It's not something I advertise."

Unlike the lavish parties he regularly attended and the endless stream of gorgeous models he escorted. Although, flying did fit with his love of extreme sports: diving, kitesurfing and snowboarding, to name a few. Zane had a well-publicized love for anything that involved adrenaline.

It occurred to Lilah, as she jammed the folder in her tote bag, out of sight, that she didn't know what Lucas liked to do in his spare time. She must make the effort to find out.

Zane shrugged out of his jacket and tossed it over the arm of the seat across the aisle. "How long have you been afraid of flying?"

Lilah tore her gaze from the snug fit of his black T-shirt and the muscular swell of tanned biceps. She was certain that beyond an intoxicating whiff of sandalwood she could detect the scent of his skin.

Her blush deepened as she was momentarily flung back to the night of The Episode. Zane had suggested they go to an empty reception room so they could indulge their mutual passion for art by studying the oils displayed on the walls.

She couldn't remember much about the garish abstracts. She would never forget the moment Zane had pulled her close.

The clean, masculine scent of his skin and the exotic undernote of sandalwood had filled her nostrils, making her head spin. When he had kissed her, his taste had filled her mouth.

Somehow they had ended up on a wide, comfortable couch. At some point the bodice of her dress had drifted to her waist, a detail that should have alarmed her. Zane had taken one breast in his mouth and her whole body had coiled unbearably tight. She could remember clutching at his shoulders, a flash of dizzying, heated pleasure, the room shimmering out of focus.

If the door hadn't popped open at that moment and Zane's date, who was also his previous personal assistant, a gorgeous redhead called Gemma, hadn't walked in, Lilah shuddered to think what would have happened next. She had dragged her bodice up and clambered off the couch. By the time she had found her clutch, which had ended up underneath the couch, Zane had shrugged into his jacket. After a clipped good-night, he had left with Gemma.

The echoing silence after the heady, intimate passion had stung. He had not suggested they meet again, which had put The Episode in its horrifying context.

Zane had not wanted a relationship; he had just wanted an interlude. Sex. He had probably thought they had been on the verge of a one night stand, that she was *easy*.

Embarrassingly, she *had* forgotten every relationship rule she had rigidly stuck to for the twelve years she had been dating.

Zane walking out so quickly then never bothering to follow up with a telephone call or text had been a blessing. It had confirmed what she had both read about him and discovered firsthand—that no matter how attractive, he could not be trusted in a relationship. If he couldn't commit to a phone call, it was unlikely he would commit to marriage.

Another shuddering crash of thunder jerked her back to the present.

Aware that Zane was waiting for an answer, she busied herself fastening her seat belt. "I've been afraid of flying forever."

Instead of sitting where he'd slung his jacket, Zane lowered himself into the seat next to hers.

She stiffened as he pried her hand off the armrest. "What are you doing?"

His fingers curled warmly through hers. "Holding your hand. Tried-and-true remedy."

Nervous tension, along with the tingling heat of his touch, zinged through her at the skin-on-skin contact. There was something distinctly forbidden about holding hands with Zane Atraeus.

Illegitimate and wild, according to the tabloids, Zane had been the instant ruination of hundreds of women, and promised to be the ruination of even more in the future. She had the shattering firsthand knowledge of exactly how that ruination was achieved.

She flexed her fingers, but his hold didn't loosen. "Shouldn't you be in the cockpit?"

"Flight deck. There's a copilot, Spiros. He doesn't need me yet."

Her stomach clenched as she was suddenly reminded that they were twenty-eight thousand feet above the ground. "How long is the flight?"

"Twenty hours, give or take. We land in Singapore to refuel. If you don't like flying, why are you going to Medinos?"

Trying to arrange her future with a steady, reliable husband who would not leave her. Trying to avoid the Cole women's regrettable tendency to fall victim to the *coup de foudre*.

Her head started to swim, and it was not just the dizzying effect of the sandalwood. She remembered that she had taken two sedatives. "Trying to get a life. I'm twenty-nine."

She blinked. She was beginning to feel as if she was swimming in molasses. Had she actually told him her age?

"Twenty-nine doesn't seem so old to me."

She smothered a yawn and frowned at the defensive note in his voice.

"What did you take?"

Her lids slid closed. She gave him the name of the sedative.

"They'll knock you out. I can remember having them as a kid. After my father found me in L.A., we flew to Medinos. I was a handful. I didn't like flying, either."

Curiosity kept her on the surface of sleep, caught in the net of his deep, cool voice and fascinated by the dichotomy of his character. She had read his story on the charity website. One of the things she admired about Zane was that he happily revealed his past in order to help homeless kids.

"Put your head on my shoulder if you want."

The quiet offer sent a warning thrill through her. She considered leaning against the window, but the thought that the shutter might slide open and she would catch a view clear down to the ground was not pleasant. "No, thank you." She struggled to stay upright. "You're nicer than I thought."

"Tell me," he muttered, "I'm curious. You've known me for two years. How did you think I would be?"

Her lids flickered open. Exactly how he had been the night of the ball. Dangerous, sexy. *Hot.*

With an effort of will, she controlled her mind, which had shot off on a very wrong tangent. Zane had probably been in intimate situations with more women than he could count. She doubted he would even remember how close they had come to making love. Or that she had actually—

She cut short that disturbing thought and searched for something polite to say. As an Atraeus, Zane was one of her employers now. She would have to adjust to the new dynamic.

Her stomach tensed at a thought she had cheerfully glossed over before. If she and Lucas married, their relationship would be even closer; he would be her brother-in-law. "Uh—for a start, I didn't think you even liked me."

"Was that after what happened on the couch or before?"

The flashback to the sensations that had flooded her that night was electrifying. From the knowing gleam in Zane's gaze, she was abruptly certain he knew exactly what had happened.

Embarrassed heat warmed her cheeks. He had been lying on top of her at the time. She would be naive to consider that he had not noticed that she had lost control and actually had an orgasm.

He had to know also that if Gemma hadn't turned up dangling car keys and making them jump guiltily apart, that she had been on the verge of making an even bigger mistake. "I'm surprised you remember."

"Lucas won't marry you."

The sudden change of topic jerked her lids open. The dark fire burning in Zane's eyes almost made her forget what she was about to say. "Lucas isn't the only one with a choice."

"Choose someone else."

Lilah's heart slammed against the wall of her chest. For a split second, she'd had the crazy thought that Zane had been about to say, "Choose *me*."

From an early age she had discovered that men liked the way she looked. Something in the slant of her eyes, the curve of her cheekbones, the shape of her mouth, spelled sexual allure. On occasion attraction had spilled over into an uncomfortable fascination, although she had never thought that Zane Atraeus would find her more than ordinarily attractive.

She dragged in a lungful of air and tried to deny the heart-pounding knowledge that behind the grim tone Zane Atraeus really did want her. "What gives you the right—?"

"This."

Zane bent toward her, his head dipped. Her pulse rate rocketed.

For two years she had tortured herself about her loss of control. Now, finally, she was being offered the chance to examine what, exactly, had gone wrong.

She caught another enticing whiff of clean skin and exotic cologne. Dimly, she noted that the concept of her ruination had receded, a dangerous sign, although she was still in control. She had time to shift in her seat. If she wanted she could turn her head—

Warm fingers gripped her chin. The pressure of his mouth on hers almost stopped her heart.

Suddenly, the electrical hum every time he looked at her coalesced into stunning truth. The double whammy of her ticking biological clock combined with prolonged celibacy was the reason she was having such a difficult time controlling her responses to Zane.

Relief surged through her. She didn't know why she hadn't thought about that two years ago. It was the logical explanation. Zane had caught her at a vulnerable moment at the charity ball. She simply hadn't had the resources to resist him.

Jerking back from the seductive softness of the kiss, Lilah gulped in air.

The experience had been so riveting that the harder she had tried to suppress the memories, the more aggressively they had surfaced—in her dreams, her painting.

She had to get a grip on herself. She could not afford to take him seriously. According to the tabloids, the youngest Atraeus brother was the dark side of the mega wealthy Atraeus family, wild and dangerous to know, the bad as opposed to the good.

Which only went to prove that her judgment when it came to men was no better than her mother's or her grandmother's before her.

A little wildly she decided that the attraction was no bigger a deal for Zane than it had been two years ago. But that didn't change the disturbing knowledge that, if anything, she was in an even more vulnerable position now. The sensations already coursing through her body had the potential to destroy the future she had mapped out for herself.

She could not let that happen.

She was strong-willed. She had steered clear of intense emotions and casual flings all of her adult life. She was not going to mess up now.

With a younger man.

Zane was twenty-four, twenty-five at most, and with no sign of tempering his fast, edgy lifestyle with the encumbrances of a wife and family. He could say what he liked about his brother, but on paper, Lucas *was* perfect. He was older, more mature, ready to commit and without the wild reputation.

Those minutes on the couch with Zane and the experience of losing control and almost giving herself to a man who had demonstrated that he did not care for her had been salutary.

She knew the danger of her weakness now. On top of the healthy sex drive that came with her Cole genes, her biological clock was ticking loudly in both ears.

The thought that Zane could make her pregnant sent a hot flash through her that momentarily welded her to the seat before she managed to dismiss the notion.

Zane was not husband material. All she had to do was ignore the magnetic power of the attraction and her raging hormones, ignore the destructive impulse to throw her wedding plan away.

And throw herself beneath Zane's naked body.

Three

After a formal family dinner at the Atraeus family's Medinian castello the following evening, Lilah excused herself from the table while coffee was being served. Lucas had left some twenty minutes earlier, during dessert. His defection had been no great surprise because through the course of the evening she had become grimly certain that he was involved with another woman.

After obtaining directions from one of the kitchen staff, she paused by the door to Lucas's private suite. Stiffening her shoulders against the chill of the Mediterranean fortress walls, she rapped on the imposing door.

Lean brown fingers manacled her wrist. "I wouldn't go in there if I were you."

Lilah spun, shocked by the deep, cool voice and the knowledge that Zane had left the dinner table and followed her.

Snatching her wrist back, she rubbed at the bare skin, which still tingled and burned from his grip.

She dragged her gaze from his overlong jet-black hair and

the trio of studs glinting in one lobe. An unwanted surge of awareness added to the tension that had gripped her ever since she had arrived at the castello that evening and seen Lucas in the arms of Carla Ambrosi.

Lucas and Carla had a short but well-publicized past, which Lilah had mistakenly believed to be invented media hype. To further complicate things, Carla was Lilah's immediate boss.

Zane indicated the closed door. "Haven't you figured it out yet? Lucas is…busy."

The startling notion that, beneath the casual facade, Zane was quietly angry was shattered by the distant sound of laughter and the tap of high heels. More guests leaving the dining table, no doubt in search of one of the castello's bathrooms.

Suddenly, the stunning risk Lilah had taken in traveling thousands of miles for a first date with an extremely wealthy man whose love life was of interest to the tabloids came back to haunt her. He had fulfilled all of the criteria of her system. Now things were going disastrously wrong.

Zane jerked his head in the direction of the approaching guests. "I take it you don't want to be discovered knocking on Lucas's bedroom door?"

A wave of embarrassed heat decimated the chill. "No."

"Finally, some sense." Zane's fingers curled around her wrist again.

The startling intimacy of the hold sent another tingling jolt through her. A split second later, heart pounding with nerves, she found herself crushed against Zane's side and flattened against the cold stone of an alcove. She inhaled, bracing herself against the effect of the sandalwood and the sudden, nervous desire to laugh.

As unpleasant as the evening had been she couldn't suppress a small thrill that Zane had come to her rescue. Now they were hiding like a couple of kids.

Zane leaned out and peered around a corner. When he settled back into place she discovered that she had missed the warmth of his body.

His dark gaze touched on hers. "What I don't get is why Lucas asked you."

Lilah stiffened at the implication that she was the last person Lucas should have asked to partner him at a family wedding.

Determinedly, she stamped on the soft core of hurt that had haunted her since she was a kid—that her illegitimate birth and the poverty of her background made her less than respectable. "You certainly know how to make a girl feel special."

He frowned. "That wasn't what I meant."

"Don't worry." She dragged her gaze free from the dangerous, too-knowing sympathy in his. "I have no problems with the reality check."

She just wished she had thought things through before she had left home. Labeled "Catch of the Year" in a prominent women's magazine, Lucas *had* been too good to be true.

Somewhere in the distance a door snapped shut, cutting off the sound of footsteps and laughter. The abrupt return to silence made Lilah doubly aware of the masculine heat emanating from Zane's body and that the pale pearlized silk of her gown suddenly seemed too thin, the scooped neckline too revealing.

Hot color flooded her cheeks as the stressed uncertainty that had driven her to go in search of Lucas, and the truth, gave way to the searing memory of the kiss on the flight out.

The sedatives she had taken had kicked in shortly afterward. She had not seen Zane again until they had landed in Singapore, where two more passengers, clients of The Atraeus Group, had boarded the jet. Courtesy of the extra passengers, the rest of the flight had been uneventful. During the customs procedures, aware that Zane had been keeping tabs on her, she had managed to separate herself from him and had taken a taxi to her hotel.

Zane checked the corridor again. "All clear, and your reputation intact."

"Unfortunately, my reputation is already shredded."

That was the risk she had accepted in traveling thousands of miles on a first date with her billionaire boss. She hadn't yet had time to formulate the full extent of the damage this would do to her marriage plan. Her only hope was that the other men on her list didn't read the gutter press.

Jaw locked, she marched to the door of Lucas's suite and rapped again.

Zane leaned one broad shoulder against the door frame, arms folded across his chest. "You don't give up easily, do you?"

Lilah tried not to notice the way the dim light of an antique wall lamp flared across his taut, molded cheekbones, the tough line of his jaw. "I prefer the direct approach."

"Just remember I tried to save you."

The door eased open a few inches. Lucas Atraeus, tall and darkly handsome in evening clothes, was framed in the wash of lamplight.

The small flare of anger that had driven her back to his door leaped a little higher. She had expected Lucas to be somehow diminished in appearance. It didn't help that he still looked heartbreakingly perfect.

The conversation was brief, punctuated by a glimpse of Carla Ambrosi, the woman Lilah realized Lucas truly wanted, hurriedly setting her clothing to rights. In that moment any idea that she could retrieve the situation and persevere with Lucas dissolved.

Gripping the door handle, Lilah wrenched the solid mahogany door closed, cutting Lucas off. In the process the strap of her evening bag flew off her shoulder. Beads scattered as the pretty purse hit the flagstones.

Silence reigned in the corridor for long, nervy seconds. Lilah tried to avoid Zane's gaze. She was so not grieving for the relationship. Somehow she had never managed to get emotionally involved with Lucas. "You knew all along."

He picked up the purse and a number of glittering beads and handed them to her. "They've got a history."

Lilah slipped the little beads into the clutch. "I read the stories two years ago. I guess I should have included the information in my—"

"Wedding planner?"

Her gaze snapped to his. "*Process*. My woman's intuition must have been taking a mini-break."

He lifted a brow. "Don't expect me to apologize for being in touch with my feminine side."

The ridiculous concept of Zane Atraeus possessing any feminine trait broke the tension. "You don't have a feminine side."

A sudden thought blindsided her. Zane in his position as The Atraeus Group's troubleshooter *was* used to handling difficult situations. And employees. "You're running interference for Lucas."

It made perfect sense. With Carla in the mix, Lucas had hedged his bets and asked Zane to fly her out. Now Zane had stepped in to stop her making a scene. It placed her in the realms of being "a problem."

"No."

The flatness of Zane's denial was reassuring. His motives shouldn't matter, but suddenly they very palpably did. She couldn't bear the thought that she was just another embarrassing, or worse, scandalous, situation that Zane was "fixing."

In the distance a door opened. The sharp tap of heels on flagstones, the clatter of dishes, broke the moment.

Zane straightened away from the wall. "You could do with a drink." His hand cupped her elbow. "Somewhere quiet."

The heat of his palm against her bare skin distracted Lilah enough that she allowed him to propel her down the corridor.

Seconds later, Zane opened a door and allowed her to precede him. Lilah stepped into a sitting room decorated in the spare Medinian way, with cream-washed walls, dark furniture and jewel-bright rugs scattered on a flagstone floor. A series of rich oils, no doubt depicting various Atraeus ancestors, decorated the walls. French doors opened out on to one of the many stone terraces that rimmed the castello, affording expansive views of a moonlit Mediterranean sea.

Zane splashed what looked like brandy into a glass. "When did you realize about Lucas and Carla?"

She loosened her death grip on her clutch. "When we arrived at the castello and Carla flung herself into Lucas's arms."

"Then why go to Lucas's room when you had to know what you would find?"

The question, along with the piercing gaze that went with it, was unsettling. She was once again struck by the notion that beneath the urbane exterior Zane was quietly, coldly angry. "I'd had enough of feeling uncomfortable and out of place. Dinner was over and I was tired. I wanted to go back to the hotel."

He pressed the glass into her hands. "With Lucas."

The brush of his fingers sent another zing of awareness through her. "No. Alone."

She sipped brandy and tensed as it burned her throat. She was not about to explain to Zane that she had not gotten as far as thinking about the physical realities of a relationship with his brother. She had assumed all of that would fall into place as they went along. "I put a higher price on myself than that."

"Marriage."

She almost choked on another swallow of brandy. "That's the general idea."

Fingers tightening on the glass, she strolled closer to the paintings, as always drawn by color and composition, the nuances of technique. Jewelry design was her trade, but painting had always been her first love.

She paused beneath an oil of a fierce, medieval warrior, an onyx seal ring on one finger, a scimitar strapped to his back. The straight blade of a nose, tough jaw and magnetic dark gaze were a mirror of Zane's.

Seated beside the warrior was his lady, wearing a parchment silk gown, her exotic gaze square on to the viewer, giving the impression of quiet, steely strength. Lilah was guessing that being married to the brigand beside her, she would need it. An exquisite diamond and emerald ring graced one slim finger; around her neck was a matching pendant.

She felt the heat from Zane's body all down one side as he came to stand beside her. The intangible electrical current that hummed through her whenever he was near grew perceptibly stronger.

Lilah swallowed another mouthful of brandy and tried to ignore the disruptive sensations. The warmth in the pit of her stomach extended to a faint dizziness in her head, reminding her that she had barely eaten at dinner and had already sipped too much wine. She stepped closer to study the jewelry the woman was wearing.

"The Illium jewels."

Lilah frowned, frustrated by the lack of fine detail in the painting. "From Troy? I thought they were a myth."

"They got sold off at the turn of last century when the family went broke. My father managed to buy them back from a private collector."

Lilah noticed the detail of a ship in the background of the painting. "A pirate?"

"A privateer," Zane corrected. "During the eighteen hundreds his seafaring exploits were a major source of wealth for the Atraeus family."

Lilah ignored Zane's smooth explanation. After a brief foray into Medinian history, she had gleaned enough information about the Atraeus family to know that the dark and dangerous ancestor had been a pirate by any other name.

She stepped back from the oil painting in order to appreciate its rich colors. The play of light over the warrior's dark features suddenly made him seem breathtakingly familiar. Exchange the robes, soft boots and a scimitar for a suit and an expensive black shirt and it was Zane. "What was his name?"

"Zander Atraeus, my namesake, near enough. Although my mother didn't have a clue about my father's family history." He turned away. "Finish your drink. I'll take you back to your hotel."

She followed Zane to the sideboard and set her empty brandy glass down. She noticed the glint of the seal ring on the middle finger of Zane's left hand. "Your ring looks identical to the one in the painting."

"It is." His reply was clipped, and she wondered what she had said to cause the cool distance.

Suddenly she understood and busied herself extracting her cell from her clutch. She knew only too well what it was like to be an illegitimate child and excluded from her father's family. As much as she had tried to dismiss that side of the family from her psyche, they still existed and the hurt remained.

"You don't have to take me back to the hotel. I can call a cab." Unfortunately, the screen of her cell was cracked and the phone no longer appeared to work. It must have happened when her purse had gone flying.

Zane checked his watch. "Even if the phone worked, you wouldn't get a cab after midnight on Medinos."

Her stomach sank. She was a city girl; she loved shops, good coffee, public transportation. All the good-natured warnings friends had given her about traveling to a foreign country that was still partway buried in the Middle Ages were coming home to roost. "No underground?"

A flash of amusement lit his dark gaze. "All I can offer is a ride in a Ferrari."

Her stomach tightened on the slew of graphic images that went with climbing into a powerful sports car with Zane Atraeus. It was up there with Persephone accepting a ride from Hades. "Thanks, but no thanks. You don't need to feel responsible for me."

Zane's expression hardened. "Lucas won't be taking you back to the hotel."

Her chin jerked up. "I did get that part." She had been stupidly naive, but not anymore. "Okay, I'll accept the lift to my hotel, but that's all."

Zane's fingers brushed hers as he took her empty glass. "Good. Don't throw yourself away on a man who doesn't value you."

"Don't worry." She stepped back, unnerved by how tempted she was to stay close. "I know exactly how much I'm worth."

She realized how cool and hard that phrase had sounded. "I didn't mean that to sound...like it did."

His expression was neutral. "I'm sure you didn't."

Another memory surfaced. Two weeks after "the kiss," at another function, Zane had found her politely trying to fend off her friend and escort's boss.

She could still remember the hot tingle down her spine, the sudden utter unimportance of the older man who had decided she was desperate to spend the night with him. For an exhilarating moment she had been certain Zane had followed her because he wanted to follow up on the shattering connection she had felt when they had kissed.

Instead, his gaze had flowed through her as if she didn't exist. He had turned on his heel and left.

In a flash of clarity she finally understood why she had agreed to travel to Medinos with a man she barely knew.

The date had been with Lucas, but it was Zane she had always wanted.

In her search for Mr. Dependable she had somehow managed to fixate on his exact opposite.

Lucas had been an unknown quantity and out of her league, but he was nothing compared to Zane. With Zane there would be no guarantees, no safety net, no commitment. The exact opposite of what she had planned for and needed in her life.

Four

Ten days later, Zane stepped into the darkened offices of The Atraeus Group's newest acquisition, Ambrosi Pearls in Sydney. He took the antique elevator, which matched the once-elegant facade of the building, to the top floor.

It was almost midnight; most of the building was plunged into darkness. Zane, who was more used to mining and construction sites and masculine boardrooms, shook his head in bemusement as he strolled into Lucas's office. The air was perfumed; the decor white-on-white. It looked like it had been designed for the editor of a high-end fashion magazine. He noted there was actually a pile of glossy fashion magazines on one end of the curvy designer desk.

Lucas turned from his perusal of downtown Sydney. His hair was ruffled as if he'd run his fingers through it, and his tie was askew. He looked as disgruntled as Zane felt coming off a long flight from Florida.

Zane checked his watch. It was midnight. By his calculations he had been awake almost thirty-six hours. "Why the cloak-and-dagger?"

Lucas stripped off his tie and stuffed the red silk into his pocket. "I've decided to marry Carla. The press is already on the hunt. I've been trying to do a little damage control, but Lilah's going to come under pressure."

Zane's tiredness evaporated. Now the midnight meeting at the office made sense. Lucas's apartment had probably been staked out by the press. "I thought you and Lilah were over."

If he had thought anything else he would not have gone back to Florida to close the land deal. He would have sent someone else.

Lucas paced to the desk, checked the screen of an ice-cream pink cell as if he was waiting for a text, then rifled through a drawer. He came up with a business card. "We are over, but try telling that to the press."

He scribbled a number on the card. "Lilah came to my apartment. She was followed."

Zane took the card. If he thought he had controlled the possessive jealousy that had eaten into him ever since Constantine's wedding, in that moment he knew he was wrong. "What was Lilah doing at your apartment?"

Lucas frowned at the pink cell as if something about it was stressing him to the max. "I'm not sure. Carla was there. Lilah left before I could talk to her. The point is, I need you to mind her for me again."

In terse sentences, Lucas described how a reporter had snapped photos of him kissing Carla out on the sidewalk, with Lilah looking on. The pictures would be published in the morning paper.

Every muscle in Zane's body tensed at the knowledge that Lucas and Lilah were still connected, even if it was only by scandal.

During Constantine's wedding, which Lilah had attended because she had not been able to get a flight out until the following Monday, she had made it clear she was "off" all things Atraeus. Zane had not enjoyed being shut out, but at least he'd had the satisfaction of knowing Lilah was over Lucas.

He wondered what had changed her mind to the extent that she had actually gone to Lucas's apartment. Grimly, he controlled the cavemanlike urge to grab Lucas by his shirtfront, shove him against the wall and demand that he leave Lilah Cole alone. "She won't like it."

Lucas's expression was distracted. "She'll adjust. She's being well compensated."

Zane went still inside. "How, exactly?"

Lucas shuffled papers. "The usual currency. Money, promotion."

Zane could feel his blood pressure rocketing. "Carla won't like that."

"Tell me about it." Lucas shot him a tired grin. "Women. It's a juggling act."

And one in which Lucas, with his killer charm, had always excelled.

Suspicion coalesced into certainty. Despite the engagement to Carla, Zane was certain that Lilah *was* still in the picture for Lucas. Maybe he had it all wrong, but he couldn't allow himself to forget that Lucas had bought Lilah an engagement ring.

He could still see the catalog picture Elena had shown him. The solitaire had been large and flawless. Personally, he had thought the chunky diamond had been a mistake. He would have chosen something antique and lavish, maybe with a few emeralds on the side to match her eyes.

Zane's jaw clenched against the fiery urge to demand to know why, now that Lucas was engaged to Carla, he couldn't leave Lilah Cole alone.

Irrelevant question. Atraeus men had a long, well-publicized history of womanizing. He should know; he was the product of a liaison.

Letting out a breath, Zane forced himself to relax. "How long do you want me to mind her this time?"

Lucas shrugged. "The weekend. Long enough to get her through the media frenzy that's going to break following the announcement at the press conference—" he checked his watch "—today."

Zane's temper frayed at the possessive concern in Lucas's voice. "Sure. We got on okay on Medinos." He drilled Lucas with another cold look. "I think she likes me."

Lucas looked relieved. "Great, I owe you one. I know Lilah isn't your normal type."

Zane's brows jerked together. "What do you mean, not my type?"

Lucas placed his briefcase on the desk and began loading files into it. "Lilah's into classical music; she's arty. I think she paints."

"She does. *I* like art and classical music."

He snapped the case closed. "She's older."

Lucas made the age gap sound like an unbridgeable abyss. "Five years is not a big gap."

Lucas's cell broke into a catchy tango.

Jaw compressed, Zane watched as Lucas snatched up the phone. "Nice tune. Bolero."

Lucas shrugged. "I wouldn't know. This is my secretary's phone. Mine's, uh, broken." He held the cell against his ear and lifted a hand in dismissal. "Hey, thanks."

"Not a problem." Jaw taut, Zane took the creaking elevator to the ground floor. If he had stayed in the office with Lucas much longer he might have lost his temper. He had learned long ago that losing control was the equivalent of losing, and with Lilah Cole he did not intend to lose.

He had to focus, concentrate.

A whole weekend. Two days, *and nights*.

With a woman so committed to marriage she had written a blueprint for success and developed a points system for the men who had scored highly enough to make it into her folder.

Lilah slid dark glasses onto the bridge of her nose and braced herself as she stepped out of her taxi into the midmorning heat of downtown Sydney. Two steps toward the impressive doors of the hotel where the press conference was being held, and a maelstrom of flashing cameras and shouted questions broke over her.

Cheeks hot with embarrassment, she tightened her grip on the ivory handbag that matched her stylish suit, and plowed forward. Someone tugged at the sleeve of her jacket; a flash blinded her. A split second later the grip on her arm and the reporter were miraculously removed, replaced by the burly back of a uniformed security guard. The mass of reporters parted and Zane Atraeus's dark gaze burned into hers, oddly calm and assessing in the midst of chaos. Despite her determination to remain calm in his presence, to forget the kiss, a hot thrill shot down her spine.

"Lilah, come with me."

For a split second she thought he had said, "Lilah, come to me," and the vivid intensity of her reaction to the low, husky command was paralyzing.

She had already had two negative experiences with Atraeus males. Now wasn't the time to redefine that old cliché by fantasizing about jumping out of the frying pan and into the fire, again.

The media surged against the wall of security, an elbow jabbed her back. She clutched Zane's outstretched hand. He released her fingers almost immediately and scooped her against his side, his muscled heat burning into her as they walked.

Three swift steps. The glass doors gleamed ahead. A camera flashed. "Oh, good. More scandal."

She caught the edge of Zane's grin. "That's what you get when you play with an Atraeus."

The hotel doors swished wide. More media were inside, along with curious hotel staff and guests. Lilah worked to keep her expression serene, although she was uncomfortably aware that her cheeks were burning. "I didn't 'play' with anyone."

"You went to Medinos. That was some first date."

The nervy thrill of Zane turning up to protect her evaporated. "I didn't exactly enjoy the experience."

As first dates went it had been an utter disaster.

Zane ushered her into an open elevator. The heat of his palm at the small of her back sent a small shock of awareness through her. Two large Medinian security guards stepped in on either side of them. A third man, blocky and muscled with a shaven head, whom she recognized as Spiros, took up a position by the door and punched buttons.

Lilah's ruffled unease at Zane's closeness increased as the elevator shot upward. "I suppose you're in Sydney for the charity art auction?"

"I'm also doing some work on the Ambrosi takeover, which is why Lucas asked me to mind you."

The last remnants of the intense thrill she had felt when Zane had come looking for her died a death. "I suppose Lucas told you what happened last night?"

"He said you found him with Carla at his apartment."

Lilah's blush deepened. Zane made it sound like she had been involved in some kind of trashy love triangle. "I didn't make it to his apartment. Security—"

"You don't have to explain."

Lilah's gaze narrowed. The surface calm she had been clinging to all morning, ever since she had seen the morning paper, shredded. "Since Medinos, I haven't been able to get an appointment to see Lucas. I got tired of waiting. I was there to resign."

The doors slid open. Adrenaline pumped when she saw the contingent of press in the lobby of the concierge floor, although these weren't the sharp-eyed paparazzi who had been out on the street. She recognized magazine editors, serious tabloids, television news crews.

She took a deep breath as they stepped out of the elevator in the wake of the security team.

Zane's fingers locked around her wrist. "If you run now, what they'll print will be worse."

"Any worse than 'Discarded Atraeus Mistress Abandoned on Street'?"

Zane's expression was grim. "You should have known Lucas was playing out of your league."

Something inside her snapped. "Is it too late to say I wish I'd never met Lucas?"

The moment was freeing. She realized she had never actually connected with Lucas on an emotional level. Marriage with him would have been a disaster.

Zane's gaze captured hers, making her heart pound. "How worried are you about the media?"

Lilah blinked. The focused heat in Zane's eyes was having a mesmerizing effect. "I don't have a TV and I canceled my newspaper subscription this morning. Dealing with the media is not my thing."

"Is this?"

His jaw brushed her forehead. Tendrils of heat shimmered through her at the unexpected contact. His hands framed her face. Dimly, she registered that he intended to kiss her. In the midst of the hum of security, press and hotel staff, time seemed to slow, stop. She was spun back two years to the seductive quiet of the empty reception room, eleven days ago to the flight to Medinos.

She dragged in a shallow breath. She needed to step back, calm down, forget the crazy attraction that zinged through her every time she was near Zane. Constantine and Lucas had both gone through gorgeous women like hot knives through butter, but Zane had a reputation that scorched.

His breath feathered her lips. She closed her eyes and his mouth touched hers, seducingly warm and soft. A shock wave of heat shimmered out from that one small point of contact.

He lifted his head. His gaze, veiled by inky lashes, locked on hers. Instead of straightening, his hands dropped to her waist. The heat from his palms burned through the finely tailored silk as he drew her closer.

The motorized whirr of cameras and the buzz of conversation receded as she clutched at Zane's shoulders and angled her jaw, allowing him more comfortable access. This time the kiss was firmer, heated, deliberate, sizzling all the way to her toes. By the time Zane lifted his mouth, her head was spinning and her legs felt as limp as noodles.

The smattering of applause and wolf whistles shunted her back to earth. She stared at the forest of microphones trying to break through the wall of security, her wild moment of rebellion evaporating.

The phrase "out of the frying pan and into the fire" once more reverberated through her. "Now they'll think I'm sleeping with you as well."

Zane's arm locked around her waist as he propelled her through the reporters and into the room in which the press conference was being held. "Think of it this way, if you're with me, at least now they'll wonder who dumped whom."

Forty-five minutes later the official part of the press conference was over. Lucas and Carla, Lucas's mother, Maria Therese, and Constantine's P.A. Tomas had left in a flurry of publicity over their engagement announcement and the further announcement that Sienna and Constantine were expecting a baby.

Zane flowed smoothly to his feet. "Now we leave."

Relieved that Lucas's announcement had taken the unnerving focus of the press off her, Lilah hooked the strap of her handbag over her shoulder.

Two steps onto the still crowded floor and an elegant blonde backed by a TV crew shoved a mike at Zane. "Can we expect another engagement announcement soon?"

"No comment." Zane lengthened his stride, bypassing the TV crew and the question as he propelled her toward the elevator.

Even though Lilah knew that Zane's lack of response was the only sensible option, his comment left her feeling oddly flat and definitely manipulated.

The end of the nonrelationship with Lucas had not mattered. Standing on the pavement the previous evening while a reporter had snapped her witnessing Lucas and Carla locked in a passionate clinch had not been a feel-good moment. But, as embarrassing as her association with Zane's brother had turned out to be, after the toe-curling intimacy of the kisses in front of the media, in that moment she felt the most betrayed by Zane.

Five

Zane hustled Lilah out into a private underground parking lot and opened the door of a gleaming, low-slung black Corvette. He waited for Lilah to climb into the passenger-side seat then walked around the vehicle and slid behind the wheel.

He had been annoyed enough with Lucas to want to stake a claim on Lilah, although he hadn't planned on doing it in quite such a public way.

He also hadn't expected Lilah to kiss him back quite so enthusiastically. Although ever since they had hit the elevator on the way down she had been cool and reserved and irritatingly distant.

He lifted a hand as Spiros and the two security guards climbed into a black sedan.

He fastened his seat belt. The back of his hand brushed Lilah's. The automatic jolt he received from the brush of her skin against his increased his irritable temper. A temper that, just days ago, he had not known he'd possessed.

The dark sedan the bodyguards had climbed into cruised

out of the parking building. Seconds later, Zane followed, emerging into the glare of daylight.

He transferred his gaze to the woman beside him. Dressed in her signature ivory and white, her hair smoothed into a loose, elegant confection on top of her head, smooth teardrop pearls dangling from tiny lobes, Lilah looked both cool and drop-dead sexy. The fact that he had kissed off her lipstick, leaving her lips bare, only succeeded in making her even more sensually alluring.

Grimly he noted that the same addictive fascination that had tempted him to lose his head two years ago was still at work. Lilah Cole was openly and unashamedly husband-hunting. She was the kind of woman he couldn't afford in his life, and yet it seemed he couldn't resist her.

Lilah stared straight ahead, her purse gripped in her lap. "I know I've been invited to lunch with your family, but with everything that's happened, maybe that isn't such a good idea. If you drop me off, I can get a taxi back to the office."

Zane's jaw tightened at the subdued, worried note in Lilah's voice. Lucas should have known better; he should have left her alone. "It's lunchtime. You need to eat."

She looked out of the passenger window. "I had cereal and toast for breakfast. I'm not exactly hungry."

Zane found the thought of Lilah crunching her way through cereal and toast before facing the press oddly endearing. He wondered what kind of cereal she ate then crushed his curiosity about her.

He braked for a set of lights. "Lucas would probably be relieved if you didn't show."

The words were ruthless, but he had gotten used to seeing Lilah calm and businesslike, with all her ducks in a row. For two years it had been a quality that had irritated him profoundly. Incomprehensibly, he now found himself looking for ways to get her back to her normal, ultraorganized self.

Her gaze snapped to his. "What Lucas wants or does not want is of no concern to me."

Zane felt suddenly happier than he had in days. The lights changed, he put the car in gear and accelerated through the intersection. "I can take you somewhere else to eat if you want."

Her head whipped around, her green gaze shooting fire. "On second thought, no."

"Good. Because we're here."

He watched Lilah study the elegant portico of the Michelin star restaurant as if the fluted columns represented the gates of Hades. "You're a manipulative man."

"I'm an Atraeus."

"Sometimes I forget."

He found himself instantly on the defensive. "Because I'm also a Salvatore?"

He did not voice the other lurking fear that had reared its head since his conversation with Lucas, that it was because he was only twenty-four.

She frowned, as if his shadowy past had not occurred to her. "Because sometimes you're...nice."

"Nice." His brows jerked together.

She looked embarrassed. "I read the article about you on the charity website. I know that you wear those three earrings to help kids relate to you when you do counseling work. You can try all you like to prove otherwise but, from where I come from, that's *nice*."

Lilah breathed a sigh of relief when Zane pulled in at her apartment's tiny parking area. Lunch had been just as stilted and uncomfortable as she had imagined. Thankfully, the service had been ultraquick and they had been able to leave early.

Zane walked around and opened her door. Lilah climbed out of the low bucket seat, acutely aware of the shadowy cleavage visible in the V of her jacket and of the length of thigh exposed by the shortness of her skirt. When she had dressed that morning, the suit had seemed elegant and circumspect but it was not made for struggling out of a low slung 'Vette.

Zane's gaze locked with hers, making her feel breathless.

She clamped down on the uncharacteristic desire to boldly meet his gaze.

Arriving at the front door of her apartment with a man was what she liked to refer to as a dating "red zone." She and Zane were not dating, but the situation had somehow become more fraught than any dating scenario she had ever experienced. After the kiss earlier, it would not be a good idea to allow Zane inside her house.

She gave him a bright, professional smile. "It's okay, you don't have to see me in. Thanks for the lift."

Zane closed the 'Vette's door and depressed the key lock. "Not a problem. I'll see you to your door."

"That won't be necessary." She aimed another smile somewhere in his general direction as she rummaged in her handbag for her door key.

Zane fell into step beside her. "If I'm not mistaken, that's a reporter staked out over there."

Lilah's head jerked up. She recognized the car that had been parked outside of Lucas's apartment the previous night. Her heart sank. "He must have followed us."

"The car was here when we arrived. According to Lucas, *you* were the one who was followed last night. The press has probably been staking you out ever since you returned from Medinos. In which case, I'd better see you safely inside."

Resigning herself, Lilah walked quickly to the large garage-style door, her cheeks warming as she saw the down-at-heel building through Zane's eyes. A converted warehouse in one of the shabbier suburbs, she had chosen the building because it had been cheerful, arty and spectacularly cheap. The ground floor apartment included a huge light-filled north-facing room that was perfect for painting.

Zane, thankfully, didn't seem to notice how shabby the exterior was, a reminder that he had not spent all of his life in luxurious surroundings.

Unlocking the door, she stepped inside the nondescript foyer, with its concrete floors and cream-washed walls.

Zane slid the door to enclose them in the shadowy space. "How many people live here?"

"A dozen or so." She led the way down a narrow, dim corridor and unlocked her front door. Made of unprepossessing sheet metal, it had once led to some kind of workshop.

She stepped into her large sitting room, conscious of Zane's gaze as he took in white walls, glowing wooden floors and the afternoon sun flooding through a bank of bifold doors at one end.

"Nice." He closed the door and strolled into the center of the room, his gaze assessing the paintings she'd collected from friends and family over the years.

He studied a series of three abstracts propped against one wall. "These are yours."

Her gaze gravitated to the mesmerizingly clean lines of his profile as he studied one of the abstracts. "How do you know that?" She had gotten the paintings ready for sale, but hadn't gotten around to signing them yet.

Faint color rimmed his cheekbones. "I've bought a couple at auction. I also saw your work in a gallery a few weeks back."

A small shock went through her that he had actually bought some of her paintings. "I usually sell most of what I paint through the gallery."

He straightened and peered at a framed photograph of her mother and grandmother. "So money's important."

Her jaw firmed. "Yes."

There was no point in hiding it. Following the recent finance company crashes, her mother's careful life savings had dissolved overnight, leaving her with a mortgage she couldn't pay. Subsisting on a part-time wage, which was all her mother could get in Broome, money had become vital.

Lilah hadn't hesitated. The regular sale of her paintings supplemented her income just enough that she was managing to pay her mother's mortgage as well as cover her rent, but only just.

Her failure to present her resignation to Lucas the previous evening was, in a way, a relief. Resigning from Ambrosi Pearls now would not be a good move for either her or her mother.

A crashing sound jerked her head around. Dropping her bag on the couch, she raced through to her studio in time to glimpse a young man dressed in jeans and a T-shirt, a camera slung over his shoulder, as he clambered out through an open window. A split second later, Zane flowed past her, stepped over a stack of canvases that had been knocked to the floor, and followed the intruder out of the window.

Zane caught the reporter as he hung awkwardly on her back fence. With slick, practiced moves he took the memory stick from the camera and shoved what was clearly an expensive piece of equipment back at the reporter's chest.

The now white-faced reporter scrambled over the fence and disappeared into the sports field on the other side.

While Zane examined the fence and walked the boundary of her tiny back garden, Lilah hurriedly tidied up the collapsed pile of canvases.

Her worst fears were confirmed when she discovered a portrait of Zane she had painted almost two years ago, after the disastrous episode on the couch. Zane had practically stepped over the oil to get out of the window. It was a miracle he hadn't noticed.

Gathering the canvases, she stacked them against the nearest wall, so only the backs were visible. She'd had a lucky escape. The last thing she needed now was for Zane to find out that she had harbored a quiet, unhealthy little obsession about him for the past two years.

Zane climbed back in the window and examined the broken catch. "That's it, you're not staying here tonight. You're coming with me. If that reporter made it into your back garden, others will."

Lilah's response was unequivocal. Given that Zane seemed to bring out her wild Cole side, going with him was a very bad idea.

Her cheeks burned as he stared at the backs of the paintings. "That won't be necessary. I'll get the window repaired. I've got a friend in the building who's handy with tools."

She led the way out of the room, away from the incriminating paintings.

His expression grim, Zane checked the locks on the windows of her main living room. "Your studio window is the least of your problems. You've got a sports field next door. That means plenty of off-road parking and unlimited access. Even with a security detail keeping watch front and back, the press won't have any problems getting pictures through all this glass."

"I can draw the curtains. They can't take pictures if there's nothing to see."

"You'll get harassed every time you walk outside or leave the house, and that fence is a major problem. Put it this way, if you don't come with me now, I'm staying here with you." He studied her plain black leather couch as if he was eyeing it up for size.

Lilah's stomach flip-flopped as images of that other couch flashed through her mind. There was no way she could have Zane staying the night in her home. The kissing had been unsettling enough. The last thing she needed was for him to invade her personal space, sleep on *her* couch. "You can't stay here."

Her phone rang and automatically went to the answering machine. The message was audible. A reporter wanted her to call him.

Lilah's gaze zeroed in on the number of messages she had waiting: twenty-three. She didn't think the machine held that many. "I'll pack."

Six

Minutes later, Lilah was packed. Zane, who had spent the time talking into a cell phone, mostly in Medinian, the low, sexy murmur of his voice distracting, snapped the phone closed and slipped it into his pants pocket. "Ready?"

The easy transition from Medinian to American-accented English was startling, pointing out to Lilah, just in case she had forgotten, that Zane Atraeus was elusive *and* complicated. Every time she tried to pigeonhole him as an arrogant, self-centered tycoon, he pushed her off balance by being unexpectedly normal and nice.

While he took her suitcase, Lilah double-checked the locks. On impulse, she grabbed one of her design sketchpads then stepped out into the sterile hall, closing the heavy door behind her.

Zane was waiting, arms folded over his chest, a look of calm patience on his face.

"I'll just leave a message for a neighbor and see if he'll fix the window."

Taking a piece of paper out of her purse, she penned a quick note. Walking a few steps along the dingy corridor, she knocked, just in case Evan was home. She didn't expect him to be in until later in the day, so she slipped the note under his door. The door swung open as she turned to walk away. Evan, looking paint-stained and rumpled, stood there, the note in his hands.

"I didn't think you'd be here until tonight."

Evan was a high-end accountant and painter, and was also a closet gay. The apartment was something in the way of a retreat for him. She had been certain he would stay clear until the press lost interest.

Evan stared pointedly past her at Zane. "It's my day off. I thought I'd come over early just in case you needed a shoulder."

"She doesn't," Zane said calmly.

Evan's expression was suspiciously blank, which meant he was speculating wildly. "Not a problem." He transferred his gaze to Lilah. "Don't worry, I'll fix the window. Call me if you need *anything* else."

Zane held the front door of the apartment building for her. "So, you're still seeing Peters."

Lilah shielded her gaze from the sun as she stepped outside. "How do you know Evan's name?"

Zane loaded her case into the limited rear space of the Corvette. "Peters has a certain reputation with commercial law. So does his boss, Mark Britten."

She could feel her automatic blush at the mention of Evan's boss, the man who had been convinced she was dying to sleep with him before Zane's appearance had ended the small, embarrassing scuffle.

She descended as gracefully as she could into the Vette's passenger seat. "Evan is a *friend*." It was on the tip of her tongue to tell Zane that Evan was gay, but that would mean breaking a confidence. "He paints in his spare time. He doesn't live here. This is just where he keeps his studio."

When they pulled away from the curb, Lilah noticed that Zane's security pulled in close behind them. The ominous black sedan, filled with blocky, muscular men—the leading henchman, Spiros, behind the wheel—looked like something off a movie set. A cream van splashed with colorful graphics idled out of the shadows and slotted in behind the sedan.

Zane glanced in the rearview mirror and made a call on his cell. When he slipped the phone back in his pocket, he glanced at her. "The van's a press vehicle."

"And Spiros is taking care of it?"

Zane's gaze was enigmatic, reminding her of the gulf that existed between his life and hers. "That's what he's paid to do."

Zane inserted the key card in the door of his hotel suite and allowed Lilah to precede him into the room.

Unlocking his jaw he finally addressed the topic that had obsessed him from the moment he had recognized Evan Peters and realized that not only were he and Lilah "friends" of long standing, they were practically living together. "How long have you known Peters?"

There was a moment of silence while she surveyed the heavy opulence of the suite. "Six years. Maybe seven. We met at a painting class."

"When did he move in next door?"

His question was somewhat lost as Lilah strolled through the overstuffed room. The suite, he realized, with its curvy furniture, swagged silk drapes and gilt embellishment might not suit him, but it was a perfect setting for Lilah. Even dressed in the modern suit, she looked lush and exotic, like the expensive courtesans that, before Medinos had become a Christian nation, had been kept closeted in luxury behind lacy wrought iron grills.

She trailed one slim hand over the back of a brocade couch. "As a matter of fact, I was the one who moved next door to him. Evan knew I was looking for a bigger place. When the apartment became available he let me know. It was ideal for what I wanted, so I snapped it up."

His jaw tightened. "And it was a bonus living so close to Peters."

Lilah dropped her purse on the couch and paused to examine an ornate oval mirror. She met his gaze in the glass. "Evan and I are not involved. As you put it, he has a certain reputation in the business world. His painting and some of his artistic friends don't fit the profile, so he keeps that part of his life under wraps."

Involvement or not, it was the knowledge that Peters had likely shared Lilah's bed that bothered him.

Although it had not been the blond accountant's portrait lying on the floor in Lilah's studio. Or Mark Britten's, or Lucas's.

The portrait had been his.

Before he could probe further, his new P.A., Elena, who occupied a single room down the corridor, appeared. Plump but efficiently elegant in a dark suit and trendy pink spectacles, Elena had a clipboard in hand. Spiros appeared in Elena's wake and carried Lilah's bag through to the spare bedroom.

Zane made brief introductions and signed the correspondence on Elena's clipboard. He suppressed his irritation at Elena's bright-eyed perusal of Lilah and the fascinated glances she kept directing his way. No doubt she had read some of the more lurid stories printed about him, which would explain why she seemed to think he needed chocolate-dipped strawberries and oysters on the half shell in his fridge. If she knew how he had lived over the past two years, he thought grimly, she would not have bothered.

When both Elena and Spiros were gone, Zane shrugged out of his jacket, tossed it over a nearby chair and strolled to the doorway of Lilah's room.

The pressing questions surrounding the portrait she had painted of him were replaced by a sense of satisfaction as he watched her unload clothing into a huge, ornate dresser. In *his* suite.

Maybe his personal assistant wasn't so far off in her opinion of him.

According to the history books, on his various raids, Zander Atraeus hadn't confined himself to stealing jewels. At that moment, he formed a grim insight into how his marauding ancestor must have felt when he had stolen away the woman he had eventually married.

Lilah glanced up, a stylish jewelry case in one hand. "Your P.A. doesn't approve."

He settled his shoulder against the door frame, curiously riveted by the feminine items she placed with calm precision on top of the dresser. "Elena had a traditional Medinian upbringing. She would probably prefer you in a separate suite for propriety's sake."

Her expression brightened. "Great idea."

"You're staying here, where I can keep an eye on you. All the suites and rooms at this end of the corridor are booked out to Atraeus staff. It's safe because no one comes in or out without security checking."

"What about the publicity?"

He shrugged. "Whether you have a separate room or share this suite, after what happened this morning, the story they print will be the same. This way, at least, *I* know where you are."

She zipped her empty case closed and placed it in the closet. "What I can't figure out is why that should be so important to you."

"I made a promise to Lucas."

Hurt registered briefly in her gaze. "Silly me," she muttered breezily. "I forgot." Pushing open the terrace door, she stepped out onto the patio.

Zane caught her before she had gone more than a few feet. "Not a good idea. The terrace isn't safe."

On the heels of the hurt that Zane was only following Lucas's orders in looking after her, Zane's grip on her arm sent a small shock of adrenaline plunging through her veins.

She took a panicked half step, at the same time twisting to free herself. In the process her heel skidded on the paver. A sharp little pain signaled that she had managed to turn her ankle.

"What is it?"

She balanced on one heel. "It's not serious." It was the shoe that was the problem; there was something not quite right with the heel.

A split second later she found herself lifted up, carried back inside and deposited on the bed.

Zane removed the offending shoe, which had a broken heel, tossed it on the floor then examined her ankle. The light brush of his fingers sent small shivers through her. "Stay there. I'll get some ice."

"There's no need, honestly."

But he had already gone.

Wiggling her foot, which felt just fine, Lilah stared at the ornately molded ceiling, abruptly speechless. Gold cherubs encircled a crystal chandelier, which she hadn't previously noticed.

She pushed up into a reclining position, and eased back into the decadent luxury of a satin quilted headboard and a plump nest of down pillows. She wiggled her ankle. There was barely a twinge, nothing she couldn't walk off.

Before she could slide off the bed, Zane appeared with a plastic bag filled with ice cubes. The enormous bed depressed as he sat down and placed the ice around her ankle.

She winced at the cold and tried not to love the fact that he was looking after her. "It's really not that bad."

He placed a cushion under her ankle to elevate it. "This way it won't get bad. Just stay put."

He rose to his feet, his expression taking on a look of blunt possession that was oddly thrilling, and that soothed the moment of hurt when she had thought he viewed her as a problem. She decided that in the rich turquoise-and-gold decadence of the room, and despite his kindness over her ankle, she had no trouble placing Zane at all.

When someone looked like a pirate and acted like a pirate, they very probably were a pirate.

An hour on the bed without anything to read and no chance of drowsing off because she was on edge at being in Zane's suite, and Lilah had had enough.

Pushing into a sitting position, she swung her legs over the edge of the bed. She put weight on the foot. A few steps, with the barest of twinges, and she judged it was perfectly sound. The ice pack, which she had taken into her bathroom as soon as Zane had left the room, was melting in the bathtub.

She checked the sitting room, relieved to see that it was empty, and noted the sound of water running, indicating that Zane was having a shower. After changing into jeans and a white camisole, she brushed her hair and wound it back into a tidy knot. Collecting her sketchpad and a pencil, she slipped dark glasses on the bridge of her nose and stepped out onto the terrace. A recliner was placed directly outside her room.

Flipping the pad open, to her horror she discovered that she had picked up the wrong pad. Instead of her latest jewelry sketches, ornate pearl items based on a set of traditional Medinian pieces, she found herself staring at a charcoal sketch of intent dark eyes beneath straight brows, mouthwatering cheekbones and a strong jaw.

Flipping through the book, she studied page after page of sketches, which she had done over a two-year period. Slamming the book closed, she stared at the blank office buildings and hotels across the street. Until that moment she hadn't realized how fixated she had become.

She had simply drawn Zane when she had felt the urge. The problem was the urge had become unacceptably frequent. It was no wonder that in the past two years she'd had trouble whipping up any enthusiasm for her dates. She had even begun to worry about her age; after all she was nearly thirty.

She had even considered dietary supplements, but clearly food wasn't the problem.

A shadow falling over the sketchpad shocked her out of her reverie.

Zane, wearing black jeans that hung low on narrow hips, his muscled chest bare. "You shouldn't be out here. I told you, it isn't safe."

Lilah dragged her gaze from the expanse of muscled flesh, the intriguing tracery of scars on his abdomen. She was abruptly glad for the screen her dark glasses provided. "We're twenty stories up, with security controlling access to this part of the hotel. I don't see how this terrace can not be safe."

"For the same reason I have bodyguards. The Atraeus family has a lot of money. That attracts some wacky types."

"Is that how you got the scars?"

He leaned down and braced his hands on the armrests on either side of the recliner, suddenly suffocatingly close. "I got the scars when I was a kid, because I didn't have either money or protection. Since my father picked me up, no one's gotten that close, mostly because I listen to what my chief of security tells me."

She stared at his freshly shaven jaw, trying to ignore the scents of soap and cologne. "Which is?"

"That no matter how sunny the day looks, there are a lot of bad people out there, so you don't take risks and you do what you're told." He lifted her dark glasses off the bridge of her nose.

She released her grip on the sketchpad to reclaim the sunglasses. Zane let her have the glasses, but straightened, taking her sketchpad with him.

Irritation at the sneaky trick, followed by mortification that he might glance through and discover her guilty secret, burned through her. "Give that back."

She caught the edge of his grin as he stepped into the shadowy interior of the sitting room. Launching off the recliner, she raced after him, blinking as she adjusted to the dimness of the sitting room. She made a lunge for the pad. Zane evaded her reach by taking a half step back.

"Why do you need it so badly?" His gaze was curiously intent, making her stomach sink.

"Those sketches are...private."

And guiltily, embarrassingly revealing.

The drawings cataloged just how empty her private life had been. He would know just how much she had thought about him, focused on him and how often.

He handed her the pad but instead of letting it go, used it to draw her closer by degrees until her knuckles brushed the warm, hard muscles of his chest.

The relief that had spiraled through her when she thought he hadn't checked out the drawings dissolved. "You *looked*."

"Uh-huh." Gaze locked with hers, he drew her close enough that her thighs brushed his and the sketchpad, which she was clutching like a shield, was flattened between them.

He lifted a dark brow. "And you would be drawing and painting me because...?"

Lilah briefly closed her eyes. The old cliché about wishing the ground would open up and swallow her had nothing on this. "You saw the painting in my apartment."

"It was hard to miss."

She drew in a stifled breath. "I was hoping you wouldn't."

"Because then you could avoid admitting that you're attracted to me. And have been ever since we met two years ago."

Gently, he eased the sketchpad from her grip. "You don't need that anymore." He tossed the pad aside. "Not when you have the real thing."

Seven

Lilah was frozen to the spot, gripped by the inescapable knowledge that if she wanted Zane, he wanted her. "Maybe I prefer the fantasy."

"Liar." His head dipped, his forehead touched hers. "What now?" The question was soft and flat.

"Nothing." She swallowed, unable to take her gaze from his mouth, or to forget the memory of the kisses that morning.

Just that morning. In the interim a lot had happened. The passage of time seemed wildly distorted, as if days had passed, not hours.

And that was when she understood what had happened.

Somehow she had done the very thing she had worked to avoid. She had allowed herself to get caught in the grip of a physical obsession. And not just any obsession.

She stared into the riveting depths of Zane's eyes. She had followed a path well-trodden by Cole women. She had fallen victim to the *coup de foudre*.

That was why she had ended up on the couch with Zane.

It explained her inability to say "no" to kissing Zane on the flight and during the press conference.

Somehow, without her quite knowing how, she had allowed sex to sabotage her life.

Zane's gaze narrowed. "Don't look at me like that."

"Like what?" But she knew.

Her guilty secret had been exposed, the emotions and longings she had kept quietly tucked away—all the better to deny them—had been forced to the surface.

And Zane wasn't helping the process. Instead of backing off, he was making no bones about the fact that he liked it that she wanted him.

He dipped his head to kiss her. Lifting up on her toes, she wound her arms around his neck and met him halfway.

It was crazy. She hardly knew him, but already she knew how to fit herself against him, how to angle her jaw so his mouth could settle against hers.

With a stifled groan, he wrapped her close. Half lifting her, he walked her backward across the sitting room. Somewhere in the distance, Lilah registered the phone ringing, then they were in his room. The back of her knees hit the edge of his bed.

He came down beside her. Conscious thought evaporated as his mouth reclaimed hers. Long minutes later, he rolled and pulled her on top of him, his fingers tangling in her hair. Charmed and utterly seduced by the clear invitation to play, to kiss him back, she framed his face and lowered her mouth to his.

His palms smoothed down the curve of her spine, pressing her against him so that she was intimately aware of every curve and plane of heated muscle, the firm shape of his arousal. On the upward journey, he peeled her camisole up until he met the barrier of her bra.

Murmuring something short and soft beneath his breath, he fumbled at the fastening then shifted his hands around to cup her breasts.

The distinctive sound of the front door opening cut through

the dizzying haze. Elena, dressed in a shimmering, ankle-length black dress and looking like a sleek well-fed raven in spectacles, appeared in the doorway to Zane's room.

Zane muttered something short beneath his breath and rolled over in an attempt to shield Lilah from his assistant's view.

Cheeks flushed, Lilah dragged her camisole back into place.

Elena dragged her fascinated gaze from Zane's chest and seemed to remember herself. She checked the dainty watch on her wrist and addressed Zane in rapid Medinian.

Zane rose to his feet and pulled on a shirt that was draped over a nearby chair. "English, please, Elena."

"The car is ready. Gemma, your, uh, *date*—" she directed an apologetic glance at Lilah "—is waiting. Providing we reach the museum in the next twenty minutes, we won't be late."

Gemma. Lilah jackknifed. She was Zane's previous personal assistant and the pretty redhead he had escorted to almost every function the charity had held over the last two years.

Hurt shimmered through her. Above all the gorgeous girls Zane had dated, Gemma reigned supreme. Zane always went back to her. If Lilah had been tempted to fantasize about any kind of a future with Zane, this was exactly the wake-up call she needed.

A second salient fact registered. The museum. And an auction of a private art collection that had been donated to the charity.

Somehow in the craziness of the past few days, she had forgotten she was supposed to attend. Frantically, she checked her wristwatch.

She should have been dressed by now and calling a taxi.

Another thought occurred to her. "Howard."

Zane's head snapped around as he shrugged into a shirt. He gave her a questioning look.

"My date." She scrambled off the bed. She was supposed to be meeting Howard outside the museum in fifteen minutes.

She dashed into her room, snatched an uncrushable cream dress off its hanger, dressed and fixed her hair. She slipped into cream heels and applied a quick dash of mascara and lip-gloss, a spray of her favorite perfume and she was ready.

Picking up her clutch, she joined Zane and Elena. The venue wasn't far away, but there was no way she would make her rendezvous with Howard in time. To compound matters, this was a first date recommended by the online dating agency she had started using just weeks ago. She had never physically met Howard. All she knew was that he had ticked all the boxes in terms of her requirements in a husband.

Now that Lucas was history, Howard was number one on her list of eligible bachelors and her most likely prospect for marriage.

She dragged her gaze from the riveting sight of Zane in a black tuxedo, and tried to gloss over the fact that she had just climbed out of his bed and was now going to meet a prospective husband. "I need a lift to the museum."

Lilah was five minutes late.

Howard White was waiting in the appointed place in the museum foyer, although at first she had difficulty picking him out because he was older than the photograph he had supplied. Mid-forties, she guessed, rather than the age of thirty-two, which he had given.

Flustered and ashamed at herself for her loss of control with Zane, and for forgetting she was even meeting Howard, Lilah resolved to overlook his dishonesty.

Howard smiled pleasantly as they shook hands. "I feel like I know you already."

Guilt burned through her as Howard continued to study her in a way that was just a little too familiar for comfort.

Her picture *had* been splashed across the tabloids. Her only hope now was that he wouldn't put two and two together when he saw Zane. She would have to do her best to make sure that they were not seen together.

As he released her hand, she couldn't help but notice that he had a pale strip across the third finger of his left hand, which seemed to indicate that Howard had been recently married.

The evening progressed at a snail's pace.

Burningly aware of Zane just a short distance away with Gemma clinging on his arm, Lilah found it hard to focus on Howard and his accounting business.

Howard placed his empty mineral water on a nearby side table and beckoned a passing waiter. "Are you sure you wouldn't like some champagne?"

"No. Thank you." Lilah was beginning to get a little annoyed at the pressure Howard was applying with regard to alcohol, especially when he had not touched anything alcoholic himself.

"Very sensible." He put his wallet away.

She tried to think of something else to say, but the conversation had staggered to a halt.

Howard jerked at his collar as if it was too tight. "My—uh, mother doesn't agree with alcohol, especially not for women."

Lilah dragged her gaze from Zane's profile. She had barely paid Howard any attention, but all of her Cole instincts were on high alert. She had received the strong impression that Howard had been about to say "wife." "Your *mother*?"

Howard's gaze shifted to the auctioneer, who was just setting up. He dragged at his tie as if he was having trouble breathing. "I live with my, uh, mother. She's a fine woman."

Feeling suddenly wary of Howard, Lilah excused herself on the grounds that she needed some fresh air before the auction started.

She stepped outside onto a small paved terrace dotted with modern sculpture. A footfall sounded behind her. Zane. Light slanted across his cheekbones, making him look even tougher and edgier.

She had been aware that he had been keeping an eye on her the entire time and had hoped he would follow her.

He jerked his head in the direction of the crowded room. "When did you meet him?"

"Tonight."

His expression was incredulous. "A blind date?"

She stared at the soaring, shadowy shape of a concrete obelisk, as if the outline was riveting. "More or less."

It was none of Zane's business that Howard had contacted her through her online dating service. His application was very recent. It had appeared in her in-box just before she had gone to Medinos. She had felt raw enough on her return that she had agreed to her first actual date.

"I don't like him, and you're not leaving with him." There was a vibrating pause. "He's old enough to be your father."

There was an oddly accusing note to Zane's voice. Lilah stared hard at a tortured arrangement of pipes at the center of the small courtyard, a piece of art that, according to a plaque, had something to do with the inner-city "vibe." "He is older than I thought."

She rubbed her bare arms against the coolness of the night, suddenly desperate to change the subject. "Where's Gemma?"

"Gemma won't miss me for a few minutes. Is that why you dated Lucas, because he was older?"

Her gaze connected with Zane's. She didn't know why he was so stuck on the issue of age. "I don't see what this has to do with anything."

"I've read your personnel file. I know how old you are, I also know that you seem to date older men. Is that a requirement for your future husband?"

Despite the chilly air it was suddenly way too hot. She tried to whip up some outrage that Zane had accessed her personal information, but the implications of his prying were riveting. She couldn't think of any reason for Zane to focus on the age of her dates unless it affected him personally. The thought that

Zane was comparing himself with her dates and that he was actually worried that he was too young, was dizzying. "No."

Something like relief flickered in his gaze. "Good."

His fingers linked with hers, drew her close.

Lilah swallowed against the sudden dryness in her mouth. After the disaster on Medinos followed by the deadening effect of Howard's company, Zane's interest in her was fatally seductive. "This is a bad idea. You're with someone else."

In theory so was she, but Howard, with his sneaky lies and deceptions, had ceased to count.

"Gemma works for The Atraeus Group. She just helps me out on occasion."

Zane's head dipped, his breath wafted over her cheek, and suddenly, irresistibly, they were back where they'd been less than two hours ago—on the verge of...something.

His lips touched hers. Heat shivered through her, she lifted up on her toes. Her palms automatically slid over his shoulders, fingers digging into pliant muscle. His hands closed on her waist.

The sound of the auctioneer taking bids flowed out into the night, but even that faded as she stepped closer, angled her chin and leaned into the kiss.

Something shifted in the shadows, flashed. Zane's head jerked up.

A second shadow flickered. A night security officer with a flashlight in one hand nodded as he walked past.

Confused, Lilah stepped back from Zane. For a moment she was certain someone had used a camera flash. She couldn't stop the gossip and the sensationalized stories, but that didn't mean she had to like the sneakiness of the reporters. "I'd better go back inside. Howard will be missing me."

Zane was still watching the shadowy figure of the security officer as he stepped into a concealed side entrance. "Are you serious about him?"

"Not anymore." Feeling a wrenching regret at leaving the courtyard, Lilah made her way back into the crowded room.

Howard was still engrossed in conversation with a knot of older men. He didn't bother to look her way. Lilah decided that Zane was right; he looked depressingly paternal.

Zane fell into step beside her. His fingers closed on hers.

Pleasure and guilty heat shooting through her, Lilah jerked her fingers free. Zane's teasing grin made her heart pound. She resisted the almost overpowering urge to smile back. "What do you think you're doing?"

The wicked grin faded. "Something I should have done before, checking out your date. I want to make sure Howard doesn't have an agenda."

"He does. I realized tonight that he's married."

Zane's expression went from irritated to remote as he slid his cell out of his pocket and spoke briefly into it.

He snapped the phone closed. "Go to the car with Gemma and Elena. Spiros has just pulled up to the curb outside. I'll deal with Howard. Your boyfriend was also out in the courtyard with a phone camera."

Lilah stared at Howard who she noticed, was now knocking back something that looked extremely alcoholic. She remembered the shuffling sound, the extra flash.

Zane inserted himself into the jovial male group with the confidence and ease that came from being a supreme predator in the business world. She saw the moment Howard realized he had been made, the automatic reach for his pocket as if he wanted to shield his cell phone.

Howard's wild gaze connected briefly with hers. With calm deliberation, Lilah turned her back on Howard and walked through to the museum lobby. She noted that she didn't feel in the least shocked or depressed by the betrayal. On the contrary, there had been something highly satisfying in watching Zane go into battle for her. Unfortunately, along with her new ruthless streak, she seemed to have also gotten used to leading a life of notoriety.

Gemma and Elena strolled out directly behind her. Spiros held the door for them while they climbed into the limousine.

Elena chatted with Spiros in Medinian, leaving Lilah with a clearly unhappy Gemma.

Seconds later Zane joined them. Gemma beamed and patted the vacant space beside her. Instead of climbing in, Zane glanced across at a group of boys Lilah had noticed loitering a small distance away from the limo.

He glanced at Lilah. "I won't be long."

Gemma, looking distinctly irritable as Zane walked over to the boys, extracted a cell from her clutch and within seconds was deep in conversation about her new job and a move overseas. Elena retrieved a romance novel from her clutch, attached an efficient looking little LED light to the back pages, and was promptly engrossed.

Lilah decided she clearly hadn't lived, because she hadn't thought to bring an activity with her that was suitable for downtime in a limousine. Absently, she noted Howard slinking off to his car, which turned out to be a sleek little hatchback with a personalized licence plate that read "HERS."

Zane terminated a cell phone conversation as he walked back to the car. "I can't come back to the hotel with you right now. I have to take care of these kids. They saw the posters for the charity auction—that's why they came."

Lilah stared across at the lean wraiths clustered around a park bench as if that small landmark was all they had. "What can you do?"

"Get them in a house for the night with state foster care. That doesn't guarantee they'll stay, but at least it's a start. I'll see you later."

Lilah watched as Zane walked back to the kids, seeing the instant brightening of their faces. She hadn't realized how personally involved he was, or how much kids liked him.

She felt like she was seeing him for the first time, not the quintessential bad boy or the exciting, elusive lover the media liked to publicize, but a committed, protective man who would make an excellent father.

With the rest of the night in Zane's hotel suite looming,

it was not a good time to discover that Zane had somehow managed to transcend the list of attributes she was searching for in a husband and had made her requirements seem petty and flawed.

Eight

Lilah's cell phone rang as she stepped in the door of the suite. It was Zane. She remembered that she had given him her number earlier.

"Stay in my room. I won't be late."

She stiffened at the invitation, as if Zane was already so sure of her he assumed she would be sleeping with him. "No."

There was a hollow pause. "Why not?"

"For a start, you already have a girlfriend."

"Gemma is not my girlfriend. Like I said, she's a company employee and she fills in as my escort on occasion. Tonight's date was organized a few weeks ago. I would have canceled if I'd had time."

Lilah's fingers tightened on the phone. "I know this might sound silly to you, but I made a certain…vow. I might have forgotten it for a few minutes this afternoon, but that doesn't change the fact that it's important to me."

There was a ringing silence, punctuated by raised voices in the background.

"I have to go," Zane said curtly. "Whatever you do, don't leave the suite. Spiros will be out in the corridor if you need anything. And don't use the hotel phone. It's not secure and the press are still camped in the foyer."

The phone clicked quietly in her ear.

Feeling suddenly flat and a little depressed, Lilah walked through to her room and showered in the opulent marble bathroom, which not only contained a large walk-in shower, but a sunken spa tub. After slipping on a silk chemise, she belted one of the fluffy hotel robes around her waist and walked back out to the kitchen.

She found a bowl of fruit and a basket of fresh rolls on the counter. The fridge was groaning with food.

Abruptly starving, because she had been too wound up to eat anything but a few canapés from the buffet at the auction, Lilah helped herself to bread and cheese and a selection of mouthwatering dishes from the fridge. To balance out the decadence, she made herself a cup of tea.

Loading her snack onto a small tray, she carried it through to the sitting room and set it down on an elegant coffee table. She flicked through TV channels until she found a local news station.

Wrong choice. She stared at the live footage of Zane with Gemma at some point during the charity auction that evening. Her arm was coiled snugly around his. Young and fresh, with an ultrasexy fuchsia gown, Gemma was the perfect foil for Zane's dark, powerful build.

Suddenly miserable, she flicked to another channel and stared blankly at an old black-and-white movie. At eleven o'clock, she turned the TV set off. Too restless to sleep and worried that her apartment might have been broken into, she decided to call Evan and check if he had managed to fix the window. She retrieved her cell from her handbag and discovered the battery was dead. In her hurry to pack, she had not included her cell phone charger.

She spent another half hour kicking her heels. Her irritation at her isolation in the fabulous suite was edged by the dreaded notion that maybe Zane hadn't yet returned because he was now with Gemma.

It wasn't as if she had a claim on Zane, or should want to make one. Despite the attraction that sizzled between them, the crazy, inappropriate sense of attachment, Zane Atraeus did not fit into her life.

The one area in which they were in complete harmony was the most dangerous part of their relationship. No matter how tempted she was to fall into bed with Zane, she couldn't forget that sex had gotten her mother and her grandmother into trouble, literally.

At eleven-thirty, she retreated to her bedroom, climbed into the Hollywood fantasy of a bed and tried to sleep.

At midnight, tired of tossing and turning in a tangle of silken bedclothes, she pushed out of bed and walked back out to the kitchenette. On impulse, she picked up the hotel directory, found out how to dial out and called Evan, who was a night owl and didn't normally go to bed until one or two o'clock.

Evan was terse and to-the-point. He *had* fixed the window, but now he was busy, entertaining a *friend*.

Cheeks burning, Lilah apologized. She was on the point of hanging up when Zane walked through the door.

Zane shrugged out of his jacket and tossed it over the back of a chair. "I thought I told you not to use the hotel phone."

Lilah said goodbye and hung up. "I had to make a call. My cell phone battery was dead."

He frowned. "Who is it? Howard?"

"No."

"Lucas?"

"I called Evan to see if he'd fixed my window."

He removed his bow tie and jerked at the buttons of his dress shirt. "Peters. Just how many male friends have you got?"

Annoyance zinged through her. "I don't know why that

should worry you, when you've got so many 'friends' yourself."

Zane's expression cleared, as if she had just said something that had cheered him up immeasurably. "I've spent half the night with a bunch of scared kids."

She stared resolutely at his jaw, desperate to avoid the softening in his gaze. "It's after midnight."

Comprehension gleamed. "And you thought I was with Gemma."

He closed the distance between them and framed her face so she was forced to meet his gaze, and suddenly there was no air. "Why do you think I became the patron of a Sydney charity, when I've been based in the States?"

Zane answered his own question. "Because I wanted you."

Zane logged the moment Lilah accepted that he genuinely wanted her.

Desire burned away the jealousy that had gripped him when he had found her talking on the phone.

He didn't *get* jealous. Ever since his early teens, he had controlled his emotions and his sex drive. He had been selective in his bed partners.

For two years, since he had severed his last short liaison, he hadn't needed a woman at all. It was not unusual for him to have periods of celibacy, but this one had stretched beyond personal preference.

Lilah's sea-green gaze locked with his.

The attraction didn't make sense. He didn't want Lilah to matter to him, but it was a fact that she did.

Bending his head, he touched his mouth to hers.

Long, drugging seconds passed. He lifted his head before he lost it completely. He was male, he loved women, their softness and beauty; he just didn't trust them.

Until now, he'd had no interest in changing.

The thought that he could change, that he wanted to trust Lilah, made his heart pound.

Her fingers slid into his hair. The faint, tugging pressure

as she lifted up and pressed her mouth to his was stunningly erotic. A wave of intense, dissolving pleasure shimmered through him. Dimly, he noted that he was on the edge of losing control.

Lilah lifted up on her toes, pressing closer to Zane. Subconsciously, she realized she had been waiting for this ever since Elena had interrupted them that afternoon.

With a stifled groan, Zane took a half step forward, pinning her against the edge of the counter.

She felt him tugging at her thick, fluffy robe, the coolness of the air against her skin as the robe slipped to the floor. He dipped his head and took one breast in his mouth through the silk of her chemise, and sensation jerked through her.

A split second later, the room tilted as he swung her into his arms. Depositing her on the soft cushions of one of the elaborate, overstuffed couches, he came down alongside her.

Blindly, she fumbled at his shirt until she found naked skin. She tore open the final buttons and impatiently waited while he shrugged out of the shirt.

She felt the heat of his palms gliding along her thighs, the warm silk of her chemise puddling around her hips.

In twelve years of dating, this was the closest she had come to feeling anything like the intensity that friends wept over and talked about, that she had absorbed second hand through books and movies.

Being desired, she discovered, was infinitely seductive; it undermined her defenses, dissolved every last shred of resistance. Even the idea of holding on to her virginity seemed vague and abstract. Especially in light of the fact that she had already more or less surrendered to Zane two years ago. After grimly hanging on to that bastion of purity for so long she couldn't help thinking it might actually be a relief to get rid of it.

Zane's fingers hooked in the waistband of her panties. Driven by desire and an intense curiosity, instead of resisting, Lilah lifted her hips and assisted the process. Cool air was instantly replaced by the muscular heat of Zane's body as he came down between her legs.

As wrong as her logical mind told her it was to allow Zane to make love to her, the man who was holding her, cradling her as if she was precious to him, *felt* right. She had never felt more alive; she couldn't help adoring every minute. In that moment she understood why both her mother and grandmother had risked all for passion. She couldn't believe she had waited this long to find out.

In an effort to help out, she tugged at the fastening of his pants, and felt him hot and silky smooth against her. His heated gaze locked with hers. For a moment, time seemed to stand still. Then he surged inside her.

Zane froze.

His gaze locked with Lilah's again. Comprehension sliced through the spiraling pleasure that for the past few minutes had numbed his brain. "You're a virgin."

Her expression was distracted, although she didn't seem overly upset. "Yes."

He wasn't wearing a condom. That was another first.

Zane's jaw clenched as wave after wave of raw desire washed through him. He had never lost control before. He needed to pull free and call a halt to the primitive rush of satisfaction that Lilah had only ever been his.

Lilah moved restlessly beneath him, the subtle shimmy easing the pressure and drawing him deeper. He gritted his teeth. "That's not helping."

Every muscle tensed as Lilah tightened around him, locking him into her body. Incredibly, he felt her climax around him. Burning, irresistible pleasure swamped Zane again. His jaw clenched as his own climax hit him, shoving him over the edge.

Long minutes passed while they lay sprawled together on the couch. Eventually, driven by an electrifying thought, Zane lifted his head.

He could make Lilah pregnant.

Not "could make," he thought grimly. That was something that happened in the future. He was pretty sure they were in the realm of "making pregnant" as in *now*.

Lilah was loathe to move, loathe to separate herself from Zane because she was certain that, as singular and devastatingly pleasurable as the lovemaking had been, despite a little initial discomfort, Zane was less than impressed.

He hadn't liked learning that she was a virgin.

Guilt flooded her when she remembered the shameless way she had clenched around him, holding him in her body.

A reflexive shiver went through her at the memory.

Zane's gaze was oddly flat. "Why didn't you tell me you were a virgin?"

Warm color flooded her cheeks. "There wasn't exactly time for a conversation."

"If I'd known, I would have done things…differently."

"I hadn't exactly planned on this, myself."

He propped himself on his elbows. "Neither had I. Otherwise I would have used a condom. Which is the second issue. How likely are you to get pregnant?"

She felt her flush deepen, although this time the surge of heat wasn't solely because of the very pertinent pregnancy question. "Don't worry, there's no danger of a pregnancy." She tried for a breezy smile, a little difficult when she had just tossed away what her grandmother had always termed her Most Valued Possession. "I take a contraceptive pill."

There was a moment of vibrating silence. Somewhere in the hush of the suite Lilah could hear the ponderous tick of a clock. Outside, somewhere in the distance a siren wailed.

Zane's expression was oddly frozen. "It's a relief someone was in control of the situation. For a minute there I thought we could be parents."

"No chance." She tried not to be riveted by the three very fascinating studs in his lobe. "The one thing I've never planned on being is a single parent."

There was another heavy silence. She got the impression that Zane was not entirely happy with her answer.

"Since you've taken care of the protection so efficiently..." He dipped his head and lightly kissed her then systematically peeled off the chemise. Satisfaction registered in his gaze as he tossed the scrap of silk onto the floor and cupped her breasts, his thumbs sweeping across her nipples.

Lilah's eyes automatically closed as the delicious sensations started all over again.

The rapid shift back into mind-numbing passion set off alarm bells. It occurred to her that now that they had made love, she was in a very precarious position with regard to marriage. Zane was not an option. He had never been an option. His aversion to relationships in general and marriage in particular was well publicized. *She* still wanted marriage, and she couldn't in all good conscience continue with her marriage plans while she had a lover. Regretfully, she did her utmost to dampen down on the desire.

She felt as if she was surfacing from a dream. She had been shameless and had acted with abandon. Her face burned at the memory. She had actively *encouraged* Zane to have unprotected sex with her.

She had clung to him when he had wanted to put a stop to the process and withdraw, then it had been too late and over in seconds.

It was as if, in a weird way, even though she had been sensible enough to guard herself with contraception, a wild, irresponsible part of her had actually courted the very thing she feared most.

Guilt and fatalism churned in her stomach. The sheer weight of her family history and conditioning, the years of guarding against these types of liaisons, should have been enough to stop her.

"We can't do this again." Pressing at Zane's shoulders, she wriggled free, grabbed at her chemise and dragged it on.

Zane's gaze seared over her as she belted the thick robe

around her waist. "All you had to do was say no." The tinge of outrage in his voice stopped her in her tracks.

She flushed guiltily at the truth of that, since she had been the one who hadn't wanted to stop in the first place. She dragged her gaze away from the bronzed, muscular lines of his body as he pulled on dark, fitted trousers. With his strong profile, his black hair tumbling to his broad shoulders, he was beautiful in an untamed, completely masculine way.

Disbelief flooded her that she had actually made love with him. Although the evidence was registering all over her body in tingling aches and the faint stiffening of muscles.

Zane retrieved his shirt. "There's one other thing you don't have to worry about. STD's."

Frowning, Lilah dragged her gaze from the mesmerizing sight of Zane's six-pack.

Zane's gaze snapped to hers. "Sexually transmitted diseases. I don't have any. If tonight was a first for you, it was a first for me. I've never had unprotected sex with a woman before."

Her stomach tightened at the clinical mention of another danger she had failed to consider, and the relegation of their lovemaking to sex. "Um…thanks."

She could feel her face, her whole body, flaming. At twenty-nine, she was probably more naive than the average fifteen-year-old and Zane's reputation with women was legendary. She had been so wrapped up in what she was experiencing she had failed to consider what Zane had to be thinking—that she was hopelessly gauche and naive.

Depression settled around her like a shroud. *Way to go, Lilah Cole. Living up to the family crest. Abandon all thought of responsibility until it's too late.* "If you'll excuse me, I'm going to bed now."

He folded his arms over his chest, his gaze cool. "I'll see you in the morning."

Not if she could help it.

Lilah closed her bedroom door behind her, relieved that

she was finally alone. She checked the bedside clock and an unnerving sense of disorientation set in. It wasn't yet one o'clock. Barely thirty minutes had passed since Zane had walked through the door. Thirty minutes in which her life had drastically altered.

She used her en suite bathroom to freshen up, this time hardly noticing the gorgeous fixtures. Instead of climbing into the elegant four-poster, she changed into jeans, a cotton sweater and sneakers, her fingers fumbling in their haste to get into casual, everyday clothes and restore some semblance of normality.

When she was dressed, she rewound her hair, which had ended up in an untidy mass, into a coil, stabbed pins through to lock the silky strands in place and systematically packed. Twenty minutes after entering her room, she was ready to leave.

Forcing herself to calm down, she sat on the edge of the bed and listened. She had heard Zane's shower earlier, but now the suite was plunged into silence.

Taking a deep breath, she walked to her door and opened it a crack. The sitting room was in darkness. There didn't appear to be any light filtering under the door of Zane's bedroom or flowing out on to the terrace, signaling that he was still awake.

Lifting her bag, she tiptoed to the door and let herself out into the hall. She was almost at the elevator when Spiros loomed out of an alcove and stopped her.

His fractured English almost defeated her. When he picked up his cell and she realized he was going to call Zane, she summoned up a breezy smile, as if the fact that she was sneaking out in the middle of the night was all part of the plan. "Nessuno." She jabbed at the call button and carefully enunciated each word as she spoke. "No need to call Zane, he's sleeping."

He frowned then nodded, clearly not happy.

Forty minutes later, Lilah paid off the taxi that had delivered her back to her apartment and walked inside.

She checked the messages on her phone. They were all

from tabloids and women's magazines wanting interviews. She had expected that Spiros, who had been uneasy about the fact that she had left at such an odd hour, would have caved and woken Zane up. Clearly, that hadn't happened, because there was no message from Zane.

Feeling oddly let down that she hadn't heard from Zane, she deleted them all.

Pulling the drapes tight, just in case someone was lurking outside with a camera, she changed into a spare chemise in pitch darkness and fell into bed.

She slept fitfully, waking at dawn, half expecting the phone to ring, or for Zane to be thumping on her door.

She got up and made a cup of tea, collapsed on the couch and watched movies. By ten o'clock, when Zane hadn't either called or come by, exhausted from waiting, she dropped back into bed and slept until two in the afternoon.

When she got up, her stomach growling with hunger, she checked her phone. There were a string of new messages but, again, they were all from reporters.

Stabbing the delete button, she erased them all and finally decided to put herself out of her misery by taking the phone off the hook. On impulse, she checked her cell phone, but it wasn't in her bag. She must have left it in Zane's suite.

To keep the cold misery at bay that Zane didn't appear to have any interest in contacting her, she opened a can of soup and made toast. Evan knocked on her door, wanting to return her spare key and check that she was okay. At four o'clock a second visitor knocked.

A courier. He handed her a package and requested she sign for it.

She scribbled her name, closed the door then ripped the package open. Her stomach dropped like a stone as her fingers closed around her cell phone.

From the second she had left Zane's suite, she realized, she had been waiting for him to come after her, to insist that he wanted her back. That what they had shared had been as special for him as it had been for her.

That clearly wasn't the case.

Zane hadn't even bothered to include a note with the phone. All he had done was return her property in such a way that made it clear he no longer wanted contact.

Feeling numb, she put the phone on charge. Almost immediately, it beeped. Crazy hope gripped her as she opened the message.

It was Lucas, not Zane. He wanted her to call him.

Using the cell, she put the call through. Lucas picked up immediately. The conversation was brief. Thanks to her boosted media profile, she had just won a prestigious design award in Milan, which would give Ambrosi an edge in the market. A week ago, she had applied for the job of managing the new Ambrosi Pearl facility, which was to be constructed on the island of Ambrus, one of the smaller islands in the Medinian group. If she wanted the job, it was hers.

The job was a promotion with a substantial raise in her salary plus a generous living allowance. If she took it, paying her mother's mortgage would no longer be a problem. She would even be able to save.

The only problem was, Zane lived on Medinos. Although, with the amount of travel he did, most of it to the States, she doubted their paths would often cross.

A bonus would be that she could leave Sydney and all of the media hype behind. She would have a fresh start.

Away from her latest sex scandal.

Taking a deep breath, she took the plunge and affirmed that she would take the job.

Lucas rang back a few minutes later. He had booked a flight, leaving in two days. Her accommodation, until a house could be arranged, was the Atraeus Resort on Medinos.

Reeling from the sudden change of direction her life had taken, Lilah rang her mother and told her the good news, carefully glossing over the bad parts.

After she had hung up, she cleared her answering machine and disconnected the phone. She also turned her cell phone off. She didn't know how long it would take the media to discover that Lucas had offered her a job on Medinos, but given the added hype behind the Milan award, she didn't think it would take long.

Too wound up to try and relax again, she decided to take one of her finished paintings to the gallery that handled her work.

When she walked into the trendy premises, the proprietor, Quincy Travers, a plump, balding man with a shrewd glint in his eyes, greeted her with open arms.

With glee he took the abstract she'd painted and handed her a check for an astounding amount. "As soon as I saw the story in the paper I contacted some collectors I know and put an extra couple of zeroes on the price of the paintings. I sold out within thirty minutes."

"Great." Lilah's delight at the check, which was enough to pay off her mother's mortgage and still leave change, went into the same deep, dark hole that had snuffed out her delight at the Milan award and her promotion.

She shoved the check in her purse. Just what she needed to brighten her day. Like her jewelry design, any value her art now had was tied to her notoriety.

Quincy propped the painting on an empty display easel and rubbed his hands together. "No need to put a price on this. I've got buyers waiting. Sex sells. What else have you got, love? You could scribble with crayons and we'd still make a fortune."

"Actually, I'm leaving town for a while, so that will be the last one for the foreseeable future."

Quincy looked crestfallen. "If I'd known that, I would have asked more for the other paintings." He rummaged beneath his counter and came up with a battered address book. "But all is not lost. If the buyers know this is the last one, they'l pay." He flipped it open and reached for his phone. "By the way, did you really, er, *date* both brothers at the same time?"

Lilah could feel herself turning pink. She was suddenly fiercely glad she was leaving town in two days. "No." Ducking her head, she walked quickly out of the gallery.

She had just slept with the one.

Nine

Two days later, fresh off a flight from Broome in Western Australia and frustrated that he had not been able to get any reply from either Lilah's work or home phone, or cell, Zane swung the Corvette into the parking space outside her building.

He buzzed the apartment. While he waited for a response, the electrifying moments on the couch replayed in his mind. The enthusiastic way Lilah had clung to him, the explosive moment when he had known for sure that she had never made love with Lucas, Peters or any other man. The fierce way she had locked him into her body when he had attempted to withdraw, as if she hadn't wanted to let him go.

The brain freeze that had hit him, because he hadn't wanted to stop, either.

When he'd discovered that Lilah had sneaked out on him during the night, he had been both furious and relieved.

The fact that he had made the monumental mistake of making love to her without protection, that he could have made her pregnant, still stunned him.

It had been right up there with finding out that she had been a virgin.

A day spent kicking his heels, trying to decide if those out-of-control moments had been unscripted and spontaneous or if he had been neatly manipulated by a consummate operator had been enough.

Every time he had examined what had happened, he had come to the same inescapable conclusion. Whatever Lilah's motives had been in surrendering her virginity to him, she had taken care of the contraception, which argued her innocence.

He had done a background check on Lilah, even going so far as to fly to her hometown, Broome. When he'd found out that, like him, she was illegitimate, several pieces of the puzzle that was Lilah Cole had fallen into place.

He knew how a dysfunctional upbringing could influence decisions. Lilah had been brought up by her single mother, whose health was poor. Consequently, the financial burden had now fallen on her. She not only paid her own costs in Sydney, she paid her mother's mortgage and medical bills.

The knowledge put Lilah's search for a well-heeled husband into an irritatingly practical light. It had also exposed how potentially vulnerable Lilah could be to an "arrangement" should some man try to step into her life.

He leaned on the buzzer again. Since Lilah wasn't answering any calls, he had reasoned that she had most probably taken some time off work and was inside, hiding out from the press.

His frustration level increasing when there was still no response, he cut through the adjacent property, another shabby warehouse, and pushed through the broken fence into Lilah's backyard.

He examined the bifold doors and windows, which were locked and blanked out by thick drapes. He rapped on the door and tried calling. When there was no answer he walked back around to the front door and pressed buzzers until he got an answer from one of the other apartments.

A voice like a rusty nail being slowly extracted from a sheet of iron informed him that Lilah had left the country. Her apartment was now empty, if he wanted to rent it.

Zane terminated the conversation and strode back to the Corvette. A quick call to Lucas answered the question that was threatening to aggravate his newly discovered anger problem.

"Lilah has flown to Medinos. She's agreed to head up the new Ambrosi Pearls facility."

Zane's fingers tightened on his cell. "Who made the arrangement?"

"I did. I'll be flying out to Medinos in the next few days to check that she's settling in."

A snapping sound informed Zane that he had just broken one of the hinges that attached the LCD screen to the body of his phone. "Carla won't be happy."

That was an understatement. Carla Ambrosi was known for her passionate outbursts. But whatever Carla might feel about Lucas's continuing involvement with Lilah didn't come close to Zane's level of unhappiness.

"After the crazy stuff the tabloids have been printing," Lucas said grimly, "the less Carla knows about Lilah the better. I'm organizing for her to spend some time with her mother here when I fly out to Medinos."

Zane's stomach tightened. Which meant Carla would be conveniently out of the way for Lucas's meeting with Lilah. "When did Lilah leave?"

"Today."

Zane terminated the conversation and placed a call to Elena. Within seconds she had located the information he wanted. The only flight out of Sydney to Medinos that day had already departed.

Tossing the phone on the passenger seat, Zane slid behind the wheel and accelerated away from the curb. Lilah had left that morning, but her flight was long, with a three-hour stopover in Singapore and another shorter stop in Dubai. Using the Atraeus private jet, he would easily reach Medinos before her.

Whatever ideas his brother might have of conducting a clandestine affair with Lilah, Zane was certain of one fact. Lilah hadn't chosen to give herself to Lucas; she had given herself to him.

He, also, had made a choice when he had made love with Lilah. He wanted her, and after two years, one night had not been enough. One thing was certain: he was not about to let Lucas entice Lilah away.

Satisfaction curled in his stomach as the decision settled in. If he'd had any reservations, in that moment they were gone.

The complication of Lilah's virginity and marriage plan aside, he was finally going to live up to the reputation of his marauding ancestor.

Lilah was his, and he was taking her.

Lilah stepped into the air-conditioned terminal on Medinos.

Almost immediately she was accosted by a uniformed security guard, a holstered gun on one thigh.

Exhausted from the long nerve-racking flight, during which she had only been able to sleep in snatches, she accompanied the officer to a small, sterile interview room. Several fruitless questions later, because the guard's English was limited and her Medinian was close to nonexistent, she resigned herself to wait. The one piece of information she had gleaned was that, apparently, they were waiting for a member of the Atraeus family.

Minutes later, her frustration levels rising, her luggage, along with a foam cup of coffee, was delivered to the interview room and an airport official showed up to personally process her arrival papers. As the official handed her stamped passport back, the door opened. Zane, dressed in dark jeans and a loose white shirt, his hair ruffled as if he'd dragged his fingers through it repeatedly, strolled into the room.

For a confused moment Lilah had difficulty grasping that

Zane was actually here, then the meaning of his presence sank in. "You're the Atraeus who had me detained."

The official left, the door closing quietly behind him.

Zane frowned. "Who were you expecting? Lucas?"

The flatness of Zane's voice was faintly shocking. Lilah couldn't help thinking it was a long way from the teasing grin and the seductive huskiness of Saturday night. "As far as I know, Lucas is still in Sydney."

Zane placed a newspaper, which had been tucked under one arm, down on the desktop.

The glaring headline, *Lucas Atraeus Installs Mistress on Isle of Medinos,* made her bristle. When she had flown out of Sydney, she had hoped she was leaving all of that behind.

Folding the paper over, she threw it in the trashcan beside the desk. "I haven't seen that one. They don't hand out Sydney gossip sheets as part of the in-flight entertainment."

Zane perched on the edge of the desk, arms folded across his chest. "Who knew that you were flying out to Medinos?"

Lilah located her handbag and stored her passport in a secure pocket. Making a quick exit lugging a large suitcase, a carry-on bag, her laptop and her handbag would be difficult, but she was ready to give it a go. "Quite a lot of people. It wasn't a secret."

Zane looked briefly irritated as she tried to harness her laptop to the suitcase using a set of buckles that was clearly inadequate for the job. "That's not helpful."

"It wasn't meant to be." She hauled on a dainty strap and finally had the laptop secure.

"So who do you think could have leaked the information that you were moving to Medinos to the press?"

She moved on to the carry-on case, which posed a problem. She was going to need a trolley after all.

"You don't have to worry about the luggage. I'll carry it for you."

Anger flowed through her at the implication that *she* could have sold the story. "I prefer to manage on my own."

"You don't have to, since I'm here to pick you up." With efficient movements, Zane unhooked the laptop and used the straps to neatly attach the carry-on case to the large suitcase.

Lilah reclaimed her laptop. "I don't get it. You didn't come around or call, and now—"

"I called. Your phone didn't seem to be working."

She tried to get her tired brain around the astounding fact that Zane hadn't abandoned her, entirely. Although, there was nothing loverlike about his demeanor now. A lightbulb went on in her head. "Don't tell me you thought I could have leaked the story because I'm angling to be Lucas's mistress?"

"Or to break Lucas and Carla up."

For a vibrating moment she struggled against the desire to empty what was left of her coffee down his front. Instead, she set her laptop down and, stepping close, ran her finger down Zane's chest, pausing over the steady thud of his heart. "Why would I, when as you so eloquently put it, I've already got the real thing?"

Heat flared in his gaze. His fingers closed around her wrist, trapping her palm against the wall of his chest. "Past tense, Lilah. You were the one who walked out."

Shock reverberated through her that he could possibly have wanted her to stay. "I didn't think you were…serious."

His gaze was unnervingly steady. "One-night stands are not exactly my thing."

The heat from his chest burned into her palm. "So all those stories in the press about you and who knows how many gorgeous women are untrue?"

His free hand curled around her nape. He reeled her in a little closer. "Mostly."

Honest, but still dangerous. Distantly, she registered that this was what she had so badly wanted from Zane two days ago. He had finally come after her and in true pirate fashion was seemingly intent on dragging her back to bed. "So, in theory then, the press could have lied about me."

He leaned forward; his lips feathered her jaw sending a hot tingle of sensation through her. "It's possible."

"I'm not interested in breaking Lucas and Carla up."

"Good, because I have a proposition for you." He bit down gently on her lobe. "Two days on an island paradise. You and me."

Sensation shimmered through her, briefly blanking her mind. So that was what it was like, she thought a little breathlessly. She had read that the earlobe was an erogenous zone. Now, finally, she could attest to that fact.

She took a deep breath and let it out slowly. The idea of an exciting interlude with Zane before she started work and became once more embroiled in her search for a stable, trustworthy husband, was unbearably seductive. There were no good reasons to go, only bad ones. "Yes."

She caught the quick flash of his grin before his mouth closed on hers, and for long seconds she forgot to breathe.

Ten minutes later, Lilah found herself installed in the rear seat of a limousine, Zane beside her and the familiar figure of Spiros behind the wheel. A short drive later and they pulled into a picturesque marina.

She examined the ranks of gleaming superyachts, launches and sailboats tied up to a neat series of jetties. "This doesn't look like the Atraeus Resort."

"It's a nice day. I thought you might enjoy the boat ride."

Spiros opened her door, distracting her. When she turned back to Zane, the seat next to her was empty. Zane was already out of the limousine, his jacket off and draped over one shoulder. Following suit, she climbed out, wincing at the dazzling brightness of sunlight reflecting off white boats. Finding her sunglasses, she slid them onto the bridge of her nose.

By that time, Spiros, who she had noticed had not met her gaze once during the last few minutes, had her cases out of the trunk. Zane was already halfway down the jetty and untying ropes. The boat trip to the resort seemed to be a fait accompli, so Lilah followed in Spiros's wake, determined to enjoy the sunny day and the spectacular sea views.

By the time she reached the sleek white yacht, her cases were already stowed. Zane extended his hand and helped her climb aboard.

Almost instantly the engine hummed to life. Spiros walked along the jetty, released the last rope and tossed it over the stern. Lilah couldn't help noticing that he seemed to be in a hurry. When he didn't climb aboard she frowned. "Isn't Spiros coming?"

"Not on this trip." With deft skill, Zane maneuvered the yacht out of its berth.

Minutes later, they cleared the marina and the boat picked up speed, wallowing slightly in the chop. Feeling faintly queasy with the motion, Lilah sat down and tried to enjoy the scenery.

Twenty minutes later, her unease turned to suspicion. Instead of hugging the coastline they seemed to be heading for open sea. The coastline of Medinos had receded, and the island of Ambrus loomed ahead.

Dragging strands of hair out of her eyes, she pushed to her feet, gripping the back of her seat to stay upright. "This is not the way to the resort."

"I'm taking you to Ambrus."

"There's nothing *on* Ambrus."

His gaze rested briefly on hers. "That's not strictly true. There's an unfinished resort on the northern headland."

The yacht rounded a point and sailed into calmer water. Lilah stared at the curve of the beach ahead and the tumbled wreckage of the old pearl facility, which had been destroyed in the Second World War. It was, literally, a bombsite. In a flash, Spiros's odd behavior and his hurried exit made sense. Zane had planned this. She gestured at the looming beach. "I didn't agree to that. You said two days. Paradise."

Zane throttled back on the engine. "Maybe I wasn't talking about the scenery."

An instant flashback to the heated few minutes on Zane's couch made her blush. "I didn't exactly find paradise in your hotel room."

"There wasn't time. If you'll recall, you ran out on me."

Her jaw firmed. When she had landed on Medinos her life had been firmly under control. Somehow in the space of an hour everything had gone to hell in a handbasket again. "I'm booked in at the Atraeus Resort. That's where I'm staying for the next few weeks."

"You agreed. Two days." His jaw tightened. "Or did you want another media furor when Lucas arrives tomorrow?"

She stared at the tough line of his jaw. The dazzling few moments in the customs interview room when she'd been weak enough to allow him to kiss her replayed in her mind. That had been her first mistake. "I assumed you were taking me to my suite at the Atraeus Resort."

"I apologize for the deception," he said bluntly, although there was no hint of apology in his gaze. "I'll take you to Medinos in two days' time. Once Lucas leaves."

She stared at the deserted stretch of coastline then back at the distant view of Medinos. She had wanted out of the media circus and she had wanted peace and quiet. It looked like now she was getting both, with a vengeance. "Is there power, an internet connection?"

"There's a generator. No internet."

"Then we need to go back to Medinos. I'll be missed. People will be concerned. Questions will be asked."

Zane frowned. "Who, exactly, is going to ask these questions?"

Lilah stared fixedly at the horizon, aware that the conversation had drifted into dangerous waters. "I have…friends."

"It's only two days."

A little desperate now, Lilah tried for a vague look. "Online friends. I need to keep in touch."

Zane's gaze was unnervingly piercing. "And being away from an internet connection for two days is an issue?"

She crossed her arms over her chest, refusing to be drawn. "It could be."

After the disappointment with Lucas she had felt an urgency to move along with her marriage project and had committed to a series of dates with her list of potentially perfect husbands. Howard had only been the first. Up until that moment she had been too busy with making arrangements to leave Sydney, and preparing herself for a new life and a new job, to stop and think about the upcoming series of dates she had arranged for a scheduled holiday back home in two weeks' time.

The sound of the engine changed as they neared shore. The reality of what was happening sank in as the huge, deserted sweep of the crescent bay underlined their complete isolation. "You're kidnapping me."

Zane's brows jerked together. "That's a little dramatic. We're staying at a beach house where we can spend some time together, uninterrupted."

Against all the odds her heart thumped wildly at his bad-tempered, rather blunt statement, which definitely indicated a desire to keep her to himself. She guessed she could excuse him, although not right away.

He had *kidnapped* her.

She clamped down on the dizzying delight that he wanted her enough to actually commit a crime. After Zane's behavior in Sydney and her misery when he had failed to come after her, it was a scenario she hadn't dared consider.

The engine dropped to a low hum. Zane stabbed at a button. The rattle of a chain cut through the charged silence as he dropped anchor.

Lilah watched the grim set of Zane's shoulders as he studied the chain for a few seconds to make sure the anchor had taken hold. "I suppose on Medinos, trying to get a conviction against an Atraeus is impossible."

Zane went very still. When he straightened, she realized

the faint shaking of his shoulders was laughter. He grinned, suddenly looking rakish. "Not impossible, just highly improbable."

Ten

The inflatable boat scraped ashore on the pristine white-sand beach. With a fluid movement, Zane climbed out and held it steady against the wash of waves. Ignoring the hand he offered her, Lilah clambered over the side, shoes in one hand, handbag gripped in the other.

Ankle-deep water splashed her calves, surprisingly cold as she stepped onto the firmly packed sand at the shoreline. With muscular ease, Zane pulled the inflatable higher on the beach, unwound rope and tied it to an iron ring attached to a weathered post.

Shielding her eyes from the sun, which was almost directly overhead, Lilah examined the bay. Beyond the post was an expanse of tussock grass interspersed with darker patches of wild thyme and rosemary. Farther back, and to the right, she could see, following the broad curve of an estuary, the remains of sheds. To the right, flanked by a grove of gnarled olive trees, was the ivy-encrusted remnant of what must have once been a grand villa. She instantly knew that this had to be

Sebastien Ambrosi's villa. Sienna and Carla Ambrosi's grandfather had left Medinos in the 1940s and settled in Broome, Australia, where he had reestablished the Ambrosi Pearls business. "The house looks smaller than I imagined."

"You knew Sebastien Ambrosi?"

"My mother used to work for him in Broome, seeding and grading pearls. He was very kind to us." She lifted her shoulders. "I've always been fascinated by Ambrosi Pearls, and I've always longed to see Ambrus."

While Zane unloaded their cases, she walked along the beach. From here nothing was visible except the misty line where sea met sky, no land, no Medinos or any other island, just water and isolation.

She studied the Atraeus beach house, which was set back into a curve in the jagged cliffs. Built on three levels, it wasn't, by any stretch of the imagination, a cottage. Planes of glass glinted in the sun. The teaklike wood and the jutting curves and angles gave it the appearance of a gigantic ship flowing out of the rock. Sited higher than the beach, it no doubt commanded a magnificent view.

"Are you all right?"

She whirled. "You're holding me prisoner. Other than that, I guess everything is just fine."

Any hint of amusement winked out of his gaze. "You are not a 'prisoner.' I've asked a Medinian couple, Jorge and Marta, to stay over for a couple of days. Jorge is a trained butler, and Marta is a chef. I'm trying to keep this as PC as I can."

"A PC kidnapping."

His jaw set in an obdurate line. "If you're hungry, Marta will have lunch ready up at the house."

Zane breathed a sigh of relief when Lilah appeared, fresh and cool after showering and changing into a white shift, to join him on one of the enormous decks for lunch.

Marta had set out a tempting array of salads and meats. As Zane watched Lilah eat, curiously at home in the wild setting, a sense of possessiveness filled him.

The house on Ambrus was a luxury retreat. He could have brought any number of women he had known here, but he had never been even remotely tempted. Lilah was his first guest. Not that she had seen it that way.

He realized he wasn't just attracted to Lilah; he liked her, even down to the way she pushed his buttons. She had given him a hard time from the minute he had caught up with her in the airport.

His decision to do whatever it took to keep her with him settled in. She wasn't ready to admit it yet, or surrender to him, but he was confident he could change that. Deny it as she might, she couldn't hide the fact that she wanted him.

Until that moment, he hadn't known how this would work, but now the equation was simple. Lucas had had his chance, and made his choice. He was no longer prepared to allow his brother, or any other man, near her.

Emotion expanded in his chest. After living an admittedly wild, single life, it was something of a U-turn. Until that moment he hadn't known how much he wanted to make it. He still didn't know how exactly they would work out a relationship, how long it would last—or if Lilah was even prepared to try, given her agenda—but he was finally prepared to try.

Lilah placed her fork down and smothered a yawn. "I think I'll go take a nap."

Zane watched her walk back into the house and determinedly squashed the desire to go after her.

After detaining her at the airport then kidnapping her, carrying her to bed would not improve on the impression he had made. Given that he wanted more than a short-lived liaison, he needed to take a different, more mature, approach.

As much as he wanted to follow up on the promise of those rushed few moments on the couch, he would have to wait.

She didn't trust him yet. At this point trust was a commodity neither of them possessed.

When Lilah woke, the sun had gone down and she could smell something savory cooking. Pushing back the sheet, which was the only covering she had needed in the balmy heat, she walked through to the lavish marble en suite bathroom to freshen up.

It seemed that even when the Atraeus family holidayed at the beach, it was done with style. After washing her face, she ran a comb through her hair and coiled it into a loose knot on top of her head. Eyes narrowed, she surveyed her crumpled wardrobe. If she was launching herself into a two-day venture of passion, she needed to dress the part.

In the end she changed into a simple but elegant ivory cotton dress with an intriguingly low cut neckline that she usually teamed with a thin silk camisole.

She inserted pearl studs in her ears and spent a good ten minutes on her makeup. The results weren't exactly spectacular, but Zane hadn't given her much notice. Feeling buoyed up but more than a little on edge, she strolled out to the main sitting room.

For the next two days she had a guilty kind of permission to put her marriage plans to one side and immerse herself in a passionate experience. Unfortunately, she was going to have to play it by ear. Nothing in her extensive research on dating with a view to marriage had prepared her to cope with a rampant love affair with a totally unsuitable man.

Zane was already on the deck dressed in fitted dark pants that outlined the muscular length of his legs and a loose, gauzy white shirt. On another man the semitransparent shirt might have looked soft and effeminate, but on Zane the effect of muslin clinging to broad shoulders was powerful and utterly masculine. With his hair sleeked back in a ponytail, the studs in his ear were clearly visible, making him look even more like his piratical ancestor.

Somewhere classical music played softly. Marta had set the table, but this time it was glamorously romantic with white damask, gleaming gold cutlery and ornate gold candlesticks. Lit candles provided a soft, flickering glow, highlighting the Lalique glassware. With the deck floating in darkness above the rocks and the sea luminous and gleaming below, it was easy to fantasize that she was standing in the prow of a ship.

Dinner was a gazpacho-style soup with fresh, warm rolls, followed by a rich chicken casserole with pasta. Desert was a platter of honeyed pastries, fresh figs and soft white cheese.

Marta and Jorge cleared away. When Zane indicated they should go inside, she preceded him gladly, grateful for the distraction from the growing awareness that they were finally alone.

Feeling even more nervous now, Lilah walked around the huge sitting room, studying the artwork on the walls. She stopped at a beautifully executed watercolor of a rocky track, which culminated in a cave.

Zane's deep, cool voice close to her ear sent a tingling jolt of awareness through her. "That came from the old villa. One of the few possessions that survived the World War Two bombing."

She forced herself to study the familiar signature at the bottom right-hand corner of the painting, although with Zane behind her she was now utterly distracted. "Of course, one of Sebastien's."

"You might recognize a couple of landmarks." He reached past her to indicate a familiar headland, then farther in the background, a high peak. "It's a painting of an area behind the old villa."

She tensed at Zane's proximity. It was ridiculous to be so on edge. It wasn't as if they hadn't kissed a number of times, made love.

The warmth of his breath on her nape sent a shivery frisson down her spine. "Would you like a drink?"

When she turned, he had already moved away and was at the drinks cabinet, a decanter of brandy in one hand, a balloon glass in the other. "No. Thanks."

He splashed brandy in the glass and gestured at the comfortable leather couches. "Have a seat.

Lilah chose an armchair close to the fire, sank into the

cloud of leather and tried to relax. She blushed when she registered Zane's gaze lingering in the area of her neckline, and tried to brazen out the moment.

"Why didn't you tell me that Peters was gay?"

She stiffened at the question. "And how would you know that?"

"I was interested. I made a few inquiries."

Outrage stiffened her spine. She knew what Zane did for a living. He was The Atraeus Group's fixer. If there was a difficult situation or a problem with personnel, Zane took care of it along with a sinister clutch of characters, one of whom happened to be Spiros. "You mean you had me, and Evan, investigated."

Irritation gleamed in his dark eyes. "I asked a few questions in the Ambrosi office. That girl who works in PR? What's her name?"

"Lisa."

"That's it. She told me."

Lilah let out a breath. She should have guessed. Lisa, who was a romantic at heart, would have been dazzled by Zane. She would have hemorrhaged information in the belief that Zane was truly interested in Lilah. "I agreed to be Evan's date on a few occasions to help him keep up the charade that he was straight for his accounting firm, that's all."

Zane positioned himself to one side of the fireplace, the brandy balloon cradled in one hand. "And what about Evan's boss?"

Her mind flashed back to a moment at the charity's annual art auction two years ago when Zane had found her fending off Britten after she had asked him a few leading questions on the subject of marriage and he had gotten the wrong idea.

"I thought you were involved with both Peters and Britten."

"Climbing the corporate ladder?" Which explained why he had practically ignored her for two years.

"Something like that." He finished his brandy and set the glass down on the mantel.

Lilah kept her gaze glued on the flames. "And after we made love, when you knew I hadn't slept with Evan or Britten, or Lucas, why didn't you bother to contact me?"

"I figured we both needed some time. Besides, I needed to go out of town. Broome, to be exact."

Lilah's head came up at the mention of her hometown. "To check out the pearl farms?"

"I wasn't interested in the pearls on that trip. I went to see your mother. I needed her permission."

For a moment she actually considered that Zane had done something crazily old-fashioned and had declared his intention to ask for her hand. Almost instantly she squashed that idea. Firstly, he hadn't asked her anything remotely like that, and since he'd walked into the interview room at the airport there had been plenty of time. Secondly, he would have to both want her *and* love her to propose marriage. "Permission to do what?"

"To pay off your mother's mortgage and outstanding loans."

She shot to her feet, any idea of a romantic idyll gone. "You've got no right to meddle in my family affairs, or offer my mother money."

"The agreement has nothing to do with you and me. Or our relationship."

"We don't *have* a relationship, and my mother is in no position to repay you."

"I don't want the money back."

She went still inside. "What do you want, then?"

"I already have it. Peace of mind."

She frowned. "How can paying off my mother's house give you peace of mind?"

"Because it takes financial pressure off you. Your mother was worried about you." Reaching into his pocket, he produced a slip of paper.

Lilah recognized the check she had written out and expressed to her mother so she could make arrangements with her bank to pay off her mortgage. Clearly, the check had never been cashed.

He dropped the check on the coffee table. "You can give that back to Lucas."

The coolness of his voice jerked her chin up. "It isn't Lucas's money. Although indirectly he, and you, did help me earn it."

Zane's brows jerked together. "The money didn't come from Ambrosi, I made sure of that."

"No. Some of my paintings sold. With the notoriety of my being involved with Lucas, then you, the gallery owner put huge prices on the works and sold out in one day." She picked up the check. "This was the result."

He took it from her fingers, crumpled it in his fist and tossed it into the fire. "Do you know what it did to me to see that check? I thought Lucas was helping you out financially."

Lilah was on her feet now. "And that it was…what? Some kind of down payment on my becoming his mistress?"

"Maybe not right now, but it could have been, eventually."

She let out a breath and tried to calm down. So…okay. She could understand his thinking, because she knew something of his background. She knew his mother had fallen from the glamorous life of an A-list party girl into drug addiction and had depended on a string of less than A-list men to support her and her son. It had been a precarious existence, and Zane had been forced to live it until he was fourteen. "What I don't get is, why you could think that?"

He stepped close and threaded his fingers through her hair. She felt the pins give, moments later her hair slipped down around her shoulders. "You traveled to Medinos for a first date with Lucas. Now you're here, a resident, and Lucas is planning on having a couple of days on Medinos…without his bride-to-be."

She frowned. "Lucas is my boss, that's all. The only thing I really liked about him was that he looks like you."

The bald statement hung in the air, surprising her almost as much as it surprised Zane.

"You hardly knew me."

She gripped the lapels of his shirt and absently worked a button loose. "But then that's how it works."

Zane tilted her face so she was looking directly at him. "You're losing me."

"Fatal attraction. The *coup de foudre,* the clap of thunder."

"Still lost."

"Sex," she muttered baldly. "As in…an affair."

His expression turned grim. He released his grip on her. "A dangerously unstable affair. With a younger man."

She blinked at the grim note in his voice. "Uh—more or less."

A split second later she was free altogether and Zane was several feet away, gripping the back of a leather chair. "Before we go any further let's get one thing clear. I didn't bring you here for a quick, meaningless thrill. If you want me to make love to you, we're going to go about it in a normal, rational, *adult* way."

Instead of throwing herself at him like some desperate, love-starved teenager. The way she had the last time.

The way she had been about to do about thirty seconds ago.

Lilah's cheeks burned. Zane was still gripping the back of the chair. As if *he* needed the protection.

She had known this was going to be a sticky area, and she had messed up, again. She was beginning to understand what had gone so disastrously wrong for Cole women over the years. With their naturally passionate natures they tried too hard to be "good" then got caught in an uncontrollable whiplash of desire. "Now that you mention it, I don't think this is the greatest time to make love."

His gaze was as cool and steady as if those heated moments had never happened. "Then, good night. If you need anything, I'm just down the hall. Or, if you prefer, you can call on Jorge and Marta who are sleeping in the downstairs apartment, although they don't speak any English."

The words *But what if I change my mind?* balanced on the tip of her tongue. She hastily withdrew them as he padded across to the ornate liquor cabinet and splashed more brandy into a clean glass.

She had already made a string of rash decisions with regard to Zane. Before she made even more of a fool of herself, she needed to think things through.

Although the fact that she *was* going to make a fool of herself again was suddenly, glaringly, obvious.

Eleven

The following morning, Lilah woke, exhausted and heavy-eyed after a night spent tossing and turning.

She had lain awake for hours, listening to the sounds of the sea and Zane's footsteps when he had finally gone to bed in the small hours. Aware of Zane, a short distance away in the next bedroom, she had eventually dropped off, only to wake periodically, thump her pillow into shape and try to sleep again.

Kicking the sheet aside, she padded to her bathroom and stared at her pale face and tangled hair in the mirror.

Zane's withdrawal had created an odd reversal in her mind. Sexually, the ball was in her court. If she wanted him, it was clear she would have to make the first move. No more excuses or deception about who was driving what.

His demand had succeeded in focusing her mind. Now, instead of trying to talk herself out of a wild fling with Zane, she was consumed with how, exactly, one went about asking a man for sex.

Lilah showered and dressed in a white camisole and a pair of board shorts, a bikini beneath, in case she felt like a swim.

After applying sunscreen, she walked out to the kitchen, only to discover that the nervous tension that had dogged her all morning had been unnecessary. Zane had left the house early. According to Marta's gestures and the few words Lilah could recognize, he had gone sailing.

Feeling relieved and deflated at the same time, she walked out on the deck where the table was set for breakfast. One glance at the empty sweep of the bay confirmed that the yacht was gone.

After breakfast she walked down to the beach and went for a swim. After sunbathing until she was dry, she walked back to the house, showered off the salt and changed back into the camisole and boardies.

To fill in time, she strolled through the house, examining the art on the walls, pausing at the watercolor that had been done by Sebastien Ambrosi.

Zane had said the painting was an actual place on the island, behind the villa. From the distant peaks included in the landscape, the cave was set on high ground. On impulse, she decided to see if she could find the cave and, at the same time, see if her cell phone would work.

Pulling on a pair of trainers, she slipped her cell in a pocket and indicated to Marta that she was going to walk to the place in the painting.

A few minutes exploring around the old villa site and she found the entrance to a narrow track that ran up through the steep hills behind the villa.

Twenty minutes of intermittent walking and climbing and she topped a rise. The view was magnificent. In the distance she could even make out hazy peaks that formed part of the mountainous inland region of Medinos. She hadn't seen any evidence of the cave.

Sitting down on a rocky outcropping, she tried the phone, but the screen continued to glow with a "No Service" message.

Instead of feeling trapped and frustrated, she felt oddly

relieved. She had done her duty, attempted to make contact with the outside world, and had failed.

She was clambering down a steep, rocky slope when she saw Zane's yacht dropping anchor in the bay. Her heart skipped a beat as she watched Zane toss the inflatable over the side. In the same instant her foot slipped. A sharp pain shot up her ankle. She tried to correct her footing and ended up sliding the rest of the way down the bank.

Sucking in a breath, she tested her ankle, the same one she'd turned in Sydney. Annoyed with the injury, which, while minor, would make the trip down slow, she began to hobble in an effort to walk off the injury.

It started to rain. She was congratulating herself on traversing the narrowest, most precipitous part of the track with steep slopes on both sides, when she glimpsed Zane walking toward her and slipped again, this time landing flat on her back. She lay on the wet ground, eyes closed against the pelting rain, and counted to ten. When her lids flipped open, Zane was staring down at her, water dripping from his chin, wet T-shirt plastered to his torso faithfully outlining every ridge and muscle. "Two days. Paradise, you said."

"It would have been if we'd spent the time in bed."

"Huh." She pushed into a sitting position and checked her ankle and in the process realized that the white camisole she was wearing was now practically invisible.

Zane crouched down beside her. Lean brown fingers closed around her ankle.

"Ouch. Don't touch it." Despite the slight tenderness, a jolt of purely sensual awareness shot through her.

His expression was irritatingly calm. "It's not swollen, so it can't be too sore. How did you do it?"

"I saw you and slipped. Twice."

The accusation bounced off him. "Can you walk?"

"Yes."

"Too bad." He pulled her up until she was balanced on one foot then swung her into his arms.

The rain began to pelt down. She clutched at his shoulders. "I'm heavy."

He glanced pointedly at her chest. "There are compensations."

He continued on down the hill but instead of taking a broad track to the beach, he veered left heading for a dark tumble of rocks. They rounded a corner and a low opening became visible. "Sebastien's cave."

"I thought it might be near."

The mouth to the cave was broad, allowing light to flow into the cavern. Ducking to avoid the rock overhang, Zane set Lilah down on one of the boulders that littered the opening. He shrugged out of the rucksack he had strapped to his back, unfastened the waterproof flap and extracted a flashlight. The bright beam cut through the gloom, revealing a dusty brass lantern balanced on a natural rock shelf and an equally dusty brass lighter lying beside it.

He crouched down and examined her ankle again. "A bandage would help."

She retracted her ankle from his tingling grip. "I can wait for a bandage. Really, it isn't that bad."

"Bad enough that it's starting to swell." He peeled out of his T-shirt.

Murky light gleamed on ridged abs and muscled pecs, the darker striations of the two thin scars that crisscrossed his abdomen. One was shorter and lighter, as if it hadn't been so serious, the other more defined and longer, curling just above one hip.

She dragged her gaze from the mesmerizing expanse of bronzed, sculpted muscle, abruptly aware that he knew exactly the effect he was having on her and that he was enjoying it. "Don't you need to wear that?"

"It's either my T-shirt or your top. You choose."

She concentrated on keeping her gaze rigidly on the wadded T-shirt. "Yours."

"Thought you'd say that."

Using his teeth, he ripped a small hole near the hem of the shirt then tore a broad strip, working the tear until he ended up with a continuous run of bandage. Clasping her calf, he began to firmly wind the bandage around her ankle.

"Don't tell me, you were a Boy Scout."

"Sea Scout." He ripped the trailing end of the bandage into two strips and tied it off.

"*Ouch*. Figures."

He wound a finger in a damp strand of her hair and tugged. "Goes with the pirate image?"

She reclaimed her hair and tried to repress the brazen impulse to wallow in the jolt of killer charm and flirt back. "Yes."

Rising to his feet before he gave in to temptation and kissed Lilah, Zane examined the lantern, which still contained an oily swill of kerosene.

He found a plastic lighter in the rucksack and tried to light it. Frustratingly, the lighter wouldn't ignite. On closer inspection he discovered that the cheap firing mechanism had broken. Tossing the lighter back in the rucksack, he tried the old brass lighter, which had to date back before World War II. It fired instantly. Seconds later, the warm glow of the lantern lit up the cave. "Close on seventy years old and it still works. They should keep making stuff like this."

Zane caught the quick flash of Lilah's smile, and held his breath at the way it lit up her face, taking her from pale and gorgeous to high-voltage, sexily gorgeous.

She held his gaze with a boldness that took him by surprise and made his heart race then looked quickly away, her cheeks pink.

She shrugged. "Sometimes I forget you're an Atraeus."

He shrugged, his jaw clenched in an effort to control the sudden hot tension that gripped him, the desire to compound his sins by grabbing her and kissing her until she melted against him. He had to keep reminding himself he was trying for a measured, adult approach, in line with his desire to try an actual relationship. "Before I was an Atraeus I was a

Salvatore. In L.A. that meant pretty much the opposite of what Atraeus means on Medinos."

"And that's when you got the scars?"

He found himself smiling grimly. "That's right. Pre-Spiros."

Picking up the lantern, he held it high. "Wait here. I'm going to check out the rest of the cavern."

And take a few minutes to regain the legendary Atraeus control that, lately, was losing hands down to the hotheaded Salvatore kid he used to be.

When he returned, Lilah was on her feet. Automatically, he set the lantern down and steadied her, his hands at her waist.

She released the rock shelf she'd grabbed and clutched at his shoulders. "Every time I see you lately, I seem to lose my balance."

"I'm not complaining."

With a calm deliberation formulated during a sleepless night and several hours out on the water, he eased a half step closer, encouraging her to lean more heavily on him. "That's better."

She wound her arms around his neck with an automatic, natural grace that filled him with relief. Despite the disastrous conversation the previous night, she still wanted him.

Her breasts flattened against his chest, sending another jolt of sensual heat through him, but he couldn't lose his cool. He had said that the next time they made love they were going to go about it in a rational, adult way, and he was sticking to that.

Lilah met his gaze squarely. "Why did you sail away on your own?"

A chilly gust of wind laced with rain swept into the cave.

"I wanted to give you time to think things through. If you had wanted off the island that badly, I would have taken you, but—"

"I don't."

His mouth went dry at her capitulation. A split second later thunder crashed directly overhead.

Lilah lifted a brow.

"Come and see what I found." An uncomplicated satisfaction flowed through Zane as he picked up the lantern and helped Lilah through to the rear part of the cavern, which narrowed and curved then widened out to form a second room.

The cavern was furnished with a table and two chairs, a small antique dresser and a chaise longue. As dusty and faded as the furniture was, the overall effect was elegant and dramatic, like a set for an old Valentino movie.

"What is this place?"

Zane set Lilah down on one of the chairs and stripped what proved to be a dustcover off the chaise longue revealing red velvet upholstery. "I'd guess we've found the location of Sebastien Ambrosi's love nest."

Lilah touched the velvet. She had heard the tale from her grandmother, who had known Sebastien quite well. According to Ambrosi family history Sebastien had asked for Sophie Atraeus's hand, but in order to save the then failing Atraeus finances, Sophie had been engaged to a wealthy Egyptian businessman. "Where he was supposed to meet with his lover, Sophie Atraeus."

"You know your history."

Zane's gaze was focused and intent as he pulled pins out of her hair. Heart pounding, she clutched at his sleek shoulders. With slow deliberation, his mouth settled on hers. Automatically, she lifted up on her good foot and wound her arms around his neck.

The kiss was firm, but restrained. After a night of tortured wrestling with her values, all undermined by a fevered anticipation that had kept her from sleeping, it was not what she had expected.

Wry amusement glinted in his eyes. "I'm trying to slow things down a little."

"Under the circumstances, it's a little late to worry about being PC."

His hands closed on her hips, pulling her in close against him. "Is that un-PC enough for you?"

She buried her face against his throat, breathing in his scent, reassured by his tentativeness, charmed by his consideration and the touches of humor. "What are you afraid of? That you might lose control and we'll end up having unprotected sex?"

He reached into his pocket. Moments later he pressed a foil packet into her hand. "That won't happen again."

Suddenly the murky afternoon was hot and airless.

His mouth captured hers again, this time frankly hungry. She felt the hot glide of his palms on her chilled skin as he peeled the damp camisole up her rib cage. Obligingly, she lifted her arms so he could dispose of the garment altogether. Moments later her bra was gone.

She braced herself against his shoulders as he unfastened her shorts and peeled them along with her panties down her legs.

When he straightened, she unfastened and unzipped his jeans. He assisted by toeing off his trainers and stepping out of damp, tight denim.

Lacing her fingers with his, he pulled her close. Heat flooded her at the intimacy of skin on skin.

The sound of the wind increased, damp air stirred through the cavern, raising gooseflesh on her skin. Zane wrapped her close. "This is no place to make love."

She buried her face in the muscled curve of shoulder and neck and breathed in his scent. "It was good enough for Sebastien and Sophie."

"Almost seventy years ago." He cupped her nape and fastened his teeth gently on the lobe of one ear, sending a bolt of heat clear through her. "I was thinking modern-day bed, silk sheets, soft music."

"Where's your sense of adventure?"

"Back in L.A.," he said drily.

Releasing her, he pulled her down with him onto the chaise

longue, their legs tangling, the weight of him shatteringly intimate. The chaise longue was narrow and unexpectedly hard, but the discomfort was instantly forgotten as the heat of his body swamped her.

She kissed him, wanting him with a fierceness that shook her. She could feel the heat and shape of him against her inner thigh and remembered the foil packet, which she was still holding. "I might need some help with this."

His teeth gleamed. He relieved her of the condom. "Leave it to me."

With expert movements, he sheathed himself, reminding her that while she was a novice, Zane operated at the other end of the scale. His experience and conquests were legendary. Seconds later, he moved between her legs. She felt the hot pressure of him, a moment of shaky vulnerability at what she was allowing, then the aching rush of pleasure.

For long seconds she couldn't think, couldn't breathe. Zane simply held himself inside her, his gaze locked with hers. And endless moment later he began to move. Not hurried and edged by anxiety, but a slow, tender rhythm that squeezed her chest tight, gathered her whole being. Lovemaking as opposed to the stormy few seconds they had shared in Sydney.

Zane's gaze locked with hers as sensation drew them together, swept her in dizzying waves, shoving her over an invisible precipice as the coiled intensity shattered.

For long minutes Lilah floated, disconnected and content, happy to wallow in the intimacy of Zane's solid weight, the heart-pounding knowledge that there was much more to lovemaking than she had ever imagined.

As if he'd read her thoughts, he lifted his head and braced himself on one elbow. He framed her face with his free hand, stroking his thumb across her bottom lip. "Next time, we're making love in a bed."

Twelve

The vibration of Zane's cell broke the warm contentment.

He extracted his phone from his jeans and checked the screen. "Sorry. Work call. The downside of a satellite connection." Pulling on his jeans, he walked out into the first part of the cavern to take the call.

Cold now that Zane was gone, Lilah found her damp clothes and quickly dressed. The squall had passed and watery sunshine filtered into the cave, relieving the oppressive gloom.

Curious about the meeting place of the two lovers who apparently had been forbidden to see each other, she studied the room. When Sophie had disappeared during a bombing raid during the war, it was rumored that Sebastien had taken her with him to Australia. Sebastien had denied the claim. The unresolved questions had been a bone of contention between the two families ever since.

Lilah opened a cupboard in the dresser and found a small wooden box and a letter. The box contained a missing set of bridal jewels that she instantly recognized. She had designed jewelry based on Sebastien's sketches of this very set. They had belonged to the Atraeus family, and Sebastien had been blamed for stealing them.

Heart speeding up, she extracted a piece of fragile, yellowed paper. She could read a little Medinian, better than she could speak it, enough to know she was looking at a love letter.

Zane strolled in, sliding the phone into his jeans pocket. She showed him the jewels then handed him the letter.

"Sophie Atraeus's final love letter to Sebastien Ambrosi." He set the letter down beside the casket of jewels. "Well, that solves the mystery. Sophie boarded one of the ships that sank with all hands. She was lost at sea."

"And she left the bridal jewels here."

"Probably for safekeeping. When the islands were evacuated, a lot of families hid their valuables in caves. To Sophie it would have made perfect sense."

Lilah touched her fingertips to a delicate filigree necklace. "These are more than jewels, they're history. And a record of love."

Zane's dark, assessing gaze rested on her.

Feeling faintly embarrassed, she closed the box and tested her weight on her sore ankle. "I think I can walk now."

Zane took the box from her, set it down on the table and drew her close. "Not yet. Later."

By the time they left the cave, the storm had cleared and it was twilight. A slow walk down the hillside, heavily assisted by Zane, and they reached the house on sunset. The fairy-tale quality of the afternoon extended into the evening with another candlelit dinner beneath the stars.

The tension of the previous night seemed a distant memory as the dishes were cleared away. When Zane pulled back her chair and linked his fingers with hers, it seemed the most natural thing in the world to go to bed together.

When Lilah woke the next morning, she was alone. Feeling disappointed, because she had looked forward to waking up with Zane, she quickly showered and dressed in a white halterneck top and muslin skirt. When she walked out onto the deck, still limping slightly, Zane was seated at the table, drinking coffee and answering emails.

Zane got to his feet and held her chair. "Your ankle's still swollen."

"Only a little. The stiffness should wear off while I walk." Feeling let down that he hadn't kissed her, but reasoning that Zane was probably distracted by whatever work situation he was dealing with, she sat and poured herself a glass of freshly squeezed orange juice.

"You won't need to walk much." Zane bent down and kissed her on the mouth.

The warm pressure, the sudden intensity of his gaze, broke her tension. The dire suspicion implanted by a number of women's magazine articles, that now they had made love and she was a "sure thing" Zane was losing interest, receded.

Zane checked his watch as he returned to his seat. "We're going back to Medinos. I've called in a ride."

By ride, Zane had meant the Atraeus family's private helicopter. Concerned about her ankle and despite her objections, Zane insisted she should get it checked out by a doctor. The helicopter set them down in the grounds of the Castello Atraeus. Zane transferred their luggage to his car and drove her to a private clinic located in downtown Medinos.

They were greeted by a plump and cheerful doctor. A few minutes later they were back out on the street. Lilah, now almost free of the irritating limp, walked as briskly as she could toward the car.

Now that they were back on Medinos, she was aware that as wonderful and earth-shattering as her time with Zane was, it had to be over. She couldn't afford to abandon her arrangements just because Zane wanted to be with her for a few days.

Zane insisted on helping her into the passenger-side seat then slid behind the wheel with a masculine grace she doggedly ignored. She would have to get used to viewing him as one of her bosses again, although with the sleek width of his shoulders almost brushing hers and the hot scent of his skin it was going to be difficult.

"Okay," he said flatly. "What's wrong?"

Lilah ignored the flash of irritation in his eyes and tried to focus on her happy place, which at present was the bland fence that encircled the parking lot. "Nothing. I need some processing time."

He actually had the gall to pinch the bridge of his nose as if he was under extreme stress. "This would be a feminine thing."

Her gaze clashed with his and the fact that she had not only made love with Zane *a number of times* but was actually considering canceling the series of blind dates she had set up for next week, for him, hit her forcibly.

She stared at the masculine planes of his face, the narrowed eyes and tough jaw, the moment of disorientation growing.

He was too wealthy, too attractive and too used to getting exactly what he wanted. The wild fling had been a mistake. She must have been out of her mind thinking that she could ever control any part of a relationship with Zane. "We've had the two days, it has to be over."

His brows jerked together. "We could spend a few more days together. I know you have vacation time coming up, but you don't fly back to Sydney until the end of next week."

She felt her brain scramble. "An affair wasn't on my priority list. I have things to do—"

"Like checking out online marriage prospects."

There was a ringing silence. "I don't know how you knew that, but yes."

"Stay with me until the end of the week." He started the engine and put the car in gear.

Her chest squeezed tight as he turned on to the spectacular coast road with its curvy white-sand beaches and sea views. After which time she would seldom see Zane, if at all, because he worked mostly in the States.

"Talk to me, Lilah."

She turned her head, which was a mistake, because Zane's gaze was neither cool nor distant, but contained a flash of vulnerability that tugged at her heart. For a split second she was filled with the dizzying knowledge that Zane truly wanted to be with her. "I don't know that it's a good idea to continue."

Lilah's fingers clenched on her handbag. The last thing she had expected was that Zane, with his freewheeling approach to love, would try to keep her with him, even if only for a few days.

She should hold firm and finish it now. Staying with Zane could wreck her plans for the secure marriage she needed. She was already distinctly unmotivated at the thought of meeting the men in her file.

But it was also a fact that since she had undertaken the search for a husband a great many things had changed; *she* had changed.

She was now financially secure and no longer based in Sydney. The financial pressure of her mother's mortgage was gone.

She was no longer a virgin.

The difference that made was unexpectedly huge. She now knew that if she was not passionately attached to her prospective husband, she would not be able to go through with the physical side of the relationship.

She was aware that this restriction would drastically reduce her chances of finding someone. She was almost certain that none of the men on her list would fulfill her new requirement, but she was no longer worried. She could marry, or not. It was her choice.

The sense of freedom that came with that thought was huge.

She still wanted a stable marriage, but she no longer felt she *had* to marry in order to be happy or secure. Now she had a much more important goal: she wanted to be loved.

Zane turned into the drive that led to the Atraeus Resort and pulled in under the elegant portico.

Lilah signed the register then followed Zane to the bank of elevators. "What if I say 'no' to more time together?" The instant the question was out she knew it was a fatal mistake.

Elevator doors slid open.

Zane gestured that she precede him. "I'm counting on the fact that, when it comes to us, you don't have a big track record with 'no.'"

The abrupt switch to teasing charm, and Zane's use of the word *us* threw her even more off balance. "A gentleman wouldn't say that."

He hit the button to close the door. "But then, as we both know, I'm no gentleman."

No. He was mad and bad and dangerous to know. He had turned her life upside down, and he was still doing it.

Almost a whole week with Zane before she committed herself fully to the tricky business of finding a husband. The thought was dizzying, tempting.

She couldn't say no.

"All right," she said huskily. "Six more days."

"And then it's over."

She tensed, stung by the neutrality of his tone, the implication that he would be relieved when the affair came to an end. "You make it sound like the resolution to a problem." One of his troubleshooting projects.

Zane bent his head and brushed her mouth with his. "It is a problem, and it has been for two years."

Six days.

She no longer wanted to concentrate on the men she had planned to meet and date next week. But neither could she afford to abandon her series of interviews altogether.

Zane was not abandoning his life for her. She still needed to plan for the future. She would need something to hold on to when he had gone.

The doors of the elevator opened. Lilah stepped out into the expensively carpeted corridor of the penthouse level. Zane opened the door to a suite.

Decorated in subtle champagne-and-pink hues with elegantly swagged curtains, the suite was both gorgeous and spacious. A glass coffee table held a display of lush pink roses, tropical fruits, a plate of handmade chocolates and an ice bucket with champagne and two flutes.

There were two bedrooms.

Lilah was aware of Zane talking to a bellhop who had delivered their luggage.

While Zane tipped the bellhop she continued to check out the rooms.

Except for the colors, the suite was a mirror image of the one they had shared in Sydney. The separate bedrooms contained identical four-poster beds swathed in diaphanous champagne silk and gorgeous en suite bathrooms. Everything was carefully arranged so that two people could live separate lives in the same suite.

She sensed his presence behind her a split second before she heard the sound of her case being placed on the stand just inside the door. She caught Zane's reflection in a large ornate mirror and her heart turned over in her chest.

When she turned, one broad shoulder was braced against the door frame. He had brought just the one suitcase, she noted, hers. She realized he had already placed his case in the other bedroom.

She set her handbag down on the end of the bed. "This is a two-bedroom suite."

His gaze was neutral. "I prefer to sleep alone."

Her stomach and her heart plunged.

Desperate for a distraction, Lilah switched her gaze to her cases. "Oh good, you've brought my laptop."

She forced a bright, professional smile and grabbed the lifeline of an internet connection.

"You're going to work?"

Blinking back a sudden urge to cry, she picked up the computer case. "I have some private correspondence to see to."

Blindly, she walked past Zane out into the sitting room

and headed in the direction of an elegant writing desk. Placing the case on the glass-topped surface, she busied herself setting up the laptop.

Zane's clinical approach to their sleeping arrangements, his rejection of any depth of intimacy, was a reminder she badly needed. Now more than ever, she needed to carry through with her schedule for the following week.

Zane frowned as he watched Lilah. The blank look in her eyes tugged at him, warring with his habit of carefully preserving his emotional distance. He was almost certain she was crying.

Instead of backing off, he found himself irresistibly drawn as she booted up the computer. "I thought we could go out for lunch."

"That sounds nice."

Zane frowned at the brisk note in Lilah's voice. He glanced at her laptop screen. The separate rooms dilemma suddenly evaporated. "Are these online 'friends' all male?"

"As it so happens, yes."

The emotional calm he had worked so hard to maintain since the riveting hours in the cave was abruptly replaced by the same fierce, unreasoning jealousy he had experienced when he had found out that Lucas was taking Lilah to Constantine's wedding. "Have you dated any of them?"

She fished spectacles out of her handbag, pushed them onto the bridge of her nose and leaned a little closer to the screen as if what she was reading was of the utmost importance. "Not yet."

Dragging his gaze from the fascinating sight of the spectacles perched on the delicate bridge of Lilah's nose, he studied the list of men she was perusing. The lineup of photographs portrayed a selection of Greek gods, some flashing golden tans and overly white teeth, some dressed with *GQ* perfection. The one exception was a slightly battered, bleach blond surfer type.

Lilah scrolled and he glimpsed the logo of the matchmaking agency. The lightbulb flared a little brighter. "But you intend to?"

"That's right. Next week when I have my annual vacation."

His gaze snagged on the four men who had withdrawn. He noted the dates. Just days after the scandal had erupted into the newspapers.

He also noted that the flood of new applications had all come in at a similar time. "How many?"

"Fifteen so far." She scrolled down to a chat page, which had several comments posted. "Seventeen if two other very good prospects come on board."

The corporate-speak momentarily distracted him. He had to remind himself that the businesslike approach was entirely consistent with Lilah's view of marriage. She didn't just want a man, she wanted a paragon, someone who would tick every one of the boxes on her corporate marriage sheet.

Someone who possessed all of the steady, reliable qualities that he clearly did not. "This is why we only have a week. You're fitting me in before you go back to Sydney to find a husband."

Her gaze remained glued to the screen. "If I'm seeing someone from the agency I can't be involved."

Involved. He suddenly knew the meaning of stress.

Lilah could feel Zane's displeasure as he studied the emails pouring into her mailbox.

Abruptly, she found herself spun around in her chair. Irritation snapped in his gaze and she realized she had pushed him too far with the list.

"Is that all this is?"

She dragged her spectacles off. "You said it yourself. Marriage doesn't come into our equation."

"I thought we had an agreement."

"We do, but long-term commitment is the one thing I do want. The reason I haven't been able to settle on anyone is because you've always been in the picture just often enough to blot out any other prospects."

The expression in his gaze was suddenly remote. "Are you saying I'm responsible for your decision to advertise for a husband?"

"No." *Yes.* She stared at the screen and tried to pinpoint what had driven her to such an extreme. It had been after the last charity auction, she realized. Zane had been there with Gemma.

Lilah had spent an entire agonizing evening trying not to be aware of Zane and failing. Afterward, she had decided she needed to deal with the fixation by making plans for the future. It had been a relief to come up with a workable plan.

It was not a good time, she realized, to acknowledge that her approach had been naive and too simplistic. The strength of her plan had relied on the screening process of a matchmaking company and the integrity of the men who had replied, which was a fatal flaw. With her family history, she should have known better. "I've tried normal dating. This seemed a more…controllable option."

Grimly, Zane decided that he shouldn't be pleased he had effectively blotted out the other men in Lilah's life. Neither should he be annoyed that Lilah dismissed him as secure relationship material, when that was the stance he had always maintained.

He should be more concerned with distancing himself. Given that they only had six days left to douse the fatal attraction that threatened to ruin both of their lives, it was not a good time to feel fiercely possessive.

Emotionally, he did not get involved; he had learned the hard way that love had conditions. It literally took him years to trust anyone, and he could count those he did trust on one hand.

That ingrained wariness of people made him good at his job. He didn't take anything for granted. His approach was often perceived as clinical and heartless. Zane didn't bring emotion into the process; he simply did the job he was paid to do.

But somehow, despite his background and his mind-set, he *was* involved. "Just what do you think every one of those guys who answered your ad wants?"

"A steady, stable relationship."

"Do you believe in the tooth fairy?"

"This is not a good time to be sarcastic."

"Then don't believe in this. It's not real."

He straightened and stabbed a finger at one of the photos of a bronzed, sculpted torso. The handsome, chiseled face rang a bell. He couldn't be sure, but he had a suspicion it belonged to a male model, probably from some underwear billboard. "*They* are not real."

"Which is exactly why I intend to conduct one-on-one interviews next week. If they're not genuine, I'll know."

There was a moment of vibrating silence. "This is the reason you have to be back in Sydney?"

"Yes."

"Where, exactly, do you intend to conduct these interviews?"

"At restaurants and cafes. They're not interviews exactly. More a series of…blind dates. After I conduct online interviews to screen candidates."

Blind dates. Suddenly Zane needed some air.

Thirteen

Pacing to a set of French doors, he jerked them open, although he was more interested in Lilah's reflection in one of the panes than the sun-washed balcony. "Did you give them your real name?"

"Yes. And a photograph."

"Along with your occupation." Lilah was nothing if not thorough. His tension ratcheted up another notch. "When the recent publicity hit the newspapers, they would all have instantly recognized you."

Lilah could feel herself going cold inside. Of course she had considered that angle, but she had been guilty of hoping that the original list of five steady, reliable men she had assembled would be too sensible to read the gutter press, or to connect the wild stories with her resume.

Zane's gaze, reflected in the glass, was neutral enough to make her feel distinctly uncomfortable. "The whole point of the exercise is marriage. What did you expect me to do? Pretend to be someone I wasn't?"

"Like the guys who replied."

Her gaze was inescapably drawn to a couple of the photos, which she suspected were of male models and not the candidates. In the case of one particularly stunning man, she was almost certain she had seen him on an underwear billboard. "I'm well aware that some of the applications are not honest."

There was a vibrating silence. "I have resources. If you want I can have them screened by the private investigative firm The Atraeus Group uses in Sydney."

For long seconds she wavered, but given the media exposure that had made her temporarily notorious, she couldn't afford not to have Zane's help. He was in the business of checking and double-checking on the integrity of businesses and personnel. She did everything she could to research the candidates, but with limited time and resources, she couldn't hope to do any in-depth checking in the span of a few days. "Okay."

Lilah brought up her file of applicants and vacated the chair. Zane sat down and began to scroll through, the silence growing progressively deeper and more charged as he read. "Do you mind if I email the file to my laptop?"

"Go ahead."

Seconds later, he exited her mail program and rose from the chair. "I'm going to have these names checked out. The firm I use has access to criminal files and credit records. I'll order lunch in, it shouldn't take more than a couple of hours to get some basic details back." An hour and a half later, Lilah stared at the list of men on her dating site, her stomach churning at the thought of what Zane could turn up. While she had waited for the results of his investigation, she had eaten one of the selection of salads that had been delivered by room service then made herself coffee in the small kitchenette.

She sipped the coffee, barely tasting it. Six days together. She blinked back a wave of unexpectedly intense emotion. It wouldn't be six days of making love; it would be six days of saying goodbye.

Jaw set, she forced her attention back to her laptop screen and began reading through all of the mail. She had expected to have a few withdrawals—what she hadn't expected was for four of her five vetted men to have quit her page and the raft of new applications.

A prickling sense of unease hit her. She had compiled her previous list of stable, steady men over months from the unenthusiastic trickle of replies to her dating agency application. In the span of two days she had lost four of the five steady prospects she had intended to meet the following week and had received fifteen new "expressions of interest." Not good.

She scrolled through the emails, flinching at some of the subject lines.

Clearly, it had been an easy matter to connect the scandalous stories in the press with her matchmaking page. Most of her solid prospects had quit and she was now being targeted by men attracted by her notoriety.

Zane strolled into the suite. "A handful of the applicants checked out." He tossed a pile of papers down on the desk. "Don't reply to any of these. If you do, you can count on my presence at any interviews you conduct because, honey, I'll be there."

Lilah swallowed the impulse to argue a point she was in one hundred percent agreement with herself. She did not want to end up at the mercy of some kind of kinky opportunist or worse, a reporter trying to generate another smutty story. "I don't see how. You won't be in Sydney next week."

Zane strolled toward his bedroom, unbuttoning his shirt and shrugging out of it as he walked. "For this, I'll make a point of it."

Lilah dragged her gaze from Zane's broad back, and the unsettling, undermining intimacy of watching him undress. With an effort of will, she squashed the impulse to walk up behind him, wrap her arms around his waist, lean into his heady warmth and breathe in the scent of his skin. "I don't see why when you made it clear you don't want anything more than a temporary arrange—"

"You want more than the one week time limit?"

Lilah tried to squash the heart pounding thought that they could extend their affair for weeks, maybe months. The reason she was keeping the time so short was to get the fixation with Zane out of her system. She couldn't in all honesty enter into a marriage with someone else if she was still attracted to Zane.

Although, she was already certain she had made a fundamental mistake. The desperate fixation *had* faded somewhat, but it had been replaced with something much more insidious.

She was beginning to *like* Zane. Neither her mother nor her grandmother had ever mentioned liking their lovers. There had simply been the dangerously out-of-control passion, which had been dispensed with when the pregnancies had become apparent.

She avoided answering him and instead stared at the papers Zane had tossed down on the desk. On the top was the underwear ad guy. In reality, he was a forty-five-year-old, twice-divorced mechanic who had somehow managed to make his application from a minimum-security prison cell.

According to the detective firm Zane had employed, he was currently serving a two-year sentence for car theft. With time out for good behavior, he could be out in six months.

The sound of running water in Zane's shower broke the heavy silence that seemed to have settled around her. She skimmed the information on the rest of the applicants Zane had blacklisted. Logging back on to the matchmaking site, she deleted them from her page. That left her with six applicants in total, one from her previous batch of applicants, and five new ones. Three were depressingly unsuitable, so she deleted them. That left her with three.

The sound of the shower stopped.

She tried to concentrate on the photos and profiles of the three remaining men on her dating list. Jack, Jeremy and John, the three J's.

They were all pleasant, attractive men in solid jobs. John Smith, wearing a crisp, dark suit, looked like an ad for *Gentleman's Quarterly*. Listed as the CEO of his own company, he fitted the profile she had put together for a husband perfectly.

The one applicant who had not deserted her following the scandal in the newspaper, Jack Riordan, had been high on her list. He wasn't perfect, but it was heartening that her top pick apart from Howard, who had not worked out, was still on board.

Taking a deep breath she decided she needed to reward Jack Riordan's loyalty for sticking with her despite the scandal, take the plunge and commit to an initial date.

She typed in a suggested meeting time and place and hit the return key. Her computer made a small whooshing sound as the reply was sent. A split second later her message appeared on her page.

Stomach tight, pulse hammering, she stared at the neat print. After months of lurking online, reluctant to commit to anything more than a little window-shopping, she felt she was finally moving forward with her plans. She ought to feel positive that, while she wouldn't have Zane in her life, at least she had the possibility of having *someone*.

There were no strings, she reminded herself. Half an hour in a coffee shop or over a lunch table, and if she didn't like Jack, or vice versa, they need never contact one another again.

The thought was soothing. On impulse she quickly typed in affirmatives for the other two men. Now more than ever, with the end of her time with Zane set and the knowledge that hurt was looming, it was important to stay focused.

She stared at the three messages on screen and her stomach did a crazy flip-flop. The decision shouldn't feel like a betrayal of Zane, but suddenly, very palpably, it did.

With a jerky movement, she pushed back from the desk, rose from her seat and strolled to the French doors. She stared out at the serene view of sea and the distant, floating shape of Ambrus.

A shiver went through her as she remembered the hours spent making love to Zane on Ambrus, then further back to the stormy interlude in Sydney.

Unhappy with the direction of her thoughts, she walked through to the bedroom and began to unpack. Long seconds ticked by as she emptied her suitcase and tidied it away in a large closet.

Despite trying to put a positive spin on the process of finding a husband, every part of her suddenly recoiled from the idea of replacing Zane in her life.

In her bed.

She walked back out into the sitting room and began to pace, too upset to settle. Her stomach was churning; she actually felt physically sick. She had the sudden wild urge to erase the messages she had sent, because she knew with sudden conviction that no matter how wonderful or perfect any one of the three J's might be she was no longer sure she was ready to offer any of them a relationship. The thought of sharing the same intimacies with another man that she had shared with Zane made her recoil. She couldn't do it.

The truth sank in with the same kind of absolute clarity she experienced when she knew a painting was finished or a jewelry design was completed. It was a complication she should have foreseen. She had tried to get Zane out of her system, but she had done the exact opposite of what she had planned to do. She had fallen wildly, irrevocably in love with him.

In retrospect, the damage had been done two years ago when she had first met him at the charity art auction.

She wondered why she hadn't seen it from the first. Clearly she had been so intent on burying her head in the sand and denying the attraction that she had failed to recognize that it was already too late.

She had been a victim of the *coup de foudre*. Struck down somewhere between the first intense eye contact when she had strolled into the ballroom that night over two years ago and the passionate interlude at the end of the evening.

With her history she should have sensed it, should have *known*. Her only excuse was that neither her mother nor her grandmother had ever mentioned a lingering fascination or liking coming into the equation. Cole women were notoriously strong-willed. As soon as the pregnancies, and their lovers' unwillingness to commit, had become apparent, the relationships had ended.

If she'd had any sense, as soon as she had registered the unusual power of the attraction she would have gotten as far away from Zane Atraeus as she could. Instead, she had offered to donate more paintings to his charity, gotten involved with fundraising, even volunteered to help with the annual art auctions. Every step she had taken had ensured further contact with Zane.

It was no wonder she had not been able to let go of the fixation. In her heart of hearts that was the last thing she had wanted. She had hung around him like a love-struck teenager, secretly sketching and painting him.

She had compounded the problem by legitimizing the affair as an exercise to get Zane out of her system. Instead she had succeeded in establishing him even more firmly in her life, to the extent that now she didn't want anyone else.

She had been in love with Zane for two years. There was no telling how long she would remain in love, but given the stubborn streak in her personality, it could be for years. Quite possibly a *lifetime*.

She still wanted a stable marriage and a happy family life. She wanted love and security and babies, the whole deal. But she no longer wanted them with some unknown mystery man in her future.

She wanted them with Zane.

Zane strolled out as she headed back to the desk, dressed in a soft white shirt and a pair of faded, glove-soft jeans.

Aware that the screen of her laptop portrayed the appointments she had made, and which she was now desperate to retract, Lilah made a beeline for the desk.

Zane, who clearly had the same destination in mind, reached her laptop a split second before she did.

The scents of soap and clean skin and the subtle, devastating undernote of cologne made her stomach clench.

Zane touched the mouse pad. The screen saver flickered out of existence, revealing the three postings she had made.

To Lilah's relief there were no replies, yet. In Sydney it would be midmorning. All three J's would be at work.

"You've made times to meet." Zane's voice was soft and flat.

Lilah stiffened at his remoteness; it was not the reaction she had expected. The lack of annoyance, or even irritation, that she was progressing with her marriage plans was subtly depressing.

With the suddenness of a thunderbolt his cool neutrality settled into riveting context. She had seen him like this only once before, when he had been dealing with a former treasurer of the charity who had "borrowed" several thousands of dollars to pay for an overseas trip. Zane had been deceptively quiet and low-key, but there had been nothing either soft or weak about his approach. Potter had taken something that mattered to Zane, and he wasn't prepared to be lenient.

Zane had quietly stated that if the money wasn't back in the account and Potter's resignation on his desk by the end of the day, charges would be laid and Zane would personally pay for and oversee the litigation.

Potter had paled and stammered an apology. He hadn't been able to write the check fast enough.

Lilah had always been aware of Zane's reputation for taking no prisoners in the business world. The element that had struck her most forcibly was that the charity had mattered to him *personally*.

Hope dawned. She knew she mattered to Zane; he had admitted as much. As hard as she had struggled to stay away from him, he had struggled to stay away from her, and failed

Because she mattered to him on a level he could not dismiss.

By his own admission, he had become more involved with the charity than he had planned because she was there. They had ended up together on Medinos and in Sydney. They'd had unprotected sex. For a man who was intent on staying clear of entanglements, that in itself was an admission.

Then there was the small matter of Zane virtually kidnapping her for two days.

She felt like a sleeper just waking up. She had been so involved in the minutiae of day-to-day events and her own plans for marriage that she had failed to step back and look at the bigger picture.

Zane cared for her. He said he cared about who she was with next. Although it was a blunt fact that Zane did not have a good track record with helping her to find love. He had gotten rid of Howard and a raft of dating applicants. He had effectively made sure that Lucas remained in her past.

There was only one conclusion to be drawn: Zane was jealous.

The tension that gripped Lilah eased somewhat as possibilities she hadn't considered opened up, expanded.

If Zane was jealous, then maybe, just maybe, there was a chance that he could overcome his phobia about intimate relationships and commit to her.

The possibility condensed into a breathtaking idea.

Relationships were not her strong area; hence the marriage plan. It had not been successful, but at least it had given her a framework—a system—to move forward with, and that was what she needed with Zane.

Not a marriage plan. The stakes were suddenly dizzyingly, impossibly high. She needed a strategy to encourage Zane to fall in love with her.

It was a leap across a fairly wide abyss, but in that moment of realization she had already mentally taken that leap. The future stretched out before her in dazzling, Technicolor brilliance. Not just a steady, reliable marriage, but one based on true love.

Once Zane fell for her, she was confident the whole marriage thing would take care of itself. There was a risk involved, but when Zane succumbed to love, the intensity of the emotion should be powerful enough to dissolve whatever objections he had to marriage.

Heart pounding, Lilah stared at the incriminating dates on the screen. It occurred to her that the proposed dates had a positive angle. They could generate the pressure that was needed to convince Zane that he couldn't bear to let her go.

The about-face in thinking was a little disorienting but she was already adjusting to the new direction. The sudden itch to sit down with a pad and pen and start formulating a plan was the clincher.

She could do this.

She had no choice.

She would begin by waiting a day or so before she canceled with the three J's. Taking a deep breath, she smiled pleasantly and answered Zane's question. "I didn't see much point in waiting around."

Zane's brows jerked together. "There's every point. You should have waited for the in-depth security checks."

Lilah's mood soared at his bad temper. "You didn't mention a further check. In any case, other than the very thorough checks you've already conducted there's nothing more that can be done unless you intend to put them under twenty-four-hour surveillance—"

She was caught and held by the complete absence of expression on Zane's face. "That is what you were planning on doing, isn't it?"

Zane's gaze met hers for a searing moment. "Yes."

The small, delighted shock wave she felt at his admission was replaced by a sudden breathless anticipation as he studied the screen. Lilah felt like a kid at Christmas, waiting to unwrap a gift. The surveillance only proved her point. It was the kind of extreme thing one did when they were falling in love.

The discovery made her feel like dancing a jig around the sunny room. She had clung to the depressing view that Zane was elusive and superficial and absolutely not good husband material. Now wasn't a good time to feel that, despite all the areas they did not fit, crazily, he was perfect for her.

Zane stabbed a key and began studying profiles. "You've chosen Appleby, Riordan and Smith. I wouldn't trust Smith. His first name's John—that makes him close to invisible in terms of security information."

Lilah kept her expression smooth and professional. "The initial dates, are just a meet and greet, they do not imply commitment."

There was a vibrating silence, broken by the near silent sound of an indrawn breath. With controlled movements, Zane picked up the hotel folder, which lay next to her laptop and flipped to the page of restaurant listings as if food was suddenly paramount. "You could withdraw from the process."

The barely veiled command in his voice made her want to fling her arms around his neck and hug him. To prevent herself from looking deliriously happy, she picked up a pen and pad and started working on her new plan of action by making an important note. She could not afford any over-the-top displays of affection until Zane capitulated. She allowed her brows to crease, as if she had just remembered that Zane had said something but was too distracted to recall his exact words. "Why should I do that?"

Zane, who seemed more interested in the restaurant he was choosing than their conversation, picked up the sleek phone on the desk, although his grasp on the phone was gratifyingly white-knuckled. "Given the recent publicity, I'm not inclined to trust any of the three. If you won't accept surveillance reports then I'm going to have to insist on being present at the interviews."

Lilah tapped her pen on the notepad. "Let me get this right.

You don't want a relationship with me, yet you'll take time off to make sure I'm..."

"*Safe* is the word you're looking for."

Lilah was momentarily sidetracked by the stormy look in Zane's eyes. A quiver of anticipation zinged down her spine then she registered Zane's emphasis of the protection angle. She was certain he was using it as a handy excuse to avoid admitting to anything else. "You can't come to the interviews."

She had no problem being firm on that point since she intended to cancel all three dates. "What would I tell the applicants?"

Zane froze in the act of dialing the hotel restaurant. "Tell them you're no longer available."

Fourteen

Zane allowed the singular truth that he was burningly, primitively possessive of Lilah to settle in.

With a sense of incredulity, he realized that he had made the kind of rash, male, territorial move he had only ever observed in other men.

He had crossed a line and now there was no going back.

He eased his grip on the phone and set it back on its rest a little more loudly than he had intended.

Lilah, who was in the process of shutting down her computer, was oddly composed. There was a distinct air of expectation that made his jaw compress.

She closed the laptop with a gentle click. "What exactly do you mean by 'no longer available'?"

Her gaze was carefully blank, but he detected the hopeful gleam in her eye. He knew with utter certainty that she wanted him to say marriage.

Bleak satisfaction that he had finally made it on to Lilah's list of marriage candidates was tempered with irritation that it had taken so long, and the old, ingrained wariness. He could feel the jaws of Lilah's feminine trap poised to snap shut.

As much as he wanted Lilah, he would not be maneuvered into a relationship that would leave him vulnerable. Years had passed since his mother had abandoned him, not once, but a number of times in pursuit of well-heeled lovers or husbands. He would never forget how it had felt to have the rug pulled out emotionally, to be relegated to last place on her list when he had needed to be first. By the time his father, Lorenzo, had found him at age fourteen, he'd had difficulty forming any relationships at all.

Remembering the past was like staring into a dark abyss. The level of trust involved in committing to any kind of intimate relationship still made him go cold inside. The progress he had made over the past few years was monumental but he was not capable of moving any further forward with Lilah now unless he could be absolutely, categorically certain of her love.

Unfortunately, Lilah's continued focus on finding a steady, reliable husband suggested that he was not even close to being number one in her life.

Grimly, he realized that part of his wariness revolved around the certainty that, because of his shadowy past and inner scars, a breakup was inevitable. And when it happened, *he* would most likely be the instigator of the betrayals.

"What exactly do you mean by 'no longer available'?"

Grimly, he examined Lilah's question, and the demand that had surprised them both.

Unlocking his jaw, he answered her question. "I think we should try...living together."

"For how long?"

Zane, arrested by Lilah's calm response, watched as she strolled to the kitchenette and extracted a bottle of water from the fridge. He had the sudden, inescapable feeling that he had ventured into a maze and was being herded by a master strategist.

To his surprise he found there was an element of relief to

the thought that Lilah would try to ruthlessly manipulate him into an even deeper commitment. He had always viewed her methodical approach to getting what she wanted from relationships as calculating. Now, it occurred to him that with his past he could not afford to go into a relationship with a woman who was too weak or too frightened to try to hold on to him. "I don't know."

She poured a glass of water and walked sedately in the direction of the bedroom. "Let me think about it."

The door to her bedroom closed quietly behind her.

Zane stared at the closed door for long seconds.

His heart was pounding, his jaw locked. He was aware that Lilah had just pulled off a feat that no one in either his professional or his personal life had attempted in a good ten years.

She had put him on hold.

She had kept her three agency dates, with him on the side.

For the first time since he was a teenager on the streets he experienced what it felt like to be shut out, although the feeling was somewhat…different.

As a teenager, he had been running on survival skills and desperation. That was not the case now. In his job as the Atraeus Group's troubleshooter, he had spent years dealing with people who were intent on closing doors in his face.

Probably the most important skill his father had taught him was that when it came to negotiating there was always a way. He either found another door or he made his own, whatever got the job done.

It was an odd moment to realize that his time as a homeless kid had created qualities in him that had uniquely fitted him out for problem solving. For one thing, he did not give up easily. He was also used to operating from a losing position, and winning.

Something in him cleared, healed.

He was aware of a sense of lightening. He was no longer fourteen and at the mercy of forces and people he could not control. Ten years on, he had a certain set of life skills and a considerable amount of money. Those two factors provided him with an edge that had been formidably successful in business.

A sense of relief filled him. In the business arena he had never been defeated no matter how unpromising the situation. He did not see why he couldn't apply the same strategies that had been so successful in business to a relationship. The only wonder of it was that he had never thought of that before.

His decision made, he strolled to his computer and found the details the security firm had supplied for the three men Lilah had chosen.

Strolling into the kitchenette, Zane opened the fridge. It was depressingly empty. He had missed lunch and his stomach felt hollow and empty. Now hungry as well as frustrated, he pulled out a beer and called down to room service for a pizza.

He walked back to his computer, intending to catch up on some correspondence. On the way, he noticed that Lilah had forgotten to take the bridal-white leather-bound folder with her.

The last time he had seen the contents of the folder had been when Lilah had dropped it on the floor of the jet on her first flight out to Medinos. He had only read snatches; just enough to understand that it contained the kind of inside information that would be very useful to him right now.

The sound of the shower in Lilah's en suite bathroom was the decider. The phrase "all is fair in love and war" took on a new resonance as he picked up the folder and carried it out to the terrace to read.

Setting the beer on the table, Zane pulled out a chair, sat down and began flipping through the pages. There was a formatted set of profiles, complete with photographs, a series of neatly handwritten notes including underlined notations highlighting domestic prowess, and a punitive points system.

A failed marriage carried a penalty of ten points. The total any one man could earn was twenty. Divorce wasn't complete disaster, but close.

That was one blot that couldn't be entered against his name, however his sense of gratification evaporated when he read the next line. Serial dating was penalized almost as heavily, carrying a maximum demerit of eight.

The scoring range from four to eight indicated there was room for movement in that category depending on the seriousness of the misdemeanor.

There was a zero tolerance for fathering an illegitimate child. Immediate disqualification was indicated.

The list went on, including a number of ways in which points could be earned. Gifts were good; a maximum of five points could be redeemed. The scoring wasn't based on the value of the item, which could be as simple as a flower. Apparently, the ability to *personally* select gifts was key. Jewelry was a time-honored indicator because it spoke to emotional value. Significant jewelry was a sign about how the rest of the relationship would go.

He had just taken the last swallow of beer when his gaze snagged on the last item on the demerit list. A penchant for junk food and beer indicated a lack of nutritional responsibility that could carry over into Other Areas.

Directly below the demerit list, typed in boldface so it couldn't be missed, was a notation: three strikes and you're out.

His fist closed on the now-empty beer can. Absently, he placed the crushed aluminum on the patio table. From inside he heard a knock on the door. Room service, no doubt, with the pizza he had ordered.

He paid the young waiter, added a generous tip and told him to give the pizza to a family with young kids he had noticed staying farther down the hall. Somewhere between demerit items eight and nine, his appetite had faded.

The shower was still running, so he walked back out to the patio, got rid of the beer can in the kitchen trash then sat down and flipped through to the end of the folder. There were a number of rejected profiles at the back. Lucas and Howard were the most recent additions to that section.

The final sheet was a list of discarded Possibles: men who Lilah knew through business and social connections or the dating website, but who had not made it through to the selection process.

Snapping the folder closed, Zane replaced it on the table and paced to the terrace railing. Gripping the wrought iron edge, he stared out at the stunning view of the bay.

The contents of the folder had given him an insight into what Lilah wanted from a man. However, the most significant fact from his point of view was that *he* did not even make it into the folder.

Lilah had not even considered him in her discarded possibles list.

Jaw tight, he strode back to the table and flipped through to the points system. He was aware of his shortcomings, but he did not think he was that bad. It annoyed him that Lilah had not even considered him as a possible.

As if all he was good for was a quick thrill.

He found the merit list and the notation he wanted: number five, gifts.

A visual of the large solitaire ring Lucas had gotten Elena to order from an online store flashed into his mind. Lucas's instincts had been good, although he had fallen down with his inability to personally select the ring.

Flipping back to Lucas's rejected profile, he noted that Lucas had not scored in the gifts area. Somehow he had managed to amass *nineteen* points without presenting Lilah with any kind of gift.

Bleakly, he wondered what Lucas had done with the ring he had bought. If it fell into Carla's hands, Lucas would have some fast talking to do.

Not that Zane was interested in obtaining the solitaire, or anything like it.

He had a better idea.

* * *

Lilah had expected dinner in the hotel restaurant to be a little tense after she had left Zane strategically hanging. However, instead of the frustration she had glimpsed that afternoon, Zane seemed relaxed and oddly preoccupied, as if his mind was on other things.

Twice he had taken calls on his cell, getting up from the candlelit patio table to pace around the enormous floodlit infinity pool, looking taut and edgy in black pants and a loose black shirt.

To make matters worse, Gemma, who Lilah had thought was based in Sydney, was seated at a nearby table. According to Zane, his former P.A. had just transferred to a position on Medinos, and now worked for the manager of the resort. She started her new job at the end of the week.

Looking young and sexy in a minuscule hot orange dress that should have clashed with her titian hair but somehow didn't, Gemma succeeded in making Lilah feel staid and old-fashioned in the classic white silk sheath she had chosen.

Every time Lilah's gaze was drawn to Gemma, the weight of every one of her twenty-nine years seemed to press in on her. Gemma looked far more Zane's type than she could ever be. It was a depressing fact that in the dating game, classic Hepburn just did not cut it with Lolita. Her sexuality had finally been released, but it was clear that if she wanted to keep Zane's eyes on her, she was going to have to update her wardrobe.

She stared bleakly at the exquisite table arrangement of pink roses. Panic gripped her at the thought that she *had* overplayed her hand. That instead of giving their relationship a discreet nudge toward marriage, she had pushed too hard and Zane was now cooling off.

Zane finished his call and returned to the table. Their dessert, an island specialty he had insisted on ordering, was delivered with a flourish. Lilah tried to show an interest in the exquisite platter of almond pastries and sweetmeats sprinkled with rose petals, but she had lost her appetite.

A wine waiter materialized beside the table with a bottle of very expensive French champagne. As if they had something to celebrate.

Candlelight, roses, champagne, all the classic elements of a grand romantic gesture.

The depression that had settled on her like a dark shroud dissipated, wiped out by a sudden dizzying sense of anticipation. Her heart began to pound. She felt like she was on an emotional roller coaster ride. Her instincts were probably all wrong, but she couldn't blot out the sudden, wild notion that Zane was about to propose.

Zane leaned forward and the subtle but heady scent of his skin and the devastating cologne made her head swim. "Do you see anything you like?"

Her gaze was caught and held by the piercing quality of his eyes. In the candlelight his irises were midnight dark with an intriguing velvety quality. He frowned and she realized he wanted her to look at the dessert that had just been delivered.

She surveyed the dessert tray. Almost instantly, she saw the glitter of jewels in the center.

Her excitement evaporated. Not an engagement ring; a diamond bracelet.

The standard currency for mistresses.

At that moment, Gemma, who was leaving with her escort, stopped at their table.

Her gaze moved from the discreet pop of the champagne cork to the bracelet. She smiled brightly. "Diamonds." She waggled one slim, tanned wrist, displaying a narrow gold bangle that shimmered with tiny stones. "Doesn't Zane give the *best* presents?"

While the waiter poured flutes of champagne, Gemma lingered, introducing her date. She eventually left in a flurry of lace ruffles and floral perfume.

Zane handed Lilah a flute of champagne, which she noted

was pink, to match the rose petals. She tried to be upbeat about that fact. Zane had gone to a great deal of effort to create a special occasion, and he had brought her a gift, which was significant.

Unfortunately, somewhere between discovering the bracelet and the conversation with Gemma, the sizzle of excitement had gone.

His gaze held a hint of impatience. "Do you like it?"

Lilah set the champagne down without tasting it. Grandma Cole had gotten a diamond bracelet from her lover, shortly before he had left her. She had used it as a down payment on a small cottage for her and the baby.

Reluctantly, she extracted the bracelet from its nest of confectionary and petals. It was unexpectedly heavy for such a delicately, intricately constructed piece. Her breath caught as she noted the cut and the quality of the emeralds interspersed between the diamonds. Not new, but old. Make that *very* old.

She frowned. The design was hauntingly familiar. She was certain she had seen something like it before, although, in the flickering light of the candles, she couldn't be sure. Curiosity briefly overrode her disappointment as she studied the archaic design.

She itched to put her spectacles on and examine the bracelet more closely, but she couldn't afford either the professional or the emotional attachment. Not when it looked like a bracelet was Zane's standard form of dating gift.

Despite all of the reasons she could not accept the bracelet, a small part of her didn't want to relinquish it. The value of the stones didn't come into it. The bracelet could have been made of plastic. What mattered was that Zane had thought to give her a gift, a keepsake of their time together.

Unfortunately, old or new, she couldn't risk accepting the bracelet in case Zane took that as her tacit agreement to a relationship with him on his terms.

As his temporary live-in lover.

After the way he had interfered with her dating program

that afternoon, she knew that if she weakened, Zane would be relentless.

Reluctantly, she placed the bracelet on the table.

Zane frowned. "Aren't you going to try it on?"

"It's lovely, but I can't accept it."

"If this is about Gemma, you don't have to worry. She was my personal assistant, nothing more."

"I don't think she sees it that way." Gemma's attitude toward Zane had always been distinctly proprietorial. So much so that for most of the past two years, Lilah had thought she *was* Zane's steady girl.

He looked impatient. "Which is why she isn't my P.A. anymore. The bracelet was a goodbye gift."

Lilah made an effort to calm emotions that were rapidly spiraling out of control. She had to keep reminding herself that she was with Zane now, not Gemma. "Goodbye, and she transfers to Medinos?"

It would not have been the way she would have handled the situation.

"I couldn't fire her, and she liked Medinos. It was a solution."

Lilah's fingers clenched. Gemma had clearly gotten emotionally involved and Zane had found a way of shifting her out of his work space, while still letting her have her way and stay close.

And think that she still had a chance.

It was a perfect example of Zane's nice side. From her dealings with him in the charity, Lilah knew he didn't like seeing anyone in a vulnerable situation get hurt. He would go out of his way to personally help. She loved that evidence of his compassion but she couldn't help wishing that Zane had been a bit more ruthless with Gemma.

Another unsettling thought occurred to her. If Zane had not given Gemma a definite "no" she had to wonder how many other discarded women still lingered on the fringes of his life in the hope that a relationship was still possible.

It was not a happy thought. Zane was nothing like the irresponsible, self-centered men who had abandoned her mother and grandmother, nevertheless the scenario with Gemma was unsettling in a way she hadn't quite worked out.

Ignoring the champagne and the dessert, Lilah got briskly to her feet.

Now visibly annoyed, Zane slipped the bracelet into his pocket and rose to his feet. He fell into step with her as she threaded her way between the tables, easily keeping pace.

His palm cupped her elbow, sending tingling heat up her arm. His gaze locked on hers. "Why won't you accept the gift?"

Lilah ignored the gritty demand and the pleasure that flooded her that, finally, Zane was responding in the way she had hoped. She focused on a bland section of beige wall in an effort to control the wimpy desire to give in, fling her arms around his neck and melt against him. "It's...too expensive."

"I'm rich. Money is no object."

They emerged from the restaurant. A little desperately she eyed the bank of elevators ahead. "It's not about the value, exactly."

Zane released her elbow as they reached the elevators. She caught a flash of his expression in the glossy steel doors. He looked disbelieving and grimly annoyed.

"Do I get points for trying?"

Her gaze snapped to his. "You *read* my folder."

"I needed to see what I was up against."

Lilah jabbed the elevator button. A door slid open. "That would be commitment."

After a night of passion that was curiously unsatisfying, Lilah rose early and spent time alone, adapting elements of the marriage plan to suit the new strategy. She decided the best way to show Zane that she was not fretting over the way their brief fling, apart from the heart-pounding sex, seemed to be disintegrating was to throw herself into her work.

During the early hours, she had given herself a pep talk

about the positives. Zane had responded to her elusiveness with a gift. It had been the wrong gift and he had cheated by reading her folder, which was a blot. She was prepared to overlook his behavior on the basis that he had not thought things through. The one shining factor was that he had made his choices based on the desire to win her. It was progress.

For the next two days she got up early and walked to Ambrosi's new retail center, a charming, antiquated building situated on the bustling waterfront. Interior decorating wasn't her job, but the retail center would be her temporary office until the facility on Ambrus was completed. Lilah figured that if she had to work there for the next six months she needed to like her surroundings, so she pulled rank and inserted herself into the process.

Zane, who had had to spend long hours closeted with Elena working through the raft of paperwork on a deal in Florida, had become even more remote. Despite their lovemaking, the abyss between them seemed to be widening.

With her strategy seemingly in tatters, it was hard to concentrate on paint colors and curtain samples when all she wanted to do was take a taxi back to the resort and throw herself into Zane's arms.

To avoid weakening, she had taken herself shopping during the long, somnolent lunch breaks the Medinians enjoyed. Instead of eating, she had spent a large amount of money on filmy, sexy clothes and a daring hot orange bikini that she gloomily decided she would probably never get the opportunity to wear.

New makeup that made her eyes look smoky and exotic, subtle caramel streaks in her hair and a fake tan completed the makeover. Every time she caught her reflection in glass doors or looked in a mirror, Lilah was amazed at the difference the subtle changes had made, although Zane had barely seemed to notice.

Tempted as she was to bluntly declare that she was in love with him and put an end to the tension, Lilah made a grim effort to appear sunnily content. She couldn't shake off the dreadful conviction that the instant Zane knew she had fallen for him, he would put an end to any hope of long-term commitment.

That was how it had worked with her mother and her grandmother. Once the prize was won, the passion had cooled. Their lovers hadn't been able to leave fast enough.

Zane strolled into the building chaos just short of noon. Wearing dark narrow trousers and a loose white shirt, sunlight slanting across his taut cheekbones, he managed to look both dangerously sexy and casual.

Lilah was instantly aware of her own attire. Instead of her usual low-key neutrals, today she was wearing one of her new purchases, a filmy orange blouse teamed with a tight little black camisole that revealed just a hint of cleavage and tight, white jeans. Combined with strappy orange heels and iridescent orange nail polish, the effect was unexpectedly striking.

Zane's gaze glittered over her. Lilah registered the gratifying flare of shock that was almost instantly shuttered.

Zane had finally noticed her. Although, it could simply be the orange color, which she had developed something of a fetish for lately. Orange was hard to miss.

Just minutes ago she had felt warm, but comfortable. Now, beneath the weight of Zane's gaze, despite all of the doors and windows flung wide admitting the balmy sea breeze, Lilah felt flushed and overheated.

"Are you ready to go?"

That afternoon Zane had planned a boat trip to survey Ambrosi's old oyster beds and the site for the new processing plant. The trip would be followed up by a launch function for the new enterprise at the castello.

Lilah ignored the faint edge to Zane's voice and kept her attention on Mario, the builder. She had spent the morning directing a number of contractors as they had fitted air-conditioning and lighting fixtures and erected partitioning. Mario was a little on the short side, but outrageously handsome. On a purely intellectual level she had thought she should feel something for such a good-looking man. Depressingly, the only thing she had felt had been the battle of wills as Mario had tried to improve on her floor plan. "Almost."

Zane's gaze shifted to the bronzed contractor who was hefting a dividing panel into place. Mario had already repositioned the panel for her twice. Both times the angle had not been quite right. As a consequence he was sweating, his T-shirt clinging damply to his chest.

Mario placed the partition and finally got it right. She rewarded him with a smile. "*Bene.*"

Zane's fingers interlaced with hers. A split second later she found herself pulled into a light clinch. Her heart pounded as Zane's gaze settled on her mouth. The move was masculine and dominant and, in front of the contractors, definitely territorial.

His mouth brushed over hers, sending a hot pulse of adrenaline through her. It was a claiming kiss, the kind of reaction she had wanted two days ago.

Two days. Panic made her tense. Time was sliding away, only four days left. Suddenly, it didn't seem nearly enough time for Zane to fall in love with her.

Zane's hands settled at her waist, making her feel even hotter. This close she could see the nicks of long-ago scars, the faint kink in a nose that should have been perfectly straight, the silky shadow of his lashes. She drew in a breath and just for a few seconds, gave herself permission to relax.

Zane cocked his head to one side. "Is this a 'yes'?"

She stiffened at the lethal combination of pressure and charm. "Yes, to the boat trip."

The midday sun struck down, glaringly hot on the marina jetty, as Lilah walked on ahead while Zane unloaded dive gear from the trunk of the car. She rummaged in her new string beach bag for a pair of dark glasses as she strolled, drawn by the bobbing yachts and the aquamarine clarity of the sea.

Movement on Zane's yacht drew her gaze. The bleached

surfer hair on one of the men rang an instant alarm bell, although neither of the other two men on the yacht were remotely recognizable.

Although, if it was the three J's she was looking at, she shouldn't be surprised. If most of the applicants had been scammers, the odds were not good for the three she had picked.

Suddenly any idea that Zane had been suffering the agonies of an emotional crisis for the past two days was swept away. The entire time she had been playing her waiting game, he had been busy working on a preemptive move.

By the time Zane appeared, stripped down to a pair of sleek black neoprene dive pants, his chest bare, a gear bag filled with diving equipment, there was no doubt.

Jaw set, she met his gaze. "How did you get them here? Wait, let me guess—Spiros."

What was the point in having a henchman unless he could do useful things like kidnap all three of her potential husbands?

Fifteen

The lenses of Zane's dark glasses made him look frustratingly remote and detached. "You make it sound like Spiros kidnapped them. All he did was pilot the jet."

That was like saying that all Blackbeard did was sail the ship. "How did you get them?"

The idea that they had been coerced in any way evaporated as she took in their collective grins, the clink of beers. A definite holiday air pervaded the yacht. "No wait, don't tell me, it was a corporate kidnap." She slid her dark glasses onto the bridge of her nose. "Two days. *Paradise*."

Zane shrugged. "They could have refused."

"Hah!"

His gaze narrowed. "If you don't want to spend time with them just say the word. Spiros can take them out for the afternoon, no problem."

Which was, she realized, exactly what he wanted. He hadn't brought the men here so she could get together with them. His plan was much simpler than that. He was intent on ruthlessly cutting them out of her life.

She squashed the thrill that shot through her at his un-PC behavior and jabbed a finger in the direction of his chest. "You had no right—"

He caught her hand and drew her close, his hold gentle as he pressed her palm against his bare chest. "While you're with me, I have every right. I told you I wanted to be present when you met them."

Lilah's toes curled at the fiery heat of his skin against her palm, the thud of his heart, the sneaky, undermining way he had gotten around the issue of crashing her dates. "I didn't agree."

Although, she realized that none of that mattered now, because it was clear Zane had never considered any of the men as serious contenders. If he had, he would not have brought them to Medinos.

She stared at the obdurate line of his jaw. In a moment of blinding clarity, she recognized the flip side of the situation, an even more important truth. Zane wanted her enough to eliminate the three J's in the first place. Far from ignoring her for the past two days, Zane had been focusing his energies on systematically clearing away all opposition so he could have what he wanted. As if her agreement to his proposition was a forgone conclusion.

He jerked his head in the direction of the yacht. "It's your choice. If you don't want to spend time with them, you don't have to."

Tension hummed through her along with an undermining, utterly female sense of satisfaction. It was difficult to stay mad at Zane for completely subverting her strategy when a part of her adored it that he had gone to such lengths to cut out the competition.

He wanted her, enough that he couldn't bear the thought of her having other men in the picture. It was exactly the result she had wanted; it just hadn't panned out the way she had thought.

A dazzling idea momentarily blotted out everything else. She was suddenly glad for the concealment of the dark glasses. "Not a problem," she said smoothly.

Mentally, she ticked off a number of new, exciting options all based around having three extra men in close proximity for the afternoon. "Now that they're here, why not meet them?"

Seconds later, Zane handed Lilah onto the yacht.

Jack Riordan, clearly an outdoors kind of guy and at home on the yacht in a pair of board shorts and a tank, looked exactly like his photo. Jeremy Appleby did not. Instead of tall and dark, he was blond and thin, with a goatee. He also had an impressive camera slung around his neck, which put Lilah on instant alert.

Zane's gaze touched on hers. The knowledge that he had also noted the camera formed a moment of intimacy that sent pleasure humming through her. Despite everything that was wrong between them, in that moment she felt utterly connected to Zane, as if they were a couple.

She also felt protected. Next to Zane's and Spiros's tanned, muscular frames, Appleby looked weak and weedy. Lilah would not want to be in Appleby's shoes if he tried to take photos or file a story.

Like Appleby, John Smith did not look anything like the *GQ* photograph he had supplied. With his plump build, balding head and glasses, he didn't come close.

A blond head popped out of the cabin, breaking the stilted conversation. Lilah recognized the pretty flight attendant from the jet. Though she was dressed now in a bright pink bikini teamed with a pair of low-slung white shorts, evidently Jasmine was fulfilling the same role, because she had a tray of cold drinks.

Lilah noticed that Jack Riordan seemed riveted by Jasmine's honey-blond hair and mentally crossed him off her now-defunct list.

After casting off, Spiros took the wheel. To Lilah's relief, Zane didn't leave her alone with the three men, but stayed glued to her side. Her relief was short-lived as Zane systematically questioned each of the three J's about their lives, concentrating on their finances.

An hour into an agonizingly slow trip, which bore more of a resemblance to the Spanish Inquisition than a pleasure cruise, they reached Ambrus.

Zane dropped anchor. Spiros heaved the inflatable raft into the water, preparatory to rowing to the beach. The three J's trooped below to change into their beachwear.

Lilah clamped down on her frustration and helped Jasmine take glasses and bottles to the galley. When she emerged on deck, Zane was securing the inflatable. She checked that the three J's were still below. "You had no right to interrogate them like that."

Apart from the fact that it had been embarrassing, it had utterly nixed any opportunities to make Zane jealous. She had barely been able to get a word in edgewise.

Zane knotted the rope to a cleat and straightened. "Did you really believe Appleby owned his own software company?"

When he had not seemed to know the difference between a megabyte and a gigabyte, it hadn't seemed likely. "No."

"Or that John Smith is the CEO of an accounting firm?"

She had not caught on to all of the jargon Zane, who had a double degree in business administration and accounting, had dropped into the conversation, but she had understood enough to know that John Smith had failed the test. "Jack Riordan seems genuine." His knowledge of the yacht at least seemed to back up his small boat-building business.

At that moment, the three men emerged on deck, ready to board the inflatable. Appleby and Smith, their alabaster skin slathered with sunblock, appeared to glow beneath the brassy Mediterranean sun.

If Lilah had been fooled, even for a second, that Zane was

doing this out of the kindness of his heart, that notion would have now been completely discredited.

First the inquisition, now the swimsuit contest.

When they reached the beach, Jasmine tossed her shorts on the sand, laid out a bright yellow towel and lay down to sunbathe. While Zane and Spiros assembled snorkeling gear, Lilah strolled behind a clump of shade trees to change. Setting her beach bag down on the sand, she extracted the hot orange bikini, which she had been reluctant to change into on the yacht.

Before her courage deserted her altogether, she quickly changed then knotted the turquoise sarong that went with the bikini around her hips. She frowned at the lush display of tanned cleavage and considered changing back into her white jeans, camisole and shirt.

Even as the thought passed through her mind she knew she could not afford to do that now. She had lost the leverage of the three J's and she was almost out of time. Unfortunately, the bikini was now a crucial part of her strategy.

Zane almost had a heart attack when Lilah emerged onto the beach. He was glad Spiros had taken the three J's on a snorkeling expedition. It was an easier solution than the medieval threats he would have been forced to issue just in case any one of them decided it was okay to look.

The cut of the outrageously sexy bikini somehow managed to make Lilah's narrow hips and delicate curves look mouth-wateringly voluptuous. Added to that, after just a few days on Medinos, her skin had taken on a tawny glow that made her green eyes look startlingly light, her cheekbones even more exotic. In the span of a few minutes, Lilah had gone from mysterious and reserved to lusciously, searingly hot.

If she had bought the bikini for the specific purpose of driving him crazy, Zane thought grimly, she had achieved the result. "When did you get the bikini?"

Lilah, who seemed more interested in laying out a bright turquoise towel and rummaging through her trendily matching beach bag, gave him a distracted, too innocent look as if she hadn't quite registered who had spoken.

Zane's jaw clamped tighter as she abandoned arranging a neat line of possessions, one of which, suspiciously, was a *red* folder, and finally seemed to become aware of his presence.

She directed a smile in his general direction. "Two days ago."

After their discussion.

Zane folded his arms across his chest so that he wouldn't repeat the cavemanlike behavior he had displayed on the jetty and simply grab Lilah. He eyed the red folder and wondered what new scheme she was cooking up now. "Have you come to a decision yet?"

She lifted a hand to her eyes and stared out to sea as if she was more interested in the four heads bobbing in the water than having an actual conversation with him. "I'm still thinking it over."

His jaw clamped. If he wasn't mistaken the smile she had given him was the same smooth, professional smile she had given the builder earlier on in the day. "The way I see it, we have three days left." He jerked his head in the direction of the swimmers. "And we're wasting time."

Lilah's cheeks went instantly pink. "Is sex all you're interested in?"

He noted with satisfaction, any suggestion that she was disinterested in him evaporated. "At the moment, yes."

Lilah glanced around distractedly. Her gaze came to rest on Jasmine, who was flipping through a magazine.

Zane frowned. It was not the response he had wanted. Living with Lilah for the past two days had been like living with a professionally cheerful automaton. The passionate nights aside, he was now officially frustrated. "Jasmine can't hear a thing. She's listening to her iPod. If she registered anything short of an explosion it would be a miracle."

She glared at him and he realized something else that was different about Lilah. She'd had light streaks put in her hair.

His hold on his temper slipped another notch. He had never thought of himself as a controlling person; his motto was Live and Let Live. However, when it came to Lilah he didn't feel anything that came even remotely close to flexibility. He found himself supremely irked that she had changed her hair without even bothering to mention it to him. "You've changed your hair."

From her beach bag Lilah fished out another object, which seemed much more rivetingly interesting than the conversation he was trying to have with her. "Yesterday. I didn't think you had noticed."

The bright turquoise iPod, which signaled that Lilah had found a new way to block him out, was the last straw, literally. In two years Lilah had never been trendy; she had remained tantalizingly, coolly the same. "Honey, I'm noticing now."

Lilah's gaze flashed to his, the deep anger in their depths electrifying, and suddenly the air was charged.

For two years he had been burningly aware of Lilah's underlying sensuality, the latent feminine power buried beneath the tempting reserve and bland, virginal white.

The reserve, like the white clothing, was long gone, replaced by hot, passionate colors, cutting-edge fashion and way too much skin.

He had been so absorbed with his own reactions to the new confident, sexy Lilah that he hadn't stopped to think about what was driving the change.

The answer was terrifyingly simple. Lilah was no longer a virgin. Thanks to him, she was now a mature woman of experience. Single. Available. And, if he wasn't mistaken, ready to shop around for what she wanted.

Taking into consideration the wish list in her white folder, he had to assume that the kind of man she would want to extend her sexual experience with would not be a man with a dysfunctional past and an inability to commit.

He did not think she was calculatingly aware of the power

she could wield. She was still feeling her way, but he was grimly certain that it would not take her long to find out.

It was a dangerous state of affairs.

Suddenly the color of the new folder—red—took on an unsettling meaning. The thought that if he could not satisfy Lilah's needs that she could start experimenting with men—plural—made him go cold inside.

Jack Riordan popped out of the surf, a speargun in one hand, a silvery fish flapping on the end.

Feeling embattled, Zane studied Riordan with new eyes. He was the least good-looking of the three, but he had a lean, rugged build and the kind of mature dependability that even Zane liked.

Riordan had one other advantage; he was a mature man who was clearly looking to settle down.

It was an advantage he should have taken more note of before he had risked bringing Riordan to Medinos.

His jaw tightened. This wasn't working.

His aim had been to protect Lilah and eliminate the competition. Unfortunately, Lilah seemed to *like* Riordan, in which case his plan could have backfired.

The thought that she might start dating Riordan was a defining moment.

Over my dead body.

Flashes of white caught his eye; Smith and Appleby were also exiting the water. He scooped up the beach bag, which, if he wasn't mistaken, contained Lilah's clothes. He had played a waiting game long enough.

Lilah realized Zane's intent a bare second before he swung her up into his arms. She noted where the expensive little iPod, which she had been on the verge of working out, had fallen and clutched at his bare shoulders. She tried to repress the automatic thrill that he was actually carrying her.

She was still angry and deeply depressed at the thought that had occurred to her, that she had made a dreadful mistake in thinking that Zane cared for her. That her entire strategy was flawed.

If Zane was even the tiniest bit as obsessed as she had become, he should have noticed her hair before now.

She stared at the approaching tree line. "Where are you taking me?"

"Somewhere you can get dressed."

"I'm *wearing* clothes."

His gaze burned over the expanse of silky skin bared by the skimpy bikini, the length of her legs visible beneath the transparent gauze of the sarong. "Couldn't prove it by me."

"I'm wearing more than Jasmine." In point of fact she was wearing a great deal more. Jasmine had a microscopic bikini, with no sarong.

"What Jasmine does or does not wear is irrelevant."

Cool shade slid over her skin as he rounded the clump of trees she had changed behind earlier. Lilah blinked as her eyes adjusted to the dim light. "I don't see why."

He set her down. "Because Jasmine doesn't interest me. Which brings me to the subject of Smith, Appleby and Riordan. Get rid of them."

There was a moment of vibrating silence.

Zane was jealous.

Lilah kept her expression carefully blank, but a part of her was melting and ridiculously happy because even if Zane wasn't showing any signs of being in love with her yet, he wanted her enough to bully and coerce and demand.

And he wanted the three J's out of the picture.

"I haven't agreed to anything yet."

His gaze was hot and distinctly irritable, signaling that the cool reserve that had grown between them when she had refused to agree to his relationship terms was finally and definitely gone. "Take as much time as you need. But *we* have an agreement and we are not wasting any more time." Both hands were wrapped around the soft flesh of her upper arms now. With a slow, inevitable movement, he pulled her close. His mouth brushed hers, heat zapped through her.

Drawing in a deep breath, she planted her palms on his chest, created a small amount of overheated space and tried not to notice how gorgeous his chest looked. "I've decided to finish with the three J's."

There was a moment of tense silence. "Will you stay with me at the castello tonight?"

For a shivering, delicious second she drowned in the stormy depths of Zane's eyes. Of course, she would be present at the launch party at the castello, but Zane was asking her to stay with him at his family home. "Yes."

The last blaze of a fiery sunset illuminated the evening sky as Zane showed Lilah to her suite at the castello.

He was acutely conscious that the guest suite he had allocated Lilah, the only one next to his, also happened to be next door to Lucas's suite.

Zane unlocked the door and handed her the key.

Lilah glanced at Lucas's door, a faint flush to her cheeks. Zane's jaw tightened as he pushed the door open and stepped inside. He had been on the verge of asking Lilah to stay with him in his private suite a number of times that afternoon, but every time he approached the subject his jaw had locked and the words wouldn't come.

He carried her suitcase through to the bedroom.

Lilah unzipped her case. "What time do you need me downstairs?"

Zane checked his watch. Frustrated, he noted he was overdue at a press interview.

He had spent valuable time driving Appleby, Riordan and Smith to the airport and making sure they boarded their commercial flight out. In light of the discovery that Appleby had been a journalist, and that he had somehow gotten photos of Lilah in her bikini, wiping the memory stick of his camera had been a job he had not wanted to entrust to Spiros. "In one hour."

Zane couldn't help noticing there was no sign of Lilah's normal low-key wardrobe as she shook out a jewel-bright array of clothes and hung them in the closet.

His gaze snagged on an outrageously sexy pair of red heels. He had never been obsessed with women's clothing, but as he left the suite, Zane found himself wondering what Lilah would wear tonight. After the revelation of the orange bikini, he decided, he couldn't bank on one of the modest cream cocktail dresses she had alternated wearing to a number of charity functions.

Unlocking his own suite door, he walked into his room, which, for the first time, did not feel like a refuge. Instead it felt oddly blank and solitary. He changed into evening clothes and walked downstairs in time to meet Constantine and Lucas, who had decided to stay on Medinos for the opening of the new pearl facility.

Even knowing that Lilah didn't want Lucas, Zane would have been profoundly annoyed by his brother's presence if he hadn't known that Carla was supposed to be joining him.

As they walked into the small reception room where the interview was being held, for the first time in years Zane's mind was not on business.

He wondered how far Lilah would push him tonight.

Grimly, he decided that his biggest problem was one that had never bothered him before. Because they hadn't established firm grounds for a relationship, he didn't have any rights.

Until that afternoon he had not understood how important it was to make it very clear, publicly, that Lilah was his.

Sixteen

Lilah showered and spent some time smoothing an expensive body moisturizer into her skin. With her skin pampered and glowing, she wrapped herself in a robe and confronted her wardrobe.

Instead of wearing the classic cream cocktail dress she had originally planned on, she took out an uncrushable red halter-neck she had bought the previous day. Not her usual color, or style, the curve-hugging dress was transforming, bringing a glow to her skin and deepening the color of her eyes.

After dressing, she carefully applied her makeup, following the instructions she had been given by the beautician who had sold her the products. Instead of confining her hair in its usual coil, she brushed it out, letting it swing in loose silky waves down her back. She inserted red crystal earrings in her lobes and fastened a gold pendant around her neck. The fine gold chain was almost invisible, leaving a single red crystal suspended just above the shadowy cleavage of her breasts.

She slipped into red heels and walked over to the closet door, which had a full-length mirror.

Her heart rate, which was already too rapid, pounded a little faster. It was going to take some time getting used to the glaringly available siren who stared back at her.

She consulted her red folder, which was open at a page she had entitled "Seduction" then quickly worked through her list. Her fingers shook slightly with nerves as she draped a red silk negligee over the bed then unpacked a box of richly scented votive candles and placed them at strategic points around the room.

They had made love enough times that she shouldn't feel nervous about the idea, but she had never set out to deliberately seduce Zane before. She wanted to make everything, herself included, as irresistible and gorgeous as possible. The last touch was a bottle of very expensive French champagne in the small bar fridge.

She surveyed the room with an eagle eye. The scene was set.

If Zane finally made the kind of emotional breakthrough she had been hoping for, he could even propose. The thought made her pulse race even faster.

Taking several deep breaths to calm herself down, she remembered to spritz herself with a waft of an exotic perfume she'd bought to go with the dress, picked up a matching red clutch and strolled downstairs.

Lilah's heart sank when the first person she saw as she entered a large, elegant reception room hung with chandeliers and festooned with white roses, was Gemma.

She was mentally braced to brazen out the evening with Zane; she didn't know if she could cope with another feminine dueling match with Zane's former P.A.

Before she could slide past the younger woman, Gemma waved her over to her group and insisted on introducing her.

Lilah already knew the two buyers from a high-end European chain of stores. She kept a smooth, professional smile in place while she chatted and tried to pretend that the way she looked was not wildly different to her usual low-key style.

Gemma was bubbling over with enthusiasm for the Atraeus family, who had moved her from Sydney to Medinos.

As Gemma's enthusiasm for all things Atraeus continued unabated, including the fact that she *loved* Medinos so much she intended to settle there permanently, Lilah felt again the sense of unease that had swept through her the previous evening. It wasn't jealousy. Although Gemma was bluntly intent on making her aware of just how much she wanted Zane. The tension that gripped her was more elusive and disturbing. She couldn't quite put her finger on—

The deep cool register of Zane's voice sent a hot tingle down her spine. Bracing herself for his reaction when he saw the red dress, she turned.

The voice belonged to Lucas, not Zane. The embarrassment of the moment was limited by the fact that Lucas was talking on his cell. Judging from the blankness of his expression, he had not even recognized her.

Zane's oldest brother, Constantine, an imposing figure, was just feet away, his arm around his new wife, Sienna Ambrosi, who was pregnant and glowing.

Out of nowhere, longing, unexpected and powerful, hit Lilah. For years the idea of a pregnancy had been something she had avoided thinking about, beyond taking extreme measures to make sure it never happened to her. Now, in the space of a few seconds, everything had changed.

Sienna, Lilah realized, was the picture of everything she wanted: the protective husband, the well-loved glow, the baby. Bleakly, she faced the fact that if Zane didn't fall in love with her, it was possible that she would never achieve any of those things. If she could not imagine replacing Zane with another man, she did not see how she was ever going to progress to the point of having a baby with someone she did not love.

She refocused beyond Lucas's shoulder. Her breath caught in her throat. Zane, looking edgily gorgeous in a tuxedo, was heading straight for her.

A prosaic little fact that had been the stumbling block of

Cole women for fifty years, and which she had happily glossed over in her pursuit of Zane, was suddenly glaringly highlighted.

She could try any number of strategies and tactics, but she could not *make* Zane fall in love with her.

Zane cut through the room, his gaze caught and held by the intensity of Lilah's.

Something had happened; something had changed.

His jaw locked as he took in the spectacular red dress that clung to every curve, the lavish, silky fall of dark hair.

The only time he had seen Lilah's hair out of its neat coils had been when he had pulled out pins and threaded his fingers through it. To his knowledge she had never voluntarily undone her hair for anyone, himself included.

His attention shifted to the man standing nearby.

Lucas.

The suspicion he had never entirely managed to wipe from his mind shot to the surface. If he'd had any doubts about the concept of marriage, which he had been tossing around like a hot coal for the past hour, they were gone.

His decision to examine the whole process from a business point of view had been a major turning point. He didn't know why he hadn't thought of the idea earlier. He had never had any problem negotiating complex legal agreements and, at the end of the day, the binding nature of marriage was similar to a business contract.

The emotional side was the tricky part but, since he had already decided he wanted Lilah to live with him, he figured that with her systematic, logical approach, they could negotiate their way to an understanding.

He was clear on the main point: Lilah belonged to him and before the night was out he was determined that she would have his ring on her finger.

If she would accept him as a husband.

His jaw clenched. The thought that, after years of avoiding sexual lures and marriage traps, he would literally have to force a woman to marry him should have been amusing.

Unfortunately his sense of humor had died that afternoon on a hot beach on Ambrus.

"Zane, *babe!*"

Zane's jaw locked as Gemma, all flowing red hair and sexy black lace, blocked his view of Lilah and Lucas.

Her arms coiled around his neck. His hands clamped her waist preventing full body contact.

She winked and grinned good-naturedly. "I've been calling, but you haven't answered."

That was because he had a block on her number. "I've been busy."

Calmly, he disengaged himself and declined her invitation to join her for a drink out on the terrace.

If he had known how complicated it was going to be taking Gemma along to charity functions in Sydney as his casual date, as insurance that he wouldn't lose his head over Lilah, he never would have crossed that particular line.

Zane finally managed to disentangle himself, only to discover that Lilah had disappeared.

Lucas snapped closed the cell he had been talking into, a grin lighting his face. "Carla has just arrived at the airport. I'm on my way to pick her up."

Zane swallowed the blunt warning he had been about to deliver. If Lucas, who had entered the room just seconds before, had been on the phone to Carla then he would not have had time to talk with Lilah.

Zane skimmed the well-dressed crowd, looking for a spectacular red dress and a silky fall of dark hair. "I thought Carla wasn't well."

Lucas dug car keys out of his pocket. "She's feeling better, which is good. I've missed her like crazy."

For the first time Zane noticed the changes in Lucas. He looked relaxed and carefree. Even his clothing was different. The suit he was wearing was a cutting-edge departure from his usual classic style. The changes could mean only one thing. He had seen the phenomena often enough in friends. Relief loosened some of Zane's tension. "You love Carla."

Lucas tossed the keys in one hand and clapped him on the arm. "I'm *in* love with her. There's a difference."

Zane watched his brother leave, transfixed by the thought of all the changes Lilah had recently made. He had been so concerned with his own issues, he had somehow managed to miss the fact that Lilah had literally blossomed while they'd been together.

He wondered how he could ever have been so blind.

Lilah joined the small knot of guests and stared blindly at an exquisite display of antique Ambrosi pearls. She should have been upset at the clinch she had just witnessed. She was *not* good with the body contact, but Gemma sidetracking Zane wasn't what was upsetting her. The thing that had struck her most was Gemma's single-minded pursuit of Zane. That was, she realized, the basis of the cold unease that gripped her. Gemma's determination reminded her forcibly of herself.

Taking a deep breath, she tried to concentrate on the jewelry display. One strand of outstanding iridescent pearls, the signature product of Ambrosi, was said to be the first ever produced by the inventor of the process, Dominic Ambrosi, an alchemist who had lived in the eighteenth century.

Symbolic of the business merger, an entire section of the display was devoted to Atraeus jewels. A blank space in the display had been filled by a photograph and description of The Illium Cache, the ancient set of diamond-and-emerald jewels that for some reason had not made it into the case. Frowning, Lilah bent closer to study the photograph.

She caught a flash of Zane's reflection in the mirrored display case. Heart suddenly pounding, she straightened.

Zane's gaze seemed riveted by the red crystal suspended in the valley between her breasts. "I see you've found my ancestor's treasure trove."

Lilah blushed, acutely aware of the revealing neckline. It

wasn't as revealing as Gemma's black lace dress, but it was uncomfortably close. "Unfortunately, the most important pieces are missing."

"Ah. The fabled Illium Cache."

Off to one side of the room, a flash of red caught Lilah's eye. Gemma's hair, as bright as a flame. She paused just short of the corridor that lead to the bathrooms and the castello's private suites. Her gaze was fixed on Zane as if she was waiting for him to make eye contact. To Lilah's eyes, she looked a little desperate.

The hollow feeling she had experienced when she had seen Gemma winding herself around Zane came back to haunt her. "I just saw you with Gemma."

Zane, who barely seemed to notice Gemma's attempt to get his attention, looked impatient. "We need to talk, and we can't do it here."

Zane's grip on her elbow distracted her from the lonely figure of Gemma, waiting for Zane to notice her, as he steered her away from the jewelry cases.

Minutes later he showed her into what looked like a study filled with heavy dark furniture and an oversized desk. An entire wall was lined with leather-bound volumes; the remaining walls were decorated with oils. When she saw Zane's laptop sitting on the desk, she realized that this was his office.

Zane perched on the edge of the desk, arms folded across his chest. "You're in love with me."

The soft, flat statement took her breath. She thought she had done a thorough job of covering up her feelings. Clearly she had slipped up badly. Now that Zane knew she loved him, that didn't leave her with much leeway. "That doesn't mean I'll agree to live with you on a temporary basis."

"Because I'm terrible husband material?"

"I never said that."

"Not directly, but it's a fact that I didn't make it on to your list. Would you stay if I offered marriage?"

Lilah's fingers tightened on her clutch. She stared at the

closest painting, one of a girl holding a bunch of bright flowers. The soft expression on the girl's face as she looked directly at the painter radiated tender promise. She was in love.

As Lilah knew, firsthand, that tended to change things. "I'm not sure what you mean exactly by 'marriage.'"

His expression shifted, as if she had surprised him. "A legal marriage. I thought that was what you wanted."

Her heart pounded in her chest. Marriage was her goal—with Zane, if he could love her. "I do."

She saw his flicker of relief. "Good. If we marry, I won't touch another woman while we're together."

While we're together.

The qualifier made her stiffen. It implied an end.

In other words he was still talking about the same, temporary arrangement he had mentioned in their hotel suite, but ratified by marriage.

Suddenly Zane's businesslike approach fell into its correct context. He was not registering emotion because this was not an emotional discussion. He had reverted to business tactics in order to control the terms of the relationship.

The thought that Zane felt he needed to control her love so he could be with her was subtly wounding. She of all people could understand his emotional fears and vulnerabilities because for years she had shared them, although to a lesser degree. "Just out of interest, how long do you think this proposed marriage will last?"

Silence reigned for long seconds, filled by the tick of a mantel clock, the distant strains of music.

"I can't answer that question, but if you think I'm going to fall in love with someone else, you don't have to worry. That won't happen."

For a split second she almost managed to twist the meaning of Zane's comment into a declaration of his love for her, then his flat denial that he could fall in love registered.

As if the thought of surrendering to love was not on his personal horizon.

It was not a new concept. It was Zane's modus operandi with relationships. The fact that she could not make Zane fall in love with her was the basis that had undermined her entire strategy. "It's a common enough scenario. Women fall for you on a regular basis."

Irritation registered in his gaze. "I get partnered with women on a regular basis through company business and charitable events. That's mostly what the tabloids pick up on. The only woman I know who has certifiably fallen for me is you."

The knife twisted a little deeper. "And that makes me a sure bet."

His hands curled around her upper arms, his palms shiveringly hot against her skin. "You were a virgin, and you've got a logical, methodical approach to relationships. That's what I trust."

Jaw set, Lilah resisted the gentle pressure to step closer to Zane. She would not muddy this process any further with passion. They had already been that route. And what Zane proposed was sounding more like a business deal than a relationship.

The vibration of his cell phone broke the taut silence.

Frowning, Zane released his grip and checked the screen. He looked briefly frustrated. "I have to go. There's something I need to take care of before the official part of the evening begins."

Lilah strolled back to the party and circulated, chatting with buyers and contractors. She checked her wristwatch. Long minutes had passed since Zane had excused himself.

She walked out on the terrace just in case he had come back and she had somehow missed him. The terrace was windswept and empty.

She strolled back inside and surveyed the reception room again. Zane was not in the room.

It suddenly occurred to her that neither was Gemma, and with her flaming red hair and white skin, the younger woman was unmistakable.

The last time she had seen Gemma, she had been heading toward the part of the castello where the private suites were located, and suddenly she knew what the desperate look she had sent Zane had meant.

Feeling like an automaton, Lilah stepped out of the reception room. A ridiculously short amount of time later she found herself in the castello's darkened hallway, the chill from the thick stone walls seeping through the silk of her red gown.

She paused at the door of Zane's private quarters and lifted her hand to knock. The chink of glass on glass signaled that the suite was occupied.

A grim sense of déjà vu gripped her. She rapped once, twice.

It occurred to her that this time, unlike the incident with Lucas, Zane could not rescue her because, in a sense, she was confronting an aspect of herself that she did not like very much.

The door swung open on a waft of perfume. Gemma's tousled red hair cascaded around her white shoulders. Slim fingers clutched a silky black negligee closed over her breasts, the defensive gesture making her look young and absurdly vulnerable.

Lilah couldn't help thinking that it looked like they had both had the same idea about setting the scene for seduction.

She felt the weight of every one of her twenty-nine years crushing down on her. Her irritation with Gemma evaporated. "You should stop trying and go home. Sex won't make Zane, or any man, have a relationship with you."

"How can you know that?"

Because it had been burned into her psyche by both her mother and her grandmother. Unfortunately, she had temporarily forgotten that fact. "Logic. If you couldn't make him fall in love with you in two years, then it's probably not going to happen."

Gemma's expression went blank, as if she didn't know what to say next.

A split second later, the door snapped shut in Lilah's face.

Lilah fumbled the key into the lock of her door and let herself in. The door closed with a soft click behind her.

She stared at the glowing lamp-lit room, the sexy, filmy negligee draped over the bed.

The preparations were wrenchingly similar to Gemma's, and the end result would be the same. She could not make Zane love her, either.

She had changed, through falling in love with him, but she had to accept that for Zane the past might never be healed.

Feeling numb and faintly sick, she jammed the negligee out of sight in the case, picked up the phone and made a quick call to the airport. She managed to secure a flight to Dubai, which was leaving in an hour. She would have several hours to wait before she could get a connection to Sydney, but that didn't matter. She could leave Medinos tonight.

She arranged for a taxi then changed into clothes suitable for a long flight—cotton pants and a sleek-fitting tank, a light jacket and comfortable shoes. She caught a glimpse of the red crystal earrings dangling from her lobes in the dresser mirror as she packed. She removed them with fingers that were stiff and clumsy, wound her hair into a knot and secured it with pins.

She did a final check of the room then tensed when she realized she was lingering in the hope that Zane would come looking for her.

Swallowing against the sudden pain squeezing her chest, she walked down to the lobby of the castello. She didn't have time to stop at the hotel and collect all of her things. That would have to wait until she returned to Medinos at the end of her vacation.

Not a problem.

By the time she came back, Zane, who was involved in a set of sensitive negotiations in the States, would probably be gone. The retail outlet would be almost ready to open and construction of the pearl facility on Ambrus would be underway.

She would be busy interviewing and training staff. In theory she wouldn't have time to think.

When she reached the forecourt the taxi pulled into a space. A chilly breeze blew off the ocean, whipping strands of loose hair around her cheeks as she climbed into the backseat. She checked her wristwatch. Time was tight, but she would make her flight.

Her throat closed as the taxi shot away from the castello. She was still reeling from the speed with which she had made the decision to leave, but she could not have done anything else.

She was not a "glass half full" kind of girl and now she was in love.

Until Zane, she hadn't been even remotely tempted to break her rule of celibacy. It would have taken a bolt of lightning—literally a *coup de foudre*—to jolt her out of her mindset, and that was what had happened. She had seen Zane and in that moment she had lost her bearings. She had committed herself emotionally and now she didn't know how to undo that.

She could not accept the marriage agreement he had been clearly working toward. She refused to die a lingering emotional death, like Gemma.

She stared bleakly ahead, at the taxi's headlights piercing the dark winding ribbon of road.

There was no going back. It was over.

Seventeen

Zane knocked on Lilah's door. When there was no answer, he walked inside. A quick inventory informed him that she had packed and left.

He strode to his suite. Any idea that Lilah had made an executive decision and moved in with him died an instant death. The moment he opened the door and caught the scent of Gemma's signature perfume, his stomach hollowed out and he understood exactly what had gone wrong.

A split second later, Gemma emerged from his bedroom, fully dressed, but the filmy negligee clutched in one hand told the story.

Suppressing the raw panic that gripped him, he strode past Gemma and found his wallet and his overnight bag. "How long ago was Lilah here?"

Gemma watched from the safety of the sitting room as he flung belongings into the bag. "Fifteen minutes." She stuffed the negligee into her evening bag and sent him an embarrassed look. "You don't have to worry, I won't do this again."

Zane zipped the bag closed and walked to the door. He couldn't be angry with Gemma, not when he was responsible for this mess. He had been guilty of the same sin Lucas had committed when he had tried to keep Carla at a distance. Now his strategy had backfired on him. "Good. You should keep dating that guy you were with the other night. He's in love with you."

"How do you know?"

Zane sent her a stark look.

Gemma blinked. "Oh."

He waited pointedly at the door for Gemma to leave. He knew the boyfriend was somewhere downstairs, because Spiros had run a standard security check on him before the invitation to the castello was issued.

Once Gemma was gone, he headed for the front entrance.

He resisted the urge to check his watch. Lilah had been gone a good fifteen minutes. It only took ten minutes, max, to get a taxi out to the castello.

He reached the forecourt in time to see the red taillights of a taxi disappearing down the drive. There had been a lone occupant in the rear seat.

Constantine's aide, Tomas, who was greeting late guests, confirmed that the occupant had been Lilah.

Zane strode to the garage, found his car and accelerated after the taxi.

The repercussions of Gemma's stunt kept compounding. He hadn't touched her, but with his past and his reputation, no one, least of all Lilah, would believe him.

He reached their hotel suite and walked quickly through the rooms, long enough to ascertain that Lilah was not there, nor had she returned. That meant she had gone straight to the airport.

Using his cell, Zane checked on flights as he took the elevator down to the lobby. There was an international departure scheduled in just under an hour. He made a second call. The Atraeus Group owned a significant block of shares in the airport itself. Enough to ensure that when Zane needed assistance it was never a problem.

He reached the airport in record time and strode to the airline desk. As he spoke to the ticketing officer, his fingers automatically closed around the small jewelry case he had retrieved from the family vault before he had discovered that Lilah had left.

She loved him. He could hardly believe it.

And all he had been prepared to offer her was a loveless marriage, a business deal that would allow him to stay safe emotionally.

In retrospect the offer had been cowardly, a cover-up for his own failings and a situation he would not have been able to sustain, since a business arrangement was the last thing he wanted from Lilah.

His chest felt tight, his heart was pounding. For years he had been focused on the betrayals in his past. After all of *his* betrayals of Lilah, he was very much afraid that he had finally lost her.

The boarding call for Lilah's flight was announced as she strolled toward the gate. Buttoning her jacket against the air-conditioned chill, she joined the line of passengers.

A male voice with an American accent sent hope surging through her. She checked over her shoulder. For a split second she thought she saw Zane then she realized the man was shorter, darker.

Until that moment, she hadn't realized how badly she had wanted Zane to come after her.

Blinking back a pulse of raw misery, she kept her gaze pinned on the flight board, which was now showing a "delayed" message, and shuffled forward. She dug her boarding pass out of her purse as she neared the counter.

Behind her there was a stir. The deep register of another masculine voice that sounded even more like Zane made her tense. Determinedly, she ignored it.

Someone said "Excuse *me*," in an offended tone.

Her head jerked around, her gaze clashed with Zane's.

His eyes were dark and intense, his expression taut. "I didn't touch her."

A hot pulse of adrenaline that he *had* come for her momentarily froze her in place. "I know."

He looked baffled. His hand closed on her elbow.

Despite the fact that her heart was pounding so fast she was having trouble breathing, Lilah gently disengaged from his hold. She knew how this worked. Once Zane got her out of the line he would start taking charge and she would melt; she would have trouble saying "No."

"She wasn't there at my invitation and there never was a 'me and Gemma.' She was only ever a...convenient date."

Lilah blinked, then suddenly she knew. "For the charity functions."

Zane's gaze was level. "That's right."

She suddenly felt short of air. "If you felt you needed protection from me, why did you even bother to come?"

"The same reason I'm here now. I couldn't stay away."

An announcement came over the speaker system that the flight was delayed. Lilah made another heart-pounding connection. "*You* delayed the flight."

"Being a member of the Atraeus family has its uses."

Lilah dragged her gaze from the sexy five o'clock shadow on his jaw and tried to concentrate on the bright hibiscus-printed sundress of the woman ahead of her. "Why did you have the flight delayed?"

The woman wearing the flowered dress gave her a fascinated look.

Zane's dark gaze held hers with a soft intensity. "Because there's an important question I need to ask you."

Panic gripped her, because hope had flared back to life and she couldn't bear it if he presented her with another variation of a loveless marriage.

Boarding resumed. "I have to go and you can't come with me."

He held up his boarding pass.

There was a smattering of applause.

Lilah dragged her gaze from the grim purpose in Zane's eyes. So, okay, he could board the flight, she couldn't stop that. "What did you want to talk about?"

"It's uh—private."

A nudge in the small of her back from the passenger behind prompted her to move forward another step. She was only feet from the counter now, but boarding the jet had ceased to be a priority. Every part of her being was focused on Zane, but she was afraid to read too much into his words. "I can't accept a temporary relationship. I still need what I've always needed—commitment."

His brows jerked together. "I'm capable of commitment. Don't believe everything the tabloids print. I've dated, but since I met you there hasn't been…anyone."

For a fractured moment the ground seemed to tilt and shift beneath her. She was certain she had misheard. "Are you saying you haven't slept with *anyone?*"

He frowned, his gaze oddly defensive. "It's not unknown for men to be celibate."

Heads turned. There was a visible stirring in the gate area. Somewhere a camera flashed.

Lilah's stomach churned. Just their luck, there was a journalist in the queue.

Zane's arm curved around her waist. "Is the fact that I was celibate so hard to believe?"

Still stunned by the admission, Lilah didn't protest when he hustled her out into the relative privacy of the corridor. "No. *Yes.*"

The thought that he hadn't wanted to be with another woman since he had met her was dizzying, terrifying.

"I don't lie."

Her mouth went dry. It explained why he had lost control in Sydney. Despite her resolve to stay distant and cool, she was riveted by the thought. "What I don't get is, with all the women you could have, why me?"

Zane sent her a frustrated, ruffled look as if he was all at sea. "You're sexy, gorgeous. We have a lot in common with the business, art, our pasts. I like you. I *want* you."

Her heart squeezed in her chest. Liking and wanting, not *loving*.

He drew a velvet box from his pocket and extracted a ring.

The jewelry designer in her fell in love with the antique confection of diamonds and emeralds. The ring was heartbreakingly perfect.

And he wanted to marry her.

Lilah swallowed against the powerful desire to cave and say yes. "You chose a ring you knew I couldn't resist."

"I'll do what I have to, to get you."

Her jaw tightened at the neutral blankness of his approach. "What if I say, no?"

"Then I'll keep asking."

Once again the neutrality of his tone hit her like a fist in the chest then suddenly she saw him, suddenly she *knew*.

At age thirteen, he would have used that tone on the streets: with the gang that had cornered him and beat him; with the police and welfare workers who had shifted him from place to place; with his mother when she had finally decided to come looking for him.

It wasn't that he didn't care. It was because he did.

The strain of his expression, the paleness of the skin beneath his tan registered as he gripped her left hand, lifted it, the movements clumsy.

Raw emotion flooded her when she saw the unguarded expression in his eyes. When she didn't withdraw from his grip the flash of relief almost made her cry.

He slid the ring onto the third finger. The fit was perfect.

Lilah stared at the glitter of diamonds, the clear deep green of the emeralds, the ancient, timeless setting. But mostly what she saw was the extreme risk Zane had just taken with a heart that had been battered and bruised, and for a few years, lost.

Somewhere in the recesses of her mind, she registered that the ring he had slipped onto her finger was a part of the priceless Illium Cache of jewels that his buccaneering ancestor had once claimed as booty.

The ring matched the bracelet he had tried to give her.

She swallowed. He had been trying to tell her then.

According to the material she had read tonight the cache was a bridal set; there had always been a ring to match the bracelet. More than that, they were heirlooms: family jewels.

As a jewelry designer she knew the message of the gems themselves was purity, eternity. Love.

She met Zane's gaze and the softness there made her heart swell. "This belongs in your family."

"Which is exactly where it's staying, if you'll marry me." For a moment he looked fiercely, heartbreakingly like his ancestor.

His fingers threaded with hers, pulled her close. "I wanted to give it to you before the opening ceremony tonight. That's why I had to leave when I did. Constantine has the combination to the vault, which is down in the cellar."

He had wanted her to wear the ring in front of his family and all of their business colleagues. Her chest squeezed tight. It explained why Zane had left just when they had seemed to be getting somewhere.

"It's beautiful." Everything she could ever have wanted and more, but it was nothing compared to the real treasure Zane was offering her: his heart.

The hurt that had filled her when she had thought Zane couldn't care for her drained away. Out of self-defense she had clung to the picture the press had painted of him, but it was no more real than the picture they had painted of her.

Zane was everything she had been looking for in a husband and more. "Yes, I'll marry you."

He muttered something rough in Medinian and pulled her

close. "Thank goodness. I don't know what I would have done if you'd refused." He buried his head in her hair. "I love you."

The relief of his husky declaration shuddered through her. She wound her arms around his neck and simply held on. They had been walking toward this moment for two years, both stumbling, both making mistakes.

Zane wrapped her even closer, so tight that for a few seconds she could barely breathe. She didn't care. She was having trouble concentrating on anything but the shattering knowledge that Zane *loved* her.

His hold loosened as he talked in a low husky voice. He had been afraid that he had lost her, that he had finally driven her away with his old fear that she couldn't simply love *him*, that there would be a catch—something to be gained—that she would turn out to be dishonest and manipulative. He could bear anything but that. He had been in a terrible situation, unable to stay away from her, but afraid to be with her and discover that she had an agenda, and it wasn't loving him.

He lifted his head, looked into her eyes and the air seemed to go soft and still. "I love you."

And this time he kissed her.

Epilogue

A year later Zane proudly escorted his wife of ten months to the opening of the Ambrosi Pearl facility on Ambrus.

The ceremony, which was to be followed by champagne and a traditional Medinian celebration, with local food and music, was timed for sunset. The whole idea was that the extended twilight would bathe the new center with its large, modern sculpture of a pearl, with a soft, golden glow to celebrate the homecoming of Ambrosi Pearls. Unfortunately, clouds were interfering with the ambiance.

A large crowd of Atraeus and Ambrosi family were present along with locals, clients and of course the media. Constantine and Sienna were there, happily showing off their dark-eyed, definitely blond baby girl. Unbearably cute, Amber Atraeus had clearly inherited the luminous Ambrosi looks and a good helping of the Atraeus charisma.

Lucas and Carla, who had been married for several months, had just returned from an extended holiday in Europe. Looking happy and relaxed, they hadn't started a family yet, but Zane privately thought it wouldn't be long.

Lilah frowned at the gloomy sky, squeezed his hand and checked her watch. "It's time to start."

Glowing and serene in a soft pink dress, her hair coiled in a loose knot, she stepped up to the podium and welcomed the guests.

After providing a quick history of Ambrosi Pearls, Lilah asked a priest to bless the building then handed the proceedings over to Octavia Ambrosi, the great-aunt of both Sienna and Carla.

The oldest living Ambrosi, Octavia, affectionately known as Via, had been Sebastien Ambrosi's sister. She had lived on Ambrus with Sebastien, seen the destruction of the war and the rift that had torn the Atraeus and Ambrosi families apart when Sophie Atraeus and the bridal jewels had disappeared.

In the moment that Via was helped up to the white satin ribbon strung across the front doors of the center the sun came out from behind a cloud, flooding the island with golden light. With great grace Octavia cut the ribbon.

Later on in the evening, when guests had started to leave by the luxury launches that had been laid on by the Atraeus family, Lilah was surprised when Carla made a beeline for her. Since the tension which had erupted between them over Lilah dating Lucas, they had barely spoken, although that was mostly so now because they lived in different countries.

Carla gave her a quick hug and handed her a battered leather case. "This belonged to Sebastien. Since you and Zane will be living on Ambrus in the refurbished villa, we thought you should have it."

Zane's arm came around Lilah, warm and comforting, as she opened the case. Her eyes filled with tears as she studied the silver christening cup engraved with Sebastien's name.

Carla's expression softened as she looked at the cup. "It's of no great monetary value—"

"How did you know?" Zane said abruptly.

"That Lilah's pregnant?" Carla smiled. "It was an informed guess. You two shouldn't look so happy."

Lilah closed the case and tried to give it back to Carla. "This is a family treasure."

Carla smiled as Lucas joined them, followed by Sienna and Constantine with a sleepy Amber tucked into the crook of his arm. "In case you hadn't noticed, you are family."

* * * * *

SHACKLED TO THE SHEIKH

TRISH MOREY

To my amazing readers,

With grateful thanks and
wishing you love always,

Trish

x

CHAPTER ONE

RASHID AL KHARIM was done with pacing.

He needed something stronger.

He needed to lose himself. To dull the pain of each and every one of today's revelations, if only for a few precious hours.

To forget about a father who hadn't died thirty years back as he'd always believed, but a scant four weeks ago.

And to forget about a tiny child—a sister—who apparently was now his responsibility...

His head full of anger and torment, he let the door of his Sydney hotel suite slam hard behind him as he strode towards the lifts, stabbing the call button with intent, because he knew exactly what he needed right now.

A woman.

CHAPTER TWO

GOD, SHE HATED dingy bars. Outside this one had looked like an escape from her anger and despair, but inside it was dark and noisy and there were far too many leering men who looked way too old to be hanging out in a place where the average age of women was probably somewhere around nineteen. Tora upped the demographic just by being there, she figured, not to mention lowered the average heel height by a matter of inches, but it didn't stop the old guys leering at her just the same.

But the bar was only a few steps from her cousin's office and after an hour remonstrating fruitlessly with him, an hour where nothing—neither her arguments nor her tears—had made a shred of difference, she'd needed to go somewhere where she could drink something strong and fume a while.

One of the old guys across the bar winked at her. Ugh!

She crossed her legs and pulled her skirt down as she ordered another cocktail.

God, she hated bars.

But right now she hated her financial adviser cousin more.

Financial adviser cheating scumbag of a cousin, she revised as she waited for her drink, wondering how long it would be before the damned alcohol was going to kick in so she might stop feeling so angry.

She really needed to forget about the curl of her cousin's

lips when she'd refused to be put off any longer with his excuses and insisted he tell her when she'd be able to access the money she'd been due from her parents' estate.

She needed to forget the pitying look in his cold eyes when he'd finally stopped beating about the bush and told her that it was gone, and that the release she'd signed thinking it was the last formality before receiving a pay-out had actually been a release signing the money over to him—only now there would be no pay-out because he'd 'invested' it all on her behalf, only the investment had turned sour and there was nothing left. Nothing at all left of the two hundred and fifty thousand dollars she'd been counting on. Nothing at all left of the money she'd promised to loan to Sally and Steve.

'You should have read the small print,' he'd said ever so smugly, and she'd never had violent tendencies before but right then she'd really fancied doing someone some serious bodily damage.

'Blood is thicker than water,' her parents had insisted, when they'd chosen their nephew Matthew over the financial planner she'd nominated, the father of a woman she'd known and trusted since primary school. And Tora had shrugged and conceded it was their choice, even if her cousin had been the kind of person who'd rubbed her up the wrong way all her life and never someone she'd choose as a friend, let alone her financial adviser.

For damned fine reason, as it had turned out.

Her cocktail arrived and her fingers curled around the stem of the glass as she studied it.

Now she had to work out a way to tell Sally she wouldn't be getting the promised funds, after assuring her—because Matt had promised—that settlement was all on track and that the funds would be coming any day. She felt ill just thinking about it. They'd been counting on her—counting on this money. She shook her head. She would have to find another way, go back to the banks and try again. *Try harder.*

She lifted the glass to her lips and it was all she could do not to swallow the drink down in a rush, wanting the buzz, hoping for the oblivion it promised.

'Hi there, sweet lips. You look like you needed that. Fancy another?'

She blinked against a sudden flash of strobe and opened her eyes to see one of the leery old guys shouldering his way alongside her at the bar, this one with a decent paunch and a skinny ponytail and with a possessive arm curling its way around the back of her seat. Across the bar his friends were watching and grinning as if this was some kind of spectator sport, and their ponytailed friend might have been right about her needing another drink but not if it meant waking up next to this guy. Suddenly getting a taxi home where there was a half-empty bottle of Riesling in the fridge seemed a far better option than staying here and seeking oblivion amongst this lot. She reached for her bag.

The bar was too noisy. Too dark.

Almost immediately Rashid regretted the impulse that had seen him climb down the stairs to the noisy bar in the basement of the building alongside his hotel.

Because the questions in his mind were still buzzing, and as his eyes skated over a dance floor filled with young women wearing more make-up than clothes he wasn't convinced he was going to find the relief he needed here.

He ground his teeth together, the fingers that had been bound so tightly today already aching to curl once more into fists.

He was wasting his time here. He turned to leave, and that was when he saw the woman sitting by herself at the bar. His eyes narrowed. She was attractive, he guessed, under that bookish exterior, and she sure looked out of place here, standing out in her short-sleeved shirt in a sea of otherwise bare flesh. Too buttoned up with her brown hair pulled back into a tight bun. A glass of milk in a wine bar wouldn't have looked more out of place.

But at least she looked as if she was past puberty. At least she looked like a woman.

He watched her down half her cocktail and scowl into the glass, but not as if she was morose, more as if she was angry. So she was as unimpressed with the world as he was? Perfect. The last thing he needed was someone with stars in their eyes. Maybe they could be angry at the world together.

He was already edging his way through the crowd when a man sidled up to her and slipped his arm around her back.

Rashid suppressed a growl and turned away. He might be angry, but he wasn't about to fight over a woman.

'I'm not actually looking for company,' Tora said to her persistent would-be friend. Sure, someone sympathetic to get the whole sorry cheating-cousin saga off her chest might be therapeutic. Someone to lend her a shoulder and rub her back and say it would all be okay might be nice, but she hadn't come here looking for that and she wasn't about to consider any offers, not if the sympathetic shoulder came packaged like this one.

'Just when we were getting on so well, too,' he said, moving his bulk sideways when he saw her picking up her clutch to block her from getting up from her stool.

'I hadn't noticed,' she said, mentally adding another hate to her growing list—leery men in bars who imagined they were God's gift to women, although, to be honest, that one had always been right up there with seedy bars. 'And now if you wouldn't mind getting out of my way?'

'Come on,' he said, curling his arm closer around her back, and breathing beer fumes all over her. 'What's your rush?'

It was when she turned her head to escape the fumes that she saw him. He moved like a shadow in the dark basement, only the burst of coloured lights betraying his movements in the glint of blue-black hair and the whites of his eyes under the lights. He was tall and looked as if he was searching for someone or something, his eyes scanning the room, and, while heads turned in his wake, so far nobody seemed to be laying claim to him.

Surprising, given the way he couldn't help but be noticed if someone was waiting for him.

Not to mention convenient.

'How's about I get you another drink?' the man offered, slurring his words. 'I'm real friendly.'

Yeah, she thought, if only he were sober and could speak clearly and looked a little more like the man who'd just walked in, she might even be interested.

'I'm meeting someone,' she lied, pushing off her stool but making sure it was her shoulder that brushed past his stomach and not her breasts. Her feet hit the ground and even on her sensible heels, she wobbled. Whoa! Maybe those cocktails weren't such a total loss after all.

'He stood you up, eh?' said the man, still refusing to give up on his quarry. Still refusing to believe her. 'Lucky I'm here to rescue you from sitting on the shelf all night.'

'No,' she said, in case Mr Beer Breath decided to argue the point, 'he just walked in,' and she squeezed her way past him determined to prove it.

Half-heartedly Rashid scanned the room one last time, already knowing that he was wasting his time in this place. He turned to leave—he would find no oblivion here—when someone grabbed his arm.

'At last,' he heard a woman say above the music. 'You're late.'

He was about to say she was mistaken and shrug her off, when her other arm encircled his neck and she drew herself closer. 'Work with me on this,' she said as she pulled his head down to hers.

It was the woman at the bar—that was his first surprise—and the only thing that prevented him from pushing her away. The fact Ms Bookish had turned into Ms Bold and Brazen was the second. But she'd saved the best for last, because her kiss was the biggest and the best surprise of all. She tried to get away after a moment but her lips were soft, her breath was warm, and she tasted of fruit and alcohol, summer and citrus, all over warm, lush woman, and she wasn't going anywhere just yet. He ran his arm down her back, from her shoulder to the sweet curve of her behind, his fingers curling as they squeezed, and she arched into him as she gasped in his mouth.

Yes. This was what he needed.

This was what he'd come looking for.

Maybe coming here tonight hadn't been such a bad idea after all.

'Let's go,' she said, purposefully, if a little shakily, as she pulled away, her eyes shot with surprise as she looked from him over her shoulder to where she'd been sitting. He followed her gaze and saw the men lined up at the bar watching her, saw the slap to the back in consolation to the man who'd been talking to her, and he half wondered what the man had said to her that she seemed so shaken now. Not that Rashid really cared, as he wrapped an arm around her shoulders and cut through the crowd heading for the stairs and the exit, given he'd ended up exactly where he'd wanted.

Tora's heart was thumping so loud, she was sure it was only the thump-thump of the music in the bar that was drowning it out. She must be more affected by the alcohol than she'd realised.

Why else would she have walked up to a complete stranger and kissed him?

Though it wasn't just the alcohol fuelling her bravado, she knew. It was the anger, first for her cheating cousin, secondly for that meat market of a nightclub and a creep of a man who imagined there was any way in the world she'd want to spend even a moment with his beery self. And it hadn't been enough simply to walk away—she'd been wanting to show him she wasn't some sad lonely woman who'd be flattered to have his attention. Well, she'd sure shown him well and good.

But a peck on the lips in greeting was all she'd intended. A signal to the men watching that she wasn't alone. She hadn't expected that man to be so willing to join in her game. Nor had she expected to be sideswiped by a stranger's taste and touch in the process, leaving her dazed and confused. And the way her skin tingled and sparked when their bodies brushed as they walked side by side—well, that was interesting, too.

She willed the itching fingers on the hand she'd wrapped around his waist to be still, but, God, it wasn't easy, not when he felt so hard, so lean. Oh, wow... She needed to get outside and let the night air cool her heated skin. She needed the oxygen so she could think straight. She needed to say thank you to this stranger and get herself a taxi and go home, before she did anything else crazy tonight.

Because tonight was shaping up to be all kinds of crazy and the way this man felt, she wasn't sure she could trust herself.

And then they were out on the street and the nightclub door closed behind them and she never got a chance to say thank you because he was pulling her into the shadows of a nearby doorway and kissing her all over again and she was letting him and suddenly it wasn't the alcohol or her anger that was affecting her—it was one hundred per cent him.

Madness, she thought as his masterful lips coaxed open hers. She should put a stop to this, she thought as his tongue danced with hers. She didn't do things like this. They might be in the shadows but they were on a public street after all. What if Matt saw her on his way home?

And then her anger kicked in and she thought, damn Matt, why would she care what he thought? Let him see. And she pressed herself closer.

A moment later she stopped caring about anything but for the hot mouth trailing kisses up her throat to her mouth, his hands holding her tight to him so they were joined from their knees to their lips and every place in between felt like an erogenous zone.

'Spend the night with me,' he whispered, drawing back to whisper against her ear, his breath fanning her hair, fanning the growing flames inside her in the process, and she almost found herself wishing he'd said nothing but carted her off to his cave so she didn't have to think about being responsible. Crazy. She didn't meet strangers in bars and spend the night with them.

'I don't even know your name.' Her words were breathless, but it was the best she could manage when her mind was shell-shocked and every other part of her body was busy screaming *yes*.

'Does it matter?'

Right now? God, he had a point. He could tell her his name was Jack the Ripper and she'd have trouble caring. But still...

'I should go home,' she managed to say, trying to remember the good girl she always figured she was and the plan she'd had—something about a taxi and a bottle of

Riesling in the fridge and a cheating cousin she wanted to forget about—but she was having trouble remembering the details and wasn't that a revelation?

Wasn't that what tonight was supposed to be all about—forgetting?

He pulled away, letting her go even though the distance between them was scant inches. Even now her body swayed into the vacuum where his had so recently been. 'Is that what you want? To go home?'

She saw the tightness in his shadowed features as if it was physically hurting him to hold himself back, she felt the heat rising from his strong body and she knew what it must be costing him to leave her to decide when the power in his strong limbs told her that he was powerful enough to take whatever he wanted. The concept was strangely thrilling. The perfect stranger. Powerful, potentially dangerous, but giving her the choice.

A choice never so starkly laid out in her mind.

A choice between being responsible and playing it safe and going home and sitting stewing about what she'd missed, or being reckless for once in her life and taking what was on offer—one night with a man whose touch promised to make her forget all the things she'd wanted to forget. One night with a stranger. Her cousin would be horrified, and right now wasn't that good enough reason in itself?

Besides, all her life she'd played it safe, and where had that got her? Nowhere. She'd done nothing wrong and yet she'd lost more today than she'd ever thought possible.

Tonight was no night to play it safe.

'No,' she said, her tongue tasting an unfamiliar boldness on her lips. 'I want to spend the night with you.'

'One night,' he said, and she recognised it as a warning. 'That's all I can offer you.'

'Perfect,' she said with a smile because that was all

she wanted. 'One night is all I want.' Tomorrow she could pick up the shattered pieces of her promises and work out where she went from there.

His eyes glinted in the street lighting, a flash of victory that came with a spark of heat, and he reached out his fingers to push a wayward tendril of her hair behind her ear, making her skin tingle. 'My name is Rashid.'

'Tora,' she said, even as she trembled under his touch.

He took her hand and brought it to his mouth, pressing it to his lips. 'Come, Tora,' he said.

CHAPTER THREE

NICE, SHE REGISTERED vaguely as he swept her through the marble-floored lobby of one of the oldest and classiest hotels in Sydney. Very nice. People dreamed of spending a night at The Velatte—ordinary people, that was. Clearly the man at her side was no ordinary person. But then, she already knew that. No ordinary person had ever set her pulse racing just by his presence. No average garden-variety man had ever set fires under her skin merely with his touch.

And now it was anticipation of a night with this far from ordinary man making the blood spin around her veins and her knees feel weak.

The lift whisked them to a high floor, his arm wound tightly around her, another couple in the lift the only thing that kept him from pulling her into his kiss, if the heated look in his dark eyes she caught in their reflection in the mirrored lift walls was any indication—mirrored panels that also gave her the chance to steal a closer look at the man she'd agreed to spend the night with. The flash of strobe in the darkened bar had shown her a face of all straight lines and planes—the dark slash of brows, the sharp blade of his nose, the angles of his jaw—but now she could see the softer lines of his mouth and the fullness of his bottom lip and the curve of flesh over high cheekbones. The combination worked.

It was then she realised that his eyes weren't black but

the deepest, deepest blue, like the surface of the bottomless ocean on a perfectly calm day.

He was beautiful, way too beautiful to be by himself, and the good girl in her wondered why he was, while the bad girl in her—the newly found bad girl who drank cocktails in basement bars and threw herself at random men on a whim—rejoiced. Because right now she was the one here in this lift with him.

He opened the door to his room that turned out to be a suite because it was a sitting room they entered, decorated in modern classics in grey and cream and illuminated with standing lamps, lending the room a subtle golden glow. Oh, no, this man was definitely not ordinary. He was either loaded, or his employer's accountant was going to have a heart attack when the expense-account bill came in.

'It's huge,' she said, overwhelmed, wondering just who this man she'd met in a nightclub and with whom she'd agreed to a night with actually was.

'I got an upgrade,' he said dismissively, as if that explained a suite fit for a king, as he headed towards a phone. 'Something to drink?'

Her mouth was dry but only because every drop of moisture in her body had been busy heading south ever since he'd asked her to spend the night. 'Anything,' she said, and he ordered champagne for two and put the receiver down, the fingers of one hand already unbuttoning his shirt.

'The bedroom's through here,' he said as he led the way into a room with furniture in both gloss white and dark timber, with white louvre glass doors opening onto a terrace beyond. A super-king-sized bed with a plump quilted headrest and snowy white bed linen held pride of place against the opposite wall.

'So,' he said as he reefed off his shirt and tossed it onto a chair in the corner, exposing a chest that wouldn't have looked out of place on her annual firefighters' fundraising calendar. 'Shower first?'

She stood transfixed, drinking in his masculine perfection, the sheer poetry of tightly packed muscle under skin, until his hands moved to his belt, and with a jolt she realised she should be doing something, too, not standing around ogling him and waiting to be seduced.

This wasn't a seduction after all. Clearly he'd done his seducing in getting her here. This was more like getting down to business.

'Oh, right,' she said, her tummy a mass of flutters, the bad girl inside her overruled by the good girl who was suddenly aware of how far out of her league she was, and not just because this man came with serious money. Here he was, shedding clothes and shoes in a lighted room more easily than an autumn tree shed its leaves in the wind and no doubt expecting her to do likewise. She slid off her shoes, her fingers playing at her buttons as she remembered what she'd put on this morning, wishing she'd worn something a bit more exciting under her boring black skirt and shirt than her even more boring underwear. Not that she had a seduction collection, exactly, but she might have managed to wear something that at least smacked of lace.

She swallowed as she pulled the shirt free from the waistband of her skirt and eased it over her shoulders, feeling more self-conscious by the second as she stood there in her department-store skirt and regulation bra. 'I didn't dress for...'

He looked at her, a frown tugging at his brows, as he shrugged off his trousers, revealing denim-coloured elastic fitted boxers that fitted his hard-packed body so well, there were no bulges anywhere—except where there should be.

Oh, my...she thought, her stomach flipping over, her mouth Sahara dry, and she wondered how long the champagne would take to arrive. She didn't need the alcohol particularly, but her mouth sure could do with the lubrication.

'I'm not interested in your underwear,' he said as he padded on bare feet towards her, his steps purposeful rather than rushed. He lifted her chin with the tips of his fingers and pressed his lips lightly to hers while his other hand eased the tie from her hair, making her scalp tingle, pulling it free so that her hair tumbled heavily over her shoulders. His fingers skimmed down her throat and to her shoulder, found the strap of her bra and curled a fingertip beneath, before slipping it away down her arm. He pushed the hair back and dipped his head and pressed his lips to her bare shoulder and breath hissed through her teeth. 'I'm interested in what lies beneath.'

She shuddered on a sigh, her breasts achingly tight, as she felt his clever fingers at her back as he slid her bra away. And then her skirt was riding low and lower over her thighs before she realised he'd even unzipped it. 'Very interested,' he said, standing back to take her in, dark storm clouds scudding over the deep ocean blue of his eyes. He touched the pads of his thumbs to her bolt-like nipples and twin spears of sensation shot down deep into her belly, triggering an aching pulse between her thighs. Her groan of need was out before she could haul it back, but he didn't seem to mind as he sucked her into a deep kiss that amplified the sensations.

'What happened to the brazen woman who accosted me in a bar?'

She was a fraud. Tora swallowed. 'She was angry. She was proving a point.'

'Is she still angry?'

'Yes, but now she just wants to forget why.'

'Oh,' he said, his eyes gleaming as he swung her into his arms and headed for the shower. 'I can make you forget.'

* * *

Her stranger was true to his words. Granted, he had steam, a rainforest shower head and slippery gel on his side, but his clever hands and mouth had a way of making her forget everything besides being naked with a man she wanted to bed her with a compulsion and an urgency she'd never felt before—an urgency he didn't seem to mirror.

When he'd turned on the taps and shucked off his underwear, she'd gasped at his size, not with fear, but with anticipation. She wasn't a virgin. She knew how things worked and what generally happened and, if she was totally honest, she'd always wondered what it would be like to make love with a man so well equipped. But then he'd hooked his fingers into the sides of her underwear and pushed them down and she'd imagined that a minute or two of foreplay in the form of soaping each other's skin, and they'd be making love right here in the shower.

Apparently he wasn't in such a rush.

He kissed her again, long and deep, as she clung to his shoulders, while the torrent rained down upon them, his slippery hands in her wet hair, down her throat to cup her breasts before sliding down her sides, the touch of his long fingers relaying the dip of her waist in a way she'd never felt or seen so clearly in her mind's eye before. Every curve his fingers seemed to find, every jut of bone explored on their seemingly leisurely but purposeful way south. It almost felt as if his fingers were mapping her terrain.

She gasped again, into his seeking mouth this time, when one hand cupped her mound. She felt his lips smile around hers before his mouth dipped to her throat, to kiss her shoulder and then worship her breasts on his way down to kneeling before her, his lips traversing her belly, his fingers deep between her thighs and the pulsing flesh that lay within.

Oh, God. She shuddered as he parted her legs, turning her face up into the spray as his fingers opened her to him. Exposed her to him. She thought she knew about sex. She'd thought this would be over in a minute. But she might just as well have known nothing. She felt like a virgin all over again.

She knew nothing at all, but...

Pleasure.

It came upon her in waves as his tongue lapped at her very core, teasing her beyond existence, beyond reason, as all she knew was sensation.

His tongue. The steam. The water cascading over her and his fingers teasing, circling her aching centre.

Right now there was nothing but sensation, and the inexorable build to a place a man had never taken her. A place she'd never believed it possible for a man to take her unassisted. This man was taking her all the way.

She felt his fingers stray closer until they edged inside her. She felt the tug of his mouth on her screaming nub of nerve endings and she felt the surge coming. She bit her lip to stop from crying out but there was no stopping the wave that washed over her and the cry that came all the same as her body broke around him.

He supported her before her knees could give way and she fell, and she felt him there, at her core.

Yes, she thought, because even on her way down from the highs he'd taken her to she still wanted this—wanted him deep inside her—more than anything.

But then, just as she thought she had him, just as her muscles worked to urge him in, he pulled away on a curse and slammed open the shower door.

She blinked as he pulled a towel from a rack and wrapped it around her, swinging her into his arms.

'What's wrong?' she said, still trembling after her high

and back to the virgin she wasn't, fearful she'd done something wrong.

'Nothing,' he said as he deposited her in the centre of the big wide bed before pulling out a drawer, 'that this won't fix.'

He tore the top from the foil packet and rolled the condom down on him and suddenly it made sense and she was glad one of them was still thinking.

'Now,' he said, his face grim as he positioned himself between her legs, 'where were we?'

And the virgin inside her turned wanton as she wrapped her hand around his bucking length and felt his power and his need within her fingers, and placed him at her core. 'Right here.'

His eyes flared with heat as he growled with approval, and her heart skipped a beat as he took her hands and pinned them each side of her head, their fingers intertwined, and then with one long thrust he was inside her and sparks went off behind her eyes.

It was sex, she had to remind herself, just sex, because in that moment it had seemed that the world as she knew it revolved around that moment and that moment only.

He leaned down and kissed her then, so sweetly and reverently that she wondered if he'd felt it, too, this tiny spark of connection that went beyond physical, before he let go her hands and raised himself higher and slowly withdrew. She almost whimpered at the loss, wanting to hold him inside and keep him there, but then he was back, lunging deeper if that were possible, the slide and slap of flesh against flesh bringing with it that tidal flow of sensation, in and out and building each time until their bodies were slick with sweat. There was nowhere left to go, nowhere left to hide, and the next wave surge crashed over her and washed her away.

She clung to him as he went with her, tossed helplessly in the foaming surf of her undoing, gasping for air, not knowing which way was up.

He pressed his lips to her forehead before he slumped beside her. 'Thank you,' she heard him say between his ragged breaths, and she wondered if he could read her mind, for they were the exact same words she wanted to tell him.

He watched her sleep in the yellow-grey light, watched the slow rise of her chest and listened to the soft sigh as she exhaled, all the time wondering at a woman who had turned up exactly when he'd needed her. A woman who had made him forget the shocks of today so well that he'd almost forgotten to use protection.

When had that ever happened before?

Never, that was when.

He shook his head. He was more affected by today's revelations than he'd realised if he could forget something so absolutely fundamental. There could be no other reason for it. Other than the way she'd come apart so furiously that he hadn't wanted to wait, he'd wanted to follow her right then and there.

Propped up on his elbow, he lay alongside her, watching her eyelids flutter from time to time. Her hair splayed wild around her head and against the pillow. Tangled. Elemental. He touched a finger to one of the coils, felt the silk and steel within the shafts of hair and congratulated himself for walking down the stairs into that basement bar.

One night with a stranger had never been so desperately needed and so satisfying.

Almost.

He leaned over, pressed his lips to hers. Her eyelids fluttered open and momentary surprise gave way to a tentative smile. 'Oh, hi,' she said as her smile turned wary. 'Is it time for me to go?'

'No way,' he said as he pulled her into his arms. 'You're not going anywhere just yet.'

CHAPTER FOUR

It was still dark when her phone buzzed, only dull yellow street light filtering up from the street far below sneaking between the gaps in the curtains. Disoriented and aching in unfamiliar places, Tora took a while to work out where she was let alone manage to stumble from the bed and find where she'd left her bag. Groggily she snatched up her mobile and stole a glance over her shoulder. Behind her Rashid lay sprawled on his front, legs and arms askew as he slept. He looked magnificent, like a slumbering god, somehow even managing to make a super-king-sized bed look small.

'Yes,' she whispered, and listened while Sally apologised for calling her on her day off, but it was an emergency and could she come in?

She closed her weary eyes and put a hand to her head, pushing back her hair. How much sleep had she had? Not a lot. Not a good way to go to work, especially not when she had news to tell her friend—bad news—and she'd really wanted more time before breaking it. 'Are you sure there's nobody else?'

But she already knew the answer to that or Sally wouldn't have been calling on the first day off she'd had for two weeks. 'One more thing,' Sally said, once she'd told her she'd be there in an hour. 'Pack a bag and bring your passport. Looks like you might need them.'

'Where am I going?'

'I'm not sure exactly. I'll fill you in on what I do know when you get here.'

Tora slipped her phone away and glanced once more at the man she'd left sleeping on the bed, the man who'd blown her world apart and put it back together again more times than she would have believed possible in just one night. She shouldn't be sorry there wouldn't be one more time, she really shouldn't. No, no regrets. It was a one-night deal and now that night was over. She gathered up her discarded shirt and skirt and abandoned underwear and dressed silently in the bathroom.

Leaving this way was better for both of them. At least this way there was no chance of an awkward goodbye scene. No chance of anyone expecting too much or appearing hopeful or needy.

He seemed like the kind of man who'd be relieved she wasn't going to hang around and argue the point.

She picked up her shoes and spared one last glance towards the bed.

One night with a stranger.

But what a night.

He'd done what he'd promised to do. He'd blotted out the pain and the anger of her cousin's betrayal. He'd taken her from feeling shell-shocked and numb with grief and for a few magical hours he'd transported her away from her hurt and despair to a world filled with unimaginable pleasure.

He'd made her forget.

She let the door snick behind her.

It was going to be a hell of a lot harder to forget him.

He woke with a heavy head from too little sleep and with a dark mood brewing yet still he reached for her. There were things he had to do today, facts he had to face from which there was no escaping—headaches, each and every one of them—but the lawyer and the vizier and the headaches could wait. There was something he wanted more right now in this drowsy waking time before he had to let the cold, hard light of day hit him, as he knew it soon would. Someone he wanted more.

His searching hand met empty sheets. He rolled over, reaching further, finding nothing but an empty bed and cold sheets and not the warm woman he was looking for. He cracked open an eyelid and found no one.

Now he was wide awake. 'Tora?' he called. But there was no answer, nothing but the soft hum of the air conditioner kicking in as the temperature rose with the sun outside.

'Tora,' he repeated, louder this time, on his feet now as he checked the bathroom and the living room. He pulled back the curtains in case she'd decided to take coffee out there so as not to waken him. Morning light poured into the room, and he squinted against the rising sun, but the terrace, like every other part of the suite, was empty.

She was gone, without so much as a word.

She was gone, before he was ready.

Before he was done with her.

He growled, a vein in his temple throbbing while his dark mood grew blacker by the minute.

Until he remembered with a jolt the revelations of yesterday and his black mood changed direction. He glanced at the clock. He had a meeting to get to.

He'd been angry when the lawyer had told him that he'd arranged it—too blindsided by the lawyer's revelations to think straight, too incensed that someone other than himself was suddenly pulling the strings of his life—but now he welcomed this meeting with this so-called vizier of Qajaran. Maybe he would have the answers to his questions.

Only then, when he was convinced, would he agree to take on this baby sister—no, half-sister—the product of a father who'd abandoned Rashid as a toddler, and a woman he'd taken as his lover.

Only then would he agree to take on guardianship of her, to take responsibility for her now that both her parents were dead, and to fill the void in her life, and wasn't that the richest thing of all?

Because how the hell was he supposed to fill a void in anyone's life when there'd been nobody to fill the void in his?

Thanks for that.

He cast one last glance back towards the rumpled bed as he headed to the shower, the bed that bore the tangled evidence of their lovemaking. How many times they'd come together in the dark night, he couldn't remember, only that every time he'd turned to her she'd been there, seemingly insatiable and growing bolder each time.

No wonder he'd been angry when he'd found her gone.

No wonder he'd felt short-changed.

But one night was what he'd wanted and it was better this way. She'd more than served her purpose. He'd lost himself in her and she'd blotted out the shock and pain for a while, but now he needed a clear head and no distractions. He thought back to the night that was. She'd been one hell of a distraction and he would have been hard pressed to send her on her way. It was better that she'd saved him the effort.

Kareem was not as Rashid had envisaged. He'd imagined someone called a vizier to be a small man, wiry and astute. But the man the lawyer introduced him to in his dark-timbered library was a tall, gentle-looking giant of indeterminate age who could have been anywhere from fifty to eighty. He looked the part of a wise man, perfectly at ease in his sandals and robes amongst a city full of men wearing suits and ties.

Kareem bowed when he was introduced to Rashid, his eyes wide. 'You are indeed your father's son.'

A tremor went down Rashid's spine. 'You knew my father?'

The older man nodded. 'I did, although our dealings have been few and far between of late. I knew you, too, as an infant. It is good to meet you again after all these years.'

The lawyer excused himself then, leaving the two men to talk privately.

'Why have you come?' Rashid asked, taking no time to get to the point. 'Why did you ask for this meeting?'

'Your father's death raises issues of which you should be aware, even if I fear you may find them unpalatable.'

Rashid sighed. He was sick of all the riddles, but he was no closer today to believing that this man they were talking about actually was his father than when the lawyer had dropped that particular bombshell yesterday. 'You're going to have to try harder than that if you want to convince me. My father died when I was just a child.'

'That is what your father wanted you to believe,' the older man said.

'*Wanted* me to believe?'

'I take your point,' the vizier conceded, his big hands raised in surrender. 'It would be more correct to say that he wanted the entire world to believe he was dead. I did not mean to give the impression that he was singling you out.'

Rashid snorted. And that was supposed to be some kind of compensation?

'And my mother?' he snapped before the other man could continue. 'What of her? Is she similarly living out a life of gay abandon somewhere else in the world, having tossed her maternal responsibilities to the winds?'

The vizier shook his head. 'I almost wish I could tell you she was, but sadly no, your mother died while you were in infancy, as you are no doubt aware. I am sorry,' he said. 'I know this must be difficult for you, but there is more. Much more.'

Rashid waved the threat in those words away. 'I already know about this so-called sister, if that's what you're referring to.'

'Atiyah? Yes, she is on her way here now, I believe. But I was not referring to her.'

He frowned. 'Then what? In fact, why are you here? What do you have to do with my father's affairs anyway?'

The older man regarded him levelly, his eyes solemn. 'I know you were brought up,' he said, slowly and purposefully, as if sensing Rashid's discomfiture, 'believing your father to have been a humble tailor, killed in an industrial accident...' He paused, as if to check Rashid was still listening.

He was listening all right, although it was hard to hear with the thumping of his heart. Today he'd expected answers. Instead all he was getting was more of the madness.

'In actual case, your father was neither. Your father was a member of the Royal House of Qajar.' He paused again. 'Do you know much of Qajaran?'

Rashid closed his eyes. He knew the small desert country well enough—his work as a petroleum engineer had taken him there several times. It had a problematic economy, he was aware, like so many countries that he visited, not that he had paid this one much more attention than he paid any of them. He had learned early on in his career that it was better not to get involved in the affairs of state when one was a visiting businessman.

But for Rashid's father to have been a member of the House of Qajar—the father he'd believed to be nothing more than a tailor—then he must have been a member of the royal family...

The wheels of his mind started turning. 'So who was my father?'

'The Emir's nephew...' the vizier paused again '...and his chosen successor over his own son who he judged as being too self-centred and weak.'

His nephew? His chosen successor? 'But if what you say is true...' Rashid ground out the words, still not convinced by the story he was hearing '...why was he living here in Australia? What happened?'

The older man took a sip of his milk and returned it to its coaster, every move measured and calm and at odds with the turmoil Rashid was feeling inside.

'Your father was an accomplished polo player,' the vizier said, 'and while he was overseas competing in one of his polo competitions, the old Emir died suddenly.' He paused on a breath, the silence stretching out to breaking point. 'Some would say too suddenly, and, of course, there was some suggestion at the time that the timing was "convenient", but nothing could ever be proved. By the time your father had arrived home, the Emir's son had announced his ascension to the throne and moved the palace forces squarely behind himself. Your father knew nothing of this and was placed under house arrest the moment he returned to the palace. But your father was popular with the people and questions were inevitably asked about his disappearance—uncomfortable questions when all of Qajaran knew he was the favoured choice for Emir—and so Malik announced he was to be appointed special adviser to the Emir while deciding privately that it would be better to have him out of the way completely.'

'So they exiled him?'

'No. Malik was nowhere near that merciful. The plan was to kill him but make it look like an accident. A helicopter accident en route from the mountain palace to where the ceremony would take place.'

Air hissed through Rashid's teeth.

'Fortunately your father had a supporter in the palace.

My predecessor could not stand back and let such a crime happen. They secreted bodies from the hospital morgue and when the time came, they parachuted to safety and the helicopter duly crashed, its cargo of dead burned beyond recognition, assumed to be the pilot and the true heir to the throne. Clothing from a small child was found in the wreckage, jackals assumed to have made off with the remains.'

Rashid felt chills down his spine. 'A small child,' he repeated. *'Me.'*

The vizier nodded. 'You. The new Emir was leaving nothing to chance. But your father's life came at a cost. To protect the lives of those who had saved him and his son, he had to swear he would never return to Qajaran, and he would live his life as an exile with a false identity. Your names were both changed, your histories altered, but, even so, as a father and son you would have been too recognisable together, and so, in order to keep you safe, he had to cut you free.'

Rashid's hands curled into fists. 'I grew up alone. I grew up thinking my father was dead."

The vizier was unapologetic. 'You grew up in safety. Had Malik suspected even one hint of your existence, he would have sent out his dogs and had you hunted down.'

Rashid battled to make sense of it all. 'But Malik died, what? Surely it's a year ago by now. Why did my father keep silent then? Why did he not move to claim the throne then if he was still alive?'

The older man shrugged and turned the palms of his hands up to the ceiling. 'Because he had made a solemn promise never to return and he was a man of honour, a man of his word.'

'No, that doesn't cut it. He still could have told *me*! He could have sought me out. Why should I have been denied knowing my father was alive because of a promise he'd made to somebody else years ago?'

'I know.' The vizier exhaled on a sigh. 'Rashid, I am sorry to be the one to tell you this, but your father decided it was better that you never knew of your heritage. I sought him out after Malik died. I begged him to reach out to you—I begged him to let me reach out to you—but he refused. He said it was better that way, that you never knew the truth, that it couldn't hurt you any more than it already had. He made me promise not to contact you while he lived.'

Rashid shook his head, his jaw so tightly set he had to fight to squeeze the words out. 'So he decided to keep me in the dark—about everything. Even the fact my own father was still alive.'

'Don't you think it cost your father—to be cursed with only seeing his son from afar and searching the papers for any hint of where you were and what you were doing? But he was proud of you and all that you achieved.'

'He had a funny way of showing it.'

'He saw all that you achieved by yourself and, wrongly or rightly, he chose to let you remain on that path, unfettered by the responsibility he knew would come if you knew the truth.'

The sensation of scuttling insects started at the base of his neck and worked its way down his spine. He peered at the vizier through suspicious eyes and asked the questions he feared he already knew the answers to. 'What do you mean? What responsibility?'

'Don't you see? You are Qajaran's true and rightful ruler, Rashid. I am asking you to come back to Qajaran with me and claim the throne.'

CHAPTER FIVE

RASHID LAUGHED. He couldn't help but laugh, even though he'd half suspected something similar, but the old man was so fervent and the idea so preposterous. 'You can't be serious!'

'Please forgive me, but I am not in the habit of joking about such matters.'

Rashid got the impression the man was not in the habit of making jokes at all, the complete lack of humour in the vizier's response stopping Rashid's mirth dead. 'But I haven't lived in Qajaran since I was a boy, if what you say is true, because I certainly can't even remember a time when I did. I have visited it briefly two or three times since at the most. There must be someone better, someone more qualified?'

'There has been a power vacuum since Malik's death. A Council of Elders has taken over the basics of governing, but there is no clear direction and no one person to take responsibility. Qajaran needs a strong leader, and there can be no one more fitting than the son of the true successor. In the beginning, I know it is what your father wanted for you, to reclaim your birthright, even though with time he changed his mind and wished for you the freedom that he had found. He had made a life here, after all, and I think the longer he was away from Qajaran, the less connection he felt and the less your father felt he owed his homeland.'

'The father I never knew,' he said, not even trying to prevent the bitterness infusing his voice. 'If indeed he was my father. Why should I take your word that he was?'

The old man nodded. 'I would be concerned if you accepted too quickly the challenge that lies before you. I would think you are attracted to the concept of power, other than the benefit of our peoples.' He slipped a hand into the folds of his robes and pulled something from a pocket. 'Malik sought to destroy all likenesses of your father. This one survived.' He handed it to Rashid.

It was one of those old photo folders that opened like a card, the cardboard crinkled and dog-eared around the border but the picture inside still preserved. A photo of a man dressed dashingly in the Qajarese colours of orange, white and red, sitting proudly astride an Arab polo pony, a mallet casually slung over his shoulder as he posed for the camera.

'My God,' Rashid said, for he recognised his own features in the photograph—his own high cheekbones and forehead and the set of his jaw. The eyes the same dark blue. It could have been him sitting on that horse.

'You see it,' Kareem said. 'There is no denying it.' The old man leaned forward. 'Your country needs you, Rashid. Qajaran is at a crossroads. Thirty years of a ruler who wasted every opportunity unless it benefited him directly, thirty years of frittering the revenues that came from its industries and rich resources on follies and peccadilloes. It is more by good luck than good management that the economy of Qajaran has not been completely ruined. But now it is time to start building. There is a desperate need for strong leadership, education and reform.'

Rashid shook his head. 'Why would the people accept me as leader, when I am supposed to have died in a helicopter crash three decades ago? Why would they believe it is even me?'

'The people have long memories. Malik may have tried to wipe your father from the collective memory of the Qajarese people, but never could he wipe the love of him from their hearts. Truly, you would be welcomed back.'

'When I am supposed to be dead? How does that work?'

'Your body was never found, assumed to be taken by the desert beasts, which means there is doubt. The people of Qajaran are in desperate need of a miracle. The return of you to Qajaran would be that miracle.'

Rashid shook his head. 'This is madness. I am a petroleum engineer. That is my job—that is what I do.'

'But you were born Qajarese. You were born to rule. That is in your blood.'

Rashid stood, his legs too itchy to remain seated any longer, and crossed to a window, watching the traffic and the pedestrians rushing by in the street below. They all had somewhere to go, somewhere to be. Nobody was stopping them and telling them that their lives up till now had been founded on a lie, and that they must become someone they had never in their wildest nightmares thought they would be. Nobody was telling them they had a tiny sister they were now responsible for—let alone a nation full of people for whom they were now responsible.

He shook his head. He didn't do family. The closest he had ever come to having family was his three friends, his desert brothers, Zoltan, Bahir and Kadar, their friendship forged at university in the crucible of shared proximity and initial animosity, all of them outcasts, all of them thrust together as a kind of sick joke—the four had hated each other on sight—only for the joke to backfire when the four became friends and the 'Sheikhs' Caïque', as their rowing four was nicknamed, won every race they ran.

And even though his three desert brothers had found matches and were starting their own broods of children, it didn't mean he had to follow suit.

He had no desire for family. Even less now given he'd learned his father had lived all those years and hadn't bothered to let him know—his own son!

And what was a nation but the worst kind of family, large, potentially unruly and dependent.

He turned suddenly. Faced the man who had brought him this horror. 'Why should I do this? Why should I take this on?'

Kareem nodded. 'I have read widely of you and seen your long list of achievements and your powers of negotiation when dealing with disparate parties. You would come eminently qualified to the task of Emir.'

Rashid shook his head, and the older man held up one broad hand. 'But yes, this is no job application. This goes beyond mere qualifications. Your father was the chosen Emir before circumstances forced him into exile. You are his heir. It is therefore your duty.'

Rashid's blood ran cold. 'My duty? I thought you said I had a choice.'

And Kareem looked hard into his eyes. 'The choice is not mine to give. I am saying you have this duty. Your choice is whether you accept it.'

Duty.

He was not unfamiliar with the concept. His best friends were no strangers to duty. He had seen Zoltan take on the quest for the throne of Al-Jirad. Rashid had done his brotherly duty and had ridden together with him and Bahir and Kadar across the desert to rescue Princess Aisha, and later to snatch her sister, Princess Marina, from the clutches of Mustafa. He had always done his duty.

But never had he imagined that duty would be so life-changing—so unpalatable—for himself. Because if he did this thing, his life would undergo a seismic shift. He would never be truly free again. And if he didn't, he would be failing in his duty.

Duty. Right now the most cursed of four-letter words.

'What I tell you is not easy for a man to absorb or accept,' Kareem said. 'I can only ask that you will come and see the country for yourself. Bring Atiyah, for it is her heritage and birthright too.'

'You want me to willingly turn up on the doorstep of a place that was so happy to see my father and me dead? You expect me to take an infant into that environment?'

'Malik is gone. You have nothing to fear from him or his supporters now. Please, you must come, Rashid. Come and feel the ancient sand of our country between your toes and let it run through your fingers. See the sunrise and sunset over the desert and maybe then you will feel the heart of Qajaran beating in your soul.'

'I'll come,' Rashid said, his head knowing what he had to do, his gut twisting tighter than steel cable in spite of it. 'For now that is all I am promising.'

The vizier nodded. 'For now, it is enough. Let me call the lawyer back in and we will make the arrangements.'

'What can they be doing in there?' Tora said as she gave up pacing the lawyer's waiting room and sat down in the chair alongside her boss. She had to pace because every now and then her lack of sleep would catch up with her and she'd find herself yawning. 'Whatever can be taking so long?' she said, trying not to sound too irate so that she didn't disturb the infant in the capsule alongside. She'd had barely enough time to get home to shower and change and pack her things, before she'd met Sally at Flight Nanny's office and they'd headed off together to pick up the baby from the foster home where she'd been looked after for the last few days, only for them to have been kept sitting and waiting so long that the baby would soon need another feed.

Her boss twisted her watch around her wrist. 'I don't know, but I can't stay much longer. I've got a meeting with Steve's doctors in less than an hour.'

'I'm sure it won't be too long now,' the middle-aged receptionist assured them when Sally asked how long it would be, before disappearing to fetch refreshments.

The baby started fussing then and Tora reached down to soothe her. She was a cherub. With black curls and dark eyes with long sooty lashes and a tiny Cupid's-bow mouth, it was obvious that she'd grow up to be a beauty. But right now she was a tiny vulnerable infant without a mother or a father—or anyone who seemed to care what happened to her.

The baby wasn't about to be placated and became more restless, her little fisted hands protesting, and Tora plucked her out of the capsule to prop against her shoulder so she could rub her back, swaying from side to side in her seat as she did so.

She smiled as she cuddled the infant close, enjoying the near new baby smell. It was unusual to have such a young infant to take care of. Most of Flight Nanny's charges were small children who needed to be ferried interstate or overseas between divorced parents who were either too busy with their careers to travel with their children, or who simply preferred to avoid any contact with the other party, even if only to hand the children over. Those cases could be sad enough.

But an infant who'd been left orphaned, that was beyond tragic. That was cruel.

'You poor sweetheart,' she said as she rocked the tiny bundle in her arms, her heart breaking a little at the injustice of it all.

Sally shifted in her seat and Tora could feel the tension emanating from her friend and colleague. Something was seriously wrong. 'How is Steve?' she ventured, once the baby had settled a little, scared to ask, even more scared for the answer.

Her boss grimaced and it occurred to Tora that Sally had aged ten years in the last couple of weeks. 'He's struggling. There's a chance they won't be able get his condition stabilised enough for the flight to Germany.' She looked up then and Tora saw the desperation in her eyes, desperation laced with a flash of hope. 'Look, Tora, I didn't want to ask—I really wanted to wait for you to say something—but how did you get on with your cousin last night? Did he give you any idea when the estate might be finalised and that settlement might come through?'

And Tora's heart plunged to the floor. There was damned good reason she hadn't wanted to come to work today and it wasn't just that she'd hardly had any sleep. Without the funds from her parents' estate, she'd have nothing to lend to Sally and Steve, funds they'd been counting on to pay for his medical transport and his treatment overseas. And she'd really wanted some time to explore any other ways of raising the money before she had to come clean on the fact that the promised funds were never going to materialise—not from that particular source. 'Ah,' she said with false brightness, as if she'd only just remembered, 'I wanted to talk to you about that.'

Sally crossed her arms and Tora could see her fingernails clawing into her arms. 'Damn. I knew I shouldn't have asked you that. I don't think I could bear to hear bad news today.'

'Oh, no,' Tora lied, doing her utmost to smile. 'Nothing like that. Just paperwork and more paperwork.' She shrugged. 'You know how it goes with these things. I'm really hoping it gets resolved soon.'

Sally glanced at her watch. 'Well, sorry, but I'm going to have to leave you with some more paperwork if I'm going to make this appointment.' She reached into her satchel and pulled out a folder that she left on the seat behind her as she rose. 'I'm really sorry to leave you like this when we still don't know all the details. Will you be okay to handle everything yourself?'

'Hey, I'll be fine. If you're going to be disappearing offshore soon,' she said, trying to stay positive and not wanting to dwell on how big that 'if' was right now if she couldn't secure the funds to make it happen, 'we're all going to have to get used to doing more paperwork here at home. Don't worry, I'll email you when I know where this baby is going and scan all the documentation for you before we go anywhere. You just worry about you and Steve right now.'

Sally smiled, giving Tora a kiss on the cheek as she bent down to pick up her bag. 'Thanks.' She curled a fingertip under the baby's tiny hand. 'Look after this little poppet, okay?'

'You bet. Now get going. And give my love to Steve.'

Sally was gone by the time the receptionist returned with her iced tea, and Tora's was half drunk when the door to the office opened then, and an older gent with bushy eyebrows and a shock of white hair peeked out. 'Ah, Joan,' he said. 'We're ready for our guests now.' He looked at Tora and the bundle perched over her shoulder.

'I'm sorry,' she said, 'but Sally Barnes couldn't stay.'

'I quite understand,' he said kindly. 'This has all taken rather longer than we expected. Thank you for being so patient, Ms Burgess. Do come in. It's time for the little one to meet her guardian.'

She stood up with the baby in her arms, and the lawyer surprised her by shoving the folder Sally had left under his arm, before picking up both the baby capsule and baby bag.

'Gentlemen,' he said as he shouldered open the door and ushered her into the room, 'here is Atiyah at last, along with Ms Victoria Burgess, who comes to us highly qualified from Flight Nanny, the number one Australian business that transports unaccompanied children all around the world. Victoria will be caring for Atiyah and accompanying you both to Qajaran.'

Tora raised her eyebrows as she digested the news. So that was where she was headed? That would be a first. She'd been to many ports in Europe and Asia but so far she'd never had an assignment that took her to the smaller Middle East states. A tall, gentle-looking man wearing Arabic robes came towards her, a warm smile on his creased face as he looked benevolently down upon the child in her arms. He reached a finger to her downy cheek and uttered something in Arabic that sounded very much like a blessing to Tora. If this man was the tiny Atiyah's guardian, she was sure she would be in good hands.

'Excuse me,' he said with a bow. 'I will inform the pilot we will be on standby.' And with a swish of his robes, he left the room.

'Victoria,' someone else said from a chair in the corner of the room behind her, in a voice as dry and flat as a desert in summer—a voice she recognised as one that had vibrated its way into her bones last night with desire but that now set off electric shocks up and down her spine with fear. 'Most people would shorten that to *Tori*, wouldn't they?'

Please, God, no, she prayed, but when she looked around, it was him all right. He rose from his chair then, the man she'd spent the many dark hours of last night with naked, the man now looking at her with storm-swept eyes. Her heart lurched and she clutched the baby in her arms tighter, just to be sure she didn't drop her.

'I don't know,' she said, trying and not sure she was succeeding in keeping the tremor from her voice. 'Is it relevant?'

The lawyer looked strangely at Rashid, questions clear in his eyes. 'Yes,' he said, 'what does it matter? Come, Rashid, and see your sister and your new charge.'

His sister? Surely that didn't mean what she thought it meant? And Tora felt the cold tea in her stomach turn to sludge.

He hadn't been in a rush to get up—he might have agreed to go to Qajaran and take the child with him, but he was in no desperate hurry to meet her. He was glad he'd hung back in his chair now, glad of the time to let incredulity settle into cold, indisputable truth.

Because it was her.

The woman who'd stolen away from his bed like a thief in the night.

The woman he'd never expected to see again.

She looked almost the same as she had last night in the bar, in a beige short-sleeved shirt and hair that he now knew fell heavy like a curtain of silk when pulled out of that damned abomination of a bun, but with black trousers this time, covering legs he could still feel knotted around his back as he drove into her.

She looked almost the same in that bland mouse-like uniform she wore that he knew hid a firebrand underneath.

And it seemed that twenty-four hours of being blindsided didn't show any signs of letting up yet.

'Rashid?' the lawyer prompted. 'Don't you want to meet your sister?'

Not particularly, he thought, and least of all now when she was being cradled in the arms of a woman he hadn't begun to forget, though he supposed he should look interested enough to take a look.

He rose to his feet. Was it his imagination or did the woman appear to shift backwards? No, he realised, it wasn't his imagination. There was fear in her eyes even though the angle of her chin remained defiant. She was scared of him and trying not to show it. Scared because he knew what the nanny got up to in the night time.

She should be worried.

In spite of himself, he got closer. Close enough that the scent of the woman he'd spent the last night with curled into his senses, threatening to undo the control he was so desperately trying to hang onto. Didn't he have enough to contend with right now—a father who'd removed himself from Rashid's life, only to leave him this tiny legacy, a country that was floundering where he was expected to take up the reins—without a woman who had the power to short his senses and make him forget? He needed his wits about him now, more than ever, not this siren whose body even now seemed to call to him.

He shifted his head back out of range, and concentrated instead on the squirming bundle in her arms. Black hair and chubby arms and a screwed-up face. Definitely a baby. He didn't know a lot about babies, but then he'd never expected to need to.

'Would you like to hold her?' the woman he knew as Tora ventured, her voice tight, as if she was having trouble getting the words out.

It was his turn to take a step back. 'No.'

'She won't break.'

'I said no.' And neither, when he thought about it, did he want this woman holding her, let alone accompanying them to Qajaran. Not that he was about to take the child himself. He turned to the lawyer. 'Is there no one else you could have found for this role?'

The woman blinked up at him, her brown eyes as cold as marble. Too bad. Did she expect him to greet her like a long-lost friend? Not likely.

'Excuse me?' the lawyer asked.

'Someone more suitable to take care of Atiyah. Couldn't you find someone better to take care of my sister?'

'Ms Burgess comes to us highly qualified. She has an exemplary record with Flight Nanny. Would you like to see her credentials?'

'That's not necessary.' He'd already seen her credentials, in glorious satin-skinned detail, and they qualified her for a different type of position entirely from the one she was required for now.

'If you have some kind of problem—' she started.

'Yes, I have "some kind of problem", Ms Burgess. Perhaps we should discuss this in private and I'll spell it out for you?'

The lawyer looked at them nervously. 'If you excuse me, a moment, I'll see how Kareem is going,' and he too was gone.

Rashid took a deep breath as he strode back towards the wall of windows.

'What are you doing here? How did you find me?'

'What? I didn't find you. I was asked by my boss to take this job on. I didn't know you had anything to do with Atiyah.'

'You expect me to believe it's some kind of coincidence?'

'You can believe what you like. I was retained to care for Atiyah on her journey to wherever it is that she is going. Frankly, I'd forgotten all about you already.'

His teeth ground together. Forgotten about him already? In his world, women had always been temporary, but he'd been the one to decide when he'd had enough. He'd been the one to forget, and it grated...

'So you're a qualified child-care worker?'

'That's my primary qualification, yes, though I have diplomas in school-aged education and childhood health care along with some language skills as well.'

'You are forgetting about your *other* skills,' he growled, his lip curling as he looked out of the window, still resentful at a world going on about its business while his life didn't resemble a train that had merely changed direction, his life was on a train that had jumped tracks, and he wasn't sure he liked where it was headed.

'They're hardly relevant,' she said behind him, and around and between her words he could hear the sounds of the baby, staccato bursts of cackles and cries, and then a zipper being undone.

He spun around, angry that she seemed oblivious to the impossibility of the situation, to see her sitting down, the baby in her lap as she dripped milk from a small bottle onto her upturned wrist before putting the bottle to the baby's mouth, looking every part the quintessential mother with child.

That was a laugh. She was no Madonna. It didn't matter what she was wearing or what she was doing, he could still see her naked. He could still remember the way she'd bucked beneath him as she'd come apart in his arms.

'Impossible!' he said, and even the baby was startled, her big eyes open wide, her little hands jerking upwards, fingers splayed. 'This cannot work.'

'Hold it down,' she said, rocking the child in her arms. 'Do you think I like the situation any more than you do?'

'I want another carer.'

'Why?'

Because I don't trust myself with you. 'Because a woman like you is not fit to look after an innocent child.'

She laughed. 'A woman like me? What kind of woman is that, exactly?'

'A woman who goes whoring in the night—picking up men in bars and sleeping with them.'

She smiled up at him and he felt his ire rise. 'But a *man* who goes whoring in the night—picking up women and inviting them back to his hotel room—he is perfectly qualified to be that child's guardian. Is that what you are saying?'

'This is not about me.'

'Clearly not, or there might be a double standard at work, don't you think?'

Frustration tangled in his gut. He hated that she had seen through his arguments but he could hardly tell her the real reason—that he needed more than ever right now to be able to think clearly, without his brain being distracted with replays of last night every time he looked at her. Why couldn't she see that he didn't want her—that this would not work? 'I want somebody else to care for Atiyah!'

'There is nobody else. All Flight Nanny's employees are busy on other assignments.'

'I don't want you coming with us.'

'Do you think for a moment that I want to come? As soon as I realised it was you, I wanted to sink through a hole in the floor. So don't worry, I'm not looking for a repeat of last night's little adventure. I'm not here because of you. I'm here to take care of the baby, nothing more.'

A brief knock on the door interrupted his words, and Kareem entered with a bow, and there was no way their visitor couldn't have heard her words or misinterpreted the tone in which they were delivered. 'A thousand pardons for the interruption, but the plane will be ready to leave in two hours.'

And Tora looked up at Rashid. 'So, do you want to tell everyone why you'd prefer to find another carer, or shall I?'

Kareem looked to him expectantly, his placid features betraying only the barest hint of surprise, and Rashid cursed the woman under his breath. But he was out of time and out of options, and, besides, what was the worst that could happen? She'd accompany them to Qajaran and then her role would be complete and she would be on the next flight home and he would be rid of the constant reminders of their night of passion together, rid of the distraction of a woman who had turned an already upside-down world spinning through another three hundred and sixty degrees in the course of one night. He could hardly wait.

'I expected someone older,' he muttered, 'but I suppose this one will just have to do.'

CHAPTER SIX

BLUFF WAS A beautiful thing, when it came off.

Tora got the baby capsule secured and sank into the buttery leather of the limousine and took a deep, calming breath. Because she'd done it, she'd saved the assignment. Sally would have been devastated if she'd lost this contract—and Tora would have found it next to impossible to explain how she'd let it happen. How did one go about explaining that you'd inadvertently slept with the client after meeting them in a bar the night before your assignment? It didn't bear thinking about.

But Rashid had given himself away when he'd asked to speak to her in private. Clearly he wasn't too keen on sharing the details of exactly why he deemed her unsuitable to care for his sister. So sure, she wasn't about to go advertising the way she'd behaved last night, but it seemed she wasn't the only one with a secret to keep.

Was he married? Was that his problem? She hadn't thought to ask last night. One night he'd offered and she'd taken it, no questions asked. And maybe it didn't reflect well on her, but last night had been just about perfect as far as she was concerned, at least until she'd entered that lawyer's office today and found him lying in wait and in judgement.

He'd been a different man last night. Bold. Decisive. He'd been angry, as she had been—and she'd felt it with his every move, his every thrust. Whereas today he seemed to be on the defensive.

What was that about?

Kareem climbed into the front seat beside the driver and turned to her. 'Do you have everything you need, Ms Burgess?'

She nodded. 'Thank you,' she said as she checked the sleeping infant, a tiny milky bubble swirling in the corner of her mouth. 'We're both very comfortable.'

Kareem nodded. 'Then we shall go.'

Tora looked around. 'Where is Rashi—? Where is Atiyah's guardian?'

'His Excellency is travelling separately. He will meet us at the airport.'

She nodded dumbly and settled back into her seat as the car cruised away. *His Excellency?*

Exactly who had she spent last night with?

He was stuck with her now. At least for the next however many hours it took to fly to Qajaran.

Only a few hours, Rashid reasoned as the driver made his way towards the coast, and then she would be on her way home again. It should be easy, given he'd only known her a few hours, but the way they'd spent them, and the way she'd left so abruptly, was it any wonder that he was still aching for more?

But he didn't want more, he told himself. He didn't need the distraction. He didn't need to be reminded of his wanting her every time he saw her. He didn't need to know she was close enough to take.

A few hours? God, already they felt too long.

Rashid had the driver stop just before the road turned to the right along the cliff face, and climbed out into the full force of the wind blowing off the Pacific Ocean. In front of them the ocean waves pounded against the rocky cliffs, sending the boiling spray high into the air, while to the left sprawled a cemetery as big as several city blocks, the marble headstones and funerary ornaments marching up the hillside to the silent blare of the angels' trumpets.

It was a wild place, elemental, the blue-skied summer day's temperature turned on its head as the tiny sparkling droplets of sea water drifted down and conspired with the wind to suck your body heat away. He welcomed it as he turned up the collar of his linen jacket.

It was the perfect place to forget about her.

He started walking, gravel crunching underfoot, towards the place the lawyer had marked for him on a map. He didn't need to look at the map again, the paths were wide and the way clear, and before long he could make out the fresh mound of earth that marked the grave where his father and his lover had been laid to rest.

He stood there, at the foot of the grave with its two white markers, feeling hollow inside. He had no flowers. He wasn't here to shed tears. He wasn't even sure why he'd come, only that he'd been compelled to visit, just once before he left this country.

Wasn't sure if he'd come to pay his respects to a father who'd cast him adrift when he was but a child, or to rail against him and demand to know why he'd abandoned him. Sure, he'd heard the lawyer's version of events, and he'd heard Kareem's, but surely he'd had a right to hear it for himself?

Surely he'd had a right to ask whether his father had ever thought of him on his birthday or whether he'd ever felt a hole in his heart where his son should have been?

He stood there, battered by the breeze caused by sea slamming into rock, until in the end Rashid knew there were no answers for him here.

Yet still he stayed a while, a silent sentinel, while the wild wind tugged at his jacket and hair and the spray from the crashing waves on the cliffs behind rained like mist over him, until finally he said in a gravelly voice to a father he couldn't remember, 'I will never understand why you did what you did. And I will never forgive you.'

And then he turned and walked away.

The jet was whisper quiet, piercing the air with the maximum of speed and the minimum of fuss or inconvenience to its passengers. Tora sat wrapped in one of the enormous leather seats, still shell-shocked. She'd travelled business class with a rock star's child once, and that had seemed luxurious after usually being consigned to economy with the children, but this was more than luxurious, this was sumptuous.

Timber-panelled walls with gold trim, plum-coloured leather seats that reclined and spun and laid flat and looked more suited to a lounge room than a plane, and opulent carpets in vermilion on gold on the floor, with enough space in between the seats to swing an entire herd of cats, while fresh frangipani placed discreetly in tiny vials around the cabin walls perfumed the air.

But then, this wasn't business class and it wasn't the only reason for her shell shock. This was the royal jet of Qajaran, and her tiny charge was some kind of princess.

What did that make Rashid?

He sat across the aisle in the row ahead, deep in conversation with Kareem. She could hear their voices every now and then, Kareem's measured and calm tones, interspersed with Rashid's arguments, though she couldn't make out what they were discussing but could see that whatever they were talking about was raising temperatures—Rashid's at least. She could make out his profile—strong lines even down to the lips on a mouth that was now snapping out words. Lips that she knew could give an inordinate amount of pleasure. She squirmed a little in her seat as she watched him, remembering, tingling in places that shouldn't be tingling right now.

God, she was kidding herself if she could forget, but it would be better for everyone if she could put those particular memories aside for however long this assignment took.

And then he turned, and caught her watching him, and she held her breath as a tremor zigzagged down her spine, unable to tear her eyes away as his dark eyes gleamed and pinned her to her seat. Then he said something short to the man beside her before turning away and severing the bonds between them.

Breath whooshed out of her in a rush as she felt his hold on her release. She took a couple of restorative breaths. What was that about?

Why had he looked at her that way, not with anger or resentment exactly, but with eyes that were so cold, hard and calculated?

Beside her, Atiyah gurgled happily in the bassinet strapped to the seat, and she blinked, focusing on what was important here. Not Rashid and his clear preference that she'd disappeared into the past and stayed there when she left his bed this morning, but this tiny baby.

Tora smiled as she leaned over the bassinet. She couldn't help but smile when she looked at Atiyah's face with her big dark eyes and tiny button nose and the pink lips busy making shapes and testing sounds. Likewise, she couldn't help but feel the tug on her heartstrings when she thought about how she'd grow up never knowing her mother or father. It was so unfair. It was wrong.

She should be smiling at two months. She probably would, if she saw her mother's face. For now, she looked up with those big eyes at Tora as if everything was new again, as it must seem to her.

It was so unfair to lose her parents just when the world

was coming into focus and making sense. She needed stability now, and people to love her. Hopefully, once she was in Qajaran with a regular carer, she would remember how to smile.

Maybe Rashid might even take an interest in her by then. He'd shown precious little interest to date, treating her more as a parcel he had to convey rather than as his tiny sister. He just didn't seem interested.

What was with that?

But then, he didn't look like a man who smiled much. He seemed angry about everything.

The baby cooed and closed her eyes and took a deep breath, settling back for another brief nap. Tora reclined her chair a little and sat sideways, almost envying Atiyah's ability to turn off the outside world. She watched her sleep, the low drone of the plane's engines like white noise, and the wide chair so comfortable, and yawned, feeling her own eyelids grow heavier.

'There is just one more issue that is of concern,' Kareem said, after a welcome pause that Rashid had taken to meaning their business was over, 'that must be discussed.'

'Why, when I still haven't agreed to take on the throne?' Kareem had gone through page after page of notes to explain the path to the throne and the coronation that must take place if he did agree, while going on to outline not only the history of the tiny but resource-rich state but the current challenges, both internal and external, that it faced, and right now Rashid's head felt as if it were about to explode.

Surely there couldn't be anything else?

'I am sorry, Excellency, but, now that we are on our way home, there is a question over Atiyah, and her place in the royal family.'

Rashid shook his head. This one at least was a no-brainer. 'She is my father's daughter. She is my sister. What possible question could there be?'

The vizier nodded. 'Both true. However, the fact remains that thirty years ago your father was supposed to have been killed in a helicopter crash. A body was recovered and accepted as his. Questions will be asked if you claim Atiyah is your father's daughter. Uncomfortable questions. The people will want to know where he has been all that time and why he abandoned them to their fate with his cousin while he was enjoying his life with a young mistress the other side of the world...'

'You said he had to promise not to return!'

'He did. But you had problems accepting that truth. Magnify that doubt by the population of Qajaran...' He paused. 'And of course, there are pockets still loyal to the memory of Malik. They will not want to believe this could be true. Is it not better to let history lie so they cannot dispute? Is it not better to let the population continue to believe your father died in that helicopter crash? Your coming home will still be the miracle they need—the child who miraculously survived and was spirited away to safety.'

Rashid's head was pounding. His life was getting more complicated by the minute. 'What does it even matter?' he growled. 'I'm Atiyah's legal guardian, aren't I?'

'Technically, yes.'

'Only "technically"?'

'Guardianship of infants and minors by unmarried men is not recognised under Qajarese law.'

'So? I don't even know if I'm going to be staying all that long.'

'It is an inconvenience, I know, but Atiyah will not be able to share your palace quarters if she is not officially acknowledged as part of your family.'

He sighed, pressing his head back deep into his head

rest. He hadn't asked to be this child's guardian but it was pretty clear that he could not let her be whisked away to God knew where to be looked after for however long this thing took. 'Then what can be done?'

'There is a way.'

'Which is?'

'Adopt Atiyah. Claim her as your own, if only in public.'

Rashid sat back in his seat, his mind reeling. What was happening to him that this proposal sounded half reasonable? Minute by minute he could feel the weight of the responsibility of a tiny desert kingdom pressing down on his shoulders, and he wondered, when it all came down to it, how much choice he really had.

'All right,' he said at last. 'What needs to be done?'

'Oh, it is but a stroke of the pen. I can handle it if you so desire.'

'Fine. Do it, then.'

If he thought that was an end to the matter and he could finally close his eyes and relax, he was sadly mistaken. Kareem was still there, watching him. 'What?' he snapped.

'There is but one *tiny* formality.'

There would be. Rashid rubbed a hand over his jaw. 'And that is?'

'To adopt in Qajaran, one must be married.'

'What? Why the hell didn't you say that before? It's pointless, then.'

'There is no one you have in mind to take for your wife?'

'No! Surely there is another way?'

'There is no other way.'

'Great. And you've only just discovered this now, when we're already on our way to Qajaran?'

Kareem bowed. 'My apologies, Excellency, this is a situation without precedent—I was hoping there would be something in the texts that might provide some comfort on this issue, but no. The texts are clear—only married couples can adopt. Perhaps, if there is no one you can suggest, I might be able to procure a suitable candidate on arrival in Qajaran City?'

'You? Find me a wife?'

'If only as a temporary measure, if it pleases you.' He raised one pen-laden hand as if he were being perfectly reasonable and Rashid only had to see it. 'It would simply be a matter of convenience.'

'And then?'

'And then you can divorce the woman and she can go her own way and you would retain custody of Atiyah. Please be assured when I say that both marriage and divorce in Qajaran are arrangements that require not much more than the stroke of a pen.'

'You said the same about adoption,' Rashid growled, 'and yet it seems needlessly complicated.'

The older man had the grace to smile ruefully as he held up his hands. 'Some strokes of the pen are more straightforward than others, but if you want to protect Atiyah, this is the only way.'

Rashid found it hard to argue the point, put like that, but he had his doubts about Kareem choosing him a bride, for however long or short this marriage was to be. Just because he had never entertained the concept of marriage was no reason to hand over the responsibility of selecting a wife. 'This wife I need—what would she be required to do?'

'She would have to perform as your wife in the public arena. She would have to be by your side during the coronation, if you go through with it, of course. Similarly at any public appearances where a mixed audience is in attendance—'

'And night times, Kareem. What would she be expected to do then?'

And for the first time Kareem looked somewhere approaching nonplussed. 'A wife populates her husband's bed at night. What else would you expect of her?'

'Of course,' Rashid said, frowning for added gravitas, while absolutely determined now that Kareem would have no part of choosing him a wife. Someone to escort him to official functions was one thing, but someone to take to his bed—only he decided who that would be. 'That is how it should be.'

'So you would like me to arrange a wife?'

'No. That won't be necessary. I've got a better idea.' One that would show a certain woman that when he said he did not want her for his sister's carer she should pay heed, that she was far better off agreeing with him and vanishing from his life just as silently as she had done from his bed this morning, or he might just think they had unfinished business.

A temporary wife to populate his bed could be some kind of compensation for this whole crazy scenario.

'Perhaps,' Kareem prompted, 'you would care to share this better idea?'

Rashid suddenly swung his head around and caught Tora watching him and he smiled.

Because although it seemed the train his life was on hadn't just changed tracks, it had changed planets, for the first time in a mad day he felt as if he was back in the driver's seat.

'I'm going to marry Victoria.'

'Ms Burgess?' Kareem forgot how to be serene and fairly spluttered. 'When you were so against her caring for Atiyah?'

'I know,' he said, unable to explain because the reason he was against her coming was the reason that made her most qualified to be his temporary wife. 'It's perfect.'

CHAPTER SEVEN

'Tired, Ms Burgess?'

Tora came to with a start to see Rashid leaning down before her, as attentive and seemingly caring as any of the flight attendants as he held what looked like a pot of coffee in one hand and a cup in the other, and it wasn't the coffee she could smell. He hadn't bothered to exchange two words to her since she'd walked out of that lawyer's office in Sydney. Something was definitely up.

'I must have dozed off,' she said warily, sitting up straighter and checking her watch. No, she'd only been asleep a few minutes and one glance towards the bassinet beside her was enough to tell her that Atiyah was still sleeping, her little arms flung back either side of her head.

'Anyone would think you've been working too hard.'

Her eyes snapped back to his. There was a cunning gleam there that had her on alert. 'Anyone except you, you mean.'

'Come, come, Ms Burgess,' he said as he put the coffee down on a small table. 'I brought you coffee.'

She looked around the cabin but it was deserted, the cabin crew all discreetly tucked away wherever it was they waited between being called upon. Even Kareem had disappeared somewhere. 'Yes, I can see. What's with that? Did you sack all the flight attendants or something?'

He smiled as he swivelled the chair in front of her around and sat down, though she sensed danger in the curve of his lips. She tucked her feet under her chair. Even with the room between the seats his long legs ventured way too far into her space for her liking. 'I have something I need to discuss with you, something that might work to our mutual benefit.'

Her eyes shuttered down. Yeah, right. 'I told you I wasn't here for you. I am here for Atiyah, nothing more.'

'You have a suspicious mind.'

'You have a transparent one.'

He shook his head. 'This is not about bedding you.' He hesitated there, and she wondered what had gone unsaid. 'This concerns Atiyah.'

'How?'

He leaned forward. 'For reasons you don't need to know about, I need to adopt Atiyah.'

She looked across at him blankly. 'And how does that concern me?'

'In order to adopt, under some quaint Qajarese law, I must be married.'

She swallowed down on a lurch in her stomach because this could in no way mean what crazy idea ventured first into her mind. 'I repeat,' she said, schooling her voice to level and wishing her heart rate would also take heed, 'how does that concern me?'

'It's not for long, it's just a temporary thing. A mere formality, really, and then in a matter of months we can be divorced.'

There was that lurch again, but this time there was no misreading his words. 'We?'

'Well, you and me.'

She blinked, hoping it covered the jolt to her senses that came with his answer. 'There is no you and me.'

'There doesn't have to be, not in any real sense. All I need is a wife. Someone to play the role of Atiyah's mother temporarily. Kareem tells me the marriage must last twelve months to ensure the adoption satisfies the laws of Qajaran, but that's only if I decide to stay. Otherwise, it might be over within a week.' He smiled, as if he were asking her nothing more than the time of day. 'Like I said, it's just a formality.'

'But a year! There's a chance I have to be married to you for an entire year!'

'If it happens. But you would not need to stay in Qajaran all that time. Once the formalities were over, you could go home.'

She looked at the coffee he had poured for her. She liked coffee, but right now she felt the need for something a whole lot stronger.

She licked her lips. 'Who are you?'

'I told you. My name is Rashid.'

She shook her head. 'No. I met someone called Rashid in a hotel bar. He was just a man. An angry man wanting to let off steam the way men do. But you—' She looked around. 'You fly in a plane with a golden crown for a crest, you have staff that bow and scrape and seem to wait on your every word and call you Excellency. So, Rashid, who are you, that you think it is perfectly reasonable to ask a near stranger to marry you so you can divorce them when it suits?'

His eyes left her face, to wander a scorching trail down her body, lingering on her breasts before venturing lower. He smiled. 'Near stranger?' he questioned, his voice husky around the edges, rasping against her very soul. 'We are hardly strangers.'

She crossed her arms and legs to stop the tingling under her skin, relieved when his gaze once again found her face. 'You don't know me and I sure as hell don't know anything about you.'

'I am not asking the world, merely for a few weeks of your time and then you can go home.'

'I said I wouldn't sleep with you again and I sure as hell won't marry you.'

'Nobody said anything about sleeping with me. You served a purpose last night, but now I'm looking for something else.'

She laughed, not sure whether to be offended or not. It was so mad, she had no other option but to laugh. 'Well, as attractive as you make your proposal sound, that I pretend to be your wife, no thank you.' She glanced at the baby and assured herself she would be all right for a minute or two more, before she pushed herself up to stand. Maybe if she headed for the bathroom, it might put a stop to this ridiculous conversation. But Rashid rose too, stepping sideways and blocking her path. 'Excuse me,' she said. 'I need to use the bathroom.'

'Not yet. You haven't heard what I'm offering in return.'

'I don't need to, to say no. You made it very clear when we were in Sydney that you didn't want me to be here at all. You made it clear that you wanted nothing more to do with me and that's fine, because I don't plan on sticking around any longer than I have to in order to do this job. As soon as I hand this child over to whoever is going to be her carer in Qajaran—because I assume from your lack of interest it won't be you—I'll be heading home.'

His eyes narrowed. 'Come now, Ms Burgess, how can you say no when there is so much on offer?'

'Like what?'

'Like an all-expenses-paid holiday in Qajaran, complete with a bird's-eye view of a possible coronation and all the festivities surrounding it, along with a return flight home in the royal jet.'

A shiver ran down her spine. 'Whose coronation?'

'Mine.'

Ri—ight. So that was it. She did her best not to sway

on her feet. Did her best not to look stunned. 'So you're kind of king-in-waiting, then?'

He nodded. 'You could put it that way. Qajaran is currently without an Emir. Apparently I am next in line to the throne, if I agree to take the role on.'

A kind of king. Well, that was kind of funny when she'd thought he'd looked like a god on the bed only this morning. A demotion almost, and that thought almost brought a smile to her face when there should be none.

She shook her head. 'Sorry, not interested.'

'How much, then?'

'Excuse me?'

'How much would it take? Everyone has their price—name it.'

She shook her head. She must be dreaming. That or she'd woken up on some bizarre television game show. Any minute now and they'd be cutting to a commercial break for disposable nappies or dishwashing liquid. 'I told you, I'm not interested.'

'Name it!'

She sucked in air. She didn't want to do this. She didn't want to spend a moment longer in this man's company than she had to. The night she'd spent with him was too fresh, too raw in her mind, the passions he'd unleashed in her still making her senses hum at his proximity as if his mere presence was enough to switch them on—but then she thought about the amount her cousin had stolen from her and the money she had assured Sally she would find...

He wouldn't say yes, she told herself, there was no way he'd say yes, but if he really wanted a figure—if he really wanted to know how much it would take for her to agree to this crazy plan... 'All right, you asked—two hundred and fifty thousand dollars. That's my price.'

And his eyes might have damned her to hell and back, but he smiled—he actually smiled—and her stomach dropped to the floor like a brick even before he said his next word.

'Done.' He turned and yelled for Kareem. 'Prepare for the ceremony.'

Tora was reeling. 'But—'

'But nothing,' he said, smiling like the cat that had the cream. 'You named your price. I agreed. The deal is done.'

Kareem married them, neatly fitting the ceremony in between Tora feeding Atiyah her bottle and changing the infant's nappy, the bride's gown nothing more than black trousers and a fawn-coloured shirt with smudges of baby milk on the shoulder.

It wasn't a ceremony as such. There was nothing more to it than for the two of them to stand before Kareem in his white robes and with her hand on Rashid's, and for Kareem to utter a few words, before Rashid dropped his hand, jettisoning hers in the process, and saying, 'Right, that's that out of the way. Let's get this adoption signed off, shall we?'

Out of the way? thought Tora, feeling stunned as she returned to her seat and changed Atiyah. So that was it, then. No *You may kiss the bride*. No congratulations or champagne or even a pretence of celebration. She was married to Rashid, according to Qajarese law, and it felt—*hollow*.

Marriage wasn't supposed to feel hollow, she was sure. She'd always imagined getting married would be one of the happiest days of her life, with her father to walk her down the aisle and her mother proudly and no doubt tearfully looking on. Sure, that was before the glider accident that had killed them, but even now she would have liked to think of them somewhere up there looking down on her approvingly on her big day…

She gulped down on that bubble of disappointment before it could become something more.

This was hardly her big day though.

This was a means to an end for her, exactly as it was to him, the opportunity for her to obtain the funds she'd promised Sally, a formality in order for him to adopt Atiyah. After all, it wasn't as if she *wanted* to be married to Rashid, even if he made her feel like no more than an adjunct to the process, like a box that had been ticked or a task on a to-do list that had been crossed off.

He'd dropped her hand as if he couldn't bear to touch her. My God, what a difference, when last night he hadn't been able to stop touching her.

Then again, what had she expected? Last night might as well have been a lifetime ago. Rashid had been a different man—attentive, creative and infinitely attuned to her pleasure—and she'd been someone she didn't even recognise. Impulsive, reckless and brazen in bed. She'd behaved like a wanton.

She dragged in a breath, trying to find calm in a world that was teetering off balance. She'd shocked herself last night at just how shameless she'd been, as if the frustrations of Matt's betrayal and the despair of letting Sally and Steve down had spilled over on an effervescent tidal wave of passion that had washed away her moral values. Last night there'd been no off switch, no holding back. Talk about out of character for a girl who normally wouldn't kiss a guy until at least the second date.

Memories of that night should have been her secret thrill, something to smile privately about and wonder at her bravado and total abandonment. Not something to be constantly reminded of every minute of the day by being confronted with the star performer of her night of the pleasures of the flesh. The last thing she'd wanted was to learn that the man at the centre of her night of nights was Flight Nanny's and her very next client.

No, she wouldn't want her parents around to witness

this. One day she'd marry for real. One day she'd find a man she loved and who loved her more than anything, and they'd be married under a brilliant blue sky and her parents could look down upon her and smile.

One day.

She slipped Atiyah's legs back into her sleep suit and did up the snaps. Think of the money, she told herself. Think of Sally and Steve and the quarter of a million dollars, merely for marrying Rashid for however long it took. Even if nothing else, now she'd have the money to complete this deal, without having to beg from the banks. Now there'd be nothing stopping Sally and Steve heading for Germany and the radical new treatment that might save him. Just as soon as she managed to give Rashid the bank account details for the transfer of the promised funds.

No wonder she felt a little hollowness in her gut.

The pilot came back then, smiling as he advised them personally they would be beginning their descent soon, and to assure them all would be well.

All would be well? She held Atiyah in her arms and softly sang her a favourite nursery rhyme, wanting to cuddle the baby for as long as she could before she'd have to be strapped into her capsule on the seat for landing.

After a night with Rashid and a mad on-paper marriage, she wasn't sure things would ever be well again.

It was done.

Kareem had completed the paperwork on both the marriage and then the adoption in short order.

His faux wife was installed and Atiyah was adopted and for now he could take a deep breath. That was one crisis averted.

His friends would laugh. Rashid married, just as they had warned him. Well, he would let them laugh. It wasn't as though it was a real marriage. It wasn't as though he was in love as Bahir and Kadar had attested to be, and it wasn't that he had to marry and impregnate a wife before he could be crowned Emir, as Zoltan had been required to do by the ancient texts of Al-Jirad when he had married the Princess Aisha.

He grunted. Though if that had been a requirement, he'd already well and truly ticked that box. Memories of last night's passion rolled through him like replays of a movie, except this was a movie in which he'd had a starring role. He'd only needed to touch her hand to be reminded of the satin smoothness of her skin, and to remember the sleek feminine beauty of the curve of her hip, the dip to the gentle round of her belly and all the places above and below that his fingers, and then his lips, had traversed.

He hadn't held her hand a second longer than he'd needed to, and yet the mere touch of her had fired his memories and kindled a need that burned like coals inside him.

There was too much going on in his life without complicating it with a woman that had blown his world apart.

He looked over his shoulder, through the gap in the seats, and saw her holding the child as if she were her own, the baby all dark-eyed innocence staring up at her as she spoke words he could not make out. What was with that? Atiyah was nothing to do with her.

So why did she seem to care so much?

Atiyah was supposed to be his sister, after all, even if the sister he'd never asked for or wanted.

And the wrongness of it all got to him and something inside him snapped.

He got out of his seat, determined to tell her so, but as he drew closer he realised she wasn't talking to the child, she was singing to it, some kind of lullaby, and she was looking down at the baby so intently, she didn't hear his approach.

He didn't interrupt at first—for a moment he couldn't because he was rooted to the spot—because for some reason he recognised the music. The notes were buried, but they were there and they were true, and each note she sang was like a shovel in his gut, exposing more.

'What are you singing?' he growled, when he could wait no longer, because he had to know.

Her singing stopped, and she looked up, suspicious, her eyes wide at finding him so close. 'Just a lullaby. I think it's Persian. Why?' she said, and suspicion turned to concern as she scanned his features. 'Is something wrong?'

He didn't know. All he knew was that there was something churning in his gut that brought him out in a cold sweat and made his skin crawl. How would he know the tune to a lullaby he was sure he'd never heard before?

But the way she was looking at him, as if he were mad, or worse... He looked for something that he could talk about to cover his confusion. His eyes fell on the infant. 'How is she?' he forced out, his mind clamouring to remember why he was here. 'I thought babies were supposed to scream through flights.'

Her doubting eyes told him she knew he hadn't come back to discuss the flying habits of babies. 'She's a good baby. Have you changed your mind? Would you like to hold her a while?'

He looked away, wondering where his anger had gone. He'd been sure he was angry when he'd left his seat, but now he was wondering why.

'Only I get the impression you haven't had a lot to do with babies. Do you have no other brothers or sisters?'

'No.'

'Babies aren't hard to look after,' she said. 'They just need to know they're loved.'

Well, that was the problem right there. How was he supposed to let a child know it was loved when he wasn't entirely sure how that was supposed to work? What did he have to offer? 'Look,' he said, 'I really just came back—to make sure you were comfortable.'

Liar.

She knew it, too, and yet still she attempted a smile. A nervous smile. She snagged her bottom lip between her teeth, before saying, 'Rashid, now that you're here, can I ask you something?'

'What?'

The 'fasten seat belt' sign lit up then and she put the baby back in her capsule, fastening the clasp over her belly and checking the seat belt. When she looked back up, her teeth were scraping over her bottom lip again. 'It's just about the money. I need to have it transferred as soon as possible.'

He breathed out on a sigh as resentment seeped like black ink into his mind, banishing his confusion with something he was entirely more comfortable with. 'The money.' He nodded. Now there was something that made sense. There was something he could understand. 'We haven't been married ten minutes and you can't wait to get your hands on your precious money.'

'Excuse me? You're the one who couldn't wait to land the plane before we were married. I've upheld my end of the bargain.'

'You expect the money now?'

'Well, we're married now, aren't we? So I thought—'

'You thought?' He was happy beyond measure that she'd turned the conversation away from where he felt so challenged and vulnerable and to money, which was solid and real and which he knew. 'You thought you could suddenly start dictating the terms?' Because if she thought that, then maybe it was time to start changing them.

'You're the one who agreed to pay me if I agreed to marry you.'

'Oh, you'll get your money, Ms Burgess. But I have to say, I'm disappointed you put so low a value on your services. I would have paid a million dollars, maybe even two for the pleasure of having you in my marital bed.'

Her face flushed bright red. 'Our deal didn't include me sleeping with you. I told you that wasn't going to happen.'

He was teasing her, of course. He had no intention of touching her again; he was still raw from losing himself too much—and too deeply—but her reaction pleased him inordinately and he was enjoying it. 'But you also told me you wouldn't marry me, and look at us now, happy newly-weds.'

'You can't make me sleep with you. That's unconscionable.'

He leaned down, one hand on the back of her seat, the other toying with a tendril of hair that had come loose from her bun.

'Don't you think it's a bit late to take the moral high ground? Who was it who picked me up in a bar? And after last night I know you're no shy, retiring virgin. Far from it. Why pretend you don't want a repeat of last night as much as I do?'

She swallowed and he tracked the movement in the kick of her chin and in her throat and his fingers let go of her hair to trail a line down the same way.

'I know what you think of me—that I'm cheap and easy.'

'I think you're expensive and easy, as it happens. But I'm willing to pay the price you ask.'

'Go to hell!'

'I have no doubt that's exactly where I'll end up. But don't fret, my charming wife, your reputation—or what's left of it—is safe with me. I have no intention of a repeat of last night's performance.'

CHAPTER EIGHT

QAJARAN CITY ROSE from the golden sands of the desert as if it had sprung from it organically, the buildings fashioned from bricks made of mud, hay and the desert sand itself, so their walls sparkled in places when the light caught on the tiny crystals as they passed, but it was the people that most fascinated Tora.

From the airport the streets were lined with people waving flags and clapping their hands—happy, smiling people. A woman in colourful robes held her young child aloft to better watch them pass, a crumpled old man leaning on walking sticks had tears running down his leathery cheeks but a smile so wide it was obvious they were tears of joy. And it struck her then that this was for Rashid—the man who might soon be their Emir, ruler of Qajaran—the man who was her new husband.

The same man whom she'd spent an illicit night of sex with.

The man who had barely an hour ago assured her there would be no repeat performance.

She trembled, the muscles between her thighs clamping down on a sudden bloom of heat in spite of his assurances. It was crazy, she should be exhausted after a night of little sleep and the drag of international flight halfway around the world, even if it was in the sumptuous surroundings of a private jet, but, looking across at Rashid, never had she felt more alive, never had she felt more aware of her sexuality.

Should she believe him when he said that it wouldn't happen again? Or was it just that she didn't want to?

Oh, God, it would be so much easier if she could simply hate him. He'd railroaded her into this deal, after all. Not without her agreement, but he'd done his best to make her feel small and mercenary even with that.

But…there was still that night between them—that unimaginable night of pleasure—how could she hate a man for that? And there were those moments since then when the blustering faltered and he looked lost and lonely and so achingly sad that she wanted to reach out to him. Because who couldn't love a tiny child? What had gone wrong in his life that he felt that he couldn't?

She wished she could hate him. Then she wouldn't be drawn to him. Then she wouldn't feel this damnable pull.

He'd told her there would be no repeat performance, but, when it came down to it, if he turned to her in the night she doubted whether she'd have the strength to say no to him. When she remembered back to the night they'd spent together and the masterful man he was then and all the ways he had pleasured her, it was hard to imagine why she'd even want to.

She looked out of the window at the people lining the street, all so keen for a glimpse of this man who might rule them, feeling shallow and superficial and hating herself right now. There was history being made here today and, even in her unsubstantial way, she was part of it, yet all she could think about was sex.

Well, that was Rashid's fault, too. That night they'd spent in each other's arms had a lot to answer for.

'Did you arrange this welcome committee?' she heard Rashid ask Kareem, and Tora looked at him, because his voice sounded as tight as his jaw looked, and as uncomfortable as it must feel. And for the first time, she saw Rashid looking like a man who was uncertain with his place in the world, and she was intrigued. He didn't seem like a man who would doubt himself.

'Good news has a way of getting out,' Kareem answered, with a shrug of his white-robed shoulders. 'Even in Qajaran, where the Internet is not as readily accessible as it is in the west. The people have waited a long time to see the Qajarese flag flying on a royal limousine. Your return is welcome.'

'If I am to do this,' Rashid said, 'I am going to need help,' and if Tora wasn't mistaken there was a sheen of sweat on his forehead in this very much air-conditioned car.

Kareem smiled even as he bowed his head, as if Rashid had said exactly what he'd wanted him to. 'I am at your disposal, of course.'

'Thank you,' Rashid acknowledged. 'And I have a friend who had to lead his country unexpectedly. I would like to seek his advice.'

'You refer to Sheikh Zoltan, the King of Al-Jirad.'

'Yes. You know him?'

'But of course. Al-Jirad and Qajaran have been friends since ancient times. He would be most welcome here. It would further cement the bonds between our two countries.'

Rashid seemed to relax then, taking a deep breath and lifting his hand in acknowledgment as they passed the cheering onlookers. He looked the other way and caught Tora watching him as his gaze drifted past hers. His eyes immediately snapped back. 'What?'

'Nothing,' she said, shaking her head, for the first time feeling a little sorry for this man, who appeared to have been thrust into a world not of his making. Nothing she could tell him or that he would want to hear at any rate.

* * *

The limousine slowed as it waited for a set of high metal gates, sculpted to look like twin peacocks, to be opened. 'I have taken the liberty of installing you in the Old Palace,' Kareem said as they started along a long palm-lined driveway. 'Emir Malik built six new palaces during his reign, all of which are more modern, and you are more than welcome to make one of the others your base, but, for your comfort and the sake of tradition, I feel the Old Palace will be more suitable.'

Tora swallowed as she caught glimpses of a building out of her window through the garden of palms and greenery, the curve of a domed roof here, a peep of a decorative window arch there, snippets that held the promise of fantasy.

But of course, they would be heading for a palace. Where else would an Emir live?

And then the palms parted and the car rolled slowly past a fountain that was the size of a small lake, featuring stallions made of gleaming marble and standing tall on their hind legs, their manes alive to an unfelt breeze as they pranced in the tumbling water that sparkled like jewels in the sun.

But while the fountain was spectacular, it was a mere accessory to the palace. Tora took one look and knew she'd left her old world behind and stepped into the pages of a fairy tale. Surely it was the most beautiful building she'd ever seen, with decorative arches and rows of columns and a golden dome adorning the roof, and the whole effect was as romantic as it was impressive.

The limousine rolled to a stop under a colonnaded entrance shaded from the weather and before a flight of stairs where a dozen uniformed men, wearing the colours of the flags she'd seen waved in the streets, stood waiting.

'Welcome home, Excellency, Sheikha,' Kareem said

with a nod as one of the guards stepped forward to open the door.

Sheikha? Tora swallowed as she unfastened Atiyah's capsule and prepared to enter this strange new world. But of course, she supposed, she must be a sheikha if she was married to a sheikh.

And then she caught a glance of Rashid's grimly set jaw. She was married to this man. As good as shackled to the sheikh. *A fairy tale?* And suddenly Tora wasn't so sure.

'If you please, Sheikha Victoria,' Kareem said with a bow as he gestured her to enter, 'this is your suite.'

Tora was reeling. She'd thought the outside of the palace was breathtaking, but then she'd stepped inside into air scented with jasmine and musk and known she was in some kind of fantasy land. Walls were decorated in gilt and mosaic, chairs and tables inlaid with mother of pearl. It was a feast for the eyes, and everywhere she looked another work of art demanded her attention. It was all she could do not to gape.

It was all she could do not to run. Still dressed in her serviceable, travel-weary uniform while everything around her was exotic and beautiful, she had never felt more out of place.

And now Kareem was showing them a suite that would swallow up her entire house in Sydney and still leave enough room to live in, and that was without taking into account the terrace overlooking the pool and garden outside her windows where the now setting sun was bathing everything including a row of mountains far in the distance in a ruby glow. It was utterly magical, and that was only the outside.

The bedroom itself was enormous, hosting a magnificent gilt four-poster bed, and there was a room prepared for Atiyah along with another room for Yousra, a local girl who'd been assigned to be her nursery maid, and the main bathroom had a bath that put some of the lap pools at home to shame.

Her suite. All hers. Which meant that Rashid would be sleeping elsewhere, and for the first time since arriving Tora started to relax. If she wanted to avoid Rashid, she need never leave the safety of her room.

She eyed the four-poster bed longingly. Weary from both the travel and the emotional roller coaster of the last however many hours since she'd walked into her cousin's office, already she imagined herself lost in blissful sleep amongst the cushions and the pillows. Tomorrow would be soon enough to chase up the funds Rashid had promised and let Sally know they were coming. By then she might be able to sound convincing when she told Sally that her delay in returning home was caused by nothing more than a simple request to stay while Atiyah settled in. Not that anyone was likely to believe her if she did tell them the truth.

But that could wait until tomorrow. Once Tora had bathed and fed Atiyah and seen her comfortable, bed was the first place she was headed.

'And through this door,' Kareem continued, opening a door of exquisitely carved timber, 'is Your Excellency's suite. The rooms are interconnecting, of course.'

'But of course,' said Rashid with a smirk in Tora's direction.

He was teasing her again, she realised. No more than taunting her. And yet all of a sudden Tora's sprawling apartment didn't seem anywhere near big enough.

Atiyah cried out, growing restless, and Tora saw her chance.

'If that is all?' she asked, not interested in venturing into Rashid's apartments. 'I will take care of Atiyah. She's had a long day.'

'Cannot Yousra take care of the child for you?' Kareem asked. 'Would you not like to dine together with us?'

While the girl's eyes looked up at her hopefully, Rashid's dark eyes gleamed, his lips turned up in one corner. He knew she was avoiding him and right now she didn't care.

'I will welcome Yousra's assistance, of course,' Tora said, smiling at the girl so as not to offend her, but also because she really would appreciate the help, especially when sleep tugged so hard at her, 'but Atiyah has been through many changes recently, and until she's settled in I'd like to keep some routine in her life. Besides, I'm sure you and Rashid have many matters to discuss that don't require my input.'

'As you wish,' Kareem said with a bow, and Tora was surprised to see what looked like approval in his eyes. 'I will have your meal sent up.' He touched his fingers to Atiyah's brow, uttered a blessing to the child and wished Tora goodnight.

'I'll see you later,' said Rashid.

'Seven in the morning for breakfast?' Tora suggested, refusing to acknowledge the implicit threat in his words. 'That would be perfect. We have some details to discuss also. Goodnight.'

And the flash of his eyes and the flare of his nostrils told her he did not like her dictating when they would meet or being so summarily dismissed. No doubt, he didn't like being reminded about his end of the bargain either. Tough. He had promised, he could pay up. 'Come,' said Tora, turning to Yousra. 'Let's give Atiyah her bath now.'

With a swish of Kareem's robes, she heard him disappear with Rashid through the interconnecting door and Tora could breathe again.

Zoltan was coming. Rashid felt the tight bunching ache in his gut loosen a fraction, but it was fraction enough to be able to breathe more deeply than he had since arriving in Qajaran. He gazed out from his terrace over the gardens surrounding the expansive pool below. Around him the palace slept. Night had fallen fast and now the sky above was a velvet shroud of blue black.

Zoltan would arrive in three days, to be joined by Aisha and the children, and Bahir and Kadar with their own families, the day before the coronation. The last time they had been together had been in Melbourne for Kadar's wedding six months ago. It would be good for the desert brothers to be together again, although once there were just four of them, and now every time they got together there seemed to be more, wives and children swelling their numbers. He shook his head. Such an eventuality would have been unthinkable even a few years ago, one by one his brothers falling into marriage.

He alone was left. He wasn't counting his hastily contrived marriage to Tora. It wasn't as if she were a real wife. She would be gone in a matter of weeks, even if their marriage needed to last a year on paper. In some ways, it was unfortunate that his desert brothers and their wives would meet her at all, for they were bound to make something of this temporary arrangement.

He heard a sound and looked sideways towards where Tora's suite of apartments lay, but the night settled into quiet again, the rustle of the palm fronds on the barely there breeze the only sound.

He sighed. Well, let his brothers make of it what they would. He had much more important things to think about now, like a country full of people who had been offered morsels through years where the Emir had grown rich on its resource revenues. Things needed to change. Less money would be lavished on palaces and fripperies. More money would go to funding schools and hospitals, especially outside the city, where needs went unseen and often ignored when they were.

His grip on the alabaster balustrade of the balcony tightened until his knuckles hurt.

It was easy to see where the inequities and injustices lay, but there was so much to address. Could he fix the problems of the past thirty years of maladministration?

Why was he even considering it?

But then somebody had to do it—share the riches and drag this country into the twenty-first century—and he was next in line to the throne.

His gut screwed tighter all over again. God, what was he even doing here? He was a petroleum engineer by day with a reputation as a playboy by night. Apart from his DNA, what qualifications did he have to equip him to run a country?

He looked around. There was that sound again. The child, he realised. But this time there was more.

She was singing that song again.

Both drawn and repelled in the same instant, he watched as Tora emerged from her suite, the baby clutched in her arms as she sang the soft, soothing words of a lullaby he never knew and yet that somehow tugged at some deep part of him. He melted into the shadows as she swayed in the night air, singing words of comfort and peace, her hair down out of that damned bun, just the way he liked it, while the blue light from the pool below turned her long white nightdress translucent so that it floated like a cloud around her slim legs and tickled the tops of her bare feet.

He swallowed back on a surge of lust as he watched, transfixed.

The breeze toyed with the hem of her nightdress, shifting shadows and whispering promises as she sang of apricots and pigeons and waterfalls, and some of her words were wrong or mispronounced, but it didn't matter because the overall effect was still beautiful.

She was beautiful.

He stood in the shadows with his heart beating too fast at a mystery he didn't understand.

He stood there utterly bewitched.

Bewitched and rock hard.

She finished the song, the last of the sweet notes trailing away on the night air, the baby in her arms asleep. She turned to go back inside the same moment as he emerged from the shadows. She gasped.

'Tora.'

And she took a deep breath and then another. 'You frightened me. What are you doing on my terrace?'

He looked back the way he had come. 'It appears we have adjoining terraces, as well as adjoining suites.'

Her eyes blinked her disappointment before shuttering down. 'Well, goodnight.'

'Tora, wait.'

'Why? Atiyah needs to go back to bed.'

He looked at the child, her face at peace in Tora's arms, oblivious to the electricity charging the air between them. 'She's asleep.'

'Which is where I want to be.'

'Tora.'

'Why are you here?'

'I couldn't sleep.'

'No,' she said, her soft voice tremulous in the velvet night, 'why are you *here*? What do you want?'

A heartbeat later he answered. 'You.' And in that moment, Tora lost all perception of time, all cognizance of space. Because Rashid was standing there in nothing more than thin white sleep pants slung low over his hips that made no secret of his arousal. And his chest was bare and in his eyes she could see torment and right now he looked as if he'd been sculpted in shadow.

And then he drew closer and she could see there was more than torment in his dark eyes—something far more carnal.

She shuddered from the top of her head all the way to the tips of toes that curled on the cool paving stone, seeking to get a grip on a world where she was a stranger.

'Rashid...' But he was already stepping closer, stepping into her space even as she drew back, her arms protecting the baby, leaving her defenceless as his fingers laced through her hair.

'Rashid...'

And then his lips brushed hers and she breathed him in and he tasted warm and musky and male and his taste and scent sent her spinning back to the place she'd been that first night. *So good.* So very good that her body hummed into life as readily as if his lips had flicked a switch.

Oh, God.

She wasn't about to turn it off.

His lips were as soft as the night sky, the sweep of his tongue like a shooting star to her senses, and there was magic in the air all around them.

Instinctively she opened to him—she knew him—and his kiss deepened. Hardened. As he angled his head and pulled her closer.

There was a squawk. A protest from between them. And Tora's attention snapped back to the child in her arms—to where it should have been before she'd been seduced by the shadows. She turned her face away, freeing a hand to push at the hard wall of his naked chest.

'Rashid, stop.'

He blinked, feeling sideswiped all over again. This woman did things to him. She made him forget himself and his determination to lock down his emotions when he was around her. She made him forget everything. He'd been so blindsided by lust that he'd forgotten completely about the child in her arms—his own tiny sister. And he'd known all along that he would be rubbish caring for an infant, and still he felt ashamed.

'Is...is she all right?'

'She's fine,' Tora said, rocking her in her arms. 'No harm done.' Although the quake in her voice told him otherwise. 'Maybe you should go back to your suite.'

He reached out for her. He didn't want to go. 'Tora—' but she spun away.

'Stop it! Don't you care about this baby at all?'

'I adopted her, didn't I?'

'Lucky Atiyah.'

'Look,' he said, shaking his head as he turned it towards the heavens, 'I didn't ask to take on the care of an infant. I don't know the first thing about babies.'

'Well, maybe you should start learning because frankly, Atiyah deserves better. You have a ten-week-old child who has lost her parents and you treat her like something you wished you could shove away in a filing cabinet somewhere and forget about.

'Don't you understand? She's not a thing, Rashid, she's a child. A baby. She needs to be nurtured, not merely tolerated. She needs love and smiles and someone who truly cares about her. Instead, she got stuck with you—sullen, resentful, miserable you—and I can't work out why you have to be that way. Have you forgotten what it's like to be a child?'

His jaw was so tightly clenched, he felt a muscle pop. 'No, as a matter of fact I haven't, but rest assured I don't plan on sending Atiyah to boarding school to be looked after by strangers the first chance I get, so I guess I do know something about bringing up children, even if it's nowhere near your high standards. But thanks anyway, for pointing out my failings so succinctly.' He turned to leave and this time it was her that stopped him.

'Rashid,' she said, concern swirling in her gentle eyes. 'Is that what happened to you? How old were you when they sent you away?'

'It doesn't matter,' he said on a sigh, raking a hand through his hair. 'Other than the fact it makes me the most useless person ever to be appointed guardian of anyone, let alone an infant like Atiyah.' He looked down at the baby, now settled again. 'She deserves better.' He turned his eyes up to Tora's. 'I'm sorry I interrupted you. Goodnight,' he said, and he was gone.

Tora stepped breathlessly back into her suite, meeting a distraught-looking Yousra coming the other way. 'Is everything all right? I heard voices,' she said as she caught sight of the child in Tora's arms. 'Oh, no. I should have woken. Did she cry? I am so sorry not to let you sleep.'

'It's okay,' Tora soothed her. 'I would normally be awake at this time and I was only half asleep. You go back to bed.'

And the younger woman bowed. 'If it pleases you, Sheikha.'

'Call me Tora,' she said. 'I am much more comfortable with that.'

'But...?'

'Tora,' she insisted. 'As I call you Yousra. We are both looking after Atiyah after all. We should be friends.'

The young girl smiled uncertainly and bowed some more. 'If you are sure, Sheikha,' and Tora smiled as the young woman withdrew.

Tora settled Atiyah back into her bed and watched her for a while, marvelling at how placid she was in the wake of having had her world turned upside down, a world that at ten weeks she'd only just been getting to grips with.

Tora ran one fingertip across her downy cheek. She was a little sweetheart, no two ways about it.

A sweetheart with a tortured brother. What had happened that he felt so incapable of loving Atiyah? What kind of childhood had he had? Boarding school, and from an early age by the sounds. But why, when his father had only recently died? Why would he have done that?

She crawled back into her bed, and tucked her knees up under her crossed arms, trying not to think about how in Sydney it would be halfway through the afternoon instead halfway through the night, trying not to think about the meeting with Rashid at breakfast that she had asked for and that now seemed so close as the clock edged closer to a Qajarese morning.

Thinking instead of how she could help him overcome whatever failings he thought he had and bond with his tiny sister.

Thinking that she cared because she wanted Atiyah to be happy.

She stretched her legs out and laid her head back in her deep, welcoming pillows. It was nothing to do with the ache she could feel in Rashid's eyes. All she wanted was for Atiyah to be happy.

That was all.

CHAPTER NINE

THE SOFT SKY outside her windows was layered in pink and blue like cotton candy when Tora rose. Atiyah was gurgling and examining her hands and fingers when Tora peeked over the side of her cot.

'Good morning, beautiful,' she said, only to be rewarded by a big, gummy smile that made her heart sing. 'Oh, you sweetheart,' she said, lifting her up as Yousra appeared with a tray of coffee.

'She's awake?' asked the girl.

'Yes, and she's smiling. Look,' and Yousra came closer and tickled her tummy and the baby kicked her little legs and made a sound like a hiccup and both women laughed.

They played with her until it was almost time for Tora's meeting with Rashid. There were preparations being made outside on the terrace—she could hear someone giving instructions as staff set a table for two. Breakfast on the terrace overlooking the pool? That should be pleasant enough, if only it didn't remind her of what had happened on that terrace last night.

She closed her eyes as she twisted her hair into a bun and pinned it to her head, trying to keep her mind on how she was going to get Rashid and Atiyah together and not thinking about that kiss. She really would have to keep her distance, especially when the velvet shadows of the night stroked her soul and dimmed her logic. No more night-time wandering for her. No more assuming she was alone.

And definitely no more kissing. She touched a finger to her lips, wondering how a man who could be so hard and cold could feel so gentle and warm...

She shook her head to banish the thought. Oh, no. She wouldn't go making that mistake again. If she hadn't been holding Atiyah, she didn't know how it might have ended.

Liar. She knew exactly how.

On her back.

Or in the shower.

No! She could not afford to think of that night in Sydney. That was in the past, when they had been nothing more than strangers in the night. Things were different now. She had a job to do and she would show him that he could not just click his fingers to get his way. If she achieved nothing else before she left, she would show him that he could love Atiyah.

She gave her hair and make-up a final check before adding a slick of neutral lip gloss. There, cool and professional on the outside at least, just the way she needed to be for this meeting. She wouldn't let him rattle her today. Besides, she was too happy to be rattled. Because Atiyah had smiled.

Rashid was already seated at the table reading some papers when she approached. The sun was still low enough not to cause them any grief, but there was the promise of heat in the air. He glanced up disapprovingly. 'Haven't you got anything else to wear?'

Tora sighed as she sat down. If she'd thought that his opening up to her a little last night might have made his attitude towards her less adversarial, she was wrong. The walls between them were up again, not that she was about to let him spoil her good mood. 'Good morning to you, too. I trust you slept well.'

He grunted as a waiter appeared, laying a napkin

across her lap and fetching a dish with yoghurt and fruit before enquiring if she'd like tea or coffee. She smiled and asked for coffee, waiting for it to be poured while all the time she was aware of the man opposite simmering where he sat.

'It's a beautiful morning,' she said, when the waiter had departed.

'You can't expect to wear—' he nodded disdainfully in the direction of her clothes, ignoring what she'd said '—*that* every day.'

Tora looked down at her clothes, at her short-sleeved shirt and skirt, both fresh and, as far as she knew it, baby-spew free. 'What's wrong with what I'm wearing?'

'Nothing, if you've got a thing about those boring shirts you probably call a uniform. For the record, I don't.'

'*You're* wearing a shirt.' Although, to be fair, it was one hell of a lot sexier than hers, the white cotton so fine she could see his skin tone and the darker circles of his areolae where the fabric skimmed his chest. *Damn.* She looked away and concentrated on her coffee.

'Couldn't you find something more appropriate?'

'It's a funny thing,' she said with a smile, refusing to be pulled into Rashid's dark cloud of a mood, 'but, for some strange reason, I seem to have left all my resort wear at home. Go figure.' She shrugged. 'Besides I actually like my uniform. It's comfortable, practical and it scares men away—well, it usually scares men away... present company excepted, of course.' Her friend Sally had always joked that she'd worn her uniform as a form of self-defence against unwanted attention, and she wasn't right exactly, but it generally didn't bring Tora too much interest from the opposite sex. 'Men aren't supposed to like bookish-looking women. Come to think of it, did you miss that memo?'

He scowled. 'What's got you so cheerful?'

'You mean aside from seeing you?' she said, smirking as she sipped her coffee, savouring the heady aroma of the spiced brew, before she continued, 'Red letter day. Atiyah smiled this morning. Maybe you should try taking a leaf out of her book some time.'

'She smiled,' he said, frowning a little. 'Is that good?'

'It's better than good, it's great. It's the first smile I've seen her give. You want her to be happy, don't you?'

'Of course,' he said, with as much conviction as if the concept had never occurred to him. And then he nodded and his eyes softened. 'Of course, yes, I want her to be happy.'

'There you go,' she said, feeling that he was not the lost cause he made out and that he would overcome whatever was holding him back from embracing his new role. 'I swear, you won't be able to resist falling in love with her when she smiles at you. I wish I'd brought her now, so you could see for yourself.'

He looked at a loss for what to say next, as if once again he was in unfamiliar territory. 'Anyway,' he said, 'you're supposed to be the wife of the Emir. You can't wear that every day—you'd look ridiculous. Kareem told me last night he'd organised an entire wardrobe of clothes for you.'

'Oh.' Is that what that was about? She'd opened the door to the walk-in wardrobe last night wondering where she could stash her suitcase and found it bursting at the seams with garments. Robes of silk and the finest cottons and in all the colours of the rainbow. And she'd shut the door again because they obviously weren't hers and found another place to leave her case. She picked up her spoon to try her yoghurt.

Rashid glanced at his watch. 'What did you want to talk to me about?'

Right. She put her spoon down again. Clearly this wasn't

a breakfast meeting where one actually expected to eat breakfast. In spite of her good mood, her heart gave a little trip at having to broach the subject again. But there was no point beating about the bush. She pulled a folded paper from her pocket. 'Here are the bank details for you to transfer the funds.'

He took it, checking the details before his eyes flicked back to hers. 'Not your account?'

'It's a trust account for a firm of solicitors.' *Matt's solicitors*, she thought, biting her lip. Damn. She really wanted nothing to do with Matt or his cronies, but it would just have to do for now.

'A trust account?' His eyebrows raised, he cast his eyes over her shirt again. 'You know, you're much more interesting that that uniform lets on. But then, we already knew that.' He put the paper down on his others. 'So, was there anything else?'

'You'll do it?' she said, hardly believing it would be that simple after the grief he'd given her on the plane. 'Today?'

His eyes narrowed, as if they were trying to find a way inside her to gain the answers he wanted, but still he said, 'It will be done today. Was that all?'

'Not quite,' she said. 'There is one more thing. I'd like Internet access. I see it's password protected.'

'You wish to Tweet that you're now sheikha of Qajaran?'

She grimaced. 'Hardly. I need to contact my work and let them know there'll be a delay in me getting home so they can start reallocating assignments.' *And tell Sally the funds are on their way.* But he didn't need to know that.

'I'll have Kareem arrange it. Just be careful what you send from the palace.'

'Of course, I will.'

'Then,' he said, collecting his papers as he rose to his feet, 'if there's nothing more, I'll leave you to it. Enjoy your breakfast.'

***

Rashid had indigestion but it had nothing to do with what he'd eaten. He strode through the palace towards the library he'd chosen last night with Kareem for his office, his stomach complaining the entire way. Cursing Tora the entire way.

Because he still had to make the biggest decision of his life and, with her around, he couldn't think straight.

And it didn't seem to matter how much he tried to block her out and tell himself that she was irrelevant, she was there, alternately smiling, needling or offering him sympathy.

He shook his head as he walked down the long passageways. Why had he told her what he had last night? His past was his business, nobody else's. It was not the kind of thing he shared with anyone, let alone a woman he'd picked up in a bar.

But then, that was not all she was. Tora was much more than a casual pick-up.

She was his sister's carer.

And now she was his wife, even if in name only.

And he wanted her despite all his claims and words to the contrary, wanted her like there was no tomorrow. Last night was proof enough of that. He'd been blind with desire and she'd come willingly into his kiss, only stopping when Atiyah had protested.

He'd beaten himself up at the time, thinking he was the one at fault, but when he'd thought about it much later, in the long hours when sleep had eluded him, he'd realised that she'd made no effort to push him away before Atiyah had cried—she'd been as much a participant in that kiss as he had been—which proved to him that he wasn't the only one feeling this way. Feeling this need.

It wasn't just one-sided. There was still unfinished business between them.

So why was he fighting it? What point was there to erecting walls between them, when they seemed so futile and no wall had yet stopped him from wanting her?

Maybe it would be better to deal with the problem head-on, rather than pretending it didn't exist. Sleep with her. Get it out of his system so he could at least think straight.

He needed to think straight.

He paused, his hands on the door to the library.

Then again, maybe he was better off keeping his distance. She was trouble. Madonna, siren and shrew all wrapped up in one irritating package.

He snorted. Yeah, he'd tried leaving her alone and look how far that had got him. But he could hardly just tell her he'd changed his mind about his hands-off policy and expect her to go for it. She'd made it plain she wasn't about to simply fall into bed with him again at a click of his fingers. But what to do?

Fed up with torturing himself over her, he pulled open the doors.

'Excellency,' said Kareem, who was waiting for him inside, already busy at his notes and making his countless plans for Rashid while he waited. 'I trust you slept well.'

'More or less,' he said, not wanting to think about how little he'd slept or any more about the why. 'So what do we have to consider today?'

'Many things,' Kareem confirmed. 'But I know it is all very dry and Sheikh Zoltan will be here soon so I thought perhaps tomorrow we might take a tour of Malik's new palaces, to see if you would prefer to use one of them for your official residence.'

'If you think it's important. How many were there again?'

'Six.'

Good grief. Rashid suppressed a sigh, feeling already weighed down with the volume of the historical and economic texts he had been given to digest. 'Are there not more important matters to consider?'

'Certainly. But if I can use an expression you might well know, Rome wasn't built in a day. You are yet to accept this role, and anyone would be foolish to expect you to conquer it overnight. There are things to be assessed in the kingdom that do not require your poring through old documents or dusty tomes twenty-four hours a day, things that might give you a broader view of the kingdom, before your possible coronation.'

'Fine,' Rashid conceded, pinching the bridge of his nose with his fingers. 'Arrange it.'

Kareem bowed. 'It will be done.'

And suddenly Rashid had a brainwave. 'What about Tora? Could she come, too?'

'Sheikha Victoria?' The vizier shook his head while he deliberated. 'I don't see why not. She would no doubt appreciate seeing some more of our architecture.'

'So long as it won't cause any problems, if people were to see Tora with me, only for her to subsequently disappear?'

Kareem looked unabashed as he weighed the air with his big hands. 'This will not be a problem. In past years, our people are used to seeing our Emir with any one of a number of consorts, and frankly they would be more surprised to think you were unmarried.'

'Excellent,' said Rashid, rubbing his hands together as he found his first smile for the day. Maybe a day out with him would prove to her he was not the sullen, resentful and miserable monster she had painted him. Maybe if they could be friends first, they could be more... 'Now, where were we?'

Tora was enjoying a day of sheer girly fun. It started in the morning, with Yousra giving her a tour of the various gardens of the palace and around the pools and fountains where the lush foliage and flowers and sprays of water combined to turn the air deliciously cool and fragrant while tiny birds darted from bush to bush. It was exotic and different and serene. And after her tense breakfast with Rashid, Tora felt that serenity seep into her bones and she could breathe again.

Just when she thought it couldn't get any better or more beautiful, Yousra showed her to the secret garden, hidden away in a courtyard and thick with trees and palms that gave way to a lily pond where small ducklings paddled. And there tucked away in the centre like a gift-wrapped jewel stood a square pavilion with ivory-coloured columns and red balustrade with a tiled roof and white curtains for walls that billowed gently from on high.

'It's beautiful,' she said, cursing the inadequacy of the description as Yousra smiled, waiting for her reaction. It was like something from a fairy tale that became more so as two peacocks emerged from the foliage and quietly wandered away. Tora was entranced by it all. 'What is it?'

'It is called the Pavilion of Mahabbah and was built by Emir Haalim when his favourite wife died. This was her favourite courtyard, you see. And he had loved her so much he had named her after the Qajarese word for love—*mahabbah*. It is said he filled this pool with his tears. Come,' she said, leading the way. 'I have arranged us to take tea there.'

'So it is the pavilion of love,' Tora said a few minutes later as she sat on one of the low sofas, thinking how appropriate it was, how romantic and how tragic, imagining the Emir standing between the curtains, looking out over the pond and remembering his beloved wife. Beside her on the rug on the floor, Atiyah played under a baby gym, kicking her legs as she swatted at the hanging toys above her with her little hands. 'He must have really loved her.'

Yousra nodded. 'The heart of a Qajarese Emir is worth the hearts of ten men. And it is said the Emir loves ten times truer.'

Tora sipped her tea, not wanting to argue, but not entirely sure that was true for all the Emirs. Malik might have loved ten times as many as other men with his palaces full of harems, and then there was Rashid.

She wanted to believe Rashid had a heart. She hadn't seen much evidence of it so far, but she so wanted it to be there, if only so his sister might grow up surrounded by love rather than indifference. And she wondered again about a man who'd let slip that his own childhood had been lacking. Something dreadful had happened to him, that much was clear, something bound up in a tortured history that had scarred him deeply and, if she wasn't mistaken, was still hurting.

She shouldn't care, she told herself. He was nothing to her but the means to fund a promise she'd made to her best friend. Nothing more to her than that—if she discounted one heated night of the best sex she'd ever had and one stolen kiss last night that she hadn't wanted to end.

She really shouldn't care.

And yet it was hard not to.

The afternoon provided a different kind of entertainment. There were just the three of them, Tora, Yousra and Atiyah, amidst a dressing room overflowing with the most amazing clothes Tora had ever seen.

Yousra sat holding Atiyah on the sofa at the end of the four-poster bed, as Tora turned model and tried on garment after garment to much applause and encouragement in between cups of honey tea and sweets made of nuts and dried figs, apricots and dates. Yousra advised her on which were more suitable for during the day, and which she might consider for night-time events like formal dinners.

How Kareem had pulled this off, Tora wondered as she slipped into another gown, she had no idea. They'd all been on their way to Qajaran when this whole mad marriage scheme had been contrived, so he would have had to have messaged ahead from the plane with his instructions.

Clearly it was a different world when one was connected to royalty.

'That one, yes!' said Yousra, as Tora turned to the young woman wearing a robe of aqua-coloured silk, embroidered around the neckline and the cuffs of the sleeves. 'That colour suits you so well. You look beautiful.'

Tora turned to the mirror and was inclined to agree. But then it was a beautiful gown, whisper-soft against her skin and so cool. 'I like it,' she said, and moved on to the next.

And after she'd exhausted both the contents of the wardrobe and tiny Atiyah, who'd been put down for a nap, Tora couldn't bear to go back to her serviceable skirt and shirt, but returned to the aqua gown that felt so deliciously cool against her skin. Yousra brushed out her hair and made up her eyes, so she had Qajaran eyes, she called them, ringed with kohl, before she hennaed Tora's feet. 'Just a little,' she said, 'for you will have your hands and feet done for the coronation.' Tora returned the favour by painting Yousra's fingernails and toenails and making the younger woman giggle as she tickled her toes.

They were both laughing as they compared the results when there was a knock on the door and Rashid entered.

'Nice to see someone having fun,' he said, his eyes sweeping the room to take in the situation. 'Won't all that noise wake the baby?'

Yousra bowed immediately, her hands clasped demurely in her lap, her painted toes tucked discreetly under her robe, as if she'd been chastised. 'Excuse me,' she said softly.

Tora saw no reason for repentance. She did see an opportunity for bringing Rashid closer towards caring for his sister. 'It's actually a fallacy babies need silence to sleep. They hear plenty of noise while in the womb and it is good for a child to grow up hearing laughter. Come and see for yourself how untroubled she is.'

His eyes raked over her. Confused eyes, as if he didn't know how to respond, so she slipped her hand in his and steered him towards Atiyah's darkened room, pulling aside the netting. Atiyah lay on her back, one hand to the side of her head as she slept. 'You see,' she said with a smile as she looked up at him. 'Sleeping like a baby. Isn't she beautiful?'

He supposed she was, with her black curls framing her face and her eyes a dark line of lashes, her lips pink and perfectly serene. He nodded. 'She is,' and only then, when he went to reach out a hand to see if the skin of her cheek was as smooth as it looked, realised Tora's hand was still in his. 'I take your point,' he said, and squeezed her fingers before he let them go, and touched fingers warmed by Tora's to his sister's cheek. So smooth. So perfect. The baby stirred slightly before sighing back into sleep, and Rashid took his hand away so he didn't disturb her more.

Tora was still smiling and it was all he could do not to pull her into his arms, but no, that was not the way. 'Kareem gave me this for you,' he said, pulling a paper from between the books he carried, and handed her the instructions for accessing the Internet.

'Thank you,' she said.

'And your money has been transferred.'

Tora closed her eyes and clutched the paper to her chest. 'Thank you so much for letting me know.'

She looked beautiful. She'd ditched the drab uniform and that too-tight bun and was wearing a silken robe that didn't cling and yet that turned her into a woman again, the woman he knew was hidden below, with breasts and hips and curves in between, and she'd done something with her eyes so they looked smoky and seductive and now, because of something he'd said, she looked radiant.

He'd been mad to ever imagine he could leave her alone.

'There's more,' he said, and his voice sounded thick even to him. 'Kareem is giving me a tour of the six new palaces tomorrow, and I came to ask you if you would like to accompany me.'

'Me?'

Her eyes had lit up, as if she wanted to say yes, but they were wary. Guarded. She didn't trust him. She had good cause. 'You.'

She looked down at the child. 'And Atiyah?'

'There is no reason to haul her around with us. We will be in and out of cars in the heat of the day. She will be much more comfortable staying here.'

'But—'

'Please, Sheikha, I can look after her.'

Tora looked at Yousra. 'Are you sure? We may be gone a long time by the sounds.'

'It is no trouble. Atiyah is a delight.'

'So, it's settled, then,' Rashid said, feeling better than he had in a long time. 'We will leave after breakfast.'

Tora looked up at him, her accentuated eyes hauntingly beautiful and her lips slightly parted. 'After breakfast, then,' she said as they walked towards the door.

But he turned back before leaving, wanting one more look at her, like this, like a woman dressed in silk and not a buttoned-up nursemaid with a bun. 'I see you found something else to wear.'

'Yes. You were right—Kareem had organised an entire wardrobe of clothes for me. Yousra's been helping me go through them.'

'I like what you're wearing,' he said, nodding at her choice. 'You look beautiful.'

And her lips moved uncertainly, but he didn't hear if she actually said anything, because he was gone.

CHAPTER TEN

THERE WERE SIX of them in all. A white palace, covered in mother of pearl shell that dazzled in the sun. A red palace with red turrets and domes that paid homage to the ruby. A palace with extensive scented gardens and called Yasmin—named after Malik's favourite of the time, they were informed—the Grand Palace that was based on a Venetian row of palazzos complete with canals and gondoliers on demand if required together with vast rooms filled to the brim with Murano glass, and a palace that looked like a double for the palace of Versailles. There was even park-cum-palace called the Fun Palace with a fantasyland theme and an expansive garden full of perfectly maintained and oiled rides that sat eerily empty, just waiting for someone to push a button.

To Tora they seemed like the folly of a boy who'd never grown up, buildings that lacked the elegant good taste of the Old Palace despite the wealth of treasures they contained, buildings that ventured into the territory of ostentatious display of wealth for wealth's sake.

'Why so many?' she asked Rashid as their convoy left the last on the list, the so-called Fun Palace, a rococo confection based on the retreats of the renaissance royals that wouldn't be out of place in the French countryside. 'Who even needs so many palaces?'

'Malik did,' he said, 'because apparently the harem in the Old Palace was nowhere near big enough.'

'So he built six additional palaces to accommodate his women?'

'Apparently he was a man of insatiable tastes. I can't think how else he could have so happily squandered so much money and so many hours when he should have been working for his people.'

'But he had no children?'

'It didn't stop him from trying,' he said drily, and Tora couldn't help but laugh.

'What?'

'You. You sounded almost funny then.'

'I'm sorry. I didn't mean to.'

'I know,' she said with a grin. 'That's what makes it so funny.'

He looked away, feigning umbrage at her laughter, when in fact he was enjoying himself immensely. It was good to get away from the endless papers and the spreadsheets filled with numbers that showed just how badly the economy had been neglected over the last three decades while its treasury had been plundered to pay for the Emir's follies.

It was good to be with her.

Surprisingly good.

He'd imagined this outing would give her the chance to see him in a better light. He hadn't expected to discover he liked her more in return.

She made a pleasant change from Kareem, who he liked and respected but whose conversation was limited to the necessary and delivered without humour.

Needless to say, she was more appealing on the eyes than Kareem, too. Much more. Today she was wearing another of those silky robes, this one coloured in ripples of yellow and orange so she looked like a shimmering sunset as she walked. He'd been right to ask her along. She made the tour a holiday excursion, expressing delight and sometimes horror at the old Emir's excesses, rather than a dry exercise of checking out the inventory.

And suddenly he didn't want it to end. They were on the outskirts of the city, only a sprinkling of buildings amidst the desert sands, and he had an idea. 'Stop the car,' he told the driver, and the vehicles rolled to a halt. Rashid climbed out to talk to Kareem and a few minutes later he was back and their car peeled away from the others and headed towards the desert proper.

'What's happening?' Tora said. 'Where are we going?'

'Seeing we are so close, I thought we should see something of the desert. Apparently there is an oasis not far from here.'

He saw her bite her lip as she glanced at her watch. 'Will it take long? We've been gone hours already and I feel bad leaving Yousra by herself for too long.' And he felt a pang of admiration for this woman who he could see wasn't using Atiyah as an excuse to get away from him, but was genuinely concerned for his sister.

'It won't take long,' he promised.

It was only a few kilometres further on through the desert sands that they found it, an oasis of palm trees, an island of green amidst the golden landscape, almost empty but for a few families picnicking on and paddling in the shores of a pond alive with waterfowl, its fringes thick with water lilies of white and pink.

'It looks idyllic,' she said as the car pulled into the shade of the palms, and they climbed outside. The desert air was hot and dry, but there was a breeze fanning through the greenery and over the water and Tora's *abaya* fluttered in the warm air as she took in the contrast between desert sands and lush greenery.

'Kareem said this was once a resting place for the caravans that traversed the dunes. Now the city has spread closer and it has been retained as a park for the people of Qajaran.'

'It's beautiful.' She turned to him then, her eyes alive and bright. 'Can we paddle, do you think? Only it's been such a long day and my feet are killing me.'

He wasn't sure why she asked when she was already slipping off her sandals and raising the hem of her *abaya* to slip her feet into the water's edge. 'Oh, it's gorgeous,' she called over her shoulder. 'Bliss. You have to try this for yourself.'

He shook his head, even as he laughed. It was crazy. He swam laps for fitness and he'd been a champion rower along with his desert brothers when he'd been at university, but he wasn't sure he'd ever paddled before. And then, because he figured there was no time like the present, he shucked off his loafers and rolled up the bottom of his trousers and joined her.

She was right. The water was cool and clear and the perfect antidote to hot feet tired from traipsing around half a dozen palaces. Tiny fish darted around his ankles while a crane stood on one leg, watching warily from a distance, and Rashid wondered at the pleasure in such a simple occupation. Tora turned around then and pointed to one of the families whose children were laughing in the shallows at their father holding up a baby whose little feet kicked at the water, giggling gleefully as he splashed himself and everyone around him. 'We should bring Atiyah here for a picnic—what do you think?'

And something shifted enough inside him that it almost sounded like a good idea. He would like to, he thought, if this woman came with them. 'Maybe,' he said as he stepped out of the water and sat on the grassy edge, looking up at the mountains in the distance, and thinking...

She came and sat down next to him. 'Thank you for bringing me here,' she said, flapping at the bottom of her wet hem while she studied the henna designs on her feet as they dried in the warm air. 'That was magic. I don't think you're ever too old to paddle.'

Alongside her he made a sound, half snort, half laughter. 'Just as well, really, given that's my first time.'

Her head swung around. 'Seriously? You've never paddled before?'

'Not that I recall.'

'But when you were a kid—you must have gone to the beach or something?'

He shook his head as he looked out over the water, his elbows on his bent knees. 'The school I went to had a pool. It's not like I didn't learn how to swim.'

But he'd never experienced the simple delights of paddling in the shallows? And she thought back to that night on the terrace when he'd told her he wouldn't send Atiyah off to boarding school, and she wondered. 'How old were you when you were sent to school?'

'I don't remember, I just remember always being there.' He shrugged. 'It was a good school, set in leafy Oxford. I can't complain.'

'But so far from home.'

'That was my home.'

'But your parents?'

'My mother died when I was in infancy. I grew up believing my father was also dead.'

A chill went down Tora's spine. Atiyah was his sister so his father had been alive... It was so horrible, she couldn't help but want it to be untrue. 'You've got to be kidding.'

And he turned and looked at her with eyes that were dark empty holes, and she regretted her words even before he spoke. 'Do you really think I'd kid about a thing like that? No, I never knew he'd been alive all that time until I was summoned to a meeting in Sydney to be told that he'd actually been alive for the thirty years I'd believed him dead, only to have been killed in a car crash weeks before. Not only that though, because I was now the proud guardian of his two-month-old child. How would you feel, learning all that?'

Under the heavy weight of his empty eyes, she knew. Gutted. Devastated. *Angry.*

And her breath caught. He'd been angry the night she'd met him. Because that was the day he'd learned the truth? God, he'd had good reason. No wonder he'd been so resentful of Atiyah, charged with the responsibility of a child of a father who'd as good as abandoned him three decades before.

She looked out over the surface of the water and the ripples that sparkled under a hot sun. 'Why would any man do such a thing to his child?'

Rashid swiped at an insect on his legs. 'Apparently he was protecting me,' he said. 'Protecting both of us.' And he told her of his father being chosen as the Emir's successor, the plot to dispose of both father and child and the exile and separation that had followed.

'And he never once contacted you in all that time.'

'No.'

'So you were brought up by strangers?'

He leaned back on his elbows. 'My houseparents were my guardians. A good couple, I suppose, but I never felt I belonged. I was never part of their family, so much as a responsibility.'

It explained so much about the man he was. No wonder he felt so ill-equipped to care for a child. 'What a hard, cold way to grow up.'

'It wasn't so bad, I guess. What they might have lacked in affection, they made up for in instilling discipline. I was the perfect student in the classroom or on the field.'

Discipline, yes. But no love. No warmth. And her heart went out to the little boy who'd grown up alone and now had the unexpected weight of a country on his shoulders. 'Will you stay, do you think? Will you become the new Emir?'

Rashid sighed. 'I'm not sure,' he said, being honest. 'My father chose not to tell me any of this—I think he valued his freedom in the end, and he wasn't about to force me into a role he saw himself having escaped. Either that, or he thought one attempt on my life was enough.'

'Would it be dangerous?'

'Kareem says not. Apparently the longer Malik ruled, the more of a buffoon he became, interested in satisfying only his own appetites. Everyone knows the last three decades have been wasted. The people want change.'

Rashid stared into the middle distance. Why was he telling her all this? But somehow putting it into words helped. Somehow her questions helped. *Would he stay?*

Qajaran needed help, that much he'd learned these last few days, but was he the man who could turn the country's fortunes around? Zoltan would be here tomorrow to advise him, but there would be no need for that if he decided to walk away.

Could he simply walk away?

And once again his eyes were drawn to the line of mountains that lay across the sands, and he thought about the words Kareem had spoken in an office in Sydney what seemed like a lifetime ago, words that had made no sense to him at the time, words that now played in his mind to the drum beats of his heart.

'Where are you going?' she asked as he rose to his feet and walked towards the sands that lay beyond the fringe of green.

'Just something I need to do,' he said, before stepping from the grass and onto the sands, feeling the crunch of the thin surface give way to the timeless hot grains of Qajaran's sands beneath. Anyone watching would think him mad—Tora must certainly think him mad—but his heart was thumping as he walked, feeling the grains work between his toes and scour his soles. And when he'd walked far enough, he stopped and leaned down to pick up a handful of sand and let it run through his fingers while warm desert air filled his lungs and the breeze tugged at his shirt, whispering the secrets of the ages. He turned his head to listen and found his gaze looking across the desert plains, back to where the blue mountains rose in the distance, and, with a juddering bolt of sensation, he saw the colour of his eyes in the distant range and he felt it then—the heart of Qajaran beating in his soul.

And he knew he was part of this place.

He was home.

His skin still tingling with the enormity of the revelation, he turned back towards the oasis. He was staying. He knew that now, and he wanted to tell Tora, to share it with her because somehow he knew she would understand.

He frowned, because there were more people gathered there where he had left her. They bowed as he drew closer, calling blessings upon him and wishing him well, their eyes full of hope, while Tora stood there in their midst, her beautiful face alight with a smile that warmed his newly found soul.

The children were less hesitant than their parents. They ran up to him, wanting to touch his hand, and he knew he didn't deserve this kind of reception, and he didn't know if he would make a good leader, but the people of Qajaran needed a good leader, and he would try.

The price of failure was too high.

Their return to the Old Palace was subdued, Rashid lost in thought as he watched the desert retreat in the face of the city. Kareem would welcome his decision, he knew, and throw himself into executing the plans for the coronation he already had mapped out. And still he wondered if it was the right decision.

'So what will you do with the palaces?' she asked. 'Unless you're planning on establishing your own harems, of course.'

Lord help him. He couldn't imagine having six women, let alone six harems. One woman was more than enough and he didn't have her. Not really. And there was another problem...

He shook his head, because there were no easy answers to anything. 'I'm not sure. But the state can't keep paying for them. Kareem wanted to show me, in case I preferred one of them over the Old Palace.'

'I like the Old Palace,' she said. 'It has history and character. You have to keep that as the kingdom's base, surely?' And then she paused. 'Not that it has anything to do with me, of course.'

'But that still leaves the problem of what to do with the rest. Qajaran already had a Desert Palace and a Mountain Palace before Malik took it into his head to increase the number of palaces by two hundred per cent.'

'Sell them, then.'

'Not possible. They belong to the people of Qajaran. For better or worse, they are part of their heritage. Even if they could be sold, nobody would pay what Malik spent on them. The country would lose a fortune.'

'So you have six white elephants costing a fortune to upkeep?'

'That's the problem.'

'Could they be turned into boutique hotels? So many bedrooms already with en-suites—surely it couldn't be too hard.'

He looked at her. Really looked at her. 'Did someone tell you that? Did Kareem mention it while we were looking around the palaces?' Kareem had mooted it as a possibility with him just yesterday when he was going over the final details for the inspection.

She shrugged and shook her head. 'No. But what else could you do with them? You could hardly turn them all into museums—that would never pull as many tourists from overseas or earn you as much money. But think of the tourists who would flock here, wanting to tick off staying at Qajaran's quirky hotels one by one, or get married alongside a Venetian canal in the desert. And think of the employment that could be generated in servicing busy hotels rather than in maintaining six empty palaces waiting for their next visit from their Emir.'

He rubbed his chin between his thumb and his fingers, the gravel of his whiskers like a rasp against his skin. The tour had taken the better part of the day and he had a five o'clock shadow to show for it. 'Maybe it's possible.' The palaces couldn't be sold, but they could be leased to a luxury hotel chain to manage…

'Yes!' she said, cutting into his thoughts, 'but not the Fun Palace. That one would be different. You should open that one up to the people of Qajaran. The palace can still be a hotel, but the park should be free for all citizens who just want to visit with their families, not to stay in the rooms.'

'And for those that do,' he said, intrigued, 'they would have to fight the crowds to access the rides that others get free?'

'So give them two hours' exclusive use in the evening or morning. I don't know. It's not exactly my line of expertise. I'm just offering a suggestion. And while you'd probably make money if you converted them all to boutique hotels, it would just be a shame if the Qajarese people couldn't enjoy something that is their own heritage, especially when it's already a fun park.'

Not her line of expertise. So why did what she said

make so much sense? Even down to offering the Qajarese people an opportunity to sample the luxury and indulgences they had so unwittingly paid for.

'How did you come to work at Flight Nanny?' he said, wondering about this woman who looked after babies and children and who came up with solutions to problems way outside her apparent field of expertise.

'Simple,' she said. 'Sally and I went through school together and then university. When she and Steve started Flight Nanny, I jumped at the opportunity to join them.'

'They sound like good friends.'

'The best. Sally is like my sister. When my parents died, I was devastated. She kept me going. And then, when I poured my grief into a love affair with Mr Wrong that ended spectacularly badly, she was there to pick up the pieces. I owe her my sanity.'

'What happened,' he asked, 'with this Mr Wrong?'

'It was my fault just as much. I wanted it so much to work out—I needed to love someone enough to compensate for the loss of my parents and I was too needy, too demanding. I can see that now, of course. I can see that when he tried to let me down gently, I wouldn't let him go.'

'So how did it end?'

She gave a wan smile. 'Badly. He announced to the world that he was dumping me on every social media account he was signed up with, because I was "a bitch, a total cow and crap in bed". I do believe those were his exact words. Mind you, they worked.'

'You're not any of those things,' he said, 'for the record.'

She gave a half-smile. 'For the record, I thank you. And I'd rather you didn't post that anywhere, if it's all the same to you.'

It was his turn to smile. The guy was a loser—that much was clear. 'You're better off without him. Anyone who could say those things wasn't worthy of being a friend, let alone a lover, especially when you were already so low.'

'I know. Sally said the same thing.'

'So why child care?' he asked, changing the subject, because the thought of her with another man was suddenly unpalatable and not something he wanted to dwell on.

She shrugged. 'I don't know exactly. But I always loved babies and little kids—maybe because I was an only child and grew up alone. They always fascinated me. When I found out I could make a living working with them, it seemed a no-brainer.'

He nodded, although he wasn't sure he entirely understood. He'd grown up alone and he'd mostly kept to himself. If he hadn't happened upon his three desert brothers, he'd probably still be wandering the world alone.

'Have dinner with me,' he said on a whim, because he realised they were nearing the Old Palace and soon she would excuse herself and take herself off to her apartments and the care of Atiyah and he was suddenly sick of being alone.

She looked flustered, her lips parting and closing as if searching for and not finding any words.

'Just dinner.'

'Um... I have to check on Yousra and Atiyah. We've been gone a long time.'

'So check.'

'And if Yousra has had enough or is tired?'

'Bring Atiyah to dinner with you,' he said, surprising himself that he meant it. 'Bring her anyway,' he added, if that helped. Anything to postpone the time she would close herself off from him again.

She blinked. 'Why are you suddenly being so reasonable?'

He turned to her, careful not to reach out a hand and

touch her, as he'd been wanting to all day, to touch the molten sunset of her robe, to feel her heat. In the end, he reached out a hand and wrapped it around hers. No pressure, just a hand hold, warm and true. 'Because I've just had the best day I've had in a long time. And I don't want it to end.'

God, he meant it. Tora's skin bloomed all over. From just the touch of his hand. No, from the import of his words and the dark intent of his eyes. He actually meant it.

And it had been a good day. She'd had a personal tour of six amazing palaces and been both dazzled by their brilliance and appalled at their waste, in the company of a man who knew how to push her buttons, be they physical or emotional, and who now was testing out a new one, one that simply said like.

She was intensely aware they'd just entered the palace gates. Aware they'd soon have doors opened and the outside world would intrude and the moment would be gone—as maybe Rashid himself would be, whisked away to put to rights whatever problem besetting the country next needed addressing.

She didn't want the world to intrude. Not just yet.

There would be time enough for the world later.

'Yes,' she said. 'I will have dinner with you.'

'Good,' he said, drawing her hand to his mouth and pressing his lips to the back of it, while his eyes smiled and warmed her in a place she hadn't expected his eyes to warm. Because it wasn't just sex she saw there, she was sure. There was more.

And she welcomed finding more.

The car slowed, even as her heart raced. Dinner with Rashid. Could they really be friends? After today, she wanted to believe it possible.

He was still holding her hand when the car pulled up to the steps. She liked the feel of her hand in his. She liked the way it made her feel, liked that today their hitherto stumbling relationship had advanced to another level, one that involved both trust and respect.

There was someone there waiting for them, standing on the steps in addition to the guard of honour that seemed to grace their every entry and exit. Someone tall and broad-shouldered with deep black hair and he was looking at their car and smiling.

'Who is that man?' she said, and Rashid looked to where she was indicating.

'Zoltan!' he said, with a wide smile. A man Rashid was clearly beyond excited to see from the way he didn't notice when she slipped her hand from his, and Tora figured the dinner invitation was off.

'Zoltan!' Rashid called as he jumped from the car. 'You're early.'

Rashid ran up the steps and pulled his friend into a hug. 'I was told you were arriving tomorrow.'

Zoltan laughed. 'I thought I'd surprise you.'

'It is a good surprise. Thank you for coming. You don't know what this means to me.'

'To me, too. Whoever thought a humble orphan child turned petroleum and gas billionaire would ever finally make good?' he joked before turning serious. 'You have had a rough ride of it lately, I understand.'

Rashid shook his head. 'I am glad you could come. There is so much to tell you.'

'Tell me over dinner.'

And Rashid suddenly remembered and looked around, to where the cars of the convoy were spilling their contents, but with Tora nowhere to be seen.

'Tora,' he said. He'd asked her to have dinner with him and now she was gone and he felt her absence like a sudden hole in a perfect day.

'What did you say?' Zoltan asked, and Rashid once again felt the jolt of pleasure that his brother was here. It was probably for the best that she'd gone, he thought, given the circumstances. At least it saved an awkward introduction. With any luck, Zoltan wouldn't have heard he was married. He'd save that gem for later. There were more important matters to discuss right now.

'So tell me,' he said, turning his back on the hollow feeling in his gut as he led Zoltan into the palace. 'How are Aisha and the family?'

It was for the best, Tora told herself as she made her way back to her suite. He was so excited to see his friend, he would have regretted asking her to have dinner with him the instant he saw him. Besides, dinner would have been pointless. It was all so pointless. She would be going home soon and leaving this world behind. Why establish links that would have to be broken?

Because when it all came down to it, this wasn't about her. This was about ensuring a bond between Rashid and Atiyah, and the signs were heartening.

It was enough.

Yousra was waiting for her in her apartments, singing to Atiyah as she rocked the baby's cradle. She looked so relieved when she saw Tora coming, Tora thought the girl was going to burst into tears.

'How was she?' Tora whispered with a frown, peeking over into the cot expecting to find a sleeping child, only to find two dark eyes that immediately locked onto hers and widened before her face crumpled and she started wailing before Tora could duck out of the way.

'I'm so sorry,' she said to Yousra, scooping the child into her arms. 'I shouldn't have left her.' After all the turmoil she'd already suffered, all the losses, Atiyah had grown used to having Tora around, only for Tora to disappear for hours, and her heart was breaking for the little girl. She should never have agreed to go with Rashid.

And she knew she couldn't afford to think that way. Knew that it was wrong. She couldn't afford to become a fixture in this child's life, and yet already it was happening. She should have returned home as she'd been supposed to. She should have handed Atiyah over and walked away. And she would have, if Rashid hadn't come up with this whole crazy marriage deal.

And now the longer she stayed, the harder it would become because the more attached to her Atiyah would become, and one day soon she'd be leaving for good and Atiyah would be hurt all over again.

She swayed as she pressed her lips to Atiyah's soft curls and felt tears sting her own eyes as Atiyah's tears threatened to rip out her heart. Staying longer was such a double-edged sword. It gave Atiyah security for a little while. But it gave Tora more time to fall in love with a precious dark-eyed child.

She'd never felt this way about one of her charges before. She'd never come so close to feeling what a mother must feel—protective and defensive and determined that she should have only the best of everything, including love. But then, she'd never had such a tiny baby to look after.

If only Rashid had been more accepting of his sister in the start. If only she hadn't felt as if she had to compensate, to give Atiyah the love she should have got from him.

Damn.

CHAPTER ELEVEN

NIGHT FELL FAST, the way it seemed to do here, the daylight hurrying away to make way for the night. Atiyah settled the same way, her bellowing cries becoming snuffles and then sniffs and before long sleep had overtaken her. Tora knew she had to wean herself off Atiyah and take a backseat role in looking after her, but still she sent Yousra to visit her family and have a night off after her trying day. She'd talk to Rashid tomorrow about getting an extra carer then. He was busy with his friend tonight and, besides, for now she was happy to sit back and relax with the meal they'd had sent up to her and check her emails.

She smiled when she found one from Sally with the subject line I love you!

After she'd read the message, she was sniffing and there were tears in her eyes for the second time tonight. Steve was doing all the right things according to his test results and he was ready to be transferred to Germany. Sally had been able to tell the doctors to get the ball rolling.

They wouldn't waste any time now. If all went well and Steve could hang in there, Sally wrote, he'd be on his way within the next day or so towards the treatment that could save his life. And there were no promises, she said, being brave, but it was the only chance he had and they were staying positive and whatever happened, she owed Tora a debt she could never repay.

Happy news, Tora thought, blinking away the tears. The

very best kind of news. And she was glad of Rashid's deal now, for all the grief it had caused her, and for all the grief it would inevitably cause her when she had to return home.

It would be worth it if the treatment worked.

It would all be worth it.

'So what's she like, this half-sister of yours?' Zoltan asked, plucking grapes from a bunch on a platter. They were seated on low sofas in one of the palace reception rooms that had doors that opened onto the gardens so that the scent of frangipani wafted in.

'I don't really know,' Rashid said. 'She's a baby.' But then he thought about Tora leading him to Atiyah's cradle to look down upon the sleeping infant and felt a pang of pride. 'She's a cute little thing, though.'

'Huh,' said Zoltan. 'That's all you can say? Spoken like a man who hasn't had children yet. Just wait until you have your own. You won't be so vague about the details then. You'll be hanging out for that first smile and that first tooth.'

Rashid snorted. 'Dream on,' he said, because even if he was warming to the child, he wasn't about to go all gooey over her any time soon. Not like Tora at least, who had been so excited about Atiyah smiling.

'That's where you're wrong, brother,' Zoltan said, waving a grape between his thumb and forefinger for emphasis, 'An Emir needs an heir. So you don't want to wait too long—you're not getting any younger.' He popped the grape between his teeth and crunched down.

Rashid shook his head. Just because he'd had some kind of epiphany out at the oasis today, didn't mean he was looking to ensure there were an heir and a spare any time soon. 'Give me a break, Zoltan. One thing at a time.'

'Not a chance. Now you'll have to find yourself a wife. Last desert brother standing, but not for long. You don't have a choice any more. Your footloose and fancy-free playboy days are toast.'

It was all Rashid could do to stop from blurting the news that in actual fact he *was* married, just to shut his friend up. Because that would be a mistake and there would be no shutting Zoltan up once he learned that particular snippet of information. What was more, he'd be off and running, firing off messages to Bahir and Kadar before they got here, get their wives all excited in the process, and Rashid would never hear the end of it.

No, he had serious stuff to get done before he let that particular cat out of the bag. He didn't want them to know about Tora just yet. He didn't want them making a bigger deal out of it than it was. Let them find out in their own good time—but by then he'd be halfway to sending her home.

Although why that left him suddenly cold, he wasn't entirely sure.

'You make marriage sound such fun,' he said, suddenly grumpy, and not just because he knew for a fact that it wasn't fun and that in his case it was nothing more than the means to an end. 'Anyway,' he said, needing to change the subject, 'I didn't ask you here to talk about my love life. Let's get to work.'

Rashid stood on his terrace, his hands spread wide apart on the balustrade, looking up at the inky sky. Below in the gardens the fountains played and the birds settled in for the night, the world at peace.

While inside him his emotions clashed and raged in a war that had forgotten what peace was. It didn't seem to matter the decision he'd made today, or maybe his emotions clashed because of it.

Duty.

Self-doubt.

Fear.
Duty.
It always came back to duty.

His heart thumped like a drum, a tattoo cursing the ever-present, inescapable duty. His stomach squeezed tight and he inhaled the dark night air in response to the bite of pain. It didn't matter what he'd decided out in the desert today, his first session with Zoltan had given him no comfort. There was so much to do. So much he needed to learn. So many doubts about what was possible to best help this country and its people...

Fear.

He wasn't used to feeling fear.

He had never failed at anything he had put his hand to, but then he had made choices that reflected his desires and wants. He'd decided his path. He'd worked hard and acted on hunches and educated guesses and he'd been successful by taking calculated risks and when those hunches had paid off. But it had always been his choice to do those things and follow that path.

Never before had he been sucked into a bottomless pit from which there was no escaping and where there was no choice.

Duty.
Self-doubt.
Fear.

Together they tangled and churned until his gut felt battered and heaving and one thing emerged victorious from the mayhem, as if that one thing had been lying in wait, ready to step into the void.

Need.

Powerful and insistent, it rose up like a mushroom cloud that reached out to fill every part of him. He turned and looked along the terrace, towards her suite, to where the glow from her lamps spilled into puddles.

Tora.

Talking to her today had been the one thing that had let him make sense of the tangled thoughts in his mind when nothing else had. She had listened and understood. She had shown him the simple fun of paddling.

And he had repaid her by leaving her cold.

And without being aware that he'd made a decision, his feet started walking.

Towards the light.

Towards Tora.

She should be sleeping. She kept telling herself to put the book down, but she was reading a book about Qajaran, about its treasures and its colourful history and the wars and crusades that had touched its shores and crossed its desert borders, and she was fascinated. And being right here, in the Old Palace that had seen so much of what she was reading, brought it all to life.

Just one more chapter, she promised herself as she glanced at the clock and turned the page anyway.

She jumped at the soft rap on the glass, her heart giving a crazy leap in her chest so that she almost didn't hear when the tap came again. She slid from the bed, her feet cool on the marble tiles, and pulled on a robe, because, whoever it was, she wasn't going to be caught on the terrace in just her nightgown again.

'Tora,' she heard, and she didn't know whether to be worried or relieved when she recognised Rashid's voice. 'Are you awake?'

The door to the terrace was open to let in the breeze, but she stayed her side of the filmy curtain, just inside the room, an invisible barrier between them. 'What do you want?'

He shook his head as if he didn't know why he was here, standing outside her door in the middle of the night. 'I don't... No, nothing. I wanted to apologise for how things worked out tonight. For leaving you in the lurch when Zoltan arrived.'

'It's okay. I understand. Your friend would be wanting to catch up with you.'

He nodded. 'And,' he said, his lips pulling to one side as he struggled with the words, his eyes troubled, 'I just wanted to see you.'

Her heart tripped and her breath caught in her throat. Her mind told her it meant nothing—but her heart...her heart wanted to believe the words he had said, just a little. 'I had a good day today, thank you.'

'Good. I didn't have a chance to thank you. For your thoughts. I will speak to Kareem tomorrow.'

And she remembered that she'd wanted to talk to Rashid, too, about changing the arrangements for Atiyah, so that she wouldn't grow too fond of her, but that could wait, because right now the night air wore a velvet glove that stroked her skin, bringing with it the scent of him, warm and musky, masculine and spicy, much like Qajaran itself.

And she remembered another night, and her head on his shoulder, drinking in that scent, thinking it would never get old, that she would never get enough of it.

'What's it like,' he said suddenly into the silence, 'when a baby smiles?'

She blinked at the question, wondering where it had come from when this was a man for whom babies didn't seem to register. 'It's like sunshine in a hug,' she said. 'It's like the world lights up and wraps you in love.'

He nodded, but his eyes looked as conflicted as ever, as if he was warring with himself, and she wondered what he'd made of what she'd said or what he'd expected to hear. 'Good. I would like to see that. I won't keep you any longer.' He turned to leave, but he looked so tortured, this man who had the weight of Qajaran on his shoulders, that she couldn't bear him to go like that, so she touched his forearm.

'Rashid?'

He looked down at her hand as if it were a foreign object. 'Yes?'

She pulled herself up, and pressed her lips to his fevered skin, a kiss that was tender and sweet, a kiss designed to soothe rather than inflame. 'Thank you, for coming by,' she said, before letting go and drawing back into the relative safety of her suite. 'Goodnight.'

He was still too keyed up to sleep. Rashid lingered on the terrace under the soft dark sky lit with its sliver of moon and sprinkle of stars and breathed deeply of the night air, air that came scented with frangipani and the blossom of lemon and lime, the ache in his belly subsided for now, the factions raging inside him finding an uneasy truce.

Only the need remained undiminished.

Need for a woman who gentled away his fears merely by her presence and her own evocative perfume and the press of her lips gentle on his cheek. Need for a woman it had taken every ounce of his self-control not to pull her to him and forcibly satisfy.

The need—and something else he couldn't quite put his finger on.

He went to sleep dreaming of Tora and her honeyed voice that played in his mind over and over, so that he woke with it still in his head.

He asked Kareem when they met over breakfast if he knew it, a lullaby about oranges and apricots and fat pigeons. 'It seems familiar but I cannot work out where I have heard it before.'

Kareem regarded him solemnly, his eyes a little sad. 'You would have heard it, of course. It is a classic Persian lullaby, very popular, very beautiful. It is a song your mother used to sing to you when you were just a baby.'

Sensation skittered down his spine like spiders' legs. 'But my mother died when I was just a few months old. Surely I couldn't remember that?'

The older man shrugged. 'Perhaps your father sang it after she was gone. Who can say? But it is something left to you from your parents—a link to your past—something to be treasured.'

He sat back in his chair with his hand to his head. Treasured? For the life of him he couldn't picture himself with his father, let alone imagine his father singing him a lullaby. He might have believed it once, but not now. It didn't fit with a man who had hidden himself from his son for thirty years.

Kareem smiled sadly. 'He loved you, Rashid. I know that it is hard for you to believe, but, for better or for worse, he did what he had to do. As you, his son, have to do.'

Rashid sighed.

His father loved him? Why did he have such a hard time believing it?

'So when can I meet her?' Zoltan asked after a heavy morning going through protocols and affairs of state with Rashid and Kareem and the Council of Elders.

Rashid's first thought was of Tora. Her kiss had haunted him last night, as he had lain on his bed waiting for sleep to claim him, her kiss and the feel of her smooth fingers on his arm and her wide cognac eyes.

'Why do you want to meet her?'

'Well, she is your sister, isn't she? You don't have to keep her locked away in a cupboard somewhere. You do let her see the light of day sometimes, don't you?'

'Oh, Atiyah,' he said, struck by Zoltan's words, because once again Tora had said something similar.

'Who did you think I meant?' asked Zoltan, and his friend looked at him as if he thought he was losing it in the desert heat.

Maybe he was. He blinked. 'I'll send for her,' he said easily, because it was a good idea, because it meant he would see Tora again, and after last night's sweet encounter he yearned to.

But when Atiyah arrived, it was not Tora's arms that bore her but Yousra's instead, and he felt a piercing stab of disappointment.

'Oh, Rashid,' Zoltan said, 'what a beauty,' and he surprised the other man by taking the baby and holding her in front of him to look at her properly. Atiyah's dark eyes were wide and uncertain, the bottom lip of her little Cupid's-bow mouth ready to start quivering. But before it could, he had the child tucked into his arms and was sitting down on the sofa again, and Rashid blinked at the ease with which he handled the child. To him she was too small, too full of traps for the unwary. 'You are going to have your work cut out for you when she becomes a young woman.'

Was he? Something else to look forward to. Wonderful.

The baby started fussing and squirming but Zoltan remained unfazed and uncovered her tiny toes and stroked the bottom of her feet with his middle finger. Tiny feet, thought Rashid, looking on, struck by life in miniature.

'Are you ticklish, little one?' Zoltan said, and Atiyah's little legs started pumping, chuckles now interspersed with her complaints. For a while it looked as if Zoltan had the baby's measure, but soon her face became redder and more screwed up and the chuckles gave way to her cries.

'Whoa,' said Zoltan, admitting defeat as her cries became bellows. 'I think it's time you went to your big brother, little one.'

And before he could say no, his tiny sister had been deposited into his hands. He stared down at the squawking bundle in his lap, wondering at the weight and her energy and the power of her lungs.

His sister.

His blood.

Who looked nothing like she had when she'd been sleeping.

And his gut churned anew as he tried unsuccessfully to quieten her.

There was no quietening her. The baby screamed and no wonder. Because what did he have to offer her? He knew nothing of what a baby would need. He had no experience—nothing but the shred of a lullaby...

'Yousra!' he snapped to the young woman who was watching helplessly on. 'Take Atiyah. There is somewhere I have to be.'

Zoltan frowned as Yousra took the child. 'Don't we have the next meeting with the council coming up shortly?'

'I won't be long.'

Tora's blood spiked with heat when she saw the name pop into her inbox. She had half a mind to delete the message straight away but the subject header stalled her—Good news.

What would he think would be good news to her— unless he'd had a change of fortunes or mind and somehow managed to recover her funds? She opened the message.

Dear Cousin Vicky

An opportunity's just come up to make some quick money, so obviously I thought of you!

I'm expecting some funds to come in and meanwhile they're promised elsewhere. I need half a million dollars fast, just to tide me over, and wondered if you might mortgage your flat for a couple of weeks to help me out? It's only temporary until those funds come in, and the good news is I'll be able to pay you a one-hundred-thousand-dollar fee guaranteed.

Let me know ASAP.
Your cousin
Matt
PS Like your folks used to say, blood is thicker than water after all!

Good news? Tora stared incredulously at the screen. Her cousin must think her stupid. First he screwed her out of her inheritance and then he wanted her home? Pigs might fly. And as for blood being thicker than water—after the way he'd betrayed the trust of her parents and of her, he was no family to her at all.

She was about to hit the delete button and send the message to the trash where it belonged. 'ASAP' be damned—let him wait for an answer that would never come.

And then she had a better idea. Much better.

So she hit Reply and changed the subject header to Better News! and started typing.

Dear Matt...

She added kisses at the end and then deleted them. No point laying it on too thick. She'd just hit Send with a satisfying click when another message pinged into her inbox. This time she was eager to open it.

We're on our way! Sally wrote. Next stop, Germany!

Yes! She fired off a quick 'good luck' reply and this time added plenty of kisses before she sent it off with a sigh. At least that was going right.

'Tora,' she heard Rashid bellowing from somewhere inside her suite. 'Tora!' He appeared at the doorway to the terrace. 'What are you doing out here?'

'You couldn't just knock like a normal person?' she said drily, wondering where the fire was.

'Why didn't you bring Atiyah when I asked for her?'

'Because you summoned Atiyah, not me. And Yousra is perfectly capable of delivering a child for your inspection. She did bring you Atiyah?'

'Yes, but that's not the point. You should have brought her.'

'Why?'

'Because you're her nanny. She's your responsibility.'

'No, Rashid. She's *your* responsibility, but you like to pass it off to me and that's a bad thing.'

'Why?'

'Because she's becoming dependent on me. She's bonding. Yesterday when I came home from our day out, Yousra was exhausted from trying to settle her.'

'She started screaming when Yousra brought her down.'

They heard her coming, still crying as Yousra entered the apartments. 'I'm sorry, Sheikha,' the young woman said as Tora went to meet her, taking the child and hugging her to her chest.

'It's okay,' Tora said, to both the baby and Yousra as Atiyah grabbed her hair in her tiny hands and her tears soaked her gown. 'It's okay.' Tora sent Yousra off to fetch some warm milk as the baby snuffled into her, her cries slowly abating.

'You see,' she said, speaking softly to Rashid as she swayed. 'I had to send her with Yousra as she's become too attached to me. You need to get more carers or take care of her yourself.'

He looked taken aback. 'But if she feels safe with you—'

'I'm leaving, Rashid. Going home as soon as our marriage can be dissolved. Or had you forgotten?'

He shook his head. 'So stay longer if Atiyah needs you. Do you need to go back straight away?'

'Stay for how long? And then what? She grows even more dependent on me. How is that going to work? That's no kind of solution.'

'How much would it take to make you change your mind?'

She sighed as Yousra returned with the milk. 'You know, Rashid, there are some things in the world that money can't fix.'

'Then show me how to do that,' he growled as Tora sat down to feed Atiyah. 'Show me how to hold her so she doesn't cry.'

Tora blinked up at him. 'Do you really mean it?'

'Of course, I mean it. She is my sister. How do you think it makes me look if I do not know how to hold her?'

And Tora looked down at the infant, still snuffling, her eyes red-rimmed and puffy from crying. She could say no now, to save Atiyah any more distress, but that would be fair to neither of them. So instead she waited until the baby was a little more relaxed, her eyelids fluttering closed as she drank. 'Then sit down and I'll pass her over to you and maybe she won't notice.'

Neither of them really believed that, but Rashid did as she suggested and Tora gently passed the baby over. Atiyah instantly jolted into awareness, her eyes wide open, her feeding stopped as she worked out what had changed in her world. 'It's okay, Atiyah, you're safe,' Tora crooned, even as she tried to show him how better to cradle the infant by relaxing and softening his arms.

Atiyah wasn't convinced and in the end they both conceded defeat, letting Tora take her back.

'I can't stay,' he said. 'I have to go.'

Tora nodded, rocking the child in her arms a little as

Atiyah resumed feeding, keeping her eyes open this time for any more tricks. 'I know,' she said. 'It will get easier, I promise,' and she couldn't help smiling as he left, because Rashid had tried.

Tora's words stayed with him as he made his way back through the palace to the meeting on foreign policy with a heavy heart made heavier by the fact that nothing seemed to work with Atiyah, even when he wanted it to. He'd tried. By God, he'd tried to do all the things Tora had told him, to relax and yet hold her securely so that she'd felt safe, to sway her gently without jerking, to comfort her.

'There are some things in the world that money can't fix.' Didn't he know it? She was preaching to the converted there. There was no amount of money he could throw at the predicament he was in and make it go away.

But surely her case was different. Why did she have to go? If she really cared about Atiyah and didn't want to upset her, surely she could agree to stay a bit longer. She didn't have to rush off. At least to give him enough time to get used to his new responsibilities.

Besides, he was intrigued by her, this woman who could be temptress, Madonna, businesswoman and even comforter. As she'd comforted him last night when he'd gone to her room with her quiet words and her sympathetic eyes.

And he didn't want her to go.

Not yet.

'Ah,' said Kareem coming out of the meeting room he was just heading into. 'We have been waiting for you to begin.'

And Rashid knew what she'd said was right. No amount of money in the world could help him now.

Tora and Yousra were sitting in the Pavilion of Mahabbah the next morning where it was still deliciously cool alongside the lake, a soft breeze stirring the curtains. Atiyah lay on a rug on her stomach on the floor attempting mini push-ups on her chubby arms. Tora was keeping out of her line of sight, but every now and then the baby would look around until she found her before resuming her exercises, assuring herself that, yes, Tora was still there. She was so alert and way too knowing for such a small bundle, Tora thought, and she was just about to disappear for a walk around the garden to see if she might forget, even for a little while, when they heard the voices, young and older.

Through the gossamer curtains Tora could see the three women, two striking dark-haired beauties and one blonde and equally stunning, heading towards the pavilion with a clutch of children in tow.

'It looks like we have visitors,' she said to Yousra. 'Do you know who they are?'

'No,' the other woman said, watching their progress. 'I've never seen them before.'

Tora forgot about hiding and scooped up Atiyah from the floor, the child gumming at her fist as the women hovered at the door. 'We're sorry to intrude, but we were told we'd find Atiyah here. We couldn't wait to meet her.'

'This is Atiyah,' said Tora, holding the baby in her lap.

'Oh, she's gorgeous,' said the first, coming closer. 'You must excuse us. We've been so excited since we heard the news that Rashid had a baby sister. We're the wives of Rashid's desert brothers—his good friends—and we've arrived for the coronation. I'm Aisha, wife to Zoltan, who has been here advising Rashid, and this is my sister Marina, wife to Bahir, and Amber, wife to Kadar. And these,' she said, gesturing to the active group around her, 'are our children.'

'It's lovely to meet you,' said Tora, introducing herself, feeling a little overwhelmed but delighted too that Atiyah would have more distractions over the coming days.

There were three toddlers and two children a little older, a girl and a boy. Other children would be the best entertainment of all. Already she was watching them eagerly, smiling when they came to say hello to her, kicking her little legs with delight.

'One more baby for the desert brothers tribe,' laughed the second dark-haired woman called Marina who was kneeling down and holding Atiyah's hands. 'And now the children have an aunty. Hello, little Atiyah,' she said with a broad smile, earning one back from the infant.

'You're Australian,' said the blonde woman called Amber, who settled herself down on the sofa next to Tora, a sizeable bump under her dress. 'Me, too. Where are you from?'

'Sydney,' Tora said.

'I'm from Melbourne.'

'And now you live—somewhere around here?'

'Kadar and I live mostly in Istanbul. We were married six months ago.' She smiled. 'It's kind of a long story.' She patted her stomach and her smile widened. 'We're expecting our own first baby in a few months. But how did you end up here, looking after Atiyah?'

It was Tora's turn to smile. 'That's kind of a long story, too. But I'm only here temporarily. I'll be going home soon.'

'Oh,' said Aisha, exchanging glances with the other women, 'for a moment I thought—I was hoping...'

'We were all hoping,' her sister said. 'As soon as we saw you, we were hoping. Rashid needs a good woman, and we thought, maybe he has found one at last.'

'He's the only desert brother left,' added Amber, 'and now he will need a woman by his side, more than ever.'

Tora said nothing, just bounced Atiyah on her knee, silently cursing this stupid marriage and the position it put her in, because it wasn't her place to say anything. Just then the peacocks put in an appearance and distracted everyone and the conversation changed direction and Tora could breathe again and enjoy being in the company of other women.

They drank honey tea and laughed and talked of their children and their husbands. They were bright and beautiful like butterflies in the garden and Tora found herself wishing she could be one of them, but that would mean marrying Rashid for real.

'Forgive me for interrupting,' Kareem said, appearing at the doorway to the pavilion with a gracious bow, 'but His Excellency would like to see you privately, Sheikha Victoria.'

Aisha's ears pricked up first. 'Sheikha?'

'I thought that's what he said,' Marina said.

Amber was staring at her strangely. 'But wouldn't that mean...?'

Tora shook her head, excusing herself as she swept past them, her face ablaze with heat. 'It's not what you think...'

'I've been thinking,' said Rashid a few minutes later, rubbing his chin as he paced the Persian rug in his big study, 'now that my friends are here with their wives and families, we need to be careful about them getting the wrong idea about us.'

He paced the other way. 'I know my friends and they'll blow it out of all proportion so I've decided it's best if I ask Kareem to be careful how he addresses you and I tell them that you're simply filling in for the role of my consort for the coronation. I think it's better that they don't know about the marriage at all.'

He suddenly stopped pacing and looked up at her, his eyes panicked. 'What do you think?'

Tora swallowed as she stood there, her fingers tangling as she selected her words carefully. 'I think it might actually be a bit late for that.'

CHAPTER TWELVE

'What?' Zoltan's head swivelled from Aisha to Rashid when the women joined them before lunch. 'You're already married? You sly dog! And you made out like it was the furthest thing from your mind.'

'But it is!'

'So how does that work when you're already married?'

'Because it's not a real marriage!'

'I want to know how come you didn't invite your best friends?' demanded Bahir.

'Yeah,' Kadar said. 'We invited you to our weddings.'

'Right, you really want to know why I didn't invite you to my fake marriage? Maybe it's because Kareem married us in the plane on the way over here. Sorry, but when you're flying at forty thousand feet it makes it a bit awkward to get the wedding invitations out.'

'But when we were talking before, you acted as if you weren't married at all,' said Zoltan. 'Like anything like that happening was years away.'

'Did any of you guys hear me? It's not a real marriage!' He gave a long sigh. He'd known this would happen. He'd damn well known it. 'Look, I had to marry someone, in order to adopt Atiyah.'

'Why did you have to adopt Atiyah?' asked Marina. 'She's your sister, isn't she?'

'Yes, but our father was supposed to have died in a helicopter crash thirty years ago and the people believe that and— Oh, what the hell does it matter why? Kareem said she had to be adopted and in order to do that, I had to be married. End of story.'

'Hardly!' snorted Bahir. 'We're just getting to the good stuff. So this woman volunteered to marry you to get you out of a tight spot, did she?'

'Tora,' said Aisha. 'Her name is Tora. I like her.'

'Me, too,' said her sister. 'And she's gorgeous.'

'She's Australian,' chimed in Amber with a grin. 'What's not to love?'

'Agreed,' said Kadar, giving his wife a squeeze as he kissed her cheek. 'This Tora must be some kind of a masochist to volunteer to marry you. What was in it for her?'

'What do you mean, what was in it for her?'

'What, she did it out of the goodness of her heart?'

'I bet it wasn't for his bedside manner.'

'Maybe it was,' suggested Kadar.

'Okay, okay,' said Rashid, who'd had enough, holding up one hand to silence his friends. 'So there may have been a financial inducement involved. We made a deal. So what?'

'Alas, poor Rashid,' Zoltan said with his hand over his heart. 'Unloved and unwanted, left on the shelf, the only one of the desert brothers who actually had to resort to paying a woman to get her to marry him.'

'Give me a break,' growled Rashid. 'Don't you guys make out you wrote the guidebook on romance—we all know that's a lie.'

'But none of us had to break out the chequebook.'

Aisha looked around. 'Why isn't Tora here? You did invite her to have lunch with us, didn't you?'

He rolled his eyes.

'You didn't!' said Marina, eyes wide with accusation. 'Don't tell me you treat her like the hired help?'

'She *is* the hired help.' But that wasn't true either, he

had to concede. She was more than that. Much more. He just didn't know what to do about it. 'Anyway, I did invite her to lunch and she declined—said she didn't want to get in the way of a desert-brothers-and-their-families reunion. Is that good enough for you?'

Nobody else thought so, which was why one minute later he was on his way to insist Tora join them for lunch.

Tora turned off her tablet still smiling. Sally had emailed with the news that Steve was installed at the clinic and that treatment had commenced and to keep her fingers and toes crossed.

Good news. She sent up a silent prayer. At least something was going right at last.

'Excuse me, Tora,' Yousra said. 'His Excellency is here to see you.'

Tora braced herself. She'd known there'd be a fallout from his friends discovering about the marriage, although for the life of her she couldn't believe how he had ever thought he'd manage to keep them from finding out.

She expected anger. What she didn't expect was him insisting she join him and his desert brothers and their wives for lunch.

'Are you sure?' she said. 'It won't give them the wrong idea?'

'They've already got the wrong idea. How about we prove them wrong and show them there's nothing going on? Besides,' he added, 'it seems you're a hit with the women. They threatened that if I failed to bring you back, then they would come and bodily drag you to lunch themselves.'

She laughed. 'In that case, how can I refuse?'

'Did you want to bring Atiyah?'

Tora shook her head. 'Yousra will have no problem. Atiyah had so much fun with the children this morning, she'll probably sleep for a week. I think the children coming is the best thing that could have happened.'

'Speaking of Atiyah,' he said as they walked down the passageway, past fabulous treasures, brightly coloured urns and dishes set in recesses in the walls, 'have you thought any more about staying on? At least until you can give me some more lessons in handling her.'

Tora sucked in a lungful of air. She hadn't for a moment believed he'd been serious when he'd suggested it and no, she hadn't given it any more thought. She couldn't stay longer and he couldn't expect her to. It wasn't fair on Atiyah and it certainly wasn't fair on her.

As it was, she was struggling to remember all the reasons she shouldn't care about Rashid. She was only a temporary fixture but the longer she was here, the more she liked him. And she didn't want to feel that way, not when it would make it harder to forget him when she was gone.

Not when it would be easier to resist him...

'Rashid—'

'No,' he said, stopping her just shy of the doors beyond which his friends waited, 'don't say anything now. Take your time to think about it. I do want the best for Atiyah, even if it doesn't seem like it. I'm learning, Tora, what she needs. Maybe too slowly for your liking, but I am determined to do right by her.'

He took her hand then, wrapping it between his own, warming her skin as his eyes were warm and tugging on her heart.

'Just promise me you'll think about it. I know it's asking a lot but I won't expect you to stay for nothing. We can work something out.

'What I want now is for Atiyah to feel secure, and she feels secure with you. So will you think about it? Will you think about what it would take to make you stay—even just a little longer?'

Tora looked up at this man, who once she thought was hard and unflinching, arrogant and overbearing, but who she knew to be trying his best.

'I'll think about it,' she promised, although she knew that whatever it would take to make her stay was nothing to how much it would ultimately cost.

'Finally,' came the cry from inside when Rashid opened the door. 'We were about to send out a posse.'

'Welcome, Tora, come and join us,' said another. 'At last, some adult company for you. It will make a nice change from Rashid, I am sure.'

Tora smiled and looked at Rashid, who was scowling. 'My desert brothers,' he said, introducing the three men, 'whom I love with my life. Apart from the times I want to kill them, that is.'

Coronation day dawned pink and clear and just about perfect, he supposed, if you didn't have a spiked cannonball rolling around in your gut.

Rashid rose early, knowing there was no putting it off, watching the layers of the early-morning sky peel away from where he took coffee on his terrace, pink giving way to blue, just as peace would give way to madness.

The day would be long—interminable at times, no doubt—a breakfast with foreign dignitaries and officials and then a long tortuous motorcade through the city to show off their new Emir before a public feast in Qajaran City's biggest square. Then while the official party headed to the formal coronation ceremony, the gates of the Fun Palace would be thrown open to the public, the ceremony relayed on big screens, before a state dinner for six hundred, all topped off with cannon fire and fireworks.

He was exhausted already.

Exhausted and still more than a little daunted.

His cup rattled against his saucer when he went to pick it up and he lifted his trembling hand to inspect it.

God, what was wrong with him? He had studied the books. He had read the histories and pored over enough economic papers and reports to sink a ship, he had listened to the advice of Kareem and Zoltan and the Council of Elders, and still he wondered what he was doing here.

Duty.

There came a knock at the door and Kareem entered with two assistants bearing the robes he would wear today. 'Excellency, it is time to prepare.'

He was dressed and taking his last few breaths as a free man when he heard the soft knock, but it wasn't Kareem this time. It came from the connecting door to Tora's apartments, the door he had never opened although temptation in the shape of a seductress lay just the other side. The door opened and a soft voice called his name, a voice that, to his fevered mind, sounded as cool as a waterfall. And then she entered, and for a moment he forgot the pain and the fever and the damnable tremble in his hands, because he had never seen anyone more beautiful.

She was dressed in a golden robe, exquisitely embroidered, with gold trim similar to his own, and with long sweeping cuffs on the sleeves and a gossamer-thin silk shawl over her hair that framed her face and floated like a cloud as she moved. She looked like something out of a medieval fantasy.

His next fantasy.

'Rashid,' she said, and her eyes opened wide as they took in the sight of him dressed in his unfamiliar robes, the first time she had seen him dressed this way. She blinked and seemed to gather herself. 'I just wanted to wish you well today,' she said, 'before it all gets crazy.'

As they both knew it would.

He nodded, because his jaw set too tight to talk and the spiked cannonball in his gut rolled and stuck its spikes in his innards, and he had to take himself to the window to ease the pressure.

For her gesture, her simple act of kindness, had almost brought him undone.

She understood a lot for a woman who wouldn't be here if he hadn't needed to adopt Atiyah and coerced her into a convenient marriage. Because she had become so much more than simply a convenient wife. Her suggestion of opening the Fun Palace to the public had led to its inclusion in the proceedings today, an inclusion he had been informed had been met by the people with huge anticipation and great excitement. He was sharing some of the riches of the state and it was he who was being lauded for it.

She understood a lot more than he had given her credit for.

She would be gone soon.

And his breath caught, as the pointed barbs of that cannonball stuck their points into his raw and wounded flesh anew.

Tora had never seen Rashid in robes—had never imagined that a man who was so at home and looked so good in western clothes could own a look so traditional and yet he did. His snowy white robes and the tunic beneath were lined with gold trim, his headpiece bound with a band of black that would be replaced with a band of gold, in the final step of the ceremony that would make him Emir.

Tall and broad-shouldered, his skin looking as if it had been burnished by the sun against so much white, he looked magnificent, as if he had been born of the desert sands—born to rule—and yet Tora could see the battle going on behind his features, could see the slight tremble in his hands that he was at pains to disguise, and she ached for him.

'You have no need to be afraid,' she said softly.

'What?' He turned sharply.

'You have no reason to fear.'

'Is that what you think? That I'm afraid?' But his voice lacked the conviction of his words and he knew it by the way he dropped his head and turned away again.

'You're strong,' she said behind him. 'You're intelligent and just and a good man, and you want to do the best for the people of Qajaran. They are lucky to have you.'

He heaved in air, and his words, when they came, might have been blasted raw by the desert sands and the hot wind. 'I was not brought up for this.'

'But it's in your blood. Your father—'

'How is finding you're suddenly responsible for the welfare and futures of millions of people in your blood?'

'You can do this, Rashid,' she said, more sternly than she'd planned. 'You would not be here if you did not believe that. Nobody who knows you, nobody here in this palace does not believe that.'

'How can you—someone who I have known for the tiniest fraction of my life—say that?'

'Because I have seen how hard you work. I have seen that a weaker man would walk away and that a greedy man would stay even if the task was beyond him. You are not like that. You can do this, and you will prevail and you will be a good Emir.'

Kareem interrupted them with a knock on the door. 'Excellency, Sheikha, if you are ready?'

She glanced at him one more time before nodding and saying she would check on Yousra and Atiyah, and had turned to go when he caught her hand before she could disappear. 'Thank you for those words. They mean more than you know.' He squeezed her hand tightly in his before he let her go. 'I just hope you are right.'

She smiled up at him in a way that warmed him from the inside out in a way the sun had never done. 'I know I am,' she said, and her words and her warmth gave him the courage to believe it.

It was exhausting but it was exciting, too. Tora sat alongside Rashid on a sofa under the shade of a tent that had been set up on a dais before a huge square that was full of the longest tables she had ever seen. They had breakfasted with the foreign dignitaries at the palace and now it was the turn of the people to meet their soon-to-be Emir before they returned to the palace for the coronation proper. Bright banners in the Qajarese colours fluttered in the air, competing with the cheerful holiday colours worn by the women and even some of the men. There was a party atmosphere as the feasting got under way, musicians and dancers providing the entertainment, and the sound of laughter was everywhere.

And not even the knowledge that theirs was a marriage of convenience, and that soon she would be heading home and no longer the sheikha, could not diminish her delight in being part of the proceedings. For now, legally at least, she was the sheikha and she would do the best job she could, even if her stomach was a mass of butterflies. But this wasn't about her, it was about Rashid, and the coronation of a new Emir, and it was a once-in-a-lifetime experience and she was going to lap up every single moment of it.

And then a young girl climbed from her seat and approached the dais, in her hands a posy of flowers, her eyes wide and a little in awe as she stood waiting at the steps. Kareem leaned low over Tora's shoulder. 'She has flowers to welcome the new sheikha, if you so wish.'

'For me?' Today was supposed to be all about Rashid,

she had thought. But still she smiled and held out her hand to urge her up and the little girl smiled back and climbed the stairs and bowed before handing over the flowers and uttering something in Qajarese.

'What did she say?'

Kareem leaned low again. 'She wished you many sons and daughters.'

'Oh,' Tora said, suddenly embarrassed, before adding *thank you* in Qajarese, one of the few words that she'd learned, feeling guilty because now she wasn't just observing the proceedings; she was a participant in them.

There were more children after that, and more blessings and more flowers, until their table was transformed into a sea of flowers, and Tora smiled at all comers, girl or boy, and their faces lit up when she thanked them.

She glanced across at Rashid at one stage and felt a sizzle down her spine when she found him watching her, his gaze thoughtful and filled with something that almost looked like respect.

Rashid watched her accept another bunch of flowers, touching her fingers to the child's face as she thanked her, and the girl skipped back to where her family were sitting, almost luminescent with delight. Tora was a stranger to this pomp and ceremony as much as he was, an observer caught up in a world not her own, but you wouldn't know it.

She was a natural with the children just as she was a constant for him, always at his side, looking calm and serene and so beautiful that his heart ached. And it was hot and there were hours to go before they could escape, and she so easily could have resented having to take part in the ceremony at all when she was no real wife of his, but she made it look easy.

She made him think anything was possible.

He could do much worse for a wife.

And later, when they were back at the palace during the coronation, when Kareem removed his black headband and lifted the gold *igal* to replace it, it was her words from this morning that he remembered. *'You're strong... You will be a good Emir.'*

Kareem then uttered the ancient words to install him and placed the crown on his head and it was done. He was the Emir.

Cheers and applause broke out across the banquet room, the loudest coming from the quarter where his desert brothers and their families were sitting, and he smiled as he let go a breath he hadn't realised he'd been holding.

He turned to her and saw the moisture there in her eyes—*the tears she'd shed for him*—and he was moved beyond measure.

But before he could tell her, before he could thank her for this morning's words and for her quiet strength today, first there was another feast, another party complete with cannon fire and fireworks, a display above the palace that was echoed all over the city and in the tiny desert and mountain villages of Qajaran.

It was after midnight by the time the festivities wound down. Yousra had taken Atiyah back to her bed hours ago—a day of formalities interspersed with playing with the children had worn her out—and now Rashid walked silently beside Tora towards their suites.

And it seemed to Tora that the very air around them was shimmering, there had been so much energy generated by the celebrations of today, energy that now turned the air electric as they moved, into currents charged by every swish of robe against robe, every slap of leather against the marble floor a metronome, beating out the time she had left.

And all she knew was she didn't want this night to end. She didn't want this feeling to end—this feeling of being at peace with Rashid, of being part of his life...an important part...if only for a day. She wanted to preserve the magic of this moment and hold it precious to her for ever.

For soon her time in Qajaran would be over. Soon she would be back in Sydney in her black skirt and buttoned-up shirt and there would be no more robes of silk to slide against her skin, no more frangipani on the air.

No more Rashid.

Her heart grew tight in her chest.

He was nothing to her really. A roll in the hay and then a quick buck—a deal made with the devil—with plenty of grief along the way. He was nothing to her—and yet her heart had swelled in her chest when he was crowned, she'd been so very proud.

Nothing to her?

And her heart tripped over itself in its rush to tell her she was a liar.

All too soon, it seemed, they were at the door that led to her apartments and she turned and looked up at him, so handsome in his robes, his features a play of dark and shadow against the stark white, the gold *igal* on his head gleaming in the low light. 'Thank you for seeing me to my rooms.'

He shook his head. 'It is you who deserves thanking, Tora. What you said to me this morning...' He trailed off, searching for the words, and she put a finger to his lips.

'I didn't say anything you didn't already know. Maybe you just needed to hear them.'

He caught her hand and pressed it hard against his mouth. 'You are a remarkable woman, Tora.'

'No, Rashid.'

'Yes, you know it's true. From the moment you arrived, you have impressed everyone you have met.

'Today, you were the star of the show, charming everyone from the tiniest child to the most important dignitary. I know our hasty marriage was foisted upon you and unwanted, but you have been one of the highlights of my return to Qajaran.'

'We had a deal, Rashid, remember? I got something out of it, too. The money—it helped a friend of mine out at a tough time.'

'It was nothing compared to all you've done. I owe you, Tora. I don't know how I can possibly repay you.'

And she knew that the moment was now, that if she wanted this night to continue she would have to be the one to make it so.

She looked up at him, at his dark eyes and his beautiful tortured features, and knew that when she left she would be leaving a part of herself right here in Qajaran.

Her heart.

'Make love with me, Rashid.'

CHAPTER THIRTEEN

THE GROWL RUMBLED up from low in his throat. But then words wouldn't come close to how he was feeling right now. He swept her into his arms and pressed his lips to hers before he carried her through to his suite where he scattered coloured cushions in all directions with one hand before he laid her reverentially in the centre of his bed.

There was no rushing as there had been that first night together. No stripping of clothes separately before they came together. This time Rashid undressed her as if he were opening a gift, taking his time to expose each part of her skin, worshipping it with his lips and his mouth— the hennaed patterns of her hands and feet, the insides of her elbows and the backs of her knees—until she was quivering with desire and need before he'd even slipped her golden *abaya* over her head.

Breath hissed through his teeth when he looked down on her. 'You're beautiful,' he told her with his words and with his adoring eyes, and warmth bloomed inside her. She felt beautiful when he looked at her that way.

He shed his robes and turned from desert ruler into her ruler. Tonight she was his kingdom and his most loyal subject. Tonight she was his queen. Tonight she was his, utterly and completely, and he gave her everything in return.

They made slow, sweet love, long into the night. Making love, she thought, not sex this time, for that tiny seed of a connection had grown into something more, something richer and more powerful.

Love.

And the thought simultaneously terrified and thrilled her, but tonight it seemed so right. She loved him.

And when he followed her into ecstasy and she heard him cry out her name on his lips, she knew he must love her, too, even just a little.

He pulled her close and kissed her and it didn't matter that he was sleeping like the dead less than a minute later. In just one night, he'd given her more than she could have ever wished for.

'I love you,' she whispered, testing the words, touching his lips with hers, before she snuggled closer and closed her eyes, still smiling.

There was a noise from beyond the interconnecting door. A cry. *Atiyah.* Tora listened in the dark, waiting, and a few seconds later came another cry, more insistent this time. Tora strained to hear Yousra's footfall on the tiled floor but heard nothing and Atiyah was working herself up to full throttle now.

Beside her Rashid slept on. He would be exhausted after the strain of the coronation and the physical excesses that followed. She should leave it to Yousra but she didn't want Rashid to be woken, so she rose from the bed, pulling on Rashid's oversized robe, and slipping into her suite.

She scooped Atiyah from her cot and held her to her chest. 'What's wrong, little one? What's the matter?'

Yousra appeared looking ill with dark shadows under her eyes and Tora sent her straight back to bed. Rashid would have to find another carer to share the load now.

Tora checked the baby's nappy and made sure there was nothing pressing in her clothes or bedding. A nightmare, she guessed, just something that spooked her in her sleep. The baby whimpered and snuffled against her chest and she massaged her back and started singing the lullaby she liked to sing to Atiyah. Eventually the little fingers of the fist holding on so tightly to her robe finally relaxed as she drifted back to sleep.

'Where did you learn that song?'

She started and turned, the baby still in her arms, to find him standing there, a towel lashed low on his hips. 'You're awake.'

'That song,' he said. 'It's beautiful. How do you know it?'

'I learnt it at the child-care centre where I worked. We had children whose families came from all over the world and we tried to learn songs from most of the major languages, even though we were never quite sure of the words.'

'Did you know it was Persian?'

She looked up at him. 'I knew it was Middle Eeastern. Why do you ask?'

'Because I've heard it before. Apparently my mother used to sing it to me. And maybe my father, too. I'd forgotten it until I heard you singing it to Atiyah, that first night on the plane.'

She stilled at his side, her heart going out to him. She couldn't begin to imagine how it must feel—the pain on discovering your parent had been alive all those years you'd thought him dead. The betrayal and the hurt would be almost too much to bear.

'Your father must have loved you a lot,' she said.

He sniffed. 'How do you figure that?'

'Because he left you Atiyah,' she said, trying to find some way of soothing his pain. 'I read that her name means gift. He left you questions without answers, I know, but he left you Atiyah, and the gift of joy and love as well, if you will only see it. He must have loved you to have entrusted her in your care.'

He blinked and reached out a hand to touch Atiyah's curls.

She watched his hand, saw the moment man connected with sleeping child, saw wonder on his face in the low lamp light, and felt a rush of joy. Baby steps, she thought, it would take one baby step at a time. But in time, she knew, he would learn to love Atiyah as he should.

She kissed the baby on the head and tucked her back into her cradle. 'Come,' she said to Rashid, and led him back to bed.

'It's strange,' he said, thinking in the dark, amazed at her wisdom. 'I feel like I know you, and yet I know nothing about you.'

She shrugged in his arms. 'There's not a lot to tell. I grew up in Sydney and became a child-care worker. And then, like I told you before, when my friend Sally and her husband opened the business, I joined Flight Nanny. End of story really.'

'What about family? Pets? Favourite colour?'

'Orange,' she said, with a smile. 'No pets. I'm away from home too much.'

'How did your parents die?'

'It was a glider crash, three years ago now. Dad was piloting when they collided with another glider and lost a wing. They were too close to the ground to have time to parachute out.'

He pulled her close, pressed his lips to her forehead. 'It must have been hard to lose them both together.'

'Yeah, and there are days when it's still hard. But overall, it gets easier with time. I was lucky enough to have them both until I was in my twenties. And I know it sounds a cliché, but it makes me feel better knowing they died doing something they both loved. Dad used to say you can never be freer than in the sky. I like to think of them soaring somewhere in the sky together.'

He squeezed her shoulders. 'Did you have any other family to help you, then?'

'I have a sprinkling of cousins but they're mostly all interstate so I hardly ever see them. Oh, except for one who lives in Sydney. But we're—well, we're not close.'

'Why's that?'

'Matt let me down badly over something.' Absently she ran her fingers through the coarse hair of his chest. 'I'm finished with him now. Sally's more family than any of them, really.'

'I'd be lost without my brothers, too. But then, they're not real brothers. Maybe that's what makes them special to us.'

'Maybe.' She squirmed and rolled over, as if the topic made her too uncomfortable. 'You know, can we talk about something else?'

'I've got a better idea,' he said, liking the way her bottom wiggled so provocatively against him and feeling his body react accordingly. 'Maybe we should *do* something else.'

'Oh,' she said, when she caught on. 'I like the way you think.'

'And I like the way you do this...' He pulled her astride him and handed her a condom, liking, too, the way her eyes widened appreciatively as she realised how aroused he already was and took him in hand. He cupped one breast and ran a palm up her thigh while her fingers worked their magic on him as slowly she rolled the condom down his hard length. She gasped when his thumb grazed her inner lips.

'Oh, my,' she said, her job complete, but not her enjoyment as his fingers explored her slick folds. 'You do make it hard for a girl to concentrate on a task.'

'Maybe,' he said as he lifted her hips over him and positioned himself at her core, 'this might make it easier?'

And he pulled her all the long way down on him until he was seated deep inside her and she was stretched up like a cat, her back arched, all curves and sleekness above him such that he could not resist running his hand up over her smooth, firm flesh.

'Oh, yes,' she said on a sigh as her muscles let him go enough to lift herself from him until she was at his very tip, 'I think I can concentrate on this,' before she lost herself as she plunged down on him again.

'Stay here in Qajaran,' he said in between breaths as he brushed her hair from her face as they lay side by side waiting for their heart rates to return to normal. 'There is no need to go home yet.'

'Atiyah is settling,' she said, relishing the tickle of his fingers on her skin. 'She is becoming more used to Yousra and her new surroundings. Find her another carer and you will not need me soon.'

'I'm not asking you to stay for Atiyah's sake,' he said. 'I'm asking you for mine.'

And like one of the bursts of fireworks she'd witnessed against tonight's sky, hope bloomed bright and beautiful in her chest.

Could it mean that he was feeling something for her, as she felt for him? Was it possible that this crazy marriage could turn out to have a fairy-tale ending after all?

'I have my work...' she said, because a crazy idea still had to be met with a rational mind and she would be leaving Sally in the lurch at the worst possible time.

'I wouldn't expect you to drop everything and walk away empty-handed.'

'It's not about money.'

'No, but money can make problems easier to sort out,'

he said, and she thought about the money that had got Sally and Steve to treatment in Germany.

'I guess that's true.'

'We'll work something out,' he said, kissing her brow.

'I haven't said I'll stay yet.'

'You haven't said you won't.'

Rashid left Tora in his bed with a smile on his face. It was perfect. She was perfect. When he'd agreed to come to Qajaran, doubt had been foremost in his mind. Need he do this, could he do this? And he'd decided to stay, and a lot of it was all down to Tora being here, right beside him all the way. When he'd been consumed by doubt, she'd been the one who'd convinced him he could be the leader Qajaran needed.

And the thought that she was leaving filled him with dread. He didn't want her gone. He wanted her to stay. More than that, when it all came down to it, he *needed* her to stay.

It was a strange feeling, this need. He'd never needed anyone in his life before, and if there was one thing his father's sudden and short-lived blip back into his life had reinforced in him, it was that he didn't need anyone else. That he was right to rely on his own devices and his desert brothers.

He knew for a fact his desert brothers would never betray him.

He'd never needed anybody else.

Until Tora.

His heart beat a little faster in his chest as he remembered how she'd looked when he'd left her. Sleep and sex tousled, her hair in wild disarray, and with a smile just for him, a smile that lit up his world.

He smiled to himself, even as he headed to work. Like the day of the ceremony, today had been declared a public holiday for everyone. Everyone, that was, who didn't happen to be the Emir or his Grand Vizier who both had work to do. He would make time later to see off Bahir and Kadar and their wives and children, who were heading off to Istanbul together. Zoltan would join him for some final talks this afternoon, before he and Aisha and the twins returned to Al-Jirad.

His thoughts returned to Tora and how he might get her to stay. The people would be happy, they clearly loved her as their sheikha, and so would his desert brothers and their wives. But he would be happier than all of them, because he wanted and needed her right there by his side.

His footsteps faltered on the marble tiles as a thunderbolt jagged through him.

Was this what his brothers always talked about, when they had found a woman to share their lives with? Was this what love felt like? Was Tora the one?

He shook his head, simultaneously baffled and in awe.

He'd never looked for love. He'd never expected to find it.

Still in a state of wonderment, he entered his office and found the unfaltering Kareem already there waiting for him.

'So, Kareem,' he said, feeling more light-hearted than he had in a long time, 'what do we have on the menu today?'

Kareem didn't seem to share his good mood. Instead he looked more troubled than Rashid had ever seen him, and older than his years, and for a moment Rashid wondered if the endurance test of the coronation had worn him out. 'Sire,' he said at length, 'I have news which may concern you.'

Rashid doubted it. Right now it would take a volcano to suddenly appear in the desert to concern him, and then only after it erupted. 'What is it?'

'A message was sent through the palace server. I did not wish to bring it to your attention yesterday. It's from Sheikha Victoria to her cousin, a man called Matthew Burgess.'

Rashid remembered her talking about her cousins and how she didn't have anything to do with one in particular—he was sure that one was called Matthew.

'That doesn't sound right. Was it definitely her cousin?'

Kareem looked tense. 'A search proved it to be true.'

He told himself that it could still be innocent, that she might just have been informing him where to contact her, although why would Kareem consider that noteworthy?

'And do I really need to read a private email from Tora to her cousin?'

'I think perhaps you should.'

And a chill descended his spine as he took the letter from his vizier's hands.

Dear Matt

Don't think twice about the quarter of a million—it's a drop in the ocean to me right now. I'm just sorry you're having a tough time of it.

As it happens, I won't need to mortgage my home to help you out—we'll never have to mortgage anything ever again!—as I've stumbled on the mother lode: a rich petroleum billionaire who has royal connections. I know! The dollar signs in my eyes lit up too! I am confident I will be able to send you at least half a million dollars in one or two days.

Hang in there and keep watching that trust account—and keep listening for the ka-ching!

It's coming!

Your cousin

Victoria

PS Yes, blood really is thicker than water.

Rashid's blood ran so thick and cold it was practically curdling in his veins. *A rich petroleum billionaire who has royal connections. The dollar signs in my eyes lit up too!*

Something new and fragile threatened to crumble inside him then, his faith in her wanting to shatter into tiny pieces to scatter on the desert winds.

'You see, Excellency,' said Kareem, 'why I thought you might be interested in reading the contents.'

He could see all right, but no, this was Tora they were talking about. 'It cannot be true.' No way could it be true. This could not be Tora writing this. And even if it was... He flicked the paper in his hand. 'Surely this is some kind of joke?'

'I am sorry, sire, we thought the same, but there is more. It seems this Matthew Burgess and a solicitor colleague are both being investigated by the financial authorities for misappropriation of client funds.'

'There must be a misunderstanding, then. If this is the cousin Tora told me about, she doesn't have anything to do with him.'

Kareem bowed his head.

'What?' demanded Rashid.

'I wish I could say there had been some kind of mistake, but the solicitor's account at the heart of the fraud case—it is the same account the sheikha had us transfer the quarter of a million dollars to.' He paused. 'And there is evidence that the sheikha had repeated visits and phone calls to her cousin's office in Sydney before she came to Qajaran.'

'But she told me that she has nothing to do with the cousin who lives in Sydney. Is there another cousin?'

Kareem bowed again. 'I am sorry, sire. There is only the one.'

And Rashid's fragile new world splintered around him, leaving him shell-shocked and raw again, just as he'd been when he'd learned of his father's three-decade deception.

But Tora's deception cut still deeper, because she'd played him for a fool.

'It's not about money,' she'd told him, after sending this message to her cousin.

It wasn't about money?

Liar.

'So her cousin is a crook,' said Rashid tightly. 'Which is no doubt why she needed the quarter of a million dollars so urgently, and another half million besides, so she could try to bail him out.'

'So it would seem, sire.'

And Rashid closed his eyes and turned his head to the ceiling. He had to hand it to her—all that talk that money couldn't fix things. All that holding out on him while all the time comforting him, reassuring him, making herself indispensable to him. All the while making out that she cared for Atiyah when it appeared now that all she had been concerned about had been riches.

His riches.

Betrayal wrapped its poisoned arms about him. There was a reason he didn't get close to anyone. There was a reason he preferred to wander this world alone.

'Kareem, as soon as the desert brothers and their wives have left today, I want you to remove Atiyah from Tora's suite and place a guard on her door. From then on until she leaves here, the sheikha is under house arrest.'

Kareem inclined his head. 'It will be done. I am sorry, sire.'

'Why are you sorry?'

'For pressing the urgency of your marriage to adopt Atiyah.'

'God, Kareem, it wasn't your fault I got lumbered with Tora. I chose her. I should have waited for you to find me a proper wife.'

'I did think, for a time, that she would make a good sheikha.'

Rashid ground his teeth together. He'd been thinking along the same lines. More fool him.

Tora took coffee and yoghurt with fruit on the terrace feeling happier than she'd felt for what seemed like ever. She ached in all kinds of places she hadn't known could ache and she didn't mind a bit because every twinge reminded her of why she ached and how she'd earned it, and every memory made her smile anew.

Because she'd spent a night making passionate love with Rashid.

Not sex. *Love.*

It was mad. She'd known Rashid for such a short time, but what she felt for him was special. Love? She didn't know, but she felt the bloom of warmth every time she thought of it. It was a new discovery, shiny and pretty and wondrous, and she wanted to take it out and examine it and hold it close to her heart.

Beside her on a rug under a sun shade Atiyah practised her push-ups, gurgling happily, and all of a sudden flipped herself over. She lay there on her back, looking totally surprised at her different view of the world.

'Oh, you clever girl,' Tora said, clapping her hands at this early milestone, and Atiyah broke into a gummy grin, suddenly delighted with herself.

And Tora couldn't wait to tell Rashid.

Surely this day could not get any more perfect?

CHAPTER FOURTEEN

THE WEATHER HAD turned humid and oppressive, the kind of day that made your clothes stick to your skin and made you want to stay in the cool inside the thick palace walls, and it was late afternoon before the two remaining women had a chance to venture outside to sit and drink tea by the pool in the courtyard before Aisha had to depart.

They had bade goodbye to Marina and Amber and their families earlier in the day and now Tora and Aisha sat in the shade, baby Atiyah lying sleeping in a cradle that Tora set swaying with a gentle push every little while, while Aisha's two-year-old twins ran around chasing each other. Jalil was bigger, and faster on his feet, but Kadija was more agile and would dart away at the last moment, shrieking in delight as her brother lunged for her and snatched only handfuls of air.

'Your children are beautiful,' Tora said, more than a little wistful that they would soon be gone. It had been hard for her to say goodbye to Marina and Amber, who had both hugged her and said they hoped to see her 'next time'. She hoped to see them again, too, but she couldn't afford to imagine herself a permanent place in Rashid's future on the strength of one night and a mere request to stay longer. No matter what this new-found emotion centred at her heart wove into wanting. It was all too new and there were too many unknowns, and what Rashid felt and wanted was the biggest unknown of them all.

Aisha beamed suddenly beside her, unable to suppress a smile. 'Thank you,' she said, putting her hand low over her belly and looking up at Tora with bright shining eyes as she reached across and squeezed Tora's hand with the other. 'I've been waiting to share the news with Zoltan ever since I had it confirmed today, but he and Rashid have been so busy. I told Marina and Amber just before they left, and I know we haven't known each other very long, but I'm bursting with the news and you feel like a friend already.' She took a breather. 'Jalil and Kadija are going to have a little brother or sister.'

'That's wonderful news,' Tora said. 'I'm so honoured that you'd tell me. Congratulations!'

'Thank you.' Aisha hugged her hands in her lap as she watched her twins. 'Zoltan will be so pleased. He thought after me getting pregnant so quickly with the twins that it would happen again just as easily.' Tora saw a glimmer of pain in her eyes and the words she hesitated over, the words she left unsaid. 'Of course, it wasn't that easy at all. But now...' and Aisha smiled again and looked radiant with it '...now he will be so thrilled.'

'You two are so much in love,' Tora said on a sigh. 'You deserve every happiness.'

Aisha nodded, adding a conspiratorial smile. 'Thank you, but, I have to admit, it didn't start out that way.'

'Really? You're both so perfect for each other, I imagined you two falling in love at first sight.'

Aisha laughed. 'That's very funny, given the first time we met I bit him on his hand, although, to be fair, he was wearing a mask so I couldn't see how handsome he was.' She seemed to think about that a second. 'No, actually that would have made no difference, because the second time we met I clawed his face with my nails, though that was after he told me we were to be married. Against my will, as it happened.'

'You were forced to marry Zoltan? That seriously happens?'

She nodded. 'Yes. It happens and I had no choice. I wanted to marry for love but my father said I had to marry Zoltan, or both our kingdoms would be compromised.'

'And so you went through with it.'

'I did. Zoltan wasn't happy though, when I refused to sleep with him on our wedding night.'

Tora was so shocked she laughed. 'You didn't?'

Aisha smiled and shrugged. 'How else could I show my displeasure at being forced into marriage? I did not know this man I was expected to fall into bed with. He was a stranger to me and I wanted a love match.'

'What happened?'

'He showed me he was a good man and I could not help but fall in love with him.'

Tora shook her head. 'Nobody would ever guess you two started out like that.'

'Don't think I'm the only one—Marina and Amber had no easy path to love either. You see, there is something you must understand about these four men, Zoltan and Bahir, Kadar and Rashid—they are like brothers, only their bond is stronger, and duty is everything to them. They may not like it, they may strain against their fate, but ultimately they know what they must do.

'But they are so focused on their duty they don't take easily to the concept of love. None of them had an easy upbringing, and they all grew up looking after themselves. They are so used to being in control of their lives and their destinies that love is foreign to them. They are caught unawares how powerful love can be, but when they do fall in love, they fall hard.

'It has been the same for Zoltan, Bahir and most recently Kadar. And now Rashid is one hundred per cent focused on his new role and, in truth, is probably still coming to terms with this change in his life, but you will see, in time, Rashid will come good, too. He will be a good husband to you.'

And Aisha sounded so certain that Tora's uncertainties came brimming to the fore. 'Except this is still a marriage of convenience. As soon as we're divorced, he'll no doubt marry a meek Qajarese woman with the right connections the first chance he gets.'

Aisha shook her head. 'No, this cannot be true. I have seen you two together. I saw you during the coronation where Rashid's eyes followed your every move. We all saw him watching you. I cannot believe he would let you go, now that he's found you.'

Tora tried not to read too much into Aisha's predictions. 'He did ask me last night, to stay longer.'

Aisha smiled. 'You see! It is happening already. Soon he will not be able to imagine living without you. Do you love him?'

And Tora looked away to escape from the other woman's direct question and even more direct gaze. 'I... I'm not sure. How do you know for sure if you love somebody?'

Aisha put a hand over her heart. 'You feel it here, and—' she touched her head '—you know it here and suddenly it consumes you and you need him with every fibre of your being. You know that without him, you can never be complete. And when you make love with the man you love, you are complete.'

Tora let go a breath she'd been holding.

Love.

That was how it had felt to her last night.

'So,' prompted Aisha. 'Is it love?'

'I think it is,' she said, smiling at the flutter in her heart as she admitted it. 'I think I've fallen in love with Rashid.'

'So here you all are.'

Tora spun around at Zoltan's voice, humiliated enough that he must have overheard her words, but no, it was worse than that, because there was Rashid, right beside him, and his eyes were as cold as the slabs of marble that lined the floor. She shivered from their impact as Zoltan leaned down and kissed his wife while the twins shrieked and came running to greet their father.

Tora looked away, busied herself looking anywhere but at Rashid and at those damning eyes.

Why would he be so angry, even if he'd overheard her? How could a few innocent words banish what they'd shared last night?

'Have you had a good day?' Zoltan asked, still leaning over his wife, their faces mere inches apart. That was love right there, thought Tora. Love in abundance.

'The best,' Aisha replied, aiming a conspiratorial smile towards Tora. 'Just wait till I tell you.'

And a glance towards Rashid saw his eyes still locked on her, so cold and hard that she was almost sure she must have imagined last night in her dreams.

And if there was any love between her and Rashid, right now, it was one-sided. He stood in the terrace doorway looking as rigid and unmoving as if he'd been planted there and sent down roots.

'Our plane is ready,' Zoltan told his wife.

'Already we must go?' she said, smiling sadly in Tora's direction. 'It's been so good to be here. So good to meet you.' And she pulled Tora into a hug that felt bittersweet, because whatever her hopes and dreams, given the dark look on Rashid's face, she had an uneasy feeling in her stomach that she would never see Aisha or the other desert wives again.

Tora went to Atiyah's cradle, ready to take her inside, when Rashid suddenly stepped forward in her path. 'No. Leave her. I will take my sister.'

And Tora's gut clenched at the tone in his voice. Something was seriously wrong.

***

Aisha and Zoltan and the children were gone and Rashid must have spirited Atiyah off somewhere because she—along with Yousra—hadn't made an appearance since she'd returned to the suite.

But what had she done between this morning and this afternoon to deserve such a cold-shouldering? Other than to be overheard saying that she loved him?

Even if she hadn't intended blurting it out as she had, was that so serious a crime?

She sat down on the sofa and switched on her tablet. Maybe there would be some good news waiting for her, something to lighten this cloud of impending doom that she'd sensed in Rashid's cold eyes.

There was an email from her cousin she groaned at but ignored—no doubt Matt wondering where the money was—because there was one from Sally that demanded her attention—one that had the subject header Prayers needed!

Feeling sick to the stomach, she opened it up and read its contents as the cloud of impending doom circling above her head rained its poison down on her.

Oh, my God—please, God, no!

And the news was so awful, so devastating, that she had to tell someone, had to share this burden. She ran to her door and pulled it open, confused when she found two palace guards waiting outside, blocking her exit. She swept tears from her cheeks as she asked, 'What are you doing here?'

'By order of the Emir,' one proclaimed, 'you must remain where you are. You are now a prisoner of Qajaran.'

CHAPTER FIFTEEN

Tora stood in the centre of her suite, too uptight to sit, too frozen by fear to move. There were guards on the terrace, too, and behind the interconnecting door to Rashid's suite. Guards everywhere, but why? On a day where it was sweltering outside, inside she felt chilled to the core.

Tora clutched at her goosebumped arms, her face still streaked with tears she'd shed in protest and shock at being arrested in a palace halfway around the world from her home.

A palace where nobody would ever find her, even if they knew where to come looking. And the vulnerability of her situation hit her. A lone woman, a long way from home, at the mercy of a man she'd thought she was beginning to understand—beginning to love.

Fool!

But what had she done to deserve being treated this way?

Nothing! She was sure of it.

She sniffed. She would make sure she told Rashid the same too.

A guard marched across the terrace in front of her windows. 'I want to see Rashid!' she called out.

The guard didn't so much as twitch in response, just kept right on marching as if she hadn't spoken.

'I *demand* to see the Emir!'

Tora waited, her heart thumping so loud in her chest, but nothing changed. Nobody was listening.

Nobody cared.

And her grief and pain and confusion coiled together inside her like the smoke from a candle flame that had been extinguished, acrid and swirling, until a new emotion rose out of it.

Fury.

It turned her shock to resolve and her tears to ice, setting her jaw to aching tight and her fingernails clawing into her arms. So the guard wouldn't tell Rashid she wanted to see him. So he wanted to make her wait. Well, let him. Because when he eventually arrived, she would be ready for him.

There was a thunder cloud hanging over him. Dark and threatening, it weighed heavily down upon him, blackening his world and poisoning his mood.

Tora.

He had not expected to be betrayed by her. Maybe at first he would have thought it possible. A woman picked up in a bar who coolly demanded a quarter of a million dollars when asked to name a price—why wouldn't he expect a woman like that to want to take advantage of the situation?

But that would have been at first.

Because since that time she'd worked her way into his life and under his skin. Floating on the air as she seemed to do in her silk robes, displaying an insight into economic and social matters he hadn't expected, telling him that he was strong.

And to top it all off, giving herself to him like a coronation gift, as if she were offering water to a man who'd been in the desert too long.

All the while it seemed she'd been scheming.

All the while waiting.

Well, now she could wait in her apartments. By the time he got to her, she would be a pathetic mess. She would apologise—profusely and with tears—and beg for his forgiveness, but there would be none. He would not fall for her ways again.

Why the hell was he waiting? He would tell her now. He stormed to his feet, upsetting a low table, and his anger went ballistic.

It was high time he told her.

Her door was flung open, and Tora held her breath. Rashid. At last!

He nodded to the guard who pulled the door shut, and then he looked grim-faced to where she stood in the middle of her room, her arms still crossed, her chin still high.

'What the hell is going on?' she demanded.

A dark eyebrow arched as he moved slowly towards her, and she could tell that if he had a shred of remorse for putting her in this situation, she couldn't see it anywhere in his stormy blue eyes. They were empty of anything but cold, hard resentment.

'Why, Sheikha, do you not like your new living arrangements? All this space to yourself, I see, and so much privacy. Who could ask for more? But if you have a complaint, there are stone cells in the floors below the palace, I believe, if these rooms are not to your satisfaction.'

Her chin ratcheted up a notch higher. 'Why am I prisoner here? What have I done?' Her voice broke on the last word and then her strength and resolve gave way. 'Rashid,' she appealed, taking a step closer even though the very air felt like bars between them. 'What is happening?'

He snorted. 'Didn't I tell you to be careful what you sent using the palace Internet? Didn't I warn you?'

He made no sense. She hadn't plastered anything up on social media. She hadn't sent anything she shouldn't.

'But then,' he continued, 'why would you listen to me? Blood *is* thicker than water, after all.'

'What?'

'Oh, come now, Sheikha, surely you can't have forgotten this little gem? *"The dollar signs in my eyes lit up too!"* Or maybe this one will strike a chord: *"keep listening for the ka-ching".*'

And like a sledgehammer it hit her. The email she'd sent to Matt. The nonsense email to get him excited and frothing at the mouth with anticipation.

'You read my emails? How dare you? That was private.'

'What did you think I meant when I warned you? Of course the palace has to monitor communication coming in and out. Did you think your little missive to your cousin would go unnoticed—a cousin you are supposedly finished with now?'

'I *am* finished with him.'

'What, after you sent him the two hundred and fifty thousand dollars, or will that be after the five hundred thousand you have promised him next?'

'What? I didn't send that money to Matt—it went to a solicitor who—' And with a sickening thud, she realised just who she'd sent the funds through—the very solicitor Matt had instructed to draw up the documents complete with the small print she'd been too naive to read and so signed her inheritance over to him. And if Matt was in some kind of financial trouble, then, chances were...

'Let me finish your sentence.' Rashid confirmed it for her. 'It went to a solicitor who is now being investigated, along with your beloved cousin, for misappropriation of funds.'

Tora squeezed her eyes shut, reeling at her naivety, cursing the rush she'd been in that she'd trusted a colleague of Matt's. What if that money, too, had been lost?

But surely Rashid couldn't believe that she'd sent the money to Matt. 'I didn't know about the charges. I didn't know any of that. Matt gave me his solicitor's name because he was dealing with my parents' estate. But the money wasn't for him. That went—'

'Then why did you tell him not to worry about it?'

'No. Listen,' she said, putting out her hands in supplication, 'you're confusing two different things. Matt cheated me out of my inheritance from my parents' estate—that was the two hundred and fifty thousand he was talking about. When he asked for more, I thought I'd send him a taste of his own medicine. What I sent him was rubbish, Rashid, to lure him in and make him think I'd stumbled on a fortune and was going to share it with him. You have to believe me.'

'Two hundred and fifty thousand dollars,' Rashid said, ignoring her explanation, 'which just *happens* to be the same amount of money you asked for and got.'

'Yes, because I had promised it elsewhere and I needed it as quickly as possible.'

'Why? What was so urgent that you were so desperate to get the money then?'

'Because Sally's husband has cancer and they needed the funds to get him to a cancer clinic in Germany. And I'd promised to loan them the money from my inheritance because they'd already mortgaged their house and they'd exhausted every other means. That's where your precious two hundred and fifty thousand dollars went, and Steve's there now lying in that clinic, fighting for his life and close to death and now it looks like everything I've done has been for nothing.'

Her vision blurred and swam and she dropped her face to the floor. She didn't know when she'd started crying, she hadn't been aware of the tears falling, but now there was no stopping the torrent coursing down her face. Because if Steve died, everything would have been for nothing.

The sound of a clap forced her head up. Followed by another. A slow clap coming from Rashid that matched the slow pace of his feet as he drew closer to where she had fallen. 'Bravo, Ms Burgess, that was an award-winning performance. It had pathos, melodrama, even tears. Unfortunately some of us recognise that was all it was—an act. I didn't see you looking too upset last night when you were coming apart in my bed. I didn't see any tears fall then.'

She sniffed. 'Sally wrote this morning with the news.'

'Oh, this morning. How convenient.'

'Steve is dying. It's the truth!'

'I don't think you'd recognise the truth if it slapped you in the face. You climbed aboard that royal jet and ever since then you've been scheming to make it worthwhile to you and your crooked cousin. You played it well. Exceptionally well. One time a siren, another a virgin Madonna, you kept ducking and weaving and spinning your web of lies so well that you almost had me convinced that you were special, that there might even be a future for us beyond this short-term deal.'

His lip curled. 'What a fool I've been.' His cold dark eyes were filled with abhorrence as they raked over her, all but scraping her skin with their intensity. 'And I must be a fool because I thought—I actually thought...' He shook his head. 'A fool. You will stay here in your rooms until it is time to send you home.'

'Rashid,' she begged as he turned to leave, because in his words was a tiny kernel, a glimmer of hope, if she could only prove to him that she was telling the truth. 'Please, I beg of you...'

His feet paused at the door. 'What?'

'There is one thing you should know. One thing you have to believe.'

'Well?'

She licked her lips, her heartbeat frantic as she prepared to lay it on the line and bare herself to him utterly. 'I couldn't do the things you say. I would never betray you. Because... Because, I love you.'

He laughed, the sound cold and jagged as it echoed around her room, until she felt as if her heart had been sliced apart. 'Nice try.'

And then he was gone.

She threw herself down onto her bed and let herself weep in great heaving sobs—because she'd only ever married Rashid to secure the funds for Steve's treatment and, somewhere along the line, she'd fallen in love with a despot in the process, a despot who'd laughed at her when she'd bared her soul to him.

And now Steve was fighting for his life in a German clinic and it had all been so pointless.

It had all been for nothing.

And she hated the man who had done this to her with all her heart.

The man she'd thought she had loved.

She loved him. Talk about desperate. As if he'd believe that. As if she'd thought it would excuse what she'd done.

Atiyah was crying when he returned to his rooms and the black cloud above his head thundered and roared.

'She won't stop,' a tearful Yousra said. 'She wants Tora.'

'Give her to me!' he demanded, and the young woman's eyes opened wide with surprise, but still she handed the bundle over. He juggled the unfamiliar weight, the arms and legs working like little pistons, the face screwed up and red, and he caught a flailing arm with one finger and tucked her in close to his chest as he tried to remember how Tora had told him to try to calm her. 'Atiyah,' he said, trying to stop the storm cloud hanging over him from making him shout over her screams, 'Calm down. Calm down.'

He walked with her one way, he walked back the other, but there was no settling her. 'Atiyah,' he said, 'little sister, you must stop this.' And on impulse, when he could not think of anything else that might help, he started humming the tune, the lullaby he'd heard Tora sing to her, the lullaby that had been dredged up from the depths of his memories. And eventually, somewhere along the line, the notes filtered through to the tiny infant and Atiyah's cries became more brief, staccato bursts between the listening moments, bursts that became hiccups. Until finally she fell silent apart from a low whimpering sound.

'Is she asleep?' Yousra whispered in awe. And he shook his head as he sang that soft lullaby, because, while her face had unscrunched, she was wide awake and staring up at him, a frown knitting her brow as she focused intently on his face, almost as if she recognised him.

He stared back at her, equally fascinated until he came to the end of the song and he smiled, and the little girl wiggled in his arms and smiled right back.

And his world turned on its axis and he knew it would never be the same.

'Like the world lights up and wraps you in love.' Tora had said that.

And yet he should have known that, because that was exactly how he'd felt when Tora had smiled at him. When she'd come apart in his arms. When he'd seen tears in her proud eyes at his coronation.

Those tears... Had she been scheming even then? How could she have known he'd turn to her in that moment? How could she have faked those tears? Tora had been the one who had got him through the coronation. Knowing she was there had been his one constant. Having her in his corner had lent him strength and made him wonder if their relationship could not be more permanent.

She'd made his duty more possible, more bearable, more palatable.

She'd made him wish she could stay by his side for ever.

She'd said she'd never betray him.

She'd said she loved him.

Oh, God, and arresting her was how he repaid her? He'd been so angry, had felt so betrayed, so manipulated, as if he'd been played for a fool from the start.

And the rank, horrible feeling in his gut told him that they had got things very wrong, and that he'd been the fool all along, he hadn't needed anyone to play him.

He had to find the truth—find the story behind the email to her cousin—there had to be proof. He owed her that much. There was an email this morning, she'd said, saying her friend was dying. It would be easy enough to check. Surely there would be something to prove or disprove her story one way or another. 'Yousra,' he said, the child still held close in his arms. 'Get me Kareem.'

An hour later, he had what he needed. A small stack of printed emails. 'Innocuous,' Kareem had labelled them. 'There was no mention of any amount of money.'

And Rashid believed him. Innocuous by themselves, but together with her story they painted a different picture... *You're a lifesaver... Next stop, Germany!* And the kick to the heart he deserved with the subject header on the email that had come overnight—*Prayers needed!*—and he knew with an icy cold rush down his spine that she'd been telling the truth.

And he dropped his head into his hands.

What the hell had he done?

And how was he ever to make amends?

CHAPTER SIXTEEN

TORA'S HEAD JERKED up from her pillow when she heard the sound of the door opening. For a moment she hoped it was Rashid so she could tell him exactly what she thought of him. She got out of bed and ran her fingers over her cheeks. Her tears had dried in the heat of her growing anger, but her skin felt tight, as if it were crusted with salt.

But it wasn't Rashid returning, but two young women, smiling shyly and holding baskets. They bid her to sit down and fed her honey tea while they brought out warm towels to wash her face and hands, and a hairbrush to brush her hair. There was even a freshly laundered gown to wear, and Tora didn't know what it meant but it was so blissful to clean the salt from her skin that she went along with it.

'Come with me, Sheikha Victoria,' the guard said, when she was feeling refreshed and human again and the women had vanished.

'What's going on?' she asked. 'Where are you taking me?' But he said nothing, just turned and led the way out.

Only one guard, she thought as she followed him. There had been four outside her doors and now only one—what did that mean?

'Where is the Emir?' she asked, but the man in front of her said nothing as he strode ahead of her through the long corridors and past the accumulated treasures of millennia and out the front doors of the palace and into an inky night.

A car idled quietly, its lights on low beam.

And there was Kareem, standing there, watching her approach. He bowed low, his hand on his chest.

'Sheikha,' he said. 'I have done you a great disservice. Please forgive me.'

And she guessed it was Kareem who had been alerted to her email to Matt and who had then alerted Rashid.

'It doesn't matter, Kareem. It was never meant to be. Can you tell me what is happening?'

'You are leaving,' he said, and, as if to support his words, her suitcase was delivered to the top of the steps. She swallowed.

'Now?' she said, caught between relief and a pang of regret for all she'd leave behind. The soft velvet night sky. Atiyah. Her heart. 'Already?'

'Already. His Excellency insisted.'

'Where is Rashid?'

'Waiting at the plane. He thought you would be happier travelling to the airport without him.'

Coward, she thought, but it was an accusation tinged with sadness. So she was to be seen off the premises like an employee who had been dismissed, her possessions hastily flung together, no chance to say goodbye to those she wished to? There was a lump in her throat the size and shape of a small child. 'You'll give Atiyah a hug for me?' she said, trying to push back on the sting of tears, and Kareem solemnly nodded.

She hauled in a breath, casting a look over her shoulder at the amazing fairy-tale palace that wasn't, before she turned back to Kareem and said with false brightness, 'Then let's go.'

He saw the headlights approach from where he stood at the foot of the stairs and felt sick to the stomach. She was leaving. Well, she'd always been going to leave, she was just leaving a little earlier, that was all.

And how could he not let her go? How could he keep her here as his prisoner and punish her for his own blind stupidity? How could he expect her to forgive him?

The car drew alongside the plane, its engines starting to whine, pulling up so the back door lined up with the red carpet that had been rolled out waiting for it, and Kareem emerged and offered his hand to the other passenger. Rashid swallowed.

Tora.

Looking like a goddess. Wearing the robe of orange and yellow she'd worn that day when they'd toured Malik's palaces. Such a few days ago and yet it seemed like a lifetime, so much had happened, so much had been felt. He saw her thank Kareem as he handed her out and retrieved her suitcase and then she glanced up and her eyes snagged on his. She looked away at her feet, and his heart snapped in two.

Well, what did he expect? It was no more than he deserved. She'd told him she loved him and he'd flung that love back in her face with a few choice insults besides. Call himself an Emir? A ruler of men? He couldn't even rule his own heart and mind. And if he couldn't make them act in consensus, how was he supposed to manage a country?

As he might have, with this woman by his side. He might have believed it was possible.

'Tora,' he said as she drew closer.

She angled her head, her eyes sharp like daggers, even if their edges seemed a little dulled with disappointment. 'Seeing me off the premises, Rashid? Making sure I don't escape with the silverware.' She held her arms out. 'Do you need to frisk me to make sure I haven't run off with any of Qajaran's treasures to pawn when I get home?'

He sucked in air that smelt of aviation fuel. He deserved that. 'I was wrong,' he said. 'And in so many ways, and I know I can never apologise for all the wrongs I have done to you. But please believe me when I say I am truly sorry for the hurt I have done to you.'

Her lips pressed tightly together. 'Well, I guess that's all right, then. So, what about my divorce?'

'You will be notified when it is finalised.'

He saw her hesitate. 'What will become of Atiyah now?'

And it struck him that even in the midst of her own private hell, she was worried about his sister. His sister, for whom Tora had cared more and been more loving. God, he'd been a fool!

'She will be fine. She smiled at me tonight.'

'She did?' And Tora smiled, too, for a moment, until she remembered why she was here. 'Excellent,' she said before her teeth found her lip, and she looked up at the stairs, putting one hand on the rail. 'I'm looking forward to being back in Sydney.'

'Tora,' he said, stopping her from taking that first step just yet, 'once upon a time, you said you loved me. Did you mean it?'

She turned her head to the velvet sky and the wide belt of stars that was more clearly visible now they were out of the city precinct. 'I thought I did. And then I was just so angry with you, that it blocked everything out. I hated you for what you had done and what you had believed of me. After everything we had been through. I was so angry.'

He closed his eyes. 'And now?'

'Now I'm just sad for what could have been.'

And he couldn't let her go without telling her. 'I know it's too late, but I am a fool where love is concerned, but I want you to know that there was love between us. There is love that I feel for you.'

She swallowed back on a sob. So good of him to tell her that now, when he was putting her on a plane to leave. 'Do you call it love to judge someone as guilty before you even ask them for the truth? Do you call it love to treat that person like a criminal? Because if you do, you have a very warped idea of love.'

'Tora, I am so sorry. I didn't want to believe it was true, but you said you had nothing to do with your cousin, and there was evidence you'd spoken to him just recently, and I felt betrayed and deceived and it was like my father all over again, except this time it was you, and that felt a hundred times worse.'

She stared at him. 'My darling cousin stole my inheritance. All the money from my parents' estate. All the money I'd promised Sally and Steve. I'd just come from a meeting with him to tell me the happy news that all the money was gone. Why do you think I was so angry that night in the bar?'

He hung his head. 'God, I'm a fool. I will never make up to you the wrongs I have done you.'

'No,' she said. 'I don't believe you will. Goodbye, Rashid.' And she turned and fled up the stairs into the plane, knowing she had to get into the safety of the cabin before she lost it completely. Knowing she had to escape while she had the chance, while she still had one last shred of dignity intact, even if her heart lay broken into tiny pieces.

Something was wrong. Tora blinked into wakefulness after a tortured sleep. 'We're coming in to land,' the flight attendant said.

'Already?' said Tora, knowing she couldn't possibly have slept for that long.

'Yes,' said the attendant, clearing away cups and plates. 'If you look outside your window, you'll see the lights of Cologne ahead.'

Cologne?

'We're landing in Germany?'

'But of course,' said the attendant. 'Didn't you know?'

* * *

Sally hugged her friend so tight when Tora reached the hospital that she thought she might snap in two but she didn't mind one little bit. 'I couldn't believe it when I heard you were coming. And now you're here!' And she hugged her again.

'How's Steve?' Tora asked, hoping above hope that Sally's happiness wasn't solely down to her arrival.

Sally smiled over clenched teeth, a tentative smile of optimism. 'We thought it was the end—it looked like the end—and the doctors suggested trying something experimental but it was so expensive and I couldn't give them the go ahead, but then some anonymous benefactor contacted the clinic just last night and asked them to pull out all stops.' She shook her head. 'You wouldn't believe the difference in him in just a few hours. It's a miracle,' she said, and fell into her friend's arms again.

Anonymous benefactor?

Tora had a clue she knew exactly who it was and why he'd done it. And a broken heart made its first tentative steps to heal and love again.

She was punch drunk when she wrote the email. High on life and one life in particular, who was looking more human every day as he made a steady recovery. High on the happiness that her friend radiated constantly.

She hit Send and turned off her tablet and sat back on the lounge chair of the tiny flat she shared with Sally, feeling the rapid beating of her heart.

Well, it was out there. Now all she could do was wait.

CHAPTER SEVENTEEN

THERE WAS A glow coming from the courtyard, coming from inside the Pavilion of Mahabbah. And when a smiling Kareem led her inside, she could see why. The pavilion was lit with a thousand candles, their flames flickering and dancing in the night breeze, and for a moment as Kareem disappeared there was just the croak and plop of frogs amongst the lily pads and the haunting cries of the peacocks as she took it all in.

And then there were footsteps, and he was standing there in the doorway, Rashid—her Rashid—his dark features and golden skin standing out in his snowy white robes. So handsome. So darkly beautiful.

'Tora,' he said, blinking as if she were some kind of vision. 'But how—?'

'Kareem helped me.'

'But you came back,' he said, as if he couldn't believe it, his eyes full of wonder as his eyes drank her in.

'How could I not come back?'

'But after everything I did, after all the wrongs I did you.'

'You did some right. You helped Sally and Steve when they had nowhere else to turn to. You did a good thing. Steve's doing well. It's a miracle and we all have you to thank.'

'What else could I do? I had to do something.'

'It was a good thing you did. A generous thing. Thank you.'

'Thank you for coming to tell me that.' He gave a small sigh, a brief smile. He was a man at a loss. 'Did you want to see Atiyah? She's sleeping now, but you can stay a little while?'

'I'd love to see her.'

'That's good.' He looked around as if for Kareem, frowning as he seemed to notice for the first time the candles and the decorations. 'I imagine Kareem's organised a suite for you?'

'Rashid.'

'What?'

'There's another reason I came.'

His eyes grew wide. 'What?'

'When I left here, I wanted to hate you. You made that harder with what you did for Sally and Steve—'

'That doesn't make up for what I did.'

'I know. But while I sat there supporting Sally, I had time to think. And I thought about all the time that I watched you struggle with responsibilities that had been thrust upon you, struggle with the demands and needs of a tiny child you'd never asked for from a father who'd cast you into the world alone, even if to protect you—I thought about all that time, and how I could see you were a good man.'

'I was not good to you.'

'Not then, it's true, but what man would act differently when he'd been subject to the turmoil of your life, when he'd felt betrayed by the most important of people, his own father? How could he trust anyone ever again?'

'I should have trusted you.'

She put a finger to his lips to silence him. 'What's done is done. Can't we draw a line under what happened in the past? Can't we start anew?'

She saw hope swirling in the deep blue depths of his eyes. 'What are you saying?'

'I'm saying that, once upon a time, you hinted that you loved me, at least a little. I'm asking if you still do, and if you would do me the honour of marrying me, for real this time.'

'Marry you?'

'Yes. Because I love you, Rashid, for better or for worse. But I hope it's for ever.'

'Yes!' he cried as he picked her up in his arms and spun her around. 'A thousand times yes. I love you so much, Tora,' Rashid said, his lips hovering over hers. 'You have turned my life from a desert into an oasis. You have given life where there should be none. I owe you everything. And I will love you to my dying day.'

Tora smiled beneath his lips. 'As I will love you, Rashid. Aisha told me you desert brothers don't fall easily, but you fall hard.'

'I never expected to fall in love. I didn't think it was possible. But now I can't imagine a day in my life without you being in it.'

'That's good,' she said, 'because I don't plan on going anywhere without you.'

'You'll never have to, ever again.'

And they made love there that night, in the Pavilion of Mahabbah, the pavilion of love, the first night in all their nights of for ever.

EPILOGUE

THEY WERE MARRIED for the second time in front of the iconic sails of the Sydney Opera House alongside the sparkling waters of the harbour on which pleasure craft made the most of a perfect sunny day. Overlooking it all sat the magnificent backdrop of the Sydney Harbour Bridge.

The bridal procession was strikingly original, a confection of sheer joy, and headed by the combined children of the desert brothers and their wives strewing rose petals and jasmine flowers, the older children holding the hands of the younger ones and guiding them back to the red carpet when they strayed off course or got distracted, to the delight of all the assembled. Behind them came the three stunning matrons of honour wearing gowns in glorious jewel colours, ruby, emerald and sapphire, the Sheikha Aisha and Princess Marina and the blonde, blue-eyed Amber.

And last came Tora, wearing a sleeveless gown of golden silk ruched over her breasts and hips with a sweeping train and with her hair piled high and studded with champagne-coloured pearls and who was walked along the foreshore to meet her groom by the three best men, Zoltan, Bahir and Kadar.

At the very front stood Rashid, waiting as each group made its way to him, waiting impatiently for the moment he would be joined by his glowing bride. Under Qajarese law, he had been a married man for six months, and Tora a married woman. Six months during which the state of Qajaran had grown up, a period full of the necessary aches and pains of change but the benefits were already there, the confidence of the economy picking up, the lacklustre tourism sector finally getting off the ground.

Six months during which he had grown up and changed and become the ruler Qajaran needed, but only, he knew, because this woman had been by his side every step of the way.

Half a year they had been together, but today was the start of their real marriage, he knew. Today what had begun as a hastily arranged marriage of convenience would become a marriage of necessity, a marriage of free choice, a marriage to last until the end of days.

He smiled at the children as they made their way closer, saw Yousra in the throng holding a growing Atiyah in her frothy white dress, a white ribbon tying up her black curls, and he knew life was good.

The three brides of his brothers, their beautiful faces beaming, stepped to his left. How was it possible for his brothers to find such remarkable women, each and every one of them, and yet to leave the pearl of the collection for him? How lucky was he?

She was drawing closer, his brothers cutting in on each other to take turns on her arms. She was laughing at something one of them said and Rashid was struck by her beauty and her joy. She was radiant. She looked up then, and the laughter died on her lips as their eyes locked. He saw the cognac-coloured eyes darken with smouldering need and the smile that she gave just to him and his heart swelled.

And then she was there before him and his three desert brothers lifted her hand to place in his, before, with a slap to his back, they peeled away to stand on his right.

'You look beautiful,' he said softly. 'I love you.'

'As I love you,' she said, unable to stop the two tears of joy that squeezed unbidden from her eyes. 'For ever.'

It was a fairy tale, it occurred to Tora in that moment as she looked up into the dark gaze of the man she loved. A tale of trials and tribulations decorated with palaces and pavilions, peacocks and fountains. A tale of the exotic. And yet a tale of the most basic human needs.

Like life.

She glanced towards her friend Sally where she sat beaming alongside Steve in his wheelchair—Steve, who was growing stronger by the day. Sally blew her a kiss and Tora smiled back, before looking up to the sky and feeling her mother and father soaring in the heights and beaming down upon her on her proudest day. They were here, she knew, and it was good.

Even better when she felt Rashid's lips on her cheek. 'You have made me the happiest man in the world,' he whispered, and she wondered just how much joy it was possible to feel before one exploded with it.

For together they had conquered the tests put before them, had overcome their own fears and confronted their own feelings, and as their reward they had won the greatest prize of all. Had earned the greatest gift of all, for even life itself was worthless without it.

Love.

'Dearly beloved,' the celebrant began then as the gulls wheeled in the sky above and the passing ferry drivers tooted their horns in celebration, 'we are gathered here today for this very special Christmas wedding...'

* * * * *

KIDNAPPED FOR THE TYCOON'S BABY

LOUISE FULLER

For Adrian.
My brother, and one of the good guys.

CHAPTER ONE

'I'M SORRY ABOUT THIS, Ms Mason. But don't worry. I'll get you there on time, just like always.'

Feeling the car slow, Nola Mason looked up from her laptop and frowned, her denim-blue eyes almost black within the dark interior of the sleek executive saloon.

Glancing out of the window, she watched a flatbed truck loaded with cones lumber slowly through the traffic lights. There had been some kind of parade in Sydney over the weekend, and the police and street cleaners were still dealing with the aftermath.

Thankfully, though, at five o'clock on Monday morning the traffic was limited to just a few buses and a handful of cars and, closing her laptop, she leaned towards her driver.

'I know you will, John. And please don't worry. I'm just relieved to have you.'

Relieved, and grateful, for not only was John punctual and polite, he also had near photographic recall of Sydney's daunting grid of streets.

As the car began to move again she shifted in her seat. Even after two months of working for the global tech giant RWI it still felt strange—fraudulent, even—having a chauffeur-driven limo at her disposal. She was a cyber architect, not a celebrity! But Ramsay Walker, the company's demanding and maddeningly autocratic CEO, had insisted on it.

Her mouth twisted. It had been the first time she'd objected to something, only to have Ramsay overrule her, but it hadn't been the last. His dictatorial behaviour and her stubborn determination to make a stand had ensured that they clashed fiercely at every subsequent meeting.

But now it was nearly over. Tomorrow was her last day in Sydney and, although, she and her partner Anna were still under contract to troubleshoot any problems in the RWI cyber security framework, they would do so from their office in Edinburgh.

She breathed out softly. And what a relief to finally be free of that intense grey gaze! Only, why then did what she was feeling seem more like regret than relief?

Glancing up at the imposing RWI building, she felt her heart begin beating hard and high in her chest. But right now was *not* the time to indulge in amateur psychology. She was here to work—and, if she was lucky, at this time of the morning she could expect a good two to three hours of uninterrupted access to the security system.

But as she walked past the empty bays in the visitor parking area some of her optimism wilted as she spotted a familiar black Bentley idling in front of the main entrance.

Damn it! She was in no mood for small talk—particularly with the owner of that car—and, ducking her chin, she began to walk faster. But she was not fast enough. Almost as she drew level with the car, the door opened and a man slid out. A woman's voice followed him into the early-morning light, together with the faintest hint of his cologne.

'But, baby, why can't it wait?' she wheedled. 'Come on—we can go back to mine. I'll make it worth your while...'

Unable to stop herself, Nola stole a glance at the man. Predictably, her breath stumbled in her throat and, gritting her teeth, she began to walk faster. She couldn't see his face, but she didn't need to. She would recognise that profile, that languid yet predatory manner anywhere. It was her boss—Ramsay Walker. In that car, at this time of the morning, it was always her boss.

Only the women were different each time.

Ignoring the sudden slick of heat on her skin, she stalked into the foyer. She felt clumsy and stupid, a mix of fear and restlessness and longing churning inside of her. But longing for what?

Working fourteen-hour days, and most weekends, she had no time for romance. And besides, she knew nobody in Sydney except the people in this building, and there was no way she would *ever* have a relationship with a colleague again. Not after what had happened with Connor.

Remembering all the snide glances, and the way people would stop talking when she walked by, she winced inwardly. It had been bad enough that everyone had believed the gossip. What had been so hurtful—so hurtful that she'd still never told anyone, not even her best friend and business partner, Anna—was that it had been Connor who'd betrayed her. Betrayed her and then abandoned her—just like her father had.

It had been humiliating, debilitating, but finally she had understood that love and trust were not necessarily symbiotic or two-way. She'd learnt her lesson, and she certainly wasn't about to forget it for an office fling.

She glanced back to where the woman was still pleading with Ramsay. Gazing at the broad shoulders beneath the crumpled shirt and the tousled surfer hair, Nola felt her heart thudding so loudly she thought one of the huge windows might shatter.

Workplace flings were trouble. But with a man like him it would be trouble squared. Cubed, even.

And anyway her life was too complicated right now for romance. This was the biggest job Cyber Angels had ever taken on, and with Anna away on her honeymoon she was having to manage alone, and do so with a brain and a body that were still struggling to get over three long-haul flights in as many weeks.

Trying to ignore the swell of panic rising inside her, she smiled mechanically at the security guard as he checked her security card. Reaching inside her bag, she pulled out her lift pass—and felt her stomach plummet as it slipped from her fingers and landed on the floor beside a pair of handmade Italian leather loafers.

'Allow me.'

The deep, masculine voice made her scalp freeze. Half turning, she forced a smile onto her face as she took the card from the man's outstretched hand.

'Thank you.'

'My pleasure.'

Turning, she walked quickly towards the lift, her skin tightening with irritation and a sort of feverish apprehension, as Ramsay Walker strolled alongside her, his long strides making it easy for him to keep pace.

As the lift doors opened it was on the tip of her tongue to tell him that she would use the stairs. But, given that her office was on the twenty-first floor, she knew it would simply make her look churlish or—worse—as though she cared about sharing the lift with him.

'Early start!'

Her skin twitched in an involuntary response to his languid East Coast accent, and she allowed herself a brief glance at his face. Instantly she regretted it. His dark grey eyes were watching her casually...a lazy smile tugged at his beautiful mouth. A mouth that had been kissing her all over every night since she'd first met him—but only in her dreams.

Trying to subdue the heat of her thoughts, praying that her face showed nothing of their content, she shrugged stiffly. 'I'm a morning person.'

'Is that right?' he drawled. 'I like the night-time myself.'

Night-time. The words whispered inside her head and she felt her body react to the darkness and danger it implied, her pulse slowing, goosebumps prickling over her skin. Only how was it possible to create such havoc with just a handful of syllables? she thought frantically.

'Really?' Trying her hardest to ignore the strange tension throbbing between them, she forced her expression into what she hoped looked like boredom and, glancing away, stared straight ahead. 'And yet here you are.'

She felt his gaze on the side of her face.

'Well, I got waylaid at a party...'

Remembering the redhead in the car, she felt a sharp nip of jealousy as stifling a yawn, he stretched his arms back behind his shoulders, the gesture somehow implying more clearly than words exactly what form that waylaying had taken.

'It seemed simpler to come straight to work. I take it you weren't out partying?'

His voice was soft, and yet it seemed to hook beneath her skin so that suddenly she had no option but to look up at him.

'Not my scene. I need my sleep,' she said crisply.

She knew she sounded prudish. But better that than to give this man even a hint of encouragement. Not that he needed any—he clearly believed himself to be irresistible. And, judging by his hit rate with women, he was right.

He laughed softly. 'You need to relax. Clio has a party most weekends. You should come along next time.'

'Surely that would be up to Clio?' she said primly, and he smiled—a curling, mocking smile that made the hairs on the back of her neck stand up.

His eyes glittered. 'If I'm happy, she's happy.'

She gritted her teeth. Judging by the photos of supermodels with tear-stained faces, papped leaving his apartment, that clearly wasn't true. Not that it was any of her business, she thought quickly as the lift stopped.

There was a short hiss as the doors opened, and then, turning to face him, Nola lifted her chin. 'Thank you, but no. I never socialise with people at work. In my opinion, the disadvantages outweigh the benefits.'

His eyes inspected her lazily. 'Then maybe you should let me change your opinion. I can be very persuasive.'

Her stomach dipped, and something treacherously soft and warm slipped over her skin as his grey gaze rested on her face. When he looked at her like that it was hard not to feel persuaded.

She drew a breath. Hard, but not impossible.

'I don't doubt that. Unfortunately, though, I always put workplace considerations above everything else.'

And before he had a chance to respond she slipped through the doors, just before they slid shut.

Her heart was racing. Her legs felt weak. Any woman would have been tempted by such an invitation. But she had been telling the truth.

Since her disastrous relationship with Connor, she had made a decision and stuck to it. Her work life and her personal life were two separate, concurrent strands, and she never mixed the two. She would certainly never date anyone from work. Or go to a party with them.

Particularly if the invitation came from her boss.

Remembering the way his eyes had drifted appraisingly over her face, she shivered.

And most especially not if that boss was Ramsay Walker.

In business, he was heralded as a genius, and he was undeniably handsome and sexy. But Ramsay Walker was the definition of trouble.

Okay, she knew with absolute certainty that sex with him would be mind-blowing. How could it not be? The man was a force of nature made flesh and blood—the human personification of a hurricane or a tsunami. But that was why he was so dangerous. He might be powerful, intense, unstoppable, but he also left chaos and destruction behind him.

Even if she didn't believe all the stories in the media about his womanising, she had witnessed it with her own eyes. Ramsay clearly valued novelty and variety above all else. And, if that wasn't enough of a warning to stay well away, he'd also publicly and repeatedly stated his desire never to marry or have children.

Not that she was planning on doing either any time soon. She and her mother had done fine on their own, but getting involved on any level with a man who seemed so determinedly opposed to such basic human connections just wasn't an option. It had taken too long to restore her pride and build up a good reputation, to throw either away for a heartbreaking smile.

Three hours later, though, she was struggling to defend both.

In the RWI boardroom silence had fallen as the man at the head of the table leaned back in his chair, his casual stance at odds with the dark intensity of his gaze. A gaze that was currently locked on Nola's face.

'So let me get this right,' he observed softly. 'What you're trying to say is that I'm being naive. Or complacent.'

A pulse of anger leapfrogged over his skin.

Did she *really* think she was going to get away with insulting him in his own boardroom? Ram thought, watching Nola blink, seeing anger, confusion and frustration colliding in those blue, blue eyes.

Eyes that made a man want to quench his thirst—and not for water. The same blue eyes that should have warned him to ignore her CV and glowing references and stick with men in grey suits who talked about algorithms and crypto-ransomware. But Nola Mason was not the kind of woman it was easy to ignore.

Refusing his invitation to meet at the office, she had insisted instead that they meet in some grimy café in downtown Sydney.

There, surrounded by surly teenagers in hoodies and bearded geeks, she had shown him just how easy it was to breach RWI's security. It had been an impressive display—unorthodox, but credible and provocative.

Only not as provocative as the sight of her long slim legs and rounded bottom in tight black jeans, or the strip of smooth bare stomach beneath her T-shirt that he'd glimpsed when she reached over to the next table for a napkin.

It wasn't love at first sight.

For starters, he didn't believe in love.

Only, watching her talk, he had been knocked sideways by lust, by curiosity, by the challenge in those blue eyes. By whatever it was that triggered sexual attraction between two people. It had been beyond his conscious control, and he'd had to struggle not to pull her across the table by the long dark hair spilling onto the shoulders of her battered leather jacket.

But it was the dark blue velvet ribbon tied around her throat that had goaded his senses to the point where he had thought he was going to black out.

Those eyes, that choker, had made up his mind. In other words, he'd let his libido hire her.

It was the first time he'd ever allowed lust to dictate a business decision. And it would be the last, he thought grimly, glancing once again at the tersely written email she had sent him that morning. He gritted his teeth. If Ms Nola Mason was expecting him to pay more, she could damn well sing for it.

Nola swallowed, shifting in her seat. Her heart was pounding, and she was struggling to stay calm beneath the battleship-grey of Ram's scrutiny. Most CEOs were exacting and autocratic, but cyber security was typically an area in which the boss was almost always willing to hand over leadership to an expert.

Only Ram was not a typical boss.

Right from that first interview it had been clear that not only was his reputation as the *enfant terrible* of the tech industry fully justified, but that, unusually, he could also demonstrate considerably more than a working knowledge of the latest big data technologies.

Truthfully, however, Ram's intelligence wasn't the only reason she found it so hard to confront him. His beauty, his innate self-confidence, and that still focus—the sense that he was watching her and only her—made her heart flip-flop against her ribs.

Her blue eyes flickered across the boardroom table to where he sat, lounging opposite her. It might be shallow, but who wouldn't be affected by such blatant perfection? And it didn't help that he appealed on so many different levels.

With grey eyes that seemed to lighten and darken in harmony with his moods, messy black hair, a straight nose, and a jaw permanently darkened with stubble, he might just as easily be a poet or a revolutionary as a CEO. And the hard definition of muscle beneath his gleaming white shirt only seemed to emphasise that contradiction even more.

Dragging her gaze back up to his face, Nola felt her nerves ball painfully. The tension in his jaw told her that she was balancing on eggshells. *Concentrate*, she told herself—surely she hadn't meant to imply that he was naive or complacent?

'No, that's not what I'm saying,' she said quickly, ignoring the faint sigh of relief that echoed round the table as she did so. She drew in a deep breath. 'What you're actually being is arrogant, and unreasonable.'

Somebody—she wasn't sure who—gave a small whimper.

For a fraction of a second Ram thought he might have misheard her. Nobody called him arrogant or unreasonable. But, glancing across at Nola, he knew immediately that he'd heard her correctly.

Her cheeks were flushed, but she was eyeing him steadily, and he felt a flicker of anger and something like admiration. She was brave—he'd give her that. And determined. He knew his reputation, and it had been well and truly earned. His negotiating skills were legendary, and his single-minded ruthlessness had turned a loan from his grandfather into a global brand.

A pulse began to beat in his groin. Normally she would be emptying her desk by now. Only the humming in his blood seemed to block out all rational thought so that he felt dazed, disorientated by her accusation. But why? What was it about this woman that made it so difficult for him to stay focused?

He didn't know. But whatever it was it had been instant and undeniable. When he'd walked into that coffee shop she had stood up, shaken his hand, and his body had reacted automatically—not just a spark but a fire starting in his blood and burning through his veins.

It had been devastating, unprecedented. At the time he'd assumed it was because she was so unlike any of the other women of his acquaintance. Women who would sacrifice anything and *anyone* to fit in, to make their lives smooth. Women who chose conformity and comfort over risk.

Nola took risks. That was obvious from the way she had dressed and behaved at her interview. He liked it that she broke the rules. Every single time he came into contact with her he liked it more—liked *her* more.

And she liked him too.

Only every single time she came into contact with him she gave him the brush-off. Or at least she tried too. But her eyes gave her away.

As though sensing his thoughts, Nola glanced up and looked away, her hand rising protectively to touch her throat. Instantly the pulse in his groin began to beat harder and faster.

He had never had to chase a woman before—let alone coax her into his bed. It was both maddening and unbelievably erotic.

At the thought of Nola in his bed, wearing nothing but that velvet choker, he felt a stab of sexual frustration so painful that he had to grip the arms of his chair to stop himself from groaning out loud.

'That's a pretty damning assessment, Ms Mason,' he said softly. 'Obviously if I thought you were being serious we'd be having a very different conversation. So I'm going to assume you're trying to shock me into changing my mind.'

Nola took a breath. Her insides felt tight and a prickling heat was spreading up her spine. Could everyone else in the room feel the tension between her and Ram? Or was it all in her head?

Stupid question. She knew it was real—and not just real. It was dangerous. Whatever this thing was between them, it was clearly hazardous—not only to her reason but to her instinct for self-preservation. Why else was she picking a fight with the boss in public?

Abruptly he leaned forward, and as their eyes met she shivered. His gaze was so intent that suddenly it felt as though they were alone, facing each other like two Western gunslingers in a saloon bar.

'Nice try! But I'm not that sensitive.'

Without warning the intensity faded from his handsome features and, glancing swiftly round the room, she knew her anger must look out of place—petulant, even. No doubt that had been his intention all along: to make her look emotional and unprofessional.

Gritting her teeth, she leaned back in her chair, trying to match his nonchalance.

Watching her fingers curl into a fist around her pen, Ram smiled slowly. 'I don't know whether to be disappointed or impressed by you, Ms Mason. It usually takes people a lot less than two months to realise I'm arrogant and unreasonable. However, they don't tend to say it to my face. Either way, though, I'm not inclined to change my mind. Or permit you to change yours. You see, I only have one thousand four hundred and forty minutes in any day, and I don't like to waste them on ill-thought-out negotiations like this one.'

Watching the flush of colour spread over her pale skin, he felt a stab of satisfaction. She had got under his skin; now he had not got under hers, And he was going to make sure it stung.

'I gave you a budget—a very generous budget—and I see no reason to increase it on the basis of some whim.'

Nola glared at him. 'This is not a whim, Mr Walker. It is a response to your email informing me that the software launch date has been brought forward by six weeks.'

Had he stuck to the original deadline, the new system would have been up and running for several months prior to the launch, giving her ample time to iron out any glitches. Now, though, the team she'd hired and trained for RWI would have to work longer hours to run all the necessary checks, and overtime meant more money.

Ram leaned forward. 'I run a business—a very successful one—that is currently paying your salary, and part of that success comes from knowing my market inside out. And this software needs to be on sale as soon as possible. And by "as soon as possible" I mean *now*.'

She blinked trying to break the spell of his eyes on hers and the small taunting smile on his lips.

Taking a breath, she steadied herself. 'I understand that. But *now* changes things. *Now* is expensive. But not nearly as expensive as it will be when your system gets hacked.'

'That sounds awfully like a threat, Ms Mason.'

She took another quick breath, her hand lifting instinctively to her throat. Feeling the blood pulsing beneath her fingertips, she straightened her spine.

'That's because it is. But better that it comes from me than them. Hackers break the rules, which means *I* have to break the rules. The difference is that I'm not about to steal or destroy or publicise your data. Nor am I going to extort money from you.'

'Not true.' The corner of his mouth lifted, as though she had made a joke, but there was no laughter in his eyes. 'Okay, you don't sneak in through the back door. You just give me one of those butter-wouldn't-melt-in-your-mouth smiles and put an invoice on my desk!'

'I can protect your company, Mr Walker. But I can't do that if my hands are tied behind my back.'

He tilted his head, his expression shifting, his dark gaze locking onto her face. 'Of course not. But, personally, I never let anyone tie me up unless we've decided on a safe word beforehand. Maybe you should do the same.'

There was some nervous laughter around the table. But before she could respond, he twisted in his seat and gestured vaguely towards the door.

'I need to have a private conversation with Ms Mason.'

Stomach churning, Nola watched as the men and women filed silently out of the room. Finally the door closed with a quiet click and she felt a ripple of apprehension slither over her skin as she waited for him to speak.

But he didn't say anything. Instead he simply stared out of the window at the blue sky, his face calm and untroubled.

Her heartbeat accelerated. *Damn him!* She knew he was making her wait, proving his power. If only she could tell him where to put his job. But this contract was not only paying her and Anna's wages, RWI was a global brand—a household name—and getting a good reference would propel their company, Cyber Angels, into the big time.

So, willing herself to stay cool-headed, she sat as the silence spread to the four corners of the room. Finally he pushed back his seat and stood up. Her pulse twitched in her throat as she watched him walk slowly around the table and come to a halt in front of her.

'You're costing me a great deal of money already. And now you're about to cost me a whole lot more.' He stared at her coolly. 'Are you sure there's nothing else you'd like, Nola? This table, perhaps? My car? Maybe the shirt off my back?'

He was looking for her to react. Which meant she should stay silent and seated. But it was the first time he had said her name, and hearing it spoken in that soft, sexy drawl caught her off guard.

She jerked to her feet, her body acting independently, tasting the sharp tang of adrenaline in her mouth.

Instantly she knew she'd made a mistake. She was close enough to reach out and touch that beautifully shaped mouth. In other words, too close. *Walk away*, she shouted silently. *Better still, run!* But for some reason her legs wouldn't do what her brain was suggesting.

Instead, she glowered at him, her blue eyes darkening with anger. 'Yes, that's right, Mr Walker. That's exactly what I want. The shirt off your back.'

But it wasn't. What she really wanted was to turn the tables. Goad him into losing control. Make him feel this same conflicted, confusing mass of fear and frustration and desire.

His fingers were hovering over the top button of his shirt, his eyes holding hers. 'You're sure about that?' he said softly.

The menacing undertone beneath the softness cut through her emotion and brought her to her senses.

At the other end of a table, surrounded by people, Ram Walker was disturbing, distracting. But up close and unchaperoned he was formidable.

And she was out of her depth.

Breathing in sharply, she shook her head, her pulse quickening with helpless anger as he gave her a small satisfied smile.

'And I thought you liked breaking the rules.'

His eyes gleamed and she knew he was goading her again, but she didn't care. Right now all she wanted was to be somewhere far away from this man who seemed to have the power to turn her inside out and off balance.

'Is there anything else you'd like to discuss?' he asked with an exaggerated politeness that seemed designed to test her self-control.

He waited until she shook her head, and then, turning, he walked towards the door.

'I'll speak to the accountants today.'

It was with relief bordering on delirium that she watched him leave the room.

Back in her office, she sat down behind her desk and let out a jagged breath.

Her hands were trembling and she felt hot and dizzy.

Leaning back in her chair, she picked up her notebook and a pencil. She knew it was anachronistic for a techie like herself to use pen and paper, but her mother had always used a notebook. Besides, it helped her clear her mind and unwind—and right now, with Ram Walker's goading words running on a loop round her head, she needed all the help she could get.

But she had barely flipped open her notebook when her phone buzzed. She hesitated before picking it up. If it was Ram, she was going to let it ring out. Her nerves were still jangling from their last encounter, and she couldn't face another head-to-head right now. But glancing at the screen, she felt a warm rush of happiness.

It was Anna.

A chat with her best friend would be the perfect antidote to that showdown with Ram.

'Hey, I wasn't expecting to hear from you. Why are you calling me? This is your honeymoon. Shouldn't you be gazing into Robbie's eyes, or writhing about with him on some idyllic beach?'

Hearing Anna's snort of laughter, she realised just how much she was missing her easy-going friend and business partner.

'I promise you, sex on the beach is overrated! Sand gets everywhere. And I mean *everywhere*.'

'Okay, too much information, Mrs Harris.' She began to doodle at the edges of the paper.

'Oh, Noles, you have no idea how weird it is to be Mrs Somebody, let alone Mrs Harris.'

'No idea at all! And planning to stay that way,' she said lightly.

Marriage had never been high on her to-do list. She was happy for Anna, of course. But her parents' divorce had left her wary of making vows and promises. And her disastrous relationship with Connor had only reinforced her instinctive distrust of the sort of trust and intimacy that marriage required.

Anna giggled. 'Every time anyone calls me that I keep thinking my mother-in-law's here. It's terrifying!'

She and Nola both burst out laughing.

'So why are you ringing me?' Nola said finally, when she could speak again.

'Well, we were at the pool, and Robbie got talking to this guy, and guess what? He's a neurosurgeon too. So you can imagine what happened next.'

Nola nodded. Anna's husband had recently been appointed as a consultant at one of Edinburgh's top teaching hospitals. He was as passionate about his work as he was about his new wife.

'Anyway, I left them yapping on about central core function and some new scanner, and that made me think of you, slogging away in Sydney all on your own. So I thought I'd give you a call and see how everything's going...'

Tucking the phone against her shoulder, Nola rolled her eyes. 'Everything's fine. There was a bit of a problem this morning, but nothing I couldn't handle.'

She paused, felt a betraying flush of colour spreading over her cheeks, and was grateful that Anna was on the end of a phone and not in the same room.

There was a short silence. Then, 'So, you and Ramsay Walker are getting on okay?'

Nola frowned.

'Yes...' She hesitated. 'Well, no. Not really. It's complicated. But it's okay,' she said quickly, as Anna made a noise somewhere between a wail and groan.

'I knew I should have postponed the honeymoon! Please tell me you haven't done anything stupid.'

Nola swallowed. She had—but thankfully only in the safe zone of her imagination.

'We had a few words about the budget, but I handled it and it's fine. I promise.'

'That's good.' She heard Anna breathe out. 'Look, Noles, I know you think he's arrogant and demanding—'

'It's not a matter of opinion, Anna. It's a fact. He *is* arrogant and demanding.'

And spoiled. How could he not be? He was the only son and heir to a fortune; his every whim had probably been indulged from birth. He might like to boast that he said no to almost everything, but she was willing to bet an entire year's salary that nobody had ever said no to him.

'I know,' her friend said soothingly. 'But for the next twenty-four hours he's still the boss. And if we get a good reference from him we'll basically be able to print money. We might even be able to pay off our loan.' She giggled. 'Besides, you have to admit that there are *some* perks working for him.'

'Anna Harris, you're a married woman. You shouldn't be having thoughts like that.'

'Why not? I love my Robbie, but Ram Walker is *gorgeous*.'

Laughing reluctantly, Nola shook her head. 'He is so not your type, Anna.'

'If you believe that you must have been looking too long into that big old Australian sun! He's *every* woman's type. As long as they're breathing.'

Opening her mouth, wanting to disagree, to deny what she knew to be true, Nola glanced down at her notepad, at the sketch she had made of Ram.

Who was she trying to kid?

'Fine. He's gorgeous. Happy now?'

But as she swung round in her seat her words froze on her lips, and Anna's response was lost beneath the sudden deafening beat of her heart.

Lounging in the open doorway, his muscular body draped against the frame, Ram Walker was watching her with a mocking gaze that told her he had clearly heard her last remark.

There was no choice but to front it out. Acknowledging his presence with a small, tight smile, she closed her notebook carefully and, as casually as she could manage, said, 'Okay, that all sounds fine. Send the data over as soon as possible and I'll take a look at it.'

Ignoring Anna's confused reply, she hung up.

Her heart was ricocheting against her ribs.

'Mr Walker. How can I help you?'

He stared at her calmly, his grey eyes holding her captive.

'Let's not worry about that now,' he said easily. 'Why don't we talk about how I can help *you*?'

She stared at him in silence. Where was this conversation going?

'I don't understand—*you* want to help *me*?'

'Of course. You're only with us one more day, and I want to make that time as productive as possible. Which is why I want you to have dinner with me this evening.'

'You mean tonight?'

Her voice sounded too high, and she felt her cheeks grow hot as he raised an eyebrow.

'Well, it can't be any other night,' he said slowly. 'You're flying home tomorrow, aren't you?'

Nola licked her lips nervously, a dizzying heat sliding over her skin. Dinner with her billionaire boss might sound like a dream date, but frankly it was a risk she wasn't prepared to take.

'That would be lovely. Obviously,' she lied. 'But I've got a couple of meetings, and the one with the tactical team at five will probably overrun.'

He locked eyes with her.

'Oh, don't worry. I cancelled it.'

She gazed at him in disbelief, and then a ripple of anger flickered over her skin.

'You cancelled it?'

He nodded. 'It seemed easier. So is seven-thirty okay?'

'Okay?' she spluttered. 'No, it's *not* okay. You can't just march in and cancel my meetings for a dinner date.'

He raised an eyebrow and took a step backwards. 'Date? Is that why you're so flustered? I'm sorry to disappoint you, Ms Mason, but I'm afraid we won't be alone.'

His words made her heart hammer against her chest, and a hot flush of embarrassment swept across her face. She was suddenly so angry she wanted to scream.

'I don't want to be alone with you,' she snapped, her hands curling into fists. 'Why would I want that?'

He smiled at her mockingly. 'I suppose for the same reason as any other woman in your position. Sadly, though, I've invited some people I think you should meet. They'll be good for your business.'

She stared at him mutely, unable to think of anything to say that wouldn't result in her being fired on the spot.

His gaze shifted from her face to her fists, grey eyes gleaming like polished pewter.

'Nothing else to say? You disappoint me, Ms Mason! I was hoping for at least one devastating comeback. Okay, I'll pick you up from your hotel later. Be ready. And don't worry about thanking me now. You can do that later too.'

'But I've got to pack!' she called after him, the bottleneck of words in her throat finally bursting.

But it was too late. He'd gone.

Staring after him, Nola felt a trickle of fury run down her spine. *Any other woman in your position.* How dared he lump her in with all his other wannabe conquests? He was impossible, overbearing and conceited.

But as a hot, swift shiver ran through her body she

swore under her breath, for if that was true then why did he still affect her in this way?

Well, it was going to stop now.

Standing up, she stormed across her office and slammed the door.

Breathing out hard, she stared at her shaking hands. It felt good to give way to frustration and anger. But closing a door was easy. She had a horrible feeling that keeping Ram Walker out of her head, even when she was back in Scotland, was going to be a whole lot harder.

CHAPTER TWO

FROM HIS OFFICE on the twenty-second floor, Ram stared steadily out of the window at the Pacific Ocean. The calm expression on his face in no way reflected the turmoil inside his head.

Something was wrong. He looked down at the file he was supposed to be reading and frowned. For starters, he was sleeping badly, and he had a near permanent headache. But worst of all he was suffering from a frustrating and completely uncharacteristic inability to focus on what was important to him. His business.

Or it had been important to him right up until the moment he'd walked into that backstreet café and met Nola Mason.

A prickling tension slid down his spine and his chest squeezed tighter.

Down in the bay, a yacht cut smoothly through the waves. But for once his eyes didn't follow its progress. Instead it was the clear, sparkling blue of the water that drew his gaze.

His jaw tightened, pulling the skin across the high curves of his cheekbones.

Two months ago his life had been perfect. But one particular woman, whose eyes were the exact shade as the ocean, had turned that life upside down.

Nola.

He ran the syllables slowly over his tongue. Before he'd met her the name had simply been an acronym for New

Orleans—or the Big Easy, as it was also known. His eyes narrowed. But any connection between Nola Mason and the city straddling the Mississippi ended there. Nola might be many things—sexy, smart and seriously good at her job. But she wasn't easy. In fact she was unique among women in that she seemed utterly impervious to his charms.

Thinking back to their conversation in the boardroom, remembering the way she had stood up to him in front of the directors, he felt the same mix of frustration, admiration and desire that seemed to define every single contact he had with her.

It was a mix of feelings that was entirely new to him.

Normally women tripped over themselves to please him. They certainly never kept him at arm's length, or spouted 'workplace considerations' as a reason for turning him down.

Turning him down! Even just thinking the words inside his head made him see every shade of red. Nobody had ever turned him down—in the boardroom *or* the bedroom.

He glanced down at the unread report, but there was no place to hide from the truth: despite the fact that his instincts were screaming at him to keep his distance, he couldn't stop thinking about Nola and her refusal to sleep with him. Her stupid, logical, perfectly justified refusal to break the rules. *Her* rules.

He closed the file with a snap. His rules too.

And that was what was really driving him crazy. The fact that up until a couple of months ago he would have agreed with her. Workplace relationships were a poisoned chalice. They caused tension and upset. And not once had he ever been tempted to break those rules and sleep with an employee.

Only Nola Mason was not just a temptation.

She was a virus in his blood.

No. His mouth twisted. She was more like malware in

his system, stealthily undermining his strength, his stability, his sanity.

But there was a cure.

His groin hardened.

He knew what it was, and so did she.

He'd seen it in the antagonism flickering in those blue eyes, heard it in the huskiness of her voice. And her resistance, her refusal to acknowledge it was merely fuelling his desire. His anticipation of the moment when finally she surrendered to him.

He tossed the file onto his desk, feeling a pulsing, breathless excitement scrabbling up inside him.

Of course, being Nola, she would offer a truce, not a surrender. Those eyes, that mouth, might suggest an uninhibited sensuality, but he sensed that the determined slant of her chin was not just a pose adopted for business but a reflection of how she behaved out of work and in bed.

Picturing Nola, her blue eyes narrowing into fierce slits as she straddled his naked body, he felt his spine melt into his chair. But truces could only happen if both parties came to the table—which was why he'd invited her to dinner. Not an intimate, candlelit tryst. He knew Nola, and she would have instantly rejected anything so blatant. But now she knew it was to be a business dinner at a crowded restaurant, she would relax—hell, they might even end up sharing a dessert.

His mouth curved up into a satisfied smile. Or, better still, they could save dessert until they got back to his penthouse.

So this was what it felt like to be famous, Nola thought as she walked self-consciously between the tables in the exclusive restaurant Ram had chosen. It was certainly an experience, although she wasn't sure it was one she'd ever want to repeat.

The Wool Shed was the hottest dining ticket in town, but even though it was midweek, and the award-winning restaurant was packed, to her astonishment Ram hadn't bothered to book. For any normal person that would have meant looking for somewhere else to eat. Clearly those rules didn't apply to Ram Walker, for now, within seconds of his arrival, the maître d' was leading them to a table with a view across the bay to the Opera House.

'I think I may have told our guests that dinner was at eight, so it's going to be just the two of us for a bit. Sorry about that.'

Nola stared at him warily. He didn't sound sorry; he sounded completely unrepentant. Meeting his gaze, she saw that he didn't look sorry either. In fact, he seemed to be enjoying the uneasiness that was clearly written all over her face.

Sliding into the seat he'd pulled out, Nola breathed out carefully. 'That's fine. It'll give you a chance to brief me on our mystery guests.'

She felt him smile behind her. 'Of course—and don't worry, your chaperones will arrive very soon. I promise.'

Gritting her teeth, she watched him drop gracefully into the chair beside her. At work it had been easy to tell herself that the tension between them was just some kind of personality clash or a battle of wills. Now, though, she could see that ever since she'd met Ram that first time, the battle had been raging inside her.

A battle between her brain and her body...between common sense and her basest carnal urges. And, much as she would have liked to deny it, or pretend it wasn't true, the sexual pull between them was as real and tangible as the bottles of still and sparkling water on the table. So much so that only by pressing her fingers into the armrests of her chair could she stop herself from reaching out to touch the smooth curve of his jaw.

Her hand twitched. It was like trying to ignore a mosquito bite. The urge to scratch was overwhelming.

But surely walking into this restaurant with him was just what she'd needed to remind her why it was best not to give in to that urge—for Ram wasn't just her boss. He was way out of her league.

In a room filled with beautiful people, he was the unashamed focus of every eye. As he'd strolled casually to their table conversations had dwindled and even the waiters had seemed to freeze; it had been as though everyone in the restaurant had taken a sort of communal breath.

And it was easy to see why.

Glancing up, she felt a jolt of hunger spike inside her.

There was something about him that commanded attention. Of course he looked amazing—each feature, from his long dark eyelashes to the tiny scar on his cheekbone, looked as though it had been lovingly executed by an artist. But it wasn't just his dark, sculpted looks that tugged at the senses. He had a quality of certainty that was unique, compelling, irresistible.

He was the ultimate cool boy at school, she decided. And now he was sitting next to her, his arm resting casually over the back of her chair, the scent of his cologne making a dizzy heat spread over her skin.

Unable to stop herself, she glanced sideways and felt her breath catch in her throat.

He was just too ridiculously beautiful.

As though sensing her focus, he turned, and the air was punched out of her lungs as his dark grey gaze scanned her face.

'What's the matter?'

'Nothing,' she lied. 'Are you going to tell me who we're meeting?' She tried to arrange her expression into that same mix of casual and professional that he projected so effortlessly. 'Are they local?'

'They're a little bigger than just Australia. It's Craig Aldin and Will Fraser. They own—'

'A&F Freight,' she finished his sentence. 'That's the—'

'The biggest logistics company in the southern hemisphere.'

His eyes glittered as he in turn finished *her* sentence, a hint of a smile tugging at his mouth. 'Maybe we should try ordering dinner this way. It would be like a new game: gastronomic consequences.'

She tried not to respond to that smile, but it was like trying to resist gravity.

'It could be fun,' she said cautiously. 'Although we might end up with some challenging flavour combinations.'

His eyes didn't leave her face. 'Well, I've never been that vanilla in my tastes,' he said softly.

Her heart banged against her ribs like a bird hitting a window. There it was again—that spark of danger and desire, her flint striking his steel.

But as he picked up the water bottle and filled her glass she bit her lip, felt a knot forming in her stomach. Flirting with Ram in this crowded restaurant might feel safe. Playing with fire, however, was never a good idea—and especially not with a man who was as experienced and careless with women as he was.

She needed to remember that the next time he made her breath jerk in her throat, but right now she needed to dampen that flame and steer the conversation back to work.

'Is A&F looking to upgrade its system?' she asked quickly, ignoring the mocking gleam in his eyes.

Ram stared at her for a moment and then shrugged.

It was the same every time. Back and forth. Gaining her trust, then losing it again. Like trying to stroke a feral cat. Just as he thought he was close enough to touch, she'd retreat. It was driving him mad.

He shifted in his seat, wishing he could shift the ache inside his body. If he couldn't persuade her to relax soon he was going to do himself some permanent damage.

His eyes drifted lazily over her body. In that cream blouse, dark skirt and stockings, and with those blue eyes watching him warily across the table, she looked more like a sleek Siamese than the feisty street cat she'd been channelling in their meeting that morning.

'Yes—and soon. That's why I want you to meet with them today.'

As he put the bottle back on the table his hand brushed against hers, and suddenly she was struggling to remember what he'd just said, let alone figure out how to reply.

'Thank you,' she said finally.

His expression was neutral. 'Of course it might mean coming back to Australia.'

Frowning, she looked into his face. 'That won't be a problem.'

'Really? It's just that you live on the other side of the world. I thought you might have somebody missing you. Someone significant.'

Nola blinked. How had they ended up talking about this? About her private life.

Ram Walker was too damn sharp for his own good. He made connections that were barely visible while she was still struggling to join the dots.

His gaze was so intense that suddenly she wanted to lift her hand and shield her face. But instead she thought about her flat, with its high ceilings and shabby old sofas. It was her home, and she loved it, but it wasn't a *somebody*. Truthfully, there hadn't been anyone in her life since Connor.

Her throat tightened. Connor—with his sweet face and his floppy hair. And his desire to be liked. A desire that had meant betraying her trust in the most humiliating way possible. He hadn't quite matched up to her father's level of unreliability, but then, he'd only been in her life a matter of months.

Of course since their break-up she hadn't taken a vow of celibacy. She'd gone out with a couple of men on more than a couple of dates and they'd been pleasant enough. But none had been memorable, and right now the only significant living thing in her flat was a cactus called Colin.

She shook her head. 'No,' she said at last. 'Anna's the home bird. I've no desire to tie myself down any time soon. I like my independence too much.'

Ram nodded. Letting his gaze wander over her face, he took in the flushed cheeks and the dilated pupils and felt a tug down low in his stomach. A pulse of heat flickered beneath his skin.

Independence. The word tasted sweet and dark and glossy in his mouth—like a cherry bursting against his tongue. At that moment, had he believed in soulmates, he would have thought he'd found his. For here was a woman who was not afraid to be herself. To stand alone in the world.

His heart was pounding. He wanted her more than he'd ever wanted anyone—anything. If only he could reach over and pull her against him, strip her naked and take her right here, right now—

But instead a waiter brought over some bread and, grateful for the nudge back to reality, Ram leaned back in his chair, trying to school his thoughts, his breathing, his body, into some sort of order.

'She's impressive, your partner,' he said, when finally the waiter left them alone.

He watched her face soften, the blue eyes widen with affection, and suddenly he wondered how it would feel to be the object of that incredible gaze. For someone to care that much about him.

The idea made him feel strangely vulnerable and, picking up his glass, he downed his water so that it hit his stomach with a thump.

She nodded eagerly. 'She was always top of the class.'

He nodded. 'I can believe that. But I wasn't talking about her tech skills. It's her attitude that's her real strength. She's pragmatic; she understands the value of compromise. Whereas you...'

He paused, and Nola felt her skin tighten. That was Anna in a nutshell. But how could Ram know that? They'd only met once, when they'd signed the contracts.

And then her muscles tensed, her body squirming with nerves at what he might be about to reveal about her.

'You, on the other hand, are a rebel.'

Reaching out, he ran his hand lightly over her sleeve and she felt a thrill like the jolt of electricity. This wasn't like any conversation she'd ever had. It was more like a dance—a dazzling dance with quick, complicated steps that only they understood.

She swallowed. 'What kind of rebel works *for* the system?'

Beneath the lights, his eyes gleamed like brushed steel. 'You might look corporate on the outside, but if I scratched the surface I'd find a hacker beneath. Unlike your partner—unlike most people, really—you like to cross boundaries, take risks. You're not motivated by money; you like the challenge.'

The hum of chatter and laughter faded around them and a pulse began to beat loudly inside her head. Reaching forward to pick up her glass, she cleared her throat with difficulty.

'You're making me sound a lot edgier than I am,' she said quickly. 'I'm actually just a "white hat".'

'Of course you are!'

Ram shifted in his seat, his thigh brushing against her leg so that her hand twitched around the stem of the glass. It was a gambler's tell—a tiny, visible sign of the tension throbbing between them.

'It's not like I'd ever catch you hanging out in some grimy internet café with a bunch of wannabe anarchists.'

He lounged back in his seat, one eyebrow lifted, challenging her to contradict him.

Remembering their first meeting, Nola felt her heart beat faster, her stomach giving way to that familiar mix of apprehension and fascination, the sense that there was something pulling them inexorably closer.

But even as she felt her skin grow warm his teasing words stirred something inside her. Suddenly the desire to tease him back was overwhelming—to put the heat on *him*, to watch those grey eyes turn molten.

'Actually, wannabe anarchists are usually pretty harmless—like sheep. It's the wolf in sheep's clothing you need to worry about.'

She kept her expression innocent, but heat cascaded down through her belly as his gaze locked onto hers with the intensity of a tractor beam. A small, urgent voice in the back of her head was warning her to back down, to stop playing Russian roulette with the man who'd loaded the gun she was holding to her head.

But then suddenly he smiled, and just like that nothing seemed to matter except being the focus of his undivided attention. It was easy to forget he was self-serving and arrogant...easy to believe that breaking the rules—*her* rules—wouldn't matter just this once.

Her heart began to beat faster.

Except she knew from experience that it *would* matter. And that smile wasn't a challenge. It was a warning—a red light flashing. *Danger! Keep away!*

Breathing in, she gave him a quick, neutral smile of her own. 'Now, this menu!' Holding her smile in place, she forced a casual note into her voice. 'My French is pretty non-existent, so I might need a little help ordering.'

'Don't worry. I speak it fluently.'

'You do?' She gazed at him, torn between disbelief and wonder.

He shrugged. 'My mother always wanted to live in Paris, but it didn't work out. So she sent me to school there.'

Nola frowned. 'Paris! You mean Paris in France?'

'I don't think they speak French in Paris, Texas.'

His face was expressionless. but there was a tension in his shoulders that hadn't been there before.

Her eyes met his, then bounced away. 'That's such a long way from here,' she said slowly.

'I suppose it is.'

Her pulse twitched.

It would have been easy to take his reply at face value, as just another of those glib, offhand remarks people made to keep a conversation running smoothly.

But something had shifted in his voice—or rather left it. The teasing warmth had gone, had been replaced by something cool and dismissive that pricked her skin like the sting of a wasp.

It was her cue to back off—and maybe she would have done so an hour earlier. But this was the first piece of personal information he had ever shared with her.

She cleared her throat. 'So how old were you?'

Along the back of her seat, she could feel the muscles in his arm tensing.

'Seven.' He gazed at her steadily. 'It was a good school. I had a great education there.'

She knew her face had stiffened into some kind of answering smile—she just hoped it looked more convincing than it felt. Nodding, she said quickly, 'I'm sure. And learning another language is such an opportunity.'

'It has its uses.' He spoke tonelessly. 'But I wasn't talking about speaking French. Being away taught me to rely on myself. To trust my own judgement. Great life lessons—and brilliant for business.'

Did he ever think of anything else? Nola wondered. Surely he must have been homesick or lonely? But the expression on his face made it clear that it was definitely time to change the subject.

Glancing down at her menu again, she said quickly, 'So, what do you recommend?'

'That depends on what you like to eat.'

Looking up, she saw with relief that the tightness in his face had eased.

'The fish is great here, and they do fantastic steaks.' He frowned. 'I forgot to ask. You do eat meat?'

She nodded.

'And no allergies?'

His words were innocent enough, but there was a lazy undercurrent in his voice that made the palms of her hands grow damp, and her heart gave a thump as his eyes settled on her face.

'Apart from to me, I mean...'

Her insides tightened, and a prickling heat spread over her cheeks and throat as she gave him a small, tight, polite smile.

'I'm not allergic to you, Mr Walker.' She bit her lip, her eyes meeting his. 'For a start, allergies tend to be involuntary.'

'Oh, I see. So you're *choosing* to ignore this thing between us?'

She swallowed, unable to look away from his dark, mocking gaze.

'If by "ignore" you mean not behave in an unprofessional and inappropriate manner, then, yes, I am,' she said crisply.

He studied her face in silence, and as she gazed into his flawless features a tingling heat seeped through her limbs, cocooning her body so she felt drowsy and blurred around the edges.

'So you do admit that there is something between us?'

His words sent a pulse up her spine, bringing her to her senses instantly, and she felt a rush of adrenaline. Damn him! She was in security. It was her job to keep out unwanted intruders, to keep important data secret. So why was it that she fell into each and every one of his traps with such humiliating ease?

She wasn't even sure how he did it. No one else had ever managed to get under her skin so easily. But he seemed not only able to read her mind, but to turn her inside out so that she had nowhere to hide. It made her feel raw, flayed, vulnerable.

Remembering the last time she had felt so vulnerable, she shivered. Connor's betrayal still had the power to hurt. But, even though she knew now that it was her ego not her heart that he'd damaged, no good was going to come of confessing any of that to Ram—a man who had zero interest in emotions, his own and other people's.

And that was why this conversation was going to stop.

Lifting her chin, she met his gaze with what she hoped was an expression of cool composure.

'I don't think a business meeting is really the right time to have this particular conversation,' she said coolly. 'But, as you have a girlfriend, I'm not sure when or where *would* be right.'

'Girlfriend?' He seemed genuinely surprised. 'If you mean Clio, then, yes, she's female. But "girlfriend"? That would be stretching it. And don't look so outraged. She knows exactly what's on offer, and she's grateful to take it.'

She stared at him in disbelief. 'Grateful! For what? For being fortunate enough to have sex with the great Ramsay Walker?'

'In a nutshell.'

He seemed amused rather than annoyed.

'You surprise me, Ms Mason. Given the nature of your job, I thought you of all people would know that it pays to look beneath the surface.' His eyes gleamed. 'You really shouldn't believe everything you read on the internet.'

A quivering irritation flickered through her brain, like static on the radio.

'Is that right? So, for example, all those times you're meant to have said you don't want to get married or have children—that was all lies? You were misquoted?'

Ram stared past her, felt the breath whipping out of him. Used to women who sought to soothe and seduce, he felt her directness like a rogue wave, punching him off his feet. Who did she think she was, to question him like this? To put him, his life, under a spotlight?

But beneath his exasperation he could feel his body responding to the heat sparking in her eyes.

Ignoring his uneven heartbeat, he met her furious blue gaze. 'I'm not in the business of explaining myself, Ms Mason. But this one time I'll answer your question. I wasn't misquoted. Everything I said was and is true. I have no desire whatsoever to marry or have children.'

That was an understatement. Marriage had never been a priority for him. Parenthood even less so. And for good reason. Both might appear to offer security and satisfaction, but it had been a long time since he'd believed in the myths they promised.

Out in the bay, the Opera House was lit up, its sails gleaming ghost-white. But it was the darkness that drew his gaze. For a moment he let it blot out the twisting mass of feelings that were rising up inside him, unbidden and unwelcome.

Commitment came at a cost, and he knew that the debt would never be paid. A wife and a child were a burden—a responsibility he simply didn't want. Had never once wanted.

And he didn't intend to start now.

Leaning back in his chair, he shrugged. 'Marriage and parenthood are just a Mobius strip of emotional scenes that quite frankly I can do without. I'm sorry if that offends your romantic sensibilities, Ms Mason, but that's how I choose to live my life.'

There was a moment of absolute silence.

Nola drew a breath. By 'romantic', he clearly meant deluded, soppy and hopelessly outdated. It was also obvious that he thought her resistance to him was driven not by logic but by a desire for something more meaningful than passion.

She felt a pulse of anger beneath her skin. Maybe it was time to disabuse him of that belief.

Eyes narrowing, she stared at him coldly. 'Sorry to disillusion you, Mr Walker, but I don't have any "romantic sensibilities". I don't crave a white wedding. Nor am I hunting for a husband to make my life complete. So if I actually had an opinion on how you live your life it would be that I have no problem with it at all.'

His watched—no—*inspected* her in silence, so that the air seemed to swell painfully in her lungs.

'But you do have a problem...' He paused, and the intent expression on his face made her insides tighten and her throat grow dry and scratchy. 'You think I say something different in private to the women you refer to as my "girlfriends".'

He shook his head slowly. 'Then it's my turn to disillusion you. I don't make false promises. Why would I?

It's not as if I need to. I always get exactly what I want in the end.'

She shook her head. 'You're so arrogant.'

'I'm being honest. Isn't that what you wanted from me?'

'I don't want anything from you,' she said hoarsely, trying to ignore the heat scalding her skin, 'except a salary and a reference. I certainly have no interest in being some accessory to your louche lifestyle.'

Watching his mouth curl into a slow, sexy smile, she felt her stomach drop as though the legs of her chair had snapped.

'So why are you blushing?' he asked softly. 'Surely not because of my "louche lifestyle". I thought you were more open-minded than that.'

She glowered at him.

'I'm as open-minded as the next woman. But not if it means being a part of your harem. That's never been one of my fantasies.'

'Sadly, I'm going to have to put your fantasies on hold,' he said softly, raising his hand in a gesture of greeting to the two tall blond men who were weaving their way towards them. 'Our guests are here. But maybe we could discuss them after dinner?'

'I think that's the first time I've seen you relax since you arrived.'

Glancing up at Ram, Nola frowned.

Dinner was over, and his limo had dropped them back at the RWI building. Now they were standing in the lift.

Like many of his remarks, it could be read in so many ways. But she was too tired to do anything but take it at face value.

'It was fun,' she said simply. 'I enjoyed the food and the company.'

He did a mock stagger. 'I'm flattered.'

Glancing up, she saw that he was smiling, and she felt a panicky rush of nerves. In daylight, Ram Walker was flawless but unattainable. Now it was night-time, and beneath the low lighting, with his top button undone and a shadow of stubble grazing his face, he looked like the perfect after-dark female fantasy.

But the point about fantasies was that they were never supposed to become reality, she told herself quickly.

Shaking her head, she gave him a small, careful smile. 'I suppose it hasn't occurred to you that I might be talking about Craig and Will?'

His eyes gleamed. 'Nope.'

She swallowed. 'They're nice people.'

'And I'm not?'

Her throat felt as though it was closing up. And, was it her imagination, or was the lift getting smaller and hotter?

'You can be,' she said cautiously. She felt her pulse twitch beneath his gaze. 'But I don't know you very well. We don't know each other very well.'

Suddenly she was struggling to breathe, and her heart was beating very fast.

He smiled. 'Oh, I think we know each other very well, Nola!'

Her stomach dropped as though the lift cable had suddenly snapped, and somewhere at the edge of her vision stars were flickering—only that couldn't be right for they weren't outside.

'And I think you're a lot like me,' he said softly. 'You're focused, and determined, and you like breaking the rules. Even when you're scared of the consequences.'

There was a tiny shift in the air…softer than a sigh.

She watched, dry-mouthed, her stomach twisting into knots as he reached out and ran his finger along her cheekbone. She could feel her heartbeat echoing inside her head like footsteps fleeing. As she should be.

Except that she couldn't move—could hardly breathe.

He moved closer, sliding his hand through her hair.

'When I met you in that café you took my breath away. You still do.'

There was silence as she struggled to speak, struggled against the ridiculous pleasure his words provoked. Pleasure she knew she shouldn't acknowledge, let alone feel. Not for her boss anyway.

But maybe she was making too big a deal about that. He might be a CEO, but he was just a man, and as a woman she was his equal. Besides, as of tomorrow he wouldn't even be her boss.

The thought jumped inside her head like popping candy, and then somehow her hand was on his arm, the magnetic pull between them impossible to resist.

'Ram...' She whispered his name and he stared down at her mutely. His eyes were dark and fierce, and she could see that he was struggling for control.

She felt a shiver of panic tumble down her spine.

But why?

What did she care if he was struggling? So was she. Like her, he was fighting himself—fighting this desire.

Desire.

The word jangled inside her head like a warning bell, for was desire a big enough reason to play truth or dare with this man? After all, she knew the risks, knew the consequences.

Her head was spinning. Memories of that first kiss with Connor were slip-sliding into an image of his face, resentful and distant, on that last day.

But there was no reason it would be the same with Ram.

Nola knew she had been reckless with Connor—clueless, really. She'd jumped off the highest board and hoped for what? Love? A soulmate? A future? But *this* was never going to be anything but lust. There was no expectation. No need to make promises.

And, most importantly, there would be no consequences. After tomorrow they would never see one another again. It would be a perfect moment of pure passion. So why shouldn't she give in to it?

But even as the question formed in her mind she knew two things. One, it was purely rhetorical. And two, it was too late.

The warmth of his body had melted away the last of her resistance; the battle was already lost.

And, as though he could read her mind, Ram leaned forward and kissed her.

Groaning softly, he reached out blindly for the wall of the lift, trying to steady himself. He'd expected to feel something—hell, how could he not after the tension that had been building between them for weeks?—but the touch of her lips on his was like being knocked sideways by a rogue wave.

His head was spinning. Somewhere, the world was still turning, but it didn't matter. All that mattered was here and now and Nola. Her body was melting into him, moving as he moved, her breath and his breath were one and the same. He felt her lips part and, deepening the kiss, he pulled her closer.

As the doors opened he pulled her against him and out of the lift. Hands sliding over each other, they staggered backwards, drunkenly banging into walls, barely noticing the impact. Somehow they reached his office, and as he pushed open the door they stumbled into the room as one.

Nola reached out for him, her fingers clutching the front of his shirt. He could feel her heart pounding, hear her breath coming in gasps. She pulled him closer and, groaning softly, he wrapped his fingers around hers and dragged her arms behind her back, holding her captive.

Ram shuddered. His heart was pounding so hard he thought it might burst and, reaching down, he jerked her closer, crushing her body against his. But it wasn't enough. He wanted more. Breathing out shakily, he nudged her backwards, guiding her towards the sofa.

As they slid onto the cushions he dragged his mouth from hers and she gazed up at him, her eyes huge and dazed.

His breath caught in his throat. He wanted her so badly, but he needed to know that she wanted what *he* wanted—what he could give.

'I don't do for ever. Or happy-ever-after. This is about now. About you and me. If you're hoping for something more than that—'

In answer, she looped her arm about his neck, gripping him tightly. 'Stop talking and kiss me,' she whispered, her fingers tugging at his arms, his shirt, his belt.

He knew that relief must be showing on his face, but for once he didn't care that he'd shown his true feelings. She had said what he wanted to hear and, lowering his mouth, he kissed her fiercely. As her lips parted he caught hold of the front of her blouse and tugged it loose.

Instantly he felt his groin harden. For a moment his eyes fed hungrily on the soft, pale curve of her stomach, and the small rounded breasts in the black lace bra.

She was beautiful—every bit as beautiful as he'd imagined.

And he couldn't wait a moment longer.

Leaning forward, he fumbled with the fastening of her bra and it was gone. Then he lowered his mouth to her bare breast, feeling the nipple harden beneath his tongue.

Nola whimpered. His tongue was pulling her upwards. She felt as if she was floating; her blood was lighter than air.

Helplessly, she let her head fall back, arching her spine so that her hips were pressing against his thighs. Her head was spinning, her body so hot and tight with need that she hardly knew who she was. All she knew was that she wanted him—wanted to feel him on her and in her.

She couldn't fight it anymore—couldn't fight herself.

Desperately she squirmed beneath him, freeing him with her fingers. She heard him groan, then a choking sound deep in his throat as she slid her hand around his erection.

For a moment he steadied himself above her, the muscles of his arms straining to hold his weight, his beautiful clean profile tensing with the effort.

Breathing out unsteadily, he gazed down at her. 'What about—?' he began. 'Are you protected?'

Nola gazed at him feverishly. She didn't want to talk. Didn't want anything to come between them—and, besides, there was no need.

'It's fine,' she whispered.

His eyes flared, his expression shifting, his face growing tauter as slowly he pushed the hem of her skirt up around her hips. She shivered, the sudden rush of air cooling her overheated skin, and then she breathed in sharply as he pressed the palm of his hand against the liquid ache between her thighs.

Helplessly, eagerly, she pressed back, and then suddenly he pulled her mouth up to meet his and pushed into her.

His fingers were bumping over her ribcage, his touch making her heartbeat stagger. She reached up, sliding her hand through his hair, scraping his scalp. The ache inside her was beating harder and faster and louder, the urge to pull him closer and deeper overwhelming her so that suddenly she was moving desperately, reaching for him, pressing against him.

She felt a sting of ecstasy—a white heat spreading out like a supernova—and then she arched against him, her breath shuddering in her throat. As her muscles spasmed around him he groaned her name and tensed, filling her completely.

CHAPTER THREE

NOLA WOKE WITH a start.

For a moment she lay in the darkness, her brain still only on pilot light, wondering what had woken her. Almost immediately the warmth of her bed began tugging her back towards sleep and, stifling a yawn, she wriggled drowsily against the source of the heat.

And froze.

Not just her body, but her blood, her heartbeat. Even the breath in her throat hardened like ice, so that suddenly she was rigid—like a tightrope walker who'd just looked down beyond the rope.

Head spinning, she slid her hand tentatively over her thigh and touched the solid, sleeping form of Ram. As her fingers brushed against him she felt him stir and shift closer, his arm curving over her waist, and instantly she was completely, fiercely awake.

Around her the air stilled and the darkness closed in on her. Someone—Ram?—had turned off the lights in the office. Or maybe they just switched off automatically. But her eyes were adjusting now, and she could just make out the solid bulk of his desk. And strewn across the floor, distorted into strange, unfamiliar shapes, were their discarded clothes.

Picturing how they had torn them off in their hurry to feel each other's naked skin, she felt her cheeks grow hot and she blew out a breath.

Finally they'd done it. They'd had sex.

Her skin tightened in the darkness, her heartbeat fluttering, as a smile pulled at her mouth.

Sex! That made it sound so ordinary, or mechanical. But it had been anything but that.

Beside her, Ram shifted in his sleep, and the damp warmth of his body sent a tremor of hot, panicky excitement over her skin.

Remembering his fierce, hard mouth on hers, his hands roaming at will over her aching, desperate body, she pressed her hand against her lips, her stomach flip-flopping as she felt the slight puffiness where he'd kissed her again and again.

She'd expected the sex to be incredible. But now, with his hard, muscular arm curled possessively around her waist, and her body still throbbing from the frenzied release of their lovemaking, she knew that what she and Ram had shared had been more than incredible.

It had been—she searched for a word—it had been *transformative*. Beautiful and wild and breathless, flaring up like a forest fire, so hot and fast that it had consumed everything in its path straight to the sea.

And then afterwards calm, a peace such as she had never known. Just the two of them glowing in each other's arms, spent, sated, their bodies seeping into one another.

It had felt so right. *He'd* felt so right.

She shivered again. Ram had been the lover she'd imagined but never expected to meet in real life. Intuitive, generous, his touch had been a masterclass in power and precision.

He had demanded more from her than she had been willing to give, but she had yielded, for it had been impossible to resist the strength of her desire. The intensity of his.

Over and over he had pulled her against him, touching her, finding the place where liquid heat gathered, using his lips, his hands, his body to stir and torment her until the blood had beaten inside her so hard and so fast she'd thought she would pass out. She had been frantic and feverish—hadn't known who or where she was. Her entire being—every thought, every beat of her heart—had been concentrated on him, on his mouth, his body, his fingertips...

A memory of exactly what he'd done with those fingers dropped into her head and she squirmed, pressing her thighs together.

She couldn't understand why she was feeling this way. Why she had responded so strongly to a man she barely knew and didn't even really like.

She'd loved Connor—or at least she'd thought she had—yet sex with him had only ever been satisfying. Whereas with Ram it had been sublime.

It made no sense.

But then, nothing she'd thought, said or done in the last twenty-four hours had even come close to making sense. Not least sleeping with the man who, for the next twelve hours or so, was still her boss.

Her breath felt thick and scratchy in her throat.

Oh, she knew why she'd done it.

Ram Walker was not your average man. Even just being in his orbit made her feel as if someone had handed her the keys to a top-spec sports car and told her to put her foot down. He was exhilarating, irresistible.

But she knew from sleeping with Connor that giving in to temptation had consequences. Messy, unexpected and painful consequences. And so she'd waited until now, until the day before her contract ended, to give in, believing that she was being smart.

Believing it would just be one perfect night of pure pleasure.

Her skin grew hot, then cold.

She'd thought it would be so easy. Not just the sex, but

the aftermath. Maybe there might be a few awkward moments. But surely nothing too dramatic or life-changing. After all, she barely knew Ram.

It had never once crossed her mind that she would feel this way—so moved, so alive.

She'd thought once would be enough. That her body would be satisfied and she could forget him and move on.

She almost laughed out loud.

Forget him!

As if she could ever forget him.

Right now, there was only him.

It was as though he'd wiped her mind—erased every memory and experience she'd ever had. And it wasn't only the past he'd obliterated. Her future would never be the same now either. How could it be after last night? She might not have a crystal ball, but she didn't need one to know that sex was never going to be as good with any other man.

But what if today was the last time she ever saw Ram?

Was she really that naive? So stupid as to imagine they were done? That she could put last night in a box, wrap it up neatly with a bow and that would be it.

Her pulse began to race.

Since breaking up with Connor she'd been so careful. She'd had a couple of short relationships, but at the first hint of anything serious she had broken them off. It had seemed safer, given her bad luck when it came to men. Or was it bad judgement?

Her father, Richard, had been charming—financially generous. But even before her parents' divorce he had been unreliable—often disappearing without explanation, and always utterly incapable of remembering anything to do with his wife and daughter, from birthdays to parents' evenings.

Then she'd met Connor—sweet, funny Connor—who

had cared about everything from saving the planet to the trainers he wore. Miraculously, he had cared about her too, so she'd thought it would be different with him.

And it had been—for a time.

Until he'd betrayed her trust...shared the most private details of their life together over a pint in the pub. And then not even stepped up to defend her reputation.

She almost laughed, but felt more as if she was about to cry.

Her reputation.

It made her sound like some foolish eighteenth-century heroine who'd let the wrong man pick up her fan. But that was what she'd felt like. Foolish and powerless. And the fact that her supposed boyfriend had sacrificed her to impress his mates still had the power to make her curl up inside with misery.

Breathing out silently, she closed her eyes.

She'd vowed never again to trust her judgement. And with Ram she hadn't needed to. Her opinion of him was irrelevant; the facts spoke for themselves.

Even before they'd met in that café in Sydney she'd known his reputation as a ruthless womaniser. Yet she'd still gone ahead and slept with him.

And why?

Because she'd become complacent.

She'd assumed, like last time, that the worst-case scenario would be the two of them having to work in the same building. Now, though, she could see that geography didn't matter, and that the worst-case scenario was happening inside her head. And it was all to do with *him*, and how he'd made her feel.

But she couldn't think about this anymore. Not with his body so warm and solid beside her.

Her breathing faltered.

It was time to leave.

Moving carefully, so as not to wake him, she slid out from beneath his arm and began groping in the darkness for her discarded bra and shoes. Her bag was harder to find, but finally she located it by one of the armchairs.

Clutching her blouse in one hand, she tiptoed to the door and gently pushed down the handle. There was a tiny but unmistakable click and she held her breath. But there was no sound from within the darkened office and slowly, carefully, she pulled open the door and slid through it into the empty corridor.

As she waited for the lift her heartbeat sounded like raindrops on a tin roof. Every second felt like a day, and she couldn't shift the feeling that at any moment she would hear Ram's voice or his footsteps in the darkness.

Pressing her forehead against the wall, she breathed out slowly. She should be feeling relief, and in some ways she was, for now she wouldn't have to go through that horrific about-last-night conversation, or the alternative—the awkward let's-pretend-it-never-happened version.

But she couldn't help feeling that somehow she was making a mistake. That what had happened between them had been so rare, so right, that she shouldn't just walk away from it.

She turned and gazed hesitantly down the darkened corridor.

Was she doing the right thing?

Or was she about to do something she'd regret?

But what would happen if she stayed?

Her heart was racing like a steeplechaser. What should she do?

She needed help. Fifty/fifty? Ask the audience?

She felt a rush of relief.

Phone a friend.

Stepping into the lift, she pulled out her mobile. It was four in the morning here, which made it two in the afternoon in Barbados. She would let it ring three times and then hang up.

Anna picked up on the second ring.

'Hi, you. This is a surprise...'

She paused, and for a moment Nola could almost picture her friend's face, the slight furrow between her eyes as she mentally calculated the time difference between the Caribbean and Australia.

'Have you been pulling an all-nighter or did you just randomly get up to watch the sunrise?'

Anna's voice was as calm as ever, but there was a brightness to it that Nola recognised as concern. And, despite everything, that made her feel calmer.

She swallowed. 'Neither. Look, I'm not hurt or anything, but...' She breathed out slowly. 'I've just done something really stupid. At least I think it was really stupid.'

There was the shortest of silences, and then Anna said firmly, 'In that case I'll get Robbie to make me a Rum Punch and you can tell me all about it.'

It was not the daylight creeping into his office that woke Ram. Nor was it the faint but aggravating hum of some kind of machinery. It was Nola.

Or rather the fact—the quite incredible fact—that at some unspecified point in the night she had gone.

Left.

Done a runner.

Hightailed it.

He felt a sudden sharp, inexplicable spasm of...of what? Irritation? Outrage? Disappointment?

No. A twitch ran down his spine and, breathing out, he sat up slowly and ran his hand over the stubble already shadowing his jaw. It was shock. That was all.

Sitting up, he stared in disbelief around the empty office. This had *never* happened. Ever. And, despite the evidence proving that it had, he still couldn't quite believe his eyes.

His heart started to beat faster. But, really, should he be that surprised? Every single time he thought he'd got Nola Mason all figured out she threw him a curveball that not only knocked him off his feet but left him wondering who she really was.

Who *he* really was.

He scowled. In this instance that should have been an easy question to answer.

He was the one who dressed and left.

He was always the one who chose the venue, and he never slept over.

Spending the night with a woman hinted too strongly at a kind of commitment he'd spent a lifetime choosing to avoid.

His face hardened. That didn't mean, though, that women upped and left him.

But, squinting into the pale grey light that was seeping into the room, he was forced to accept that on this occasion, with this woman, it did mean exactly that.

Which should be a good thing. Most women were tedious about their need to be held, or to talk, or to plan the next date, even when he couldn't have made it any clearer that none of the above was on offer.

Only for some reason Nola's departure felt premature.

Incomprehensible.

Maybe he was just overthinking it.

But why did her leaving seem to matter so much?

Probably because, although superficially she might have seemed different, he'd assumed in the end that she would behave like every other woman he knew. Only nothing about last night had turned out as he'd imagined it would.

He'd thought he was seducing her, but he'd never lost control like that.

He certainly hadn't planned to have sex with her *here*,

on the sofa in his office. But could he really be blamed for what had happened?

The tension between had been building from the moment they'd first met. In the restaurant it had been so intense, so powerful, he was surprised the other diners hadn't been sucked in by its gravitational pull.

She'd been as shaken by it as him—he was sure of it—and in the lift she had responded to his kiss so fiercely, and with such lack of inhibition, that he'd never got as far as inviting her back to his apartment.

Remembering that beat before they'd kissed, he felt his heart trip, heat and hunger tangling inside him. Watching that to-hell-with-you expression on her face grow fiercer, then soften as she melted into him, he'd wanted her so badly that he would have taken there and then in the lift if the doors hadn't opened.

Glancing round his office, his eyes homed in on his discarded shirt and he felt suddenly breathless, winded by the memory of how he'd sped her through the building with no real awareness of what he was doing, no conscious thought at all, just a need to have her in the most primitive way possible.

Reaching down, he picked his shirt up from the floor and slid his arms carelessly into the sleeves.

He hadn't hurt her. He would never do that. But he hadn't recognised himself. Hadn't recognised that fire, that urgency, that need—

The word snagged inside his head. No, not *need*.

It had been a long time since he had let himself *need* anyone. Not since he'd been a child, fighting misery and loneliness in a school on the other side of the world from his mother. Needing people, being needed, was something he'd avoided all his adult life, and whatever he might have felt for Nola he knew it couldn't have been that.

No, what he'd felt for Nola had been lust. And, like

hunger and thirst, once it had been satisfied it would be forgotten. *She* would be forgotten.

And that was what mattered. After months of feeling distracted and on edge, he could finally get back to focusing on his work.

After all, that was the real reason he'd wanted to sleep with her. To soothe the burn of frustration that had not only tested his self-control but made it impossible for him to focus on the biggest product launch of his career.

Now, though, just as he had with every other female he'd bedded, he could draw a line under her and get on with the rest of his life.

Straightening his cuffs, he stood up and walked briskly towards the door.

Ten hours later he was wrapping up the last meeting of the day.

'Right, if there's nothing else then I think we'll finish up here.'

It was five o'clock.

Ram glanced casually around the boardroom, saw his heads of department were already collecting their laptops and paperwork. His loathing of meetings was legendary among his staff, as was his near fanatical insistence that they start *and* end on time.

Pulling his laptop in front of him, he flipped it open as they began to leave the room.

The day had passed with grinding slowness.

Nothing had seemed to hold his attention, or maybe he simply hadn't been able to concentrate. But, either way, his thoughts had kept drifting off from whatever spreadsheet or proposal he was supposed to be discussing, and his head had filled with memories of the night before.

More specifically, memories of Nola—her body straddling his, her face softening as his own body grew harder than it had ever been...

He gritted his teeth. For some reason she had got under his skin in a way no woman ever had before. He'd even fallen asleep holding her in his arms. But for once intimacy had felt natural, right.

Staring down blankly at his computer screen, he felt his chest tighten. So what if it had felt right? He'd held her *in his sleep*. He hadn't even been conscious. And of course he would like to have sex with Nola again. He was a normal heterosexual man, and she was a beautiful, sexy woman.

Abruptly his muscles tensed, his eyes narrowing infinitesimally as through the open door he caught a glimpse of gleaming dark hair.

Nola! His stomach tightened involuntarily and he felt a rush of anticipation.

All day he'd been expecting to bump into her, had half imagined that she might seek him out. But now he realised that wouldn't be her way. She'd want it to play out naturally—like the tide coming in and going out again.

He breathed out sharply, his pulse zigzagging through his veins like a thread pulled through fabric, and before he even knew what he was doing he had crossed the room and yanked open the door.

But the corridor was empty.

Anger stuttered across his skin.

What the—? Why hadn't she come in to talk to him? She *must* have seen him.

Breathing out slowly, he stalked swiftly through the corridor to his office.

Jenny, his secretary, glanced up from her computer, her eyes widening at the expression on his face.

'Get Nola Mason on the phone. Tell her I want her in my office in the next five minutes.'

Slamming his office door, he strode across the room and stared furiously out of the window.

Was this some kind of a game?

Hopefully not—for *her* sake.

There was a knock at the door, and he felt a rush of satisfaction at having dragged Nola away from whatever it was she'd been doing.

'Come in,' he said curtly.

'Mr Walker—'

He turned, his face hardening as he saw Jenny, hovering in the doorway.

She smiled nervously. 'I'm sorry, Mr Walker. I was just going to tell you, but you went into your office before—'

He frowned impatiently. 'Tell me what?'

'Ms Mason can't come right now.'

'Can't or won't?' he snapped.

Jenny blinked. 'Oh, I'm sure she would if she were here, Mr Walker. But she's not here. She left about an hour ago. For the airport.'

Ram stared at her in silence, his eyes narrowing.

The airport?

'I—I thought you knew,' she stammered.

'I did.' He gave her a quick, curt smile. 'It must have slipped my mind. Thank you, Jenny.'

As the door closed his phone buzzed in his jacket and he reached for it, glancing distractedly down at the screen. And then his heart began to beat rhythmically in his chest.

It was an email.

From *Nola_Mason@CyberAngels.org*.

The corner of his mouth twisted, and then the words on the screen seemed to slip sideways as he slowly read, then reread, the email.

Dear Mr Walker

I am writing to confirm that in accordance with our agreement, today will be the last day of my employment at RWI. My colleague, Anna Harris—nee Mackenzie—and I will, of course, be in close contact with the on-site team, and remain available for any questions you may have.

I look forward to the successful completion of the project, and I wish to take this opportunity to thank you for all your personal input.
Nola Mason

Ram stared blankly at the email.
Was this some kind of a joke?
Slowly, his heart banging against his ribs like bailiffs demanding overdue rent, he reread it.
No, it wasn't a joke. It was a brush-off.
He read it again, his anger mounting with every word. Oh, it was all very polite, but there could be no mistaking the thank-you-but-I'm-done undertone. Why else would she have included that choice little remark at the bottom?

I wish to take this opportunity to thank you for all your personal input.

His fingers tightened around the phone.
Personal input!
He could barely see the screen through the veil of anger in front of his eyes, and it didn't help that he knew he was behaving irrationally—hypocritically, even. For in the past he'd ended liaisons with far less charm and courtesy.
But this was the woman he was paying to protect his business from unwanted intruders. Why, then, had he let her get past the carefully constructed emotional defences he'd built between himself and the world?

CHAPTER FOUR

Three months later

GLANCING UP AT the chalkboard above her head, Nola sighed. It was half past ten and the coffee shop was filling up, and as usual there was just too much choice. Today though, she had a rare morning off, and she wasn't about to waste the whole of it choosing a hot drink! Not even in Seattle, the coffee-drinking capital of the world.

Stepping forward, she smiled apologetically at the barista behind the counter. 'Just a green tea. Drink in. Oh, and one of those Danish, please. The cinnamon sort. Thanks.'

The sun was shining, but it was still not quite warm enough to sit outside, so she made her way to a table with a view of Elliott Bay.

Shrugging off her jacket, she leaned back in her seat, enjoying the sensation of sunlight on her face. Most of her time at work was spent alone in an office, hunched over a screen, so whenever she had any free time she liked to spend it outside. And her favourite place was right here, on the waterfront.

It was a little bit touristy. But then she *was* a tourist. And, besides, even if it did cater mainly to visitors, the restaurants still served amazingly fresh seafood and the coffee shops were a great place to relax and people-watch.

It was two weeks since she'd arrived in Seattle. And three months since she'd left Sydney. Three months of picking over the bones of her impulsive behaviour. Of wondering why she had ever thought that the consequences of sleeping with her boss would be less messy than sleeping with any other colleague?

Her pulse hopscotched forward. It was a little late to start worrying about consequences now. Particularly when one of them was a baby.

Breathing out slowly, she glanced down at her stomach and ran her hand lightly over the small rounded bump.

She had never imagined having a child. Her parents' unhappy marriage and eventual divorce had not exactly encouraged her to think of matrimony as the fairy-tale option that many of her friends, including Anna, believed it to be.

Being a mother, like being married, had always been something she thought happened to other people. Had she thought about it at all, she would probably have wanted the father of her baby to be a gentle, easy-going, thoughtful man.

She took another sip of tea.

So not Ram Walker, then.

And yet here she was, carrying his baby.

Across the café a young couple sat drinking *lattes*, gazing dotingly at a baby in a buggy. They looked like a photoshoot for the perfect modern family, and suddenly the cup in her hand felt heavy. Almost as heavy as her heart. For it was a life her child would never enjoy.

Not least because she hadn't told Ram about the baby.

And nor would she.

Had he shown any sign, any hint that he wanted to be a father, she would have told him the moment she'd found out. But some men just weren't cut out for relationships and commitment, and Ram was one of them.

He'd said so to her face, so it had been easy at first to feel that her silence was justified—especially when she was still struggling not just with the shock of finding out she was pregnant but with nausea and an exhaustion that made getting dressed feel like a tough mission.

Only now, when finally she was in a fit enough state to think, she was almost as overwhelmed with guilt as she had been with nausea.

Evening after evening had been spent silently arguing with herself over whether or not she should tell him about the baby. But with each passing day she'd convinced herself that there really was no point in letting him know.

He'd clearly stated that he didn't want to be a father, and she knew from the way he lived his life that he wasn't capable of being one.

She didn't mean biologically. He clearly could father a child—and had. But what kind of a father would he be? His relationships with women lasted days, not years—not much use for raising a child to adulthood. Their brief affair had given her first-hand experience of his limited attention span. That night in his office she had felt as though he was floating through her veins. But afterwards he'd barely acknowledged the email she'd sent him. Just sent a single sentence thanking her for her services.

Her face felt hot. Was that the real reason why she hadn't told him about the baby? Her pride? Her ego? A yearning to keep her memories of that night intact and not made ugly by the truth? The truth that he'd never wanted anything more than a one-night stand. Never wanted her *or* this baby.

She felt the hot sting of tears behind her eyes as silently she questioned her motives again. But, no, it wasn't pride or sentimentality that was stopping her from saying anything.

It was him. It was Ram.

She didn't need to confront him to know that he wouldn't want to know about the baby, or be a father, or be in their lives. Whatever connection there had been between them had ended when she'd crept out of his office in the early hours of that morning. Nothing would change that, so why put herself through the misery of having him spell it out in black and white?

She shifted in her seat. So now she was three months pregnant, unmarried, living out of a suitcase—and happy.

It was true that she sometimes got a little freaked out at the thought of being solely responsible for the baby growing inside her. But she knew she could bring a child up on her own—better than if Ram was involved.

Her mum had done it and, besides, Anna and Robbie would be there for her—when she finally got round to telling them.

She felt a twinge of guilt.

Unlike with Ram, she didn't have any doubts about telling her friends about the baby. Quite the opposite. She wanted them to know. But by the time she'd done a test she'd been in Seattle, struggling with morning sickness. Besides, she wanted to tell her friend face-to-face, not over the—

Her phone rang and, glancing down at the screen, she frowned. It was Anna. Quickly, she answered it.

'That is so weird. I was literally just thinking about you.'

Anna snorted. 'Really? What happened? Did you eat some shortbread and finally remember your old pal in Scotland?'

'I spoke to you three days ago,' Nola protested.

'And you said you'd call back. But what happens? Nothing. No text. No email...'

'I've been busy.'

'Doing what?' Anna paused. 'No, let me guess. Drinking coffee?'

Nola smiled. Since her arrival in Seattle, it was a private joke between them that Nola was drinking coffee every time her friend called.

Tucking the phone under her chin, she smiled. 'Actually, it's green tea, and it's delicious. And the Danish isn't bad either!'

'You're eating a Danish? That's fantastic.'

The relief in Anna's voice caught Nola off guard. They might barely have seen one another over the last few months but she knew her friend had been worried about her, and if she wasn't going to tell her about the baby, the least she could do was put Anna's mind at rest.

'Yeah, you heard it here first. The appetite's back. Pizzerias across the entire state of Washington are rejoicing! In fact I might even get a national holiday named after me.'

Anna laughed. 'I always said you had Italian roots.'

'Was it my blue eyes or my pale skin that gave it away?' Nola said teasingly. 'Okay, that's enough of your amateur psychology, Dr Harris. Tell me why you've rung.'

There was a slight pause.

'You mean I need something more than just being bossy?'

Nola frowned. There was something odd about her friend's voice. She sounded nervous, hesitant. 'I don't know—do you?'

There was a short silence, then Anna sighed. 'Yes. I still can't believe it happened, but...you know how clumsy I am? Well, I was out walking yesterday with Robbie, and I tripped. Guess what? I broke my foot.'

Relief, smooth and warm, surged over Nola's skin.

'Oh, thank goodness.' She frowned. 'I don't mean thank goodness you broke your foot—I just thought it was going to be something worse.' She breathed out. 'Are you okay? Does it hurt? Have you got one of those crazy boot things?'

'I'm fine. It doesn't hurt anymore and, yeah, I've got a boot. But, Noles...'

Anna paused and Nola felt the air grow still around her.

'But, Noles, what?' she said slowly.

'I can't fly for another week. It's something to do with broken bones making you more at risk of blood clots, so—'

Nola felt her ribcage contract. Glancing down, she noticed that her hands were shaking. But she'd read the email. She knew what was coming.

'So you want me to go to Sydney?'

Nola swallowed. Even just saying the words out loud made panic grip her around the throat.

'I really didn't want to ask you, and ordinarily I'd just postpone it. But the launch is so close.' There was another infinitesimal pause. 'And we *are* under contract.'

Anna sounded so wretched that Nola was instantly furious with herself.

Of course she would go to Sydney. Her friend had been a shoulder to cry on after she'd slept with Ram and generally fallen apart. She damn well wasn't going to make her sweat and feel guilty for asking one tiny favour.

'I know, and I understand—it's fine,' she heard herself say.

'Are you sure? I thought there might be a problem—'

There definitely *would* be a problem, Nola thought dully. About six feet of problem, with tousled dark hair and cheekbones that could sharpen steel. But it would be *her* problem, not Anna's.

'There won't be!' Nola shook her head, trying to shake off the leaden feeling in her chest. 'And it's me who should be sorry. Moping around and making a huge fuss about some one-night stand.'

'You didn't make a fuss,' Anna said indignantly, sounding more like herself. 'You made a mistake. And if he wasn't paying us such a huge sum of money, I'd tell him where he could stick his global launch.'

Nola laughed. 'Let's wait until the money clears and then we can tell him together. Look, please don't worry,

Anna. It'll be fine. It's not as if he's going to be making an effort to see me.'

'Oh, you don't need to worry about that,' Anna said quickly. 'I checked before I called you. He's in New York on some business trip. He won't be back for at least five days, so you definitely won't have to see him. Not that you'd have much to say to him even if he was there.'

Hanging up, Nola curled her arms around her waist protectively.

Except that she did.

She had a lot to say.

Only she had no intention of saying any of it to Ram—ever.

Glancing out of the window of his limo, Ram stared moodily up at the RWI building with none of the usual excitement and pride he felt at seeing the headquarters of his company. His trip to New York had been productive and busy—there had been the usual hectic round of meetings—but for the first time ever he had wanted to come home early.

As the car slowed he frowned. He still didn't understand why he'd decided to shorten his trip. But then, right now he didn't understand a lot of what was happening in his life, for it seemed to be changing in ways he couldn't control or predict.

Nodding at the receptionists on the front desk, he strode through the foyer and took the lift up to the twenty-second floor. Closing the door to his office, he stared disconsolately out of the window.

The launch date was rapidly approaching, but he was struggling to find any enthusiasm and energy for what amounted to the biggest day of his business career.

Nor was he even faintly excited about any of the beautiful, sexy women who were pursuing him with the determination and dedication of hungry cheetahs hunting an impala.

Why did he feel like this? And why was he feeling like it *now*?

He gritted his teeth. He knew the answer to both those questions. In fact it was the same answer. For, despite his having tried to erase her from his mind, *Nola* was the answer, the punchline, the coda to every single question and thought he'd had since she'd left Australia.

It might have been okay if it was just every now and then, but the reality was that Nola was never far from his thoughts. Even though she'd been gone for months now, every time he saw a mass of long dark hair he was still sure it was her. And each time that it wasn't he felt the same excitement, and disappointment, then fury.

There was a knock at the door, and when he was sure his face would give away nothing of what he was feeling, he said curtly. 'Come in.'

It was Jenny.

'I emailed you the data you asked for.' She handed him a folder. 'But I know you like a hard copy as well.'

He nodded. 'Anything crop up while I was away?'

'Nothing major. There were a couple of problems with some of the pre-order sites, and the live stream was only working intermittently on Tuesday. But Ms Mason sorted them out so—'

Ram stiffened. 'Ms Mason? Why didn't you tell me she called?'

Jenny's eyes widened. 'Because she didn't call. She's here.'

He stared past her, his chest tightening with shock.

'Since when?'

'Since Monday.' She smiled. 'But she's leaving tonight. Oh, and she's pr—'

He cut her off. 'And nobody thought to tell me?' he demanded.

'I thought you knew. I— Is there a problem?' Jenny stammered. 'I thought she was still under contract.'

Blood was pounding in his ears.

Glancing at his secretary's scared expression, he shook his head and softened his voice. 'There isn't, and she is.'

He could hardly believe it. Nola was in the building and yet she hadn't bothered to come and find him.

As though reading his thoughts, Jenny gave him a small, anxious smile. 'She probably thinks you're still in New York. I'm sure she'd like to see you,' she said breathlessly.

Remembering the email Nola had sent him, he felt his pulse twitch. That seemed unlikely, but it wasn't her choice.

He smiled blandly. 'I'm sure she does. Maybe you could get her on the phone, Jenny, and tell her I'd like to see her in my office. When it's convenient, of course. It's just that we have some unfinished business.'

But it wasn't going to stay unfinished for long.

Watching the door close, he leaned back in his chair, his face expressionless.

Finally she was done!

Resting her forehead against the palms of her hands, Nola stifled a yawn. It might only be four o'clock in the afternoon, but it felt as if she'd worked an all-nighter. If only she could go back to bed. Really, though, what would be the point? The fact she was sleeping badly was nothing to do with jet lag.

It was nerves.

She scowled. Not that she had any real reason to be nervous. Anna had been right—Ram was in New York on business. But that hadn't stopped the prickling sensation in the back of her neck as she'd walked into the RWI foyer, for even if the man himself wasn't in the building his presence was everywhere, making it impossible to shake off the feeling that there was still some link between them— an invisible bond that just wouldn't break.

Lowering her hands, she laid her fingers protectively over her stomach.

Not so invisible now.

For the last few weeks she'd been wearing her usual clothes, but today, for the first time, she'd struggled to get into her jeans. Fortunately she'd packed a pair of stretchy trousers that, although close-fitting, were more forgiving. She glanced down at her bump and smiled. It wasn't large, but she definitely looked pregnant now, and several people—mostly women—had noticed and congratulated her.

It was lovely, seeing their faces light up and finally being able to share this new phase of her life. But she would still be glad when it was all over and she could walk out through the huge RWI doors for the last time. And not just because of Ram's ghostly presence in the building. It felt wrong that people she barely knew—people who worked for Ram—knew that she was pregnant when he didn't.

And somehow, being here in his building, telling herself that he wouldn't want to know about the baby or be a father, didn't seem to be working anymore. He *was* the father. And being here had made that fact unavoidable.

Thankfully her train of thought was interrupted as her phone rang. Glancing at the screen, she frowned, her stomach clenching involuntarily.

It was Ram's secretary, Jenny.

'Hi, Jenny. Is everything okay?

'Yes, everything's fine, Ms Mason. I was just ringing to ask if you'd mind popping up to the office? Mr Walker would like to see you.'

Mr Walker.

She opened her mouth to say some words, but no sound came from her lips.

'I thought he was away,' she managed finally. 'On business.'

'He was.' To her shell-shocked ears Jenny's voice sounded painfully bright and happy. 'But he flew back in this afternoon. And he particularly asked to see you. Apparently you have unfinished business?'

Nola nodded, too stunned by Jenny's words even to register the fact that the other woman couldn't see her.

'Okay, well, he said to come up whenever it's convenient, so I'll see you in a bit.'

'Okay, see you then,' Nola lied.

As she hung up her heart began leaping like a salmon going upstream. For a moment she couldn't move, then slowly she closed her laptop and picked up her jacket.

Where could she go? Not her hotel. He might track her down. Nor the airport—at least not yet. No, probably it would be safest just to hide in some random café until it was time to check in.

On legs that felt like blancmange, she walked across the office and out into the corridor.

'Mr Walker? I'm just making some coffee. Can I get you anything?'

Ram looked up at Jenny.

'No, thank you, Jenny. I'm good.'

He glanced down at his phone and frowned. It was half past four. A flicker of apprehension ran down his spine.

'By the way, did you call Ms Mason?' he asked casually.

She nodded. 'Yes, and she said she'd be up in a bit.'

He nodded. 'Good. Excellent.'

He felt stupidly elated at her words, and suddenly so restless that he couldn't stay sitting at his desk a moment longer.

'Actually, I might just go and stretch my legs, Jenny. If Ms Mason turns up, ask her to wait in my office, please.'

The idea of Nola having to wait for him was strangely satisfying and, grabbing his jacket, he walked out through the door and began wandering down the corridor. Most of his staff were at their desks, but as he turned the corner into the large open-plan reception area he saw a group of people waiting for the lift.

Walking towards them, he felt a thrill of anticipation at the thought of finally seeing her again—and then abruptly he stopped dead, his eyes freezing with shock and disbelief. For there, standing slightly apart from the rest, her jacket folded over her arm, was Nola.

He watched, transfixed, as she stepped into the lift. Her long dark hair was coiled at the nape of her neck, and a tiny part of his brain registered that he'd never seen her wear it like that before.

But the bigger part was concentrating not on her hair but on the small, rounded, unmistakable bump of her stomach.

He heard his own sharp intake of breath as though from a long way away.

She was pregnant.

Pregnant.

A vice seemed to be closing around his throat. He felt like a drowning man watching his life play out in front of his eyes. A life that had just been derailed, knocked off course by a single night of passion.

And then, just as his legs overrode his brain, the lift doors closed and she was gone.

He stood gazing across the office, his head spinning, his breath scrabbling inside his chest like an animal trying to get out.

She was pregnant—several months pregnant at least—and frantically he rewound back through the calendar. But even before he reached the date when they'd slept together he knew that the baby could be his.

The blood seemed to drain from his body.

So why hadn't she said anything to him?

She'd been in the office for days. Yes, he'd been in New York when she arrived, but Jenny had spoken to her earlier. Nola knew he was in the building. Knew that he wanted to see her—

Remembering his remark about unfinished business, he almost laughed out loud.

Unfinished business.

You could say that again.

So why hadn't she said anything to him?

The question looped inside his head, each time growing louder and louder, like a car alarm. The obvious and most logical answer was that he was not the father.

Instantly he felt his chest tighten. The thought of Nola giving herself to another man made him want to smash his fists into the wall.

Surely she wouldn't—she couldn't have.

A memory rose up inside him, stark and unfiltered, of Nola, her body melting into his. She had been like fire under his skin. For that one night she had been his.

But was that baby his too?

A muscle flickered along the line of his jaw and he felt his anger curdle, swirling and separating into fury and frustration. Turning, he strode back into his office.

There was no way he could second-guess this. He had to know for certain.

'Tell Mike to bring the car round to the front of the building—*now*,' he barked at Jenny. 'I need to get to the airport.'

Ten minutes later he was slouched in the back of his limo. His head was beginning to clear finally, and now his anger was as cold and hostile as the arctic tundra.

How could she do this?

Treating him as if he didn't matter, as if he'd only had some walk-on part in her life. If he was the father, he should be centre stage.

His hands clenched in his lap. He hated the feeling of being sidelined, of being secondary to the key players in the drama, for it reminded him of his childhood, and the years he'd spent trying to fit into his parents' complex relationship.

But he wasn't a child anymore. He was man who might be about to have a child of his own.

His breath stilled in his throat.

Only *how* could he be the father? She had told him she was safe. But there was always an element of risk—particularly for a man like him, a man who would be expected to provide generous financial support for his child. Which was why he always used precautions of his own.

Except that night with Nola.

He'd wanted her so badly that he couldn't bring himself to do anything that might have risked them pausing, maybe changing their minds—like putting on a condom.

Feeling the car slow, he glanced up, his pulse starting to accelerate.

Was the baby his? He would soon find out.

Before the limo had even come to a stop, he was opening the door and stepping onto the pavement.

Dragging her suitcase through the airport, Nola frowned. She had waited as long as possible before arriving at the airport, and now she was worried she would be too late to check in her luggage.

But any worry she might be feeling now was nothing to the stress of staying at the office. Knowing he was in the building had been unsettling enough, but the fact that Ram had asked to see her—

She didn't need to worry about that now and, curving her hand protectively over her stomach, she breathed out slowly, trying to calm herself as she stopped in front of the departures board.

She was just trying to locate her flight when there was some kind of commotion behind her and, turning, she saw that there was a crowd of people pointing and milling around.

'They're shooting a commercial,' the woman standing next to her said knowledgeably. 'It was in the paper. It's for beer. Apparently it's got that rugby player in it, and a crocodile.'

'A real one?'

The woman laughed. 'Yes, but it's not here. I just meant in the advert. I don't think they'd be allowed to bring a real croc to an airport. That'd be way too dangerous.'

Nodding politely, Nola smiled—and then she caught her breath for, striding towards her, his lean, muscular body parting the crowds like a mythical wind, and looking more dangerous than any wild animal, was Ram Walker.

CHAPTER FIVE

AS SHE WATCHED his broad shoulders cutting through the clumps of passengers like a scythe through wheat Nola couldn't move. Or speak, or even think. Shock seemed to have robbed her of the ability to do anything but gape.

And as he made his way across the departures lounge towards her she couldn't decide if it was shock or desire that was making her heart feel as if it was about to burst.

Mind numb, she stood frozen, like a movie on pause. It was just over three months since she'd last seen him. Three months of trying and failing to forget the man who had changed her life completely.

She'd assumed she just needed more time, that eventually his memory would fade. Only now he was here, and she knew she'd been kidding herself. She would never forget Ram—and not just because she was pregnant with his baby.

Her body began to shake, and instinctively she folded her arms over her stomach.

A baby he didn't even know existed.

A baby she had deliberately chosen to conceal from him.

And just like that she knew his being here wasn't some cosmic coincidence: he was coming to find her.

Before that thought had even finished forming in her head he was there, standing in front of her, and suddenly she wished she was sitting down, for the blazing anger in his grey gaze almost knocked her off her feet.

'Going somewhere?' he asked softly.

She had forgotten his voice. Not the sound of it, but the power it had to throw her into a state of confusion, to turn her emotions into a swirling mass of chaos that made even breathing a challenge.

Looking up at him, hoping that her voice was steadier than her heartbeat, she said hoarsely, 'Mr Walker. I wasn't expecting to see you.'

He didn't reply. For a moment his narrowed gaze stayed fixed on her face, and then her skin seemed to blister and burn as slowly his eyes slid down over her throat and breast, stopping pointedly on the curve of her stomach.

'Yes, it's been a day of surprises all round.'

His heart crashing against his ribs, Ram stared at Nola in silence. He had spent the last two hours waiting at the check-in desk for her, his nerves buzzing beneath his skin at the sight of every long-haired brunette. At first when she hadn't turned up he'd been terrified that she'd caught another flight. But finally it had dawned on him that she was probably just hoping to avoid him, and therefore was going to arrive at the last minute.

Now that she was here, he was struggling to come to terms with what he could see—for seeing her in the office had been such a shock that he'd almost started to think that maybe what he'd seen might not even have been real. After all, it had only been a glimpse...

Maybe it had been another woman with dark hair, and after months of thinking and dreaming about her he'd just imagined it was Nola.

Now, though, there could be no doubt, no confusion.

It was Nola, and she was pregnant.

But that didn't mean he was the father.

He felt himself jerk forward—doubt and then certainty vibrating through his bones.

If that baby was another man's child, he knew she would

have met his gaze proudly. Instead she looked hunted, cornered, like a small animal facing a predator it couldn't outrun.

In other words, guilty as hell.

With an effort he shifted his gaze from her stomach to her face. Her lips were pale, and her blue eyes were huge and uncomprehending. She looked, if possible, more stunned than he felt. But right now feelings were secondary to the truth.

'So this is why you've been giving me the runaround?' he asked slowly. 'I suppose I should offer my congratulations.' He paused, letting the silence stretch between them. *To both of us.*

Watching her eyes widen with guilt, he felt new shoots of anger pushing up inside him, so that suddenly his pulse was too fast and irregular.

'I wonder—when, exactly, were you going to tell me you were pregnant?'

Looking up into his face, Nola felt her breath jerk in her throat. He was angrier than she'd ever seen him. Angrier than she'd ever seen anyone. And he had every right to be.

Had she been standing there, confronted by both this truth and the months of deception that had preceded it, she would have felt as furious and thwarted as he did. But somehow knowing that made her feel more defensive, for that was only half the story. The half that *didn't* include her reasons for acting as she had.

Lifting her chin, she met his gaze. 'Why would I tell you I'm pregnant? As of twenty minutes ago, I don't actually work for you anymore.'

Her hands curled up into fists in front of her as he took a step towards her.

'Don't play games with me, Nola.'

His eyes burned into hers, and the raw hostility in his

voice suffocated her so that suddenly she could hardly breathe.

'And don't pretend this has got anything to with your employment rights. You're having a baby, and we both know it could be mine. So you should have told me.'

Around her, the air sharpened. She could feel people turning to stare at them curiously.

Forcing herself to hold his gaze, she glared at him. 'This has got nothing to do with you.'

A nerve pulsed along his jawline.

'And you want me to take your word for that, do you?' He gazed at her in naked disbelief. 'On the basis of what? Your outstanding display of honesty up until now?'

She blinked. 'You don't know for certain if you're the father,' she said quickly, failing to control the rush of colour to her face.

His eyes locked onto hers, and instantly she felt the tension in her spine tighten like a guy rope.

'No. But *you* do.'

She flinched, wrong-footed.

How was this happening?

Not him finding her. It would have been a matter of moments for his secretary to check her flight time. But why was he here? Over the last three months she'd spent hours imagining this moment, playing out every possible type of scenario. In not one of them had he pursued her to the airport and angrily demanded the truth.

Her heart began to pound fiercely.

It would be tempting to think that he cared about the baby.

Tempting, but foolish.

Ram's appearance at the airport, his frustration and anger, had nothing to do with any sudden rush of paternal feelings on his part. Understandably, he hadn't liked finding out second-hand that she was pregnant. But that didn't mean he could just turn up and start throwing his weight around.

'I don't see why you're making this into such a big deal,' she snapped. 'We both know that you have absolutely no interest in being a father anyway.'

Ram studied her face, his pulse beating slow and hard.

It was true that up until this moment, he'd believed that fatherhood was not for him. But he'd been talking about a concept, a theoretical child, and Nola knew that as well as he did.

His chest tightened with anger.

'That doesn't mean I don't want to know *when* I am going to be one. In fact, I think I have a right to know. However, if you're saying that you really don't know who the father is, then I suggest we find out for certain.' His eyes held hers. 'I believe it's a fairly simple test. Of course it would mean you'd have to miss your flight…'

Imprisoned by his dark grey gaze, Nola gritted her teeth.

He was calling her bluff, and she hated him for it.

But what she hated more was the fact that in spite of her anger and resentment she could feel her body unfurling inside, as though it was waking from a long hibernation. And even though he was causing mayhem in her life, her longing for him still sucked the breath from her lungs.

Glancing at his profile, she felt a pulse of heat that had nothing to do with anger skim over her skin. But right now the stupid, senseless way she reacted to Ram didn't matter. All she cared about was catching that plane—and that was clearly not going to happen unless Ram found out, one way or another, if this baby was his.

So why not just tell him the truth?

Squaring her shoulders, she met his gaze. 'Fine,' she said slowly. 'You're the father.'

She didn't really know how she'd expected him to react,

but he didn't say or do anything. He just continued to stare at her impassively, his grey eyes dark and unblinking.

'I know you don't want to be involved, and that's fine. I'm not expecting you to be,' she said quickly. 'That's one of the reasons I didn't tell you.'

'So you had more than one reason, then?' he said quietly.

She frowned, unsure of how she should respond. But she didn't get a chance to reply, for as though he had suddenly become conscious of the sidelong glances and the sudden stillness surrounding them, he reached down and picked up her suitcase.

'I suggest we finish this in private.'

Turning, Ram walked purposefully across the departures lounge. Inside his head, though, he had no idea where he was going. Or what to do when he got there.

You're the father!

Three words he'd never expected or wanted to hear.

Then—*boom!*—there they were, blowing apart his carefully ordered world.

His chest grew tight. Only this wasn't just about his life anymore; there was a new life to consider now.

Through the haze of his confused thoughts he noticed two empty chairs in the corner, next to a vending machine, and gratefully sat down in one.

His head was spinning. Seeing Nola pregnant at the office, he'd guessed that he might be the father. But it had been just that. A guess. It hadn't felt real—not least because he'd spent all his life believing that this moment would never happen.

Only now it had, and he would have expected his response to be a mix of resentment and regret.

But, incredibly, what he was actually feeling was resolve. A determination to be part of his child's life.

Now all he needed to do was persuade Nola of that fact.

Glancing over to where Ram now sat, with that familiar shuttered look on his handsome face, Nola felt resentment surge through her. How could he do this? Just stroll back into her life and take over, expecting her to follow him across the room like some puppy he was training?

He had said he wanted to know the truth and so she'd told him, hoping that would be the end of their conversation. Why, then, did they need to speak in private? What else was there to say?

Her eyes narrowed. Maybe she should just leave him sitting there. Leave the airport, catch a train, or just go and hide in some nameless hotel. Show Ram that she wasn't going to be pushed around by him.

But clearly he was determined to have the last word, and trying to stop him doing so would be like trying to defy gravity: exhausting, exasperating, and ultimately futile.

The fact was that he was just so much more relentless than she could ever be, and whatever it was that drove his desire—no, his determination to win, she couldn't compete with it. Whether she liked it or not, this conversation was going to have to happen, so she might as well get on with it or she would never get on that plane.

Mutinously, she walked over to him and, ignoring the small satisfied smile on his face, sat down next to him.

Around her people were moving, picking up luggage and chatting, happy to be going home or going on holiday, and for a split second she wished with an intensity that almost doubled her over that it was her and Ram going away together. That she could rewind time, meet him in some other way, under different circumstances, and—

Her lip curled.

And what?

She and Ram might share a dizzying sexual chemistry, but there was no trust, no honesty and no harmony. Most of their conversations ended up in an argument, and the only time they'd managed to stay on speaking terms was when they hadn't needed to speak.

Remembering the silence between them in the lift, the words left unspoken on her lips as he'd covered her mouth with his, she felt heat break out on her skin.

That night had been different. That night all the tension and antagonism between them had melted into the darkness and they had melted into one another, their quickening bodies hot and liquid...

She swallowed.

But sex wasn't enough to sustain a relationship. And one night of passion, however incredible, wasn't going to make her change her mind. It had been a hard decision to make, but it was the right one. A two-parent set-up might be traditional—desirable, even—but not if one of those parents was always halfway out through the door, literally and emotionally.

Breathing out slowly, she turned her head and stared into his eyes. 'Look, what happened three months ago has got nothing to do with now...' She paused. 'It wasn't planned—we just made a mistake.'

For a moment, his gaze held hers, and then slowly he shook his head.

'We didn't make a mistake, Nola.'

'I wasn't talking about the baby,' she said quickly.

His eyes rested intently on her face.

'Neither was I.'

And just like that she felt her stomach flip over, images from the night they'd spent together exploding inside her head like popping corn. Suddenly her whole body was quivering, and it was all she could do not to lean over and kiss him, to give in to that impulse to taste and touch that beautiful mouth once again—

Taking a quick breath, she dragged her eyes away from him, ignoring the sparks scattering over her skin.

'You said you wanted to finish this, Ram, but we can't,' she said hoarsely. 'Because it never started. It was just a one-night stand, remember?'

'Oh, I remember every single moment of that night. As I'm sure you do, Nola.'

His eyes gleamed, and instantly her pulse began to accelerate.

'But this isn't about just one night anymore. Our one-night stand has got long-term consequences.' He gestured towards her stomach.

'But not for you.' She looked up at him stubbornly, her blue eyes wide with frustration. 'Whatever connection we had, it ended a long time ago.'

'Given that you're pregnant with my child, that would seem to be a little premature and counter-intuitive,' he said softly. 'But I don't think there's anything to be gained by continuing this discussion now.' He grimaced. 'Or here. I suggest we leave it for a day or two. I can take you back to the city—I have an apartment there you can use as a base—and I'll talk to my lawyers, get some kind of intermediate financial settlement set up.'

Nola gazed at him blankly.

Apartment? Financial settlement?

What was he talking about?

This wasn't about money. This was about what was best for their child, and Ram was *not* father material. A father should be consistent, compassionate, and capable of making personal sacrifices for the sake of his child. But Ram was just not suited to making the kinds of commitment and sacrifices expected and required by parenthood.

She had no doubt that financially he would be generous, but children needed more than money. They needed to be loved. To be wanted.

Memories of her own father and his lack of interest filled her head, and suddenly she couldn't meet Ram's eyes. Her father had been a workaholic. For him, business had come first, and if he'd had any time and energy left after a working day he'd chosen to spend it either out entertaining clients or with one of his many mistresses. Home-life, his wife and his daughter, had been right at the bottom of his agenda—more like a footnote, in fact.

Being made to feel so unimportant had blighted her childhood. As an adult, too, she had struggled to believe in herself. It had taken a long time, her friendship with Anna, and a successful career to overcome that struggle. And it was a struggle she was determined her child would never have to face.

But what was the point of telling Ram any of that? He wouldn't understand. How could he? It was not as if he'd ever doubted himself or felt that he wasn't good enough.

'No,' she said huskily. 'That's not going to happen.' She was shaking her head but her eyes were fixed on his face. 'I don't want your money, Ram, or your apartment. And I'm sorry if this offends your *romantic sensibilities*, but I don't want you in my baby's life just because we spent eight hours on a sofa in your office.'

Recognising his own words, Ram felt a swirling, incoherent fury surge up inside him. Wrong, he thought savagely. She had *belonged* to him that night, and now she was carrying his baby part of her would belong to him for ever.

Leaning back, he let his eyes roam over her face, his body responding with almost primeval force to her flushed cheeks and resentful pout even as his mind plotted his next move.

What mattered most was keeping her in Australia, and losing his temper would only make her more determined to leave. So, reining in his anger, he stretched out his legs and gazed at her calmly.

'Sadly for you, that decision is not yours to make. I'm not a lawyer, but I'm pretty sure that it's paternity, not romantic sensibilities, that matters to a judge. But why don't you call your lawyer just to make sure?'

It wasn't true but judging by the flare of fear in her eyes, Nola's knowledge of parental rights was clearly based on law procedural dramas not legal expertise. Nola could hardly breathe. Panic was strangling her. Why was he suddenly talking about lawyers and judges?

'Wh-Why are you doing this?' she stammered. 'I know you're angry with me for not telling you about the baby, and I understand that. But you have to understand that you're the reason I didn't say anything.'

'Oh, I see. So it's *my* fault you didn't tell me?'

He was speaking softly, but there was no mistaking the dangerous undertone curling through his words.

'*My* fault that you deliberately chose to avoid me at the office today? And I suppose it'll be my fault, too, when my child grows up without a father and spends the rest of his life feeling responsible—'

He broke off, his face hardening swiftly.

She bit her lip. 'No, of course not. I just meant that from everything you said before I didn't think you'd want to know. So I made a choice.'

Ram could hear the slight catch in her voice but he ignored it. Whatever he'd said before was irrelevant now. This baby was real. And it was his. Besides, nothing he'd said in the past could excuse her lies and deceit.

'And that's what this is about, is it? *Your* choices? *Your* pregnancy? *Your* baby?' He shook his head. 'This is not *your* baby, Nola, it's *our* baby—mine as much as yours—and you know it. And I am going be a part of his or her life.'

Nola stared at him numbly, her head pounding in time with her heart. She didn't know what to say to him—hadn't got the words to defend herself or argue her case. Not that it mattered. He wasn't listening to her anyway.

Shoulders back, neck tensing, she looked away, her eyes searching frantically for some way to escape—and then her heart gave a jolt as she suddenly saw the time on the departures board.

The next second she had snatched her suitcase and was on her feet, pulse racing.

'What do you think you're doing?'

Ram was standing in front of her, blocking her way.

'I have to go!'

Her voice was rising, and a couple of people turned to look at her. But she didn't care. If she missed this flight she would be stuck in Sydney for hours, possibly days, and she had to get away—as far away from Ram as quickly as she could.

'They've called my flight so I need to check in my luggage.'

For a moment he stared at her in silence, and then his face shifted and, leaning forward, he plucked the suitcase handle from her fingers.

'Let me take that!'

He strode away from her and, cursing under her breath, she hurried after him.

'I really don't need your help,' she said through gritted teeth.

Tucking the suitcase under his arm, he smiled blandly. 'Of course not. But you have to understand I don't fly commercial, so all this rushing around is very exciting for me. It's actually better than watching a film.'

He sounded upbeat—buoyant, almost—and she glowered at him, part baffled, part exasperated by this sudden change in mood.

'That's wonderful, Ram,' she said sarcastically. 'But I'm not here to be your entertainment for the evening.'

'If you were my entertainment for the evening you wouldn't be getting breathless from running around an airport,' he said softly. And, reaching over, he took her arm and pulled her towards him.

Her breath stuttered in her throat, and suddenly all her senses were concentrated on his hand and on the firmness of his grip and the heat of his skin through the fabric of her shirt.

'You need to slow down. You're pregnant. And besides...' he gestured towards the seemingly endless queue of people looping back and forth across the width of the room '... I don't think a couple of minutes is going to make that much difference.'

Gazing at the queue, Nola groaned. 'I'm never going to make it.'

'You don't know that.' Ram frowned. 'Why don't we ask at the desk?'

He pointed helpfully to where two women in uniform were chatting with a group of passengers surrounded by trolleys and toddlers. But Nola was already hurrying across the room.

'Excuse me. Could you help me, please? I'm supposed to be on this flight to Edinburgh but I need to check in my baggage.'

Handing over her boarding pass, she held her breath as the woman glanced down at it, and then back at her screen, before finally shaking her head.

'I'm sorry, the bag drop desk is closed—and even if we rush you through it's a good ten minutes to get to the boarding gate.' She grimaced. 'And, looking ahead, all Edinburgh flights are full for the next twenty-four hours. You might be able to pick up a cancellation, but that would mean hanging around at the airport. I'm sorry I can't be more helpful...'

'That's okay,' Nola said stiffly. 'It's really not your fault.'

And it wasn't.

Turning away, she stalked over to where Ram stood, watching her unrepentantly.

'This is your fault,' she snapped. 'If you hadn't been talking to me I'd have heard it when they called my flight and then I would have checked in my luggage on time.'

He gazed at her blandly. 'Oh, was that your flight to Edinburgh? I didn't realise it was that important. Like I said, I don't fly commercial, so—'

Nola stared at him, wordless with disbelief, her nails cutting into her hands. 'Don't give me that "I don't fly commercial" rubbish. You knew exactly what you were doing.'

He smiled down at her serenely. 'Really? You think I'd deliberately and selfishly withhold a vital piece of information?' He shook his head, his eyes glittering. 'I'm shocked. I mean, who would *do* something like that?'

She was shaking with anger. 'This is not the same at all.'

'No, it's not,' he said softly. 'I stopped you catching a flight, and you tried to stop me finding out I was a father.'

'But I didn't do it to hurt you,' she said shakily. 'Or to punish you.

And she hadn't—only how could she prove that to Ram? How could she explain to him that she had only been trying to prevent her child's future from inheriting her past? How could she tell him that life had taught her that no father was better than a bad father.

She shivered. It was all such a mess. And she didn't know what to do to fix it. All she knew was that she wanted to go home. To be anywhere but at this noisy, crowded airport, standing in front of a man who clearly hated her.

Her eyes were stinging and she turned away blindly.

'Nola. Don't go.'

Something in his voice stopped her, and slowly, reluctantly, she met his gaze.

He was staring at her impassively, his eyes cool and detached.

'Look, I don't think either of us was expecting to have this conversation, and even though I think we both know that we have a lot to talk about we need time and privacy to do it properly. I also know that I need to get home, and you need a plane. So why don't you borrow mine?'

She looked at him dazedly. 'Borrow your plane?'

He nodded. 'I have a private jet. Just sitting there, all ready to go, thirty minutes from here. It's got a proper bedroom and a bathroom. Two, in fact, so you can get a proper night's sleep. I guess I *am* responsible in part for making you miss your flight, so it's really the least I can do.'

He looked so handsome, so contrite, and clearly he wanted to make amends. Besides, all her other options involved an effort she just couldn't summon up the energy to make right now.

Biting her lip, she nodded.

Exactly thirty-three minutes later, Ram's limo turned into a private airfield.

As the car slid to a halt, Nola glanced over to where Ram sat gazing out of the window in silence. 'Thank you for letting me use your plane,' she said carefully.

Turning, he looked over at her, his eyes unreadable in the gloom of the car.

'My pleasure. I called ahead and told the pilot where to take you, so you can just sit back and enjoy the ride.'

She nodded, her heart contracting guiltily as his words replayed inside her head. He was being so reasonable—kind, even—and like a storm that had blown itself out the tension between them had vanished.

Her pulse was racing. A few hours earlier she'd been desperate to leave the country, to get away from Ram. Only now that it was finally time to go something was holding her back, making her hesitate, just as she had three months ago when she'd crept out of his office in the early hours of the morning. It was the same feeling—a feeling that somehow she was making a mistake.

She held her breath. But staying was not an option. She needed to go home, even if that meant feeling guilty. Only she hadn't expected to mind so much.

Her heart was bumping inside her chest like a bird trapped in a room and, clearing her throat, she said quickly, 'I was wrong not to tell you about the baby. I should have done, and I'm sorry. I know we've got an awful lot to discuss. But you're right—we do need time and privacy to talk about it properly, so thank you for being so understanding about me leaving.'

His eyes were light and relaxed, and she felt another pang beneath her heart.

'I'm glad you agree, and I feel sure we'll see each other very soon.'

The walk from the car to the plane seemed to last for ever, but finally she was smiling at the young, male flight attendant who had stepped forward to greet her.

'Good evening, Ms Mason, welcome on board. My name is Tom, and I'll be looking after you on this flight with my colleagues, James and Megan. If you need anything, please just ask.'

Collapsing into a comfortable armchair that bore no resemblance to the cramped seats on every other flight she'd ever been on, she tried not to let herself look out of the window. But finally she could bear it no more and, turning her head, she glanced down at the tarmac.

It was deserted. The limo was gone.

Swallowing down the sudden small, hard lump of misery in her throat, she sat back and watched numbly as Tom brought her some iced water and a selection of magazines.

'If you could just put on your seatbelt, Ms Mason, we'll be taking off in a couple of minutes.'

'Yes, of course.'

Leaning back, she closed her eyes and listened to the hum of the air conditioning, and then finally she heard the engines start to whine.

'Is this seat taken?'

A male voice. Deep and very familiar.

But it couldn't be him—

Her eyes snapped open and her heart began to thump, for there, staring down at her, with something very like a smile tugging at his mouth, was Ram.

She stared up at him in confusion. 'What are you doing here?'

'I thought you might like some company.'

Company! She frowned. Glancing past him at the window, she could see that they were starting to move forward, and across the cabin Tom and his colleagues were buckling themselves into their seats.

'I don't think there's time,' she said hurriedly. 'We're just about to take off.'

He shrugged. 'Well, like you said, we do have an awful lot to talk about.'

A trickle of cool air ran down her spine, and she felt a pang of uneasiness.

'Yes, but not now—'

She broke off as he dropped into the seat beside her.

'Why not now?' Sliding his belt across his lap, he stretched out his long legs. 'Just the two of us on a private jet…'

Pausing, he met her gaze, and the steady intensity of his grey eyes made the blood stop moving in her veins.

'Surely this is the perfect opportunity!'

CHAPTER SIX

NOLA STARED AT him uncertainly. Beneath the sound of her heartbeat she heard the plane's wheels starting to rumble across the tarmac. But she barely registered it. Instead, her brain was frantically trying to make sense of his words.

He couldn't possibly be intending to fly to Scotland with her, so it must be his idea of a joke.

Glancing up into his face, she felt her breath catch.

Except that he didn't look as if he was joking.

Taking a deep breath, trying to appear calmer than she felt, she forced herself to smile. 'I couldn't ask you to do that,' she said lightly. 'It's not as if it's on your way home.'

His grey gaze rested on her face. 'But you're not asking me, are you? Nor am I asking *you*, as it happens.'

Her face felt stiff with shock and confusion. Slowly she shook her head. 'But this isn't what we agreed. You said I could borrow your plane—you didn't say anything about coming with me.'

He gazed at her blandly. 'I thought you said we had a lot to talk about.'

'You know I didn't mean *now*.' Her voice rose.

This was madness. Total and utter madness.

Except madness implied that Ram was acting irrationally, and there was nothing random or illogical about his decision to join her on the plane. He was simply proving a point, and getting his own way just like he always did.

She felt as though she was going to throw up.

'You tricked me. You made me miss my flight and then

you offered to let me use your plane just so you could trap me here.'

And, fool that she was, she had actually believed he was trying to make amends.

Her heart began to pound fiercely. Not only that, she'd apologised to him. *Apologised* for not telling him about the baby and *thanked* him for being so understanding.

But everything he'd said had been a lie.

How could she have been so stupid—so gullible?

Her cheeks felt as if they were on fire. 'Why are you doing this to me?' she whispered.

He shrugged. 'It was your choice. I didn't make you do anything. You could have waited for a regular flight.' His mouth hardened. 'Except that would have meant talking to me. So I made a calculated guess that you'd do pretty much anything to avoid that—including accepting the offer of a no-strings flight back to Scotland.'

'Except there *are* strings, aren't there?' she snapped. 'Like the fact that you never said you were coming with me.'

He looked at her calmly. 'Well, I thought it might be a little counterproductive.'

Her pulse was crashing in her ears. 'I can't believe you're doing this,' she said hoarsely.

Leaning forward, he picked up one of the magazines and began flicking casually through the pages. 'Then you clearly don't know me as well as you thought you did.' He smiled at her serenely. 'But don't worry. Now that we have the chance to spend some time alone, I'm sure we'll get to know each other a whole lot better.'

Her hands clenched in her lap. She was breathless with anger and frustration. 'But you can't just hijack this plane—'

'Given that it's my plane, I'd say that would be almost impossible,' he agreed.

'I don't care that it's your plane. People don't behave like this. It's insane!'

'Oh, I don't think so.' He gazed at her steadily. 'You're pregnant with my child, Nola. Insane would be letting you fly off into the sunset with just your word that you'll get in touch.'

'So you just decided to come with me to the other side of the world?' she snapped. 'Yeah, I can see that's *really* rational.'

For a moment she glared at him in silence, and then her pulse began to jerk erratically over her skin, like a needle skipping across a record, as he leaned over and rested his hand lightly on the smooth mound of her stomach.

'Whether you like it or not, Nola, this baby is mine too. And until we get this sorted out I'm not letting you out of my sight. Where you go, I go.'

Blood was roaring in her ears. On one level his words made no sense, for she hardly knew him. He was a stranger, and what they'd shared amounted to so little. The briefest of flings. A night on a sofa.

And yet so much had happened in that one night. Not just the baby, but the fire between them—a storm of passion that had left her breathless and dazed, and eclipsed every sexual experience she'd had or would ever have.

She'd known that night that a part of her would always belong to Ram. She just hadn't realised then that it would turn out to be a baby. But now that he knew the truth was anything he'd done really that big a surprise? She was carrying his child, and she knew enough about Ram to know that he would never willingly give up control of anything that belonged to him.

Still, that didn't give him the right to trap her and manipulate her like this, bending her to his will as though being pregnant made her an extension of his life.

'You didn't have to do this,' she said hoarsely. 'I told you I was going to get in touch and I would have done.'

'I've saved you the trouble, then.' He gave her a small, taunting smile. 'It's okay—you don't need to thank me.'

She glowered at him in silence, her brain seething as she tried to think up some slick comeback that would puncture his overdeveloped ego.

But, really, why bother? Whatever she said wasn't going to change the fact that they were stuck with each other for the foreseeable future.

Only just because he'd managed to trick her into getting on his plane, it didn't mean that he was going to have everything his own way. Remembering his remark back at the airport, she felt her breathing jerk, and she curled her fingers into the palms of her hands. She sure as hell wasn't going to spend the rest of this flight entertaining him.

'I'd love to keep on chatting,' she said coldly. 'But it's been a long, and exhausting day, and as you can imagine I'm very tired.'

Their eyes met—his calm and appraising, hers combative—and there was a short, taut silence.

Finally he shrugged. 'Of course. I'll show you to your room.'

Her room!

'No—' She lurched back in her seat.

She would have liked to brush her teeth, and maybe put on something more comfortable, but the thought of undressing within a five-mile radius of Ram made her heart start to beat painfully fast.

'Actually, I think I'd rather stay here,' she said quickly. 'These seats recline, don't they? And I'm not really sleeping properly at the moment anyway.'

He stared at her speculatively, and she wondered if he was going to demand that she use the bedroom.

But after a moment, he simply nodded. 'I'll get you a blanket.'

Five minutes later, tucked cosily beneath a soft cashmere blanket, Nola tilted back her seat and turned her head pointedly away from where Ram sat beside her, working on his laptop.

How was he able to do any work anyway? she thought irritably. After everything that had happened in the last few hours anybody else—her included—would have been too distracted, too agitated, too exhausted.

But then wasn't that one of the reasons she'd been so reluctant to tell him about the baby? Just like her father, he always put business first, pleasure second, and then the boring nitty-gritty of domestic life last. And, having offered to fly her home in his private jet, he probably thought he'd been generous enough—caring, even.

Stifling a yawn, she closed her eyes. Ram's deluded world view didn't matter to her any more than he did. He might have been her boss, and he might be calling the shots now. But that would change as soon as they landed in Scotland. Edinburgh was her home, and she wasn't about to let anyone—especially not Ram Walker—trample over the life she had built there. Feeling calmer, she burrowed further down beneath the blanket...

She woke with a start.

For a moment she lay there, utterly disorientated, trying to make sense of the soft wool brushing against her face and the clean coolness of the air, and then suddenly she was wide awake as the previous night's events slid into place inside her head.

Opening her eyes, she struggled to sit up, her senses on high alert.

Why did it feel as though they were slowing down? Surely she couldn't have slept for that long? Picking up her phone, she glanced at the screen and frowned. It didn't make sense. They'd only been flying a couple of hours, and yet the plane seemed to be descending.

'Good, you're awake.'

Her heart gave a jolt, and she turned.

It was Ram. He was standing beside her, his face calm, his grey eyes watching her with an expression she didn't quite recognise.

'I thought I was going to have to wake you,' he said coolly.

He was holding his laptop loosely in one hand, so he must have spent the last few hours working, and yet he looked just as though he'd had a full eight hours' sleep. She could practically feel the energy humming off him like a force field.

But that wasn't the only reason her pulse was racing.

With his dark hair falling over his forehead, and his crisp white shirt hugging the muscles of his chest and arms, he looked like a movie star playing a CEO. Even the unflattering overhead lights did nothing to diminish his beauty.

Was it really necessary or fair for him to be that perfect? she thought desperately. Particularly when her own body seemed incapable of co-ordinating with her brain, so that despite his appalling behaviour at the airport her senses were responding shamelessly to his blatant masculinity.

Gritting her teeth, hoping that none of her thoughts were showing on her face, she met his gaze.

'Why are we slowing down? Are we stopping for fuel?'

'Something like that.'

He studied her face for a moment, and then glanced back along the cabin. 'I just need to go and speak to the crew. I won't be long.'

Biting her lip, she stared after him, a prickle spreading over her skin. She sat in uneasy silence, her senses tracking the plane's descent, until she felt the jolt as it landed.

Something felt a bit off. But probably it was just because she'd never flown on a private jet before. Usually at this point everyone would be standing up and pulling down their luggage, chatting and grabbing their coats. This was so quiet, so smooth, so civilised. So A-list.

Glancing out of the window, Nola smiled. They might not be in Scotland yet, but the weather was doing its best to make her feel as if they were. She could hear the wind already, and fat drops of rain were slapping against the glass.

'Come on—let's go!'

Turning, she saw that Ram was standing beside her, his hand held out towards her.

She frowned. 'Go where? Don't we just wait?'

'They need to clean the plane and do safety checks. And then the crew are going off-shift.'

She gazed up at him warily.

'So where are we going?'

'Somewhere more comfortable. It's not far.'

Her heart began to thump. Maybe it would have been better after all if she'd just waited for another flight. But it was too late to worry about that now.

It was warm outside—tropical, even—but she still ducked her head against the wind and the rain.

'Be careful.'

Ram took hold of her arm and, ignoring her protests, guided her down the stairs.

'I can manage,' she said curtly.

But still he ignored her, tightening his grip as he walked her across the runway to an SUV that was idling in the darkness.

Inside the car, he leaned forward and tapped against the glass. 'Thanks, Carl. Just take it slow, okay?'

'I thought you said it wasn't far,' she said accusingly.

Turning back to face her, he shrugged. But there was a

small, satisfied smile on his handsome face that made her heart start to bang against her ribs.

'It isn't. But this way we stay nice and dry.' His eyes mocked her. 'Despite what you may have heard, I can't actually control the weather.'

She nodded, but she was barely listening to what he said; she was too busy squinting through the window into the darkness outside.

Stopover destinations to and from Australia usually depended on the airline. It could be Hong Kong, Dubai, Singapore or Los Angeles. Of course flying on a private jet probably meant that some of those options weren't available. But, even so, something didn't feel right.

For a start there were no lights, nor even anything that really passed as a building. In fact she couldn't really see much at all, except a tangled, dark mass of trees and vegetation stretching away into the distance. Her heart began to beat faster, and she felt a rush of cold air on her skin that had nothing to do with the car's air conditioning.

She forced herself to speak. 'Where exactly are we?'

'Queensland—just west of Cairns.'

Turning, she stared at him in confusion, her mouth suddenly dry.

'What? We haven't even left Australia? So why have we stopped? We're never going to get to Scotland at this rate!'

'We're not going to Scotland,' he said quietly.

That prickling feeling had returned, and with it a sensation that she was floating—that if she hadn't been gripping the door handle so tightly she might have just drifted away.

'What do you mean? Of course, we're going to Scotland—' She broke off as he started to shake his head.

'Actually, we're not.'

His eyes glittered in the darkness, and she felt her breath catch in her throat.

'We never were. It was always my intention to bring you here.'

She stared at him in silence. Fury, shock, disbelief and frustration were washing over her like waves breaking against a sea wall.

Here? Here!

What was he talking about?

'There is no *"here"*,' she said shakily. 'We're in the middle of nowhere.'

He was mad. Completely mad. There was no other explanation for his behaviour. How could she not have noticed before?

'You and I need to talk, Nola.'

'And you want to do that in the middle of a jungle?' She was practically shouting now. Not that he seemed to care.

She watched in disbelief as calmly he shook his head.

'It's actually a rainforest. Only parts of it are classified as a jungle. And clearly I'm not expecting us to talk there. I have a house about three miles from here. It's very beautiful and completely private—what you might call secluded, in fact, so we won't be disturbed.'

Her head was spinning.

'I don't care if you have a palace with its own zoological gardens. I am not going there now or at any other time—and I'm definitely not going there with *you*.'

He lounged back against the seat, completely unperturbed by her outburst, his dark eyes locking onto hers. 'And yet here you are.'

She stared at him in shock, too stunned, too dazed to speak. Then, slowly, she started to shake her head. 'No. You can't do this. I want you to turn this car around now—'

Her whole body was shaking. This was far, far worse than missing her flight or Ram joining her on the plane.

Leaning forward, she began banging desperately on the glass behind the driver's head.

'Please—you have to help me!'

Behind her, she heard Ram sigh. 'You're going to hurt your hand, and it won't make any difference. So why don't you just calm down and try and relax?'

Her head jerked round. 'Relax! How am I supposed to relax? You're *kidnapping* me!'

Ram stretched out his legs. He could hear the exasperation and fury in her voice—could almost see it crackling from the ends of her gleaming dark hair.

Good, he thought silently. Now she knew how he felt. How it felt to have your life turned upside down. Suddenly no longer to be in charge of your own destiny.

'Am I? I'm not asking anyone for a ransom. Nor am I planning to blindfold you and tie you to the bed,' he said softly, his gaze holding hers. 'Unless, of course, you want me to.'

He watched two flags of colour rise on her cheekbones as she slid back into her seat, as far from him as was physically possible.

'All I want is for you to stop acting like some caveman.' She breathed out shakily. 'People don't behave like this. It's barbaric…primitive.'

'Primitive?' He repeated the word slowly, letting the seconds crawl by, feeling his groin hardening as she refused to make eye contact with him. 'I thought you liked primitive,' he said softly.

'That was different.' Turning her head sharply, she glowered at him. 'And it has nothing to do with any of this.'

'On the contrary. You and I tearing each other's clothes off has everything to do with this.'

'I don't want to talk about it,' she snapped, her blue eyes wide with fury. 'I don't want to talk to you about anything. In fact the only conversation I'm going to be having is with the police.'

She sounded breathless, as though she'd been running. He watched her pull out her phone and punch at the buttons.

'Oh, perhaps I should have mentioned it earlier...there's pretty much zero coverage out here.'

He smiled in a way that made her want to throw the phone at his head.

'It's one of the reasons I like it so much—no interruptions, no distractions.'

Fingers trembling with anger, she switched off her phone and pressed herself against the door. 'I hate you.'

'I don't care.'

The rest of the journey passed in uncomfortable silence. Nola felt as though she'd swallowed a bucket of ice; her whole body was rigid with cold, bitter fury. When finally the car came to a stop at his house she slid across the seat and out of the door without so much as acknowledging his presence.

Staring stonily at his broad shoulders in his dark suit jacket, she followed him through a series of rooms and corridors, barely registering anything other than the resentment hardening inside her chest.

'This is your room. The bathroom is through there.'

She glared at him. 'My room? How long are you planning on keeping me here?'

He ignored her. 'You'll find everything you need.'

'Really? You mean there's a shotgun and a shovel?'

His eyes hardened. 'The sooner you stop fighting me, Nola, the sooner this will all be over. If you need me, I'm just next door. I'll see you in the morning.'

'Unless you're going to lock me in, I won't be here in the morning.'

He stared at her impatiently. 'I don't need to lock you in. It would take you the best part of a day to walk back to the airfield. And there would be no point. There's nothing there. And if you want to get to civilisation that's a three-day walk through the rainforest—a rainforest with about twenty different kinds of venomous snakes living in it.'

'Does that include you?' she snarled.

But he had already closed the door.

Left alone, Nola pulled off her clothes and angrily yanked on her pyjamas. She still couldn't believe what was happening. How could he treat her like this?

Worse—how could he treat her like this and then expect her to sit down and have a civilised conversation with him?

She clenched her jaw. He could expect what he liked. But he couldn't make her talk or listen if she didn't want to.

Her eyes narrowed. In fact she might just stay in her room.

She would think about it properly in the morning. Right now she needed to close her eyes and, climbing into bed, she pulled the duvet up to her chin, rolled onto her side, and fell swiftly and deeply into sleep.

Ram strode into the huge open-plan living space, his frustration with Nola vying with his fury at himself.

What the hell was he doing?

He'd only just found out he was going to be a father. Surely that was enough to be dealing with right now? But apparently not, for he had decided to add to the chaos and drama of the evening by kidnapping Nola.

Because, regardless of what he had said to her in the car, this *was* kidnapping.

Groaning, he ran a hand wearily over his face.

But what choice had she given him?

Ever since she'd forced him to meet her at that internet café she had challenged him at every turn. But she was pregnant with his child now, and her leaving the country was more than defiance. Even though she'd said she would be in touch, he hadn't believed her.

His face hardened. And why should he? She had kept the pregnancy secret for months, and even when she'd had the perfect opportunity to tell him about the baby she had chosen instead to avoid him. And then tried to run away.

But Nola was going nowhere now. She certainly wasn't going to Scotland any time soon.

He breathed out slowly. In fact, make that *never*.

If she moved back to Edinburgh, then he would be cut out of his baby's life. Not only that, his child would grow up with another man as his father—with another man's name instead of his. Worse, he or she would grow up believing themselves to be a burden not worth bearing, a mistake to be regretted.

He would do whatever it took to stop that from happening.

Crossing the room, he poured himself a whisky and downed it in one mouthful.

Even kidnapping.

His chest tightened.

What had he been thinking?

But that was just it. He hadn't been thinking at all—he'd just reacted on impulse, his emotions blindly driving his actions, so that now he had a woman he barely knew, who was carrying a child he hadn't planned, sleeping in the spare room in what was supposed to be his private sanctuary from the world.

Gritting his teeth, he poured himself another whisky and drank that too.

So why had he brought Nola here?

But he knew why. He hadn't been exaggerating when he'd said that the house was secluded. It was luxurious, of course, but it was completely inaccessible to anyone without a small plane or helicopter, and on most days communicating with the outside world was almost impossible.

Here, he and Nola would be completely alone and they would be able to talk.

His fingers twitched against the empty glass.

Except that talking was the last thing he wanted to do with her. Particularly now that they were alone, miles from civilisation.

A pulse began to beat in his groin.

For a moment he stared longingly at the bottle of whisky. But where Nola was concerned it would take a lot more than alcohol to lock down his libido. A cold shower might be better—and if that didn't work he might have to go and swim a few lengths in the pool. And then maybe a few more.

He'd do whatever was necessary to re-engage his brain so that tomorrow he could tell Nola exactly how this was all going to play out.

As soon as she woke Nola reached over to pick up her phone, holding her breath as she quickly punched in Anna's number. When that failed to connect she called the office, then Anna again, and then, just to be certain, her favourite takeaway pizzeria by the harbour. But each time she got the same recorded message, telling her that there was no network coverage, and finally she gave up.

Rolling onto her side, she gazed in silence around the bedroom. It was still dark, but unless she'd slept the entire day it must be morning. She wasn't planning on going anywhere, but there was no point in lying there in the dark. Sighing, she sat up. Immediately she heard a small click, and then daylight began filling the room as two huge blinds slid smoothly up into the ceiling.

She gasped. But it wasn't the daylight or the blinds or even the room itself that made her hold her breath. It was the pure, brilliant blue sky outside the window.

Heart pounding, she scrambled across the bed and

gazed down at a huge canopy of trees, her eyes widening as a group of brightly coloured birds burst out of the dark green leaves. She watched open-mouthed as they circled one another, looping and curling in front of her window like miniature acrobatic planes, before suddenly plunging back into the trees.

She had been planning on staying in her room to protest against Ram's behaviour. But ten minutes later she had showered, dug some clean clothes out of her suitcase and was standing by her bedroom door.

Her pulse began to beat very fast. If she opened that door she would have to face Ram. But sooner or later she was going to have to face him anyway, she told herself firmly.

And, not giving herself the chance to change her mind, she stalked determinedly out of her room.

In daylight, the house was astonishingly, dazzlingly bright. Every wall was made of glass, and there were walkways at different levels, leading to platforms actually within the rainforest itself.

No doubt it had been designed that way, she thought slowly. So that the wildlife could be watched up close but safely in its natural environment.

Her heart began to thump.

Only some of the wildlife clearly didn't understand the rules, for there on the deck, standing at the edge of an infinity pool, was one of the most dangerous animals in Australia—probably in the world.

Unfortunately there was no safety glass between her and Ram.

She was on the verge of making a quick, unobtrusive retreat when suddenly he turned, and her breath seemed to slide sideways in her chest as he began slowly walking towards her.

It was the heat, she thought helplessly. Although she

wasn't sure if it was the sun or the sight of Ram in swimming shorts that was making her skin feel warm and slick.

She tried not to stare, but he was so unbelievably gorgeous—all smooth skin and golden muscles. Now he was stopping in front of her and smiling, as though yesterday had never happened, and the stupid thing was that she didn't feel as though it had happened either. Or at least her body didn't.

'Good morning.' He squinted up at the sky. 'I think it still qualifies as morning.' Tilting his head, he let his eyes drift casually over her face. 'I was going to come and wake you up. But I didn't fancy getting punched on the nose.'

She met his gaze unwillingly. 'So you admit that I've got a reason to punch you, then?'

He grinned, and instantly she felt a tug low in her pelvis, heat splaying out inside her so quickly and fiercely that she thought she might pass out.

'I'm not sure if you need a reason,' he said softly. 'Most of the time I seem to annoy you just by existing.'

She gazed at him in silence, trying to remember why that was.

'Not always,' she said carefully. 'Only some of the time. Like when you kidnap me, for instance.'

There was a short, pulsing silence, and then finally he sighed.

'We need to talk about this now, Nola. Not in a week or a month. And, yes, maybe I overreacted, bringing you here like this. But you've been building a life, a future, that doesn't include me.'

Her heart gave a thump. 'I thought you *wanted* that.'

'What if I said I didn't?'

His eyes were fixed on her face.

She breathed out slowly, the world shifting out of focus around her.

'Then I guess we need to talk.'

'And we will.' His gaze locked onto hers. 'But first I'll give you the tour, and then you'd better eat something.'

The tour was brief, but mind-blowing. The house was minimalist in design—a stunning mix of metal and glass that perfectly offset the untamed beauty of the rainforest surrounding it.

Breakfast—or was it brunch?—took longer. A variety of cold meats, cheese, fruit and pastries were laid out buffet-style in the huge sunlit kitchen and, suddenly feeling famished, Nola helped herself to a plate of food and a cup of green tea while Ram watched with amusement.

'I have a live-in chef—Antoine. He's French, but he speaks very good English. If you have any particular likes or dislikes tell him. His wife, Sophie, is my housekeeper. She takes care of everything else. So if you need anything…'

Fingers tightening around her teacup, Nola met his gaze. 'Like what?'

He gave a casual shrug. 'I don't know. What about a bikini? You might fancy a swim.'

His eyes gleamed, and she felt something stir inside her as his gaze dropped over the plain white T-shirt that was just a fraction too small for her now.

'Unless, of course, you're planning on skinny-dipping.'

Ignoring the heat throbbing over her skin, she gave him an icy stare. 'I'm not planning on anything,' she said stiffly. 'Except leaving as soon as possible. I know we have a lot to talk about, but I hardly think it will take more than a day.'

He stared at her calmly. 'That will depend.'

'On what?'

He was watching her carefully, as though gauging her probable reaction to what he was about to say. But, really, given everything that he'd already said and done, how bad could it be?

'On what happens next. You see, I've given it a lot of thought,' he said slowly, 'and I can only think of one possible solution to this situation.'

Her nerves were starting to hum. She looked over at him impatiently. 'And? What is it?'

He stared at her for a long moment, and then finally he smiled.

'We need to marry. Preferably as soon as possible.'

CHAPTER SEVEN

NOLA STARED AT him in stunned silence.

Marry?

As her brain dazedly replayed his words inside her head she felt her skin grow hot, and then her heart began to bang against her ribs. Surely he couldn't be serious.

She laughed nervously. 'This is a joke, right?'

For a moment he looked at her in silence, then slowly he shook his head.

She stared at him incredulously. 'But you don't want to get married.' Her eyes widened with shock and confusion. 'Everyone knows that. You told me so yourself.' She frowned. 'You said marriage was a Mobius strip of emotional scenes.'

Watching the pulse beating frantically at the base of her throat, Ram felt a flicker of frustration.

To be fair, her reaction wasn't really surprising. He'd spent most of the night thinking along much the same lines himself. But, as he'd just told her, marriage was the only solution—the only way he could give his child the *right* kind of life. A life that was not just financially secure but filled with the kind of certainty that came from *belonging*.

He shrugged. 'I agree that it's not a choice I've ever imagined making. But situations change, and I'm nothing if not adaptable.'

Adaptable! Nola felt her breathing jerk. What was he talking about? As soon as she'd shown the first signs of not wanting to do things his way he'd kidnapped her!

'Oh, I see—so that's what this is all about.' She loaded her voice with sarcasm. 'Dragging me out here, trying to coerce me into marrying you, is just your way of showing me how *adaptable* you are.' She gave a humourless laugh. 'You're about as adaptable as a tornado, Ram. If there's anything in your path it just gets swept away.'

'If that was true we wouldn't be having this conversation,' he said calmly.

'How is this a conversation?' Nola shook her head. 'You just told me we *need* to marry. That sounds more like an order than a proposal.'

His eyes narrowed. 'I'm sorry if you were hoping for something a little more romantic, but you didn't exactly give me much time to look for a ring.'

She glowered at him, anger buzzing beneath her skin. 'I don't want a ring. And I wasn't hoping for anything from you. In case you hadn't noticed, I've managed just fine without you for the last three months.'

His gaze didn't flicker.

'I wouldn't know,' he said softly. 'As you didn't bother telling me you were having my baby until last night.'

Pushing away a twinge of guilt that she hadn't told him sooner, she gritted her teeth. It had been wrong of her not to tell him that she was pregnant. But marrying him wasn't going to put it right.

Only, glancing at the set expression on his face, she saw that Ram clearly thought it was.

Forcing herself to stay calm, she said quickly, 'And I've apologised. But why does that mean we need to get married?'

Ram felt his chest grow tight. Did he *really* need to answer that? His face hardened and he stared at her irritably. 'I would have thought that was obvious.'

For a fraction of a second his eyes held hers, and then he glanced pointedly down at her stomach.

'Because I'm *pregnant*?' She stared at him in exasperation, the air thumping out of her lungs. How could he do this? It was bad enough that he'd tricked her into coming here in the first place. But to sit there, so handsome and smug, making these absurd, arrogant statements... And then assume that she was just going to go along with them.

'Maybe a hundred years ago that might have been a reason. But it is possible to have a baby out of wedlock. People do it all the time now.'

'Not *my* baby,' Ram said flatly, his stomach clenching swiftly at her words.

How could she be so casual about this? So dismissive? Did she really think that having a father was discretionary? A matter of preference? Like having a dog or a cat?

He studied her face, seeing the fear and understanding it. *Good*. It was time she realised that he was being serious. Marriage wasn't an optional extra, like the adaptive suspension he'd had fitted on his latest Lamborghini. It was the endgame. The obvious denouement of that night on his sofa.

Shaking his head, trying to ignore the anger pooling there, he said coolly, 'By any definition this situation is a mess, and the simplest, most logical way to clear it up is for us to marry. Or are you planning on buying a crib and just hoping for the best?'

Nola felt her heartbeat trip over itself. How *dare* he?

She didn't know what was scaring her more. The fact that Ram was even considering this as an option, or his obvious belief that she was actually going to agree to it.

Looking up into his handsome face, she felt her skin begin to prickle. She couldn't agree. She might not have planned this pregnancy, but she knew she could make it work. Marrying Ram, though...

How could that be anything *but* a disaster?

They barely knew each other, had nothing in common,

and managed to turn every single conversation into an argument. She swallowed. And, of course, they weren't in love—not even close to being in love.

Her head was spinning.

All they shared was this baby growing inside her, and one passionate night of sex. But marriages weren't built on one-night stands. And, no matter how incredible that night had been, she wasn't so naive as to believe that a man like Ram Walker would view his wedding vows as anything but guidelines.

Her fingers curved into the palms of her hands. For her—for most people—marriage meant commitment. Monogamy.

But Ram could barely manage five days with the same woman. So how exactly was he planning on forsaking all others?

Or was he expecting to be able to carry on just as he pleased?

Either way, how long would it be before he felt trapped… resentful?

Or, worse, bored?

Remembering the distracted look in her father's eyes, the sense that he was always itching to be somewhere else and her own panicky need to try and make him stay, she felt sick.

She knew instinctively that Ram would be the same.

Wanting Nola to be his wife was just the knee-jerk response of a CEO faced with an unexpected problem. But she didn't want her marriage to be an exercise in damage limitation. Surely he could understand that.

But, looking over at him, she felt a rush of panic.

He looked so calm, almost too calm, as though her opposition to his ludicrous suggestion was just a mere formality—some twisted version of bridal nerves.

And with any other woman he would probably be right

in thinking that. After all, he'd almost certainly never met anyone who had turned him down.

Her heart began to pound.

Until now.

Slowly, she shook her head.

'I can't marry you, Ram. Right now, I'm not sure I ever want to be married. But if at some point I do, it will be because the man asking me *loves* me and wants me to be his wife.'

His face was expressionless, but his eyes were cool and resolute.

'And what happens if you don't marry? I doubt you'll stay single for ever, so how will that work? Are you going to live with a man? Is he just going to spend the occasional night in your bed?'

She felt her face drain of colour.

'I don't know. And you can't expect me to be able to answer all those questions now. That's not fair—'

His eyes were locked on hers.

'*I don't know* is not a good enough answer,' he said coldly. 'And the life you're planning for our child sounds anything but fair.'

'I'm not planning anything.' She stared at him helplessly.

'Well, at least we can agree on that,' he snarled. 'Believe me, Nola, when I tell you that no child of mine is going to be brought up by whichever random man happens to be in your life at that particular moment.'

'That's not—' She started to protest but he cut her off.

'Nor is my child going to end up with another man's name because its mother was too stubborn and selfish to marry its father.'

She stood up so quickly the chair she was sitting on flew backwards. But neither of them noticed.

'Oh, I see. So you marrying me is a *selfless* act,' she

snapped. Her blue eyes flashed angrily up at him. 'A real sacrifice—'

'You're putting words in my mouth.'

'And you're putting a gun to my head,' she retorted. 'I'm not going to marry you just to satisfy your archaic need to pass on a name.'

'Names matter.'

She shivered. 'You mean *your* name matters.'

Ram felt his chest tighten. Yes, he did mean that. A name was more than just a title. It was an identity, a destiny, a piece of code from the past that mapped out the future.

His eyes locked onto hers. 'Children need to know where they come from. They need to belong.'

'Then what's wrong with *my* name?' she said stubbornly. 'I'm the mother. This baby is inside *me*. How could it belong to anyone more than to me?'

'Now you're just being contrary.'

'Why? Because I don't want to marry you?'

He shook his head, his dark gaze locked onto hers. 'Because you know I'm right but you're mad at me for bringing you here so you're just going to reject the only logical solution without a moment's consideration.'

Nola felt despair edge past her panic. His cavalier attitude to her objections combined with his obvious belief that she would crumble was overwhelming her.

'I have considered it and it won't work,' she said quickly. 'And it doesn't have to. Look, this is *my* responsibility. I should have been more careful. That's why this is on *me*.'

'This is *on you*?' He repeated her words slowly, his voice utterly expressionless.

But as she looked over at him she felt the hairs on the back of her neck stand up. His eyes were narrowed, fixed on her face like a sniper.

'We're not talking about a round of drinks, Nola. This is a baby. A life.'

She flinched. 'Biology is not a determining factor in parenthood.'

He looked at her in disbelief. 'Seriously? Did you read that in the in-flight magazine?'

She looked at him helplessly. 'No, I just meant—'

He cut her off again. 'Tell me, Nola. Did you have a father?'

The floor seemed to tilt beneath her feet. 'Yes. But I don't—'

'But you don't what?' He gave a short, bitter laugh. 'You don't want that for your own child?'

She blinked. Tears were pricking at her eyes. But she wasn't going to lose control—at least not here and now, in front of Ram.

'You're right,' she said shakily. 'I don't want that. And I never will.'

And before he had a chance to reply she turned and walked swiftly out of the kitchen.

She walked blindly, her legs moving automatically in time to the thumping of her heart, wanting nothing more than to find somewhere to hide, somewhere dark and private, away from Ram's cold, critical gaze. Somewhere she could curl up and cradle the cold ache of misery inside her.

Her feet stopped. Somehow she had managed to find the perfect place—a window looking out into the canopy of the rainforest. There was even a sofa and, her legs trembling, she sat down, her throat burning, hands clenched in her lap.

For a moment she just gazed miserably into the trees, and then abruptly her whole body stilled as she noticed a pair of eyes gazing back at her. Slowly, she inched forward—and just like that they were gone.

'It was a goanna. If you sit here long enough it will probably come back.'

She turned as Ram sat down next to her on the sofa.

She stared at him warily, shocked not only by the fact that he had come to find her but by the fact that his anger, the hardness in his eyes, had faded.

'Did I scare it?'

Ram held her gaze. 'They're just cautious—they run away when something or someone gets too close.'

Watching her lip tremble, he felt his heart start to pound. She looked so stricken...so small.

His breath caught in his throat. In his experience women exploited emotion with the skill and precision of a samurai wielding a sword. But Nola was different. She hadn't wanted him to see that she was upset. On the contrary, she had been as desperate to get away as that lizard.

Desperate to get away from *him*.

An ache was spreading inside his chest and he gritted his teeth, not liking the way it made him feel, for he would never hurt her. In fact he had wanted more than anything to reach out and pull her against him. But of course he hadn't. Instead he'd watched her leave.

Only almost immediately, and for the first time in his life, he'd been compelled to follow. He'd had no choice—his legs had been beyond his conscious control.

He stared at her in silence, all at once seeing not only the tight set of her shoulders and the glint of tears but also what he'd chosen to ignore earlier: her vulnerability.

Shifting back slightly, to give her more space, he cleared his throat.

'There's always something to see,' he said carefully. 'We could stay and watch if you want?'

He phrased it as a question—something he would never normally do. But right now getting her to relax, to trust him, seemed more important than laying down the law.

She didn't reply, and he felt an unfamiliar twitch of panic that maybe she never would.

But finally she nodded. 'I'd like that. Apart from the odd squirrel, I've never seen anything wild up close.'

'Too busy studying?'

It was a guess, but she nodded again.

'I did work too hard,' she agreed. 'I think it was a survival technique.'

Staring past him, Nola bit her lip. She'd spoken without thinking, the words coming from deep inside. Memories came of hours spent hunched over her schoolbooks, trying to block out the raised voices downstairs, and then—worse—the horrible, bleak silence that had always followed.

Ram stared at her uncertainly, hating the bruised sound of her voice. This was the sort of conversation he'd spent a lifetime avoiding. Only this time he didn't want to avoid it. In fact he was actually scared of spooking her, and suddenly he was desperate to say something—anything to make her trust him enough to keep talking.

'Why do you think that?' he asked gently.

She swallowed. 'My dad was often home late, or away, and my parents would always argue when he got home. He'd storm off, and my mum would cry, and I'd stay in my room and do my homework.'

The ache in her voice cut him almost as much as her words, for he was beginning to understand now why she was so determined to stay single, so vehemently opposed even to letting him know about the baby.

'Are they still together?'

She shook her head.

'They divorced when I was seven. At first it was better. It was calmer at home, and my dad made a real effort. He even promised to take me to the zoo in Edinburgh for my birthday. Only he forgot. Not just about the zoo, but about my birthday too.'

Ram felt as though he'd been punched hard in the face.

He felt a vicious, almost violent urge to find her father and tell him exactly what he thought of him.

She breathed out unsteadily. 'About two months later I got a card and some money. The following year he forgot my birthday again. One year he even managed to forget me at Christmas. Of course when he remembered I got the biggest, glitziest present...'

Nola could feel Ram's gaze on her face, but she couldn't look at him. She couldn't let him see what her father had seen and rejected: her need to be loved. Couldn't bear for him to guess her most closely guarded secret. That she hadn't been enough of a reason for her father to make the effort.

'I thought he'd stopped loving my mum, and that was why he left. But he didn't love me either, and he left me too.'

'And that's what you think I'd do?'

Turning her head, she finally met his eyes. 'You have to put children first. Only sometimes people just can't do that, and I'm not blaming them...'

His grey eyes were searching her face, and she felt a rush of panic. How could she expect Ram to understand? He wouldn't know what it was like to feel so unimportant, so easy to forget, so disposable.

'Sometimes you have to give people a chance too,' he said quietly.

Nola bit her lip. His voice sounded softer, and she could sense that he was if not backing down then backing off, trying to calm her. But her heart was still beating too fast for her to relax. And anyway... Her pulse shivered violently... It wasn't as though he was going to change his mind. He was just trying a different tactic, biding his time while he waited for her to give in.

Suddenly she could no longer rein in the panic rising up inside her. 'I can't do this, Ram. I know you think I'm just being difficult. But I'm not. I know what marrying the wrong person can do people. It's just so damaging and destructive. And what's worse is that even when the marriage ends that damage doesn't stop. It just goes on and on—'

'Nola.'

Her body tensed as he lifted a hand and stroked a long dark curl away from her face.

'I'm not going to behave like your father did. I'm not walking away from you, or our baby. I'm fighting to make it work. Why do you think I want to marry you?'

She shook her head. 'You want it *now*. But soon you'll start to think differently, and then you'll *feel* differently. And we hardly know each other, Ram. Having a baby won't change that, and there is nothing else between us.'

His gaze seemed to burn into hers. 'We both know that's not true.'

She swallowed. 'That was one night…'

'Was it?' Ram studied her face. He could see the conflict in her eyes, and with shock he realised that it mirrored what he was feeling himself—the longing, the fear, the confusion. The pain.

He didn't want to feel her pain, or his own. He didn't want to feel anything. And for a fraction of a second he was on the verge of pulling her into his arms and doing what he always did to deflect emotion—his own and other people's.

But something held him back—a sudden understanding that if he didn't allow himself to feel, then he would never be able to comfort Nola, and right now that was all that mattered.

Not himself, nor his business, the launch, or even getting her to agree to this marriage, but Nola herself.

In shock, clenching his hands until they hurt, he gazed past her, struggling to explain this wholly uncharacteristic behaviour.

Surely, though, it was only natural for him to care. Nola was carrying his child.

Turning, he breathed out slowly, staring down into her eyes. 'I know you don't trust me. And if I were you I'd feel exactly the same. I haven't exactly given you much reason to have faith in me, bringing you here like I have.'

He grimaced.

'I just wanted to give us some time and some privacy. I didn't think we could sort things out with everything else going on, and I still think that. But I'm not going to force you to marry me, Nola. Or even to stay here if you don't want to.'

Reaching into his pocket, he pulled out a phone and held it out to her, watching her eyes widen with confusion.

'I didn't lie to you. There is no coverage here. That's why I have this. It's a satellite phone. If you want to leave you can call the pilot. If you stay, I want it to be your choice.'

Nola stared at him, her tears beaten back by Ram's words. This was a concession. More than that, it was a chance to get her life back.

She glanced down at the phone, her brain fast-forwarding. They could handle this through their lawyers. There was probably no need even to see one another again. But was that really what she wanted? What was best for their baby?

'I'll stay.' She held his gaze. 'But I might ring Anna later, or tomorrow. Just to let her know I'm okay.'

He pocketed the phone and nodded, and then after the briefest hesitation he reached over and took her hand in his.

'I know this is a big step for both of us, Nola. But I think we can make it work if we compromise a little.'

Nola gazed at him blankly. 'Compromise?'

He frowned. 'That *is* a word, isn't it?'

She smiled weakly. 'It is. I'm just not sure you understand what it means. Maybe you're thinking of another word.'

His grey eyes softened, and she felt her pulse dip as he lifted her hand to his mouth and kissed it gently. 'Let's see... I think it means I have to stop acting like a tornado and listen to what you're saying.'

She felt her stomach drop. Ram might have been difficult to defy when he was angry, but he was impossible to resist when he was smiling.

'That sounds like a compromise,' she said cautiously. 'But what does it mean in real terms?'

'It means that I think we need time to get used to the idea of getting married and to each other.'

She bit her lip. 'How much time?'

'As long as it takes.' He met her gaze. 'I'll wait, Nola. For as long as it takes.'

Her pulse was jumping again. For a moment they stared at one another, breathing unsteadily, and then finally she gave him a hesitant smile.

'That could work.'

And maybe it would, for suddenly she knew that for the first time she was actually willing to consider marrying him.

They spent the rest of the morning together, watching lizards and frogs and birds through the glass. Ram knew a surprising amount about the various animals and plants, and she found herself not only relaxing, but enjoying herself and his company.

So much so that as she dialled Anna's number the following morning she found it increasingly difficult to remember that he was the same person who had made her feel so horribly trapped and desperate.

'So let me get this right,' Anna said slowly down the phone. 'You're staying with Ram Walker in his rainforest treehouse. Just you and him. Even though we don't work for him anymore. And you think that's normal?'

'I didn't say that,' Nola protested, glancing over to where Ram lay lounging in the sun, a discarded paperback on the table beside him. 'Obviously nothing he does is normal. He's the richest man in Australia. I just said that me being here is not that big a deal.'

Her friend gave a short, disbelieving laugh. 'Is that why I wasn't invited?'

Nola grimaced. 'You weren't invited because you're in Edinburgh. With a broken foot and a husband.'

'I *knew* it!' Anna said triumphantly. 'So there *is* something going on!'

'No!' Nola froze as Ram turned and glanced over at her curiously. Lowering her voice, she said quickly. 'Well, it's complicated...'

She badly wanted to tell her best friend the truth. Sooner or later she would have to. Her fingers gripped the phone more tightly.

'I'm pregnant, and Ram's the father.'

Her words hung in silence down the phone and she closed her eyes, equal parts of hope and fear rising up inside her. What if Anna was disgusted? Or never wanted to speak to her again?

'That's why I'm here. We're talking things through.' Breathing out shakily, she pressed the phone against her face. 'I wanted to tell you before, but—'

'It was complicated?'

Nola opened her eyes with relief. Her friend's voice was gentle, and full of love. It was going to be okay.

'I'm sorry. I just couldn't get think straight.'

Anna laughed. 'That's okay. I forgive you as long as you tell me everything now.'

She didn't tell Anna everything, but she gave her friend an edited version of the last few days. But even while she was talking she was thinking about Ram. Having finally stopped fighting him, all she wanted was to concentrate on the two of them building a relationship that would work for their child.

That was, after all, the reason she'd decided to stay.

The only reason.

Her cheeks grew hotter.

Try telling that to her body.

Her mouth was suddenly dry. Staring across the deck at Ram, she felt her breath catch fire. It was true, she *did* want a relationship with him that would work for their child. But that didn't mean she could deny the way her body reacted to his. Even now, just looking at him was playing havoc with her senses. And up close he seemed to trigger some internal alarm system, so that she felt constantly restless, her body shivering and tightening and melting all at the same time.

But her relationship with Ram was already complicated enough. So it didn't matter that no man had ever made her feel the way he had. Giving in to the sexual pull between them would only add another layer of complication neither of them needed.

Her mouth twisted.

Maybe if she told herself that often enough, she might actually start to believe it.

'So,' Ram said softly, as she sat down beside him and handed him the phone, 'is everything okay?'

She nodded. 'Yes. I told her about the baby. She was a little…' she hesitated, searching for the right word '… stunned at first, but she was cool about it.'

Ram studied her face. Since agreeing to stay, Nola had seemed more relaxed, but he couldn't shift the image from his head of her looking so small and crushed, and impulsively he reached out and ran his fingers over her arm.

'You need to be careful. Are you wearing enough sunblock?'

She grimaced. 'Loads. I used to try and tan, but it never works. I just burn and then peel, so now I am fully committed to factor fifty.'

'Is that right?' His gaze roamed over her face. 'Then I'm jealous. I only want you to be fully committed to *me*.'

Nola blinked. He must be teasing her, she decided. Ram might want to marry her in order to legitimise this pregnancy, but he didn't do commitment. And jealousy would require an emotional response she knew he wasn't capable of or willing to give. But knowing that didn't stop her stomach flipping over in response to the possessiveness in his words.

Hoping her thought process wasn't showing on her face, she said lightly, 'You've got bigger competition than a bottle of sunblock.'

His eyes narrowed. 'I do?'

He let his fingers curl around her wrist, and then gently he pulled her towards him so that suddenly their eyes were level.

'I thought you said you didn't have anyone missing you,' he said softly.

She bit her lip. 'I don't think he does miss me. He's quite self-sufficient...' Glancing up at the stubble shadowing his jaw, she smiled. 'A little prickly. A bit like you, really. Except he's green, and he's got this cute little pot like a sombrero.'

Ram shook his head. 'I can't believe you're comparing me to a cactus.'

She laughed. 'There's no comparison. Colin is a low-maintenance dream. Whereas you—'

His eyes were light and dancing with amusement. 'I'm what?'

She felt her pulse begin to flutter. 'You have a private jet and a house in the rainforest.'

'And you care about that?'

She glanced up. Something in his tone had shifted, and he was watching her, his grey gaze oddly intent.

'No, I don't,' she said truthfully. It might sound rude, or ungrateful but she wasn't going to lie just to flatter him. 'It's lovely to have all this, but it doesn't matter to me. Other things are more important.'

Her father had taught her that. His gifts had always been over the top—embarrassingly so in comparison to what her mother had chosen for her. But there had been no thought involved, nothing personal about his choice. Nothing personal about the money he'd sent either, except that it had grown exponentially in relation to his neglect.

'Like what?'

Ram was gazing at her curiously, but just as she opened her mouth to reply, his phone rang.

Glancing down at it, he frowned. 'Excuse me. I have to take this.'

Standing up, he walked away, his face tight with concentration.

She caught bits of the conversation, but nothing that gave her any clue as to who the caller might be. Not that she needed any. It would be work-related, because of course, despite what he'd said and what she'd chosen to believe, work would always come first. She just hadn't expected to have it pointed out to her quite so quickly.

Finally he hung up.

'Sorry about that.' His face was impassive, but there was a tension in his voice that hadn't been there before.

Looking up, she forced herself to smile casually, even though she felt flattened inside. 'When do they want you back?'

'Who?' He stared at her blankly.

'Work. Do you need to leave now?'

Ram didn't answer. He was too busy processing the realisation that since getting off the plane he hadn't thought about work once. Even the launch seemed to belong to another life he had once lived. And forgotten.

He shook his head.

'It wasn't work. It was Pandora. My mother. I was supposed to have lunch with my parents today, only with everything that's happened I forgot.'

Catching sight of Nola's face, he shrugged.

'It's fine—honestly. My mother's portions are so tiny it's hardly worth the effort of going, and besides it gives Guy, my father, a chance to complain about me, so—'

'You could still go,' she said hastily. 'I can just stay here and—'

She stopped mid-sentence as his eyes locked onto hers.

'Why would you stay here?'

'I don't know.' She hesitated. 'I just thought... I mean, obviously I'd like to meet them.'

Was that true? Her pulse jumped.

She was still wary of escalating their relationship too fast. But was that because her perception of marriage was so skewed by the past? Maybe lunch with Ram's family would help balance out her point of view. And, more importantly, it might give her some insight into the father of her child, for while she had talked a lot—about herself, her parents, even her cactus—Ram was still a mystery to her.

Take his parents. She didn't know anything about them. If she'd been shaped by her mother and father, then surely it was logical to assume that Ram had been shaped by his parents too. So why not take this opportunity to see what they were like? For the sake of their child, of course.

She glanced up at him hesitantly. 'Would you like me to meet them?'

Ram stared at her in silence, wondering how best to

answer that question. Nola meeting his parents had not been part of the equation when he'd brought her here. Yet clearly she was trying to meet him halfway, and as it had been he who had suggested they get to know one another better it seemed churlish to refuse.

But going to lunch with them would mean leaving the rainforest, and he didn't want to do that.

He wanted to stay here with Nola. For it to be just the two of them. There was no need to involve Pandora and Guy. Only how could he explain that without having to explain who he was and *what* he was…?

His chest tightened.

Lifting his face, he smiled coolly. 'Of course. It will give me a chance to drop in at the office. There are a couple of papers I need. I'll ring her back and see if she can do tomorrow.'

CHAPTER EIGHT

THEY FLEW BACK to Sydney the next day.

Gazing out of the window, Nola wished her thoughts were as calm as the clear blue sky beyond the glass. It was hard to believe that only a few days ago she'd fled from the RWI building. So much had happened since then. So much had changed. Not least her perception of Ram.

She had believed him to be domineering, insensitive and unemotional, but as she glanced across the aircraft to where he stood, joking with the cabin crew, she knew that he was a different man than she'd thought.

Yes, he had as good as abducted her from the airport but, seeing her upset, he had backed down, given her the option of leaving. And he'd been unexpectedly gentle and understanding when she'd told him about her father.

Shifting in her seat, she bit her lip. She still didn't really understand why she had confided in Ram. The words had just spilled out before she'd been able to stop them. But she didn't regret it, for they had both learnt something about one another as a result.

Yet now she was about to meet *his* parents, and she could feel all her old nervousness creeping over her skin. Glancing down at her skirt, she pressed her hands against the fabric, smoothing out an imaginary crease.

If only they could just stay here on the plane, circling the earth for ever...

She jumped slightly as Ram sat down beside her, and

plucked her hand from her lap. Threading his fingers through hers, he rested his grey eyes on her face.

'So, what's bothering you, then?'

'Nothing,' she protested.

'You haven't said more than two words since we got on the plane. And you're fidgeting. So let's start with the obvious first. What have I done?'

She shook her head again. 'You haven't done anything.'

'Okay. What have I said? Or not said?'

Despite her nerves, she couldn't help smiling.

'It's not you…it's nothing—' She stopped, suddenly at a loss for words. 'It's just been such a long time since I've done a family lunch, and spending time with my mum and dad was always so stressful.'

'Then you don't need to worry,' he said dryly. 'My parents are the perfect hosts. They would never do anything to make a guest feel uncomfortable.'

She frowned. There was an edge to his voice that hadn't been there before.

'Are you sure they don't mind me coming along too? I don't want to put them to any trouble.'

He smiled—an odd, twisted smile that made her heart lurch forward.

'Pandora is the queen of the charity dinner and the benefit dance. She loves entertaining, and Guy does as he's told, so you coming to lunch will be absolutely no trouble at all.'

Her heart felt as if it were high up in her chest.

'And who do they think I am? I mean, in relation to you?' She hesitated. 'Have you told them about the baby?'

His face was expressionless. 'No. They don't need to know. As to who you are—I told them you used to work for me, and that now we're seeing one another.'

As she opened her mouth to protest, he shrugged.

'You're the first woman I've ever taken to meet them.' His grey eyes watched her steadily, his mouth tugging up at the corners. 'It was either that or pretend you were coming to fix the hard drive.'

They landed in Sydney an hour later. Ram's limo was waiting for them at the edge of the private airfield, and soon they were cruising along the motorway.

But instead of turning towards the city centre, as she'd expected, the car carried on.

'Didn't you want to go to the office first?' Frowning, Nola glanced over to where Ram was gazing down at his phone.

'I changed my mind.' He looked up, his face impassive. 'I thought you might like to freshen up, and I need to pick up a car.'

'Where are we going?'

He smiled. 'We're going home.'

She frowned. 'I thought you had a penthouse in the city?'

He shrugged. 'I do. It's convenient for work. But it's not my home.'

Home.

The word made her think of her flat in Edinburgh, her shabby sofas and mismatched crockery. But home for Ram turned out to be something altogether grander—a beautiful white mansion at the end of a private drive.

Stepping dazedly out of the car, Nola felt her heart jump. She'd recognised the name of the road as soon as they'd started to drive down it. How could she not? It was regularly cited as being the most expensive place to live in the country, and Ram's house more than lived up to that reputation.

'Welcome to Stanmore.' He was standing beside her, smiling, watching her face casually, but she could sense a tension beneath his smile, and suddenly she knew that he cared what she thought—and that fact made her throat tighten so that she couldn't speak.

'It's incredible,' she managed finally.

A couple of hours ago she'd denied being intimidated by his wealth, but now she wasn't sure that was still true. For a moment she hesitated, caught between fear and curiosity, but then his hand caught hers and he tugged her forward.

'I'm glad you think so. Now, come on. I want to show you round.'

As they wandered through the beautiful interior Nola caught her breath, her body transformed into a churning mass of insecurity. How could Ram seriously expect them to marry? This was a different world from hers. And no doubt his parents would realise that the moment she walked through their door.

'My great-great-grandfather, Stanley Armitage, bought this land in 1864,' Ram said casually as he led her into a beautiful living room with uninterrupted views of the ocean. 'I'm the fifth generation of my family to live here.'

Nola nodded. 'So you grew up here?'

His face didn't change but his eyes narrowed slightly.

'My mother moved out when she got married. They live just along the road. But I spent most of my holidays here, aside from the odd duty dinner with my parents.' He paused. 'Which reminds me... We should probably think about getting ready.'

Nola gazed down at her skirt and blouse in dismay. They had looked fine when she'd put them on that morning, but after two hours of travelling she felt sticky and dishevelled.

'I can't meet your parents looking like this.'

'So don't,' he said easily.

'But I don't have anything else.'

'Yes, you do.'

Before she had a chance to reply, he was towing her upstairs, through one of the bedrooms and into a large dressing room.

'I know you acted cool about it, but I thought you might worry about being underdressed, so I spoke to my mother's stylist and she sent these over this morning.'

Hanging from a rail were at least twenty outfits in clear, protective wrappers.

Nola gazed at them speechlessly.

He grinned, obviously pleased by her reaction. 'Pick something you like. I think there are shoes as well. I'm just going to go change.'

She nodded. But picking something was not as easy as Ram's throwaway remark had implied. The clothes were all so beautiful... Finally she settled on a pale blue dress with a pretty ribbon-edged cardigan that cleverly concealed her bump. Her cheeks were already flushed, so she didn't bother with any blusher, but she brushed her hair until it lay smoothly over her shoulders, and then added a smudge of clear lip gloss.

'You look beautiful.'

Turning, she caught her breath. Ram was lounging in the doorway, his grey eyes glittering with approval.

'So do you,' she said huskily, her gaze drifting over his dark suit and cornflower-blue shirt.

Holding out his hand, he grinned. 'Who? Me? I'm just here to drive the car.'

The car turned out to be a Lamborghini, low to the ground and an eye-catching bright blue.

As they drove the short distance to his parents' house she couldn't resist teasing him about the colour. 'Did you choose the car to match your shirt?'

He gave her a heartbreaking smile. 'No, your eyes,' he said softly. 'Now, stop distracting me.'

She bit her lip, her expression innocent. 'I distract you?'

Shaking his head, he grimaced. 'More like bewitch me. Since I met you in that café I haven't been able to concentrate on anything. I've hardly done any work for months. If I wasn't me, I'd fire myself.'

Glancing out of the window, with his words humming inside her head, she felt suddenly ridiculously happy—even though, she reminded herself quickly, Ram was really only talking about the sexual chemistry between them.

Two minutes later he shifted down a gear and turned into a driveway. Nola could see tennis courts and a rectangle of flawless green grass.

'It's a putting green,' Ram said quietly. 'Guy is a big golf fan.'

She nodded. Of course it was a putting green.

But then the putting green was forgotten, for suddenly she realised why Ram had taken her to his house first.

As he switched off the engine she breathed out slowly. 'You thought all this would scare me, didn't you? That's why we went to Stanmore first.'

He shrugged, but the intensity of his gaze told her that she was right.

Reaching out, she touched his hand tentatively. 'Thank you.'

He caught her fingers in his, his eyes gently mocking her. 'I was a little concerned at how you might react. But, as you can see, I'm way richer than they are...'

She punched him lightly on the arm.

'I can't believe you said that.'

Leaning forward, he tipped her face up to his. 'Can't you?' he said softly. 'Then your opinion of me must be improving.'

For a moment time seemed to slow, and they gazed at one another in silence until finally she cleared her throat.

'Do you think we should go in?'

'Of course.' He let go of her chin. 'Let's go and eat.'

Walking swiftly through the house, Ram felt as though his chest might burst. He couldn't quite believe that he'd brought Nola here. One way or another it was asking for trouble—especially as his relationship with her was still at such a delicate stage. But avoiding his parents wasn't an option either—not if he was serious about getting Nola to trust him.

Aware suddenly that she was struggling to keep up with him, he slowed his pace and gave her an apologetic smile. 'Sorry. I think they must be in the garden room.'

The garden room! Was that some kind of conservatory? Nola wondered as she followed Ram's broad back.

Yes, it was, she concluded a moment later as she walked into a light, exquisitely furnished room. But only in the same way that Ram's rainforest hideaway was some kind of treehouse.

'Finally! I was just about to ring you, Ramsay.'

Pulse racing, Nola swung round. The voice was high and clear, and surprisingly English-sounding. But not as surprising as the woman who was sashaying towards them.

Ram smiled coolly. 'Hello, Mother.'

Nola gazed speechlessly at Pandora Walker. Tall, beautiful and blonde, wearing an expensive silk dress that showed off her slim arms and waist, she looked more like a model than a mother—certainly not one old enough to have a son Ram's age.

'You said one o'clock, and it's two minutes past,' Ram said without any hint of apology, leaning forward to kiss her on both cheeks.

'Five by my watch.' She gave him an indulgent smile. 'I'm not fussing on my account, darling, it's just that you know your father hates to be kept waiting.

Glancing past them, she pursed her lips.

'Not that he has any qualms about keeping everyone else hanging around. Or ruining the food.'

Nola stilled. Goosebumps were covering her arms. For

a fraction of second it could have been her own mother speaking.

But that thought was quickly forgotten as, shaking his head, Ram turned towards Nola and said quietly, 'The food will be perfect. It always is. Nola, this is my mother, Pandora. Mother, this is Nola Mason. She's one of the consultants I hired to work on the launch.'

Smiling politely, Nola felt a jolt of recognition as she met Pandora's eyes—for they were the exact same colour and shape as Ram's. But where had he got that beautiful black hair?

'Thank you so much for inviting me,' she said quickly. 'It's really very kind of you.'

Pandora leaned forward and brushed her cheek lightly against Nola's.

'No, thank *you* for coming. I can't tell you how delightful it is to meet you. Ram is usually so secretive. If I want to know anything at all about his private life I have to read about it in the papers. Ah, finally, here's Guy. Darling, we've all been waiting…'

Nola felt another shiver run over her skin. Pandora was still smiling, but there was an edge of coolness to her voice as a tall, handsome man with blond hair and light brown eyes strolled into the room.

'Ramsay, your mother and I were so sure you'd forget I booked to have lunch with Ted Shaw at the club. Just had to ring and cancel.' He turned towards Nola. 'Guy Walker—and you must be Nola.'

'It's lovely to meet you, Mr Walker.'

He smiled—a long, curling smile that reached his eyes.

'Call me Guy, please, and the pleasure is all mine.'

Ram might get his grey eyes from his mother, Nola thought as she followed Pandora out of the room to lunch, but he'd clearly inherited his charm from his father.

To her relief, she quickly discovered that Ram had been

telling the truth about his parents. They were the perfect hosts: beautiful, charming and entertaining. And the food was both delicious and exquisitely presented. And yet somehow she couldn't shift the feeling that there was an undercurrent of tension weaving unseen beneath the charm and the smooth flow of conversation.

'So what is it you did, then, Nola? For RWI, I mean?' Leaning forward, Guy poured himself another glass of wine.

'I'm a cyber architect. I designed and installed the new security system.'

He frowned. 'That's a thing now, is it?'

Nola opened her mouth, but before she could reply Ram said quietly, 'It's been a "thing" for a long time now. All businesses have cyber security teams. They have to. Big, global companies like RWI even more so. They're a prime target for hackers, and if we get hacked we lose money.'

Guy lifted his glass. 'By *we* you mean *you*.' He smiled conspiratorially at Nola. 'I might have given him my name but it's not a family business.'

She blinked. Taken at face value, Guy's comment was innocuous enough: a simple, statement of fact about who owned RWI. So why did his words feel like a shark's fin cutting through the surface of a swimming pool?

'Actually, I think what Ram is trying to say is that hacking is like any other kind of theft,' she said hurriedly. 'Like shoplifting or insurance fraud. In the end the costs get passed on to the consumers so everyone loses out.'

Feeling Ram's gaze on the side of her face, she turned and gave him a quick, tight smile. He nodded, not smiling exactly, but his eyes softened so that for a fraction of a second she almost felt as if they were alone.

Watching the faint flush of colour creep over Nola's cheeks, Ram felt his throat tighten.

He couldn't help but admire her. She was nervous—he could hear it in her voice. But she had defended him, and the fact that she cared enough to do that made his head spin, for nobody had *ever* taken his side. He'd learnt early in life to rely on no one but himself. Some days it felt as though his whole life had been one long, lonely battle.

Not that he'd cared.

Until now.

Until Nola.

But spending time with her over the last few days had been a revelation. Having never cohabited before, he'd expected to find it difficult—boring, even. But he'd enjoyed her company. She was beautiful, smart, funny, and she challenged him. And now she had gone into battle for him, so that the solitude and independence he had once valued so highly seemed suddenly less important. Unnecessary, unwelcome even.

'I'll have to take your word for it.' Guy laughed. 'Like I said, I might be a Walker but I'm not a hotshot businessman like my son.'

Draining his glass, he leaned forward towards Nola.

'A long time ago I used to be an actor—quite a good one, actually. Right now, though, I'm just a party planner!'

Nola stared at him confusedly. 'You plan parties?'

'Ignore him, Nola, he's just being silly.' Pandora frowned at her husband, her lips tightening. 'We're having a party for our thirtieth wedding anniversary, and Guy's been helping with some of the arrangements.'

'Thirty years!' Nola smiled. 'That's wonderful.'

And it was. Only as Ram reached out and adjusted his water glass she felt her smile stiffen, for how did that make him feel? Hearing her sound so enthusiastic about his parents' thirtieth wedding anniversary when she'd been so fiercely against marrying him.

But then Ram only wanted to marry her because he

felt he should, she thought defensively. His parents, on the other hand, had clearly loved each other from the start, and they were still in love now, thirty years later.

'Oh, you're so sweet.' Pandora gave her a pouting pink smile. "It's going to be a wonderful evening, but there's still so much to sort out. Only apparently *my* input is not required.'

So that was why she and Guy were so on edge.

Glancing over to see Guy was pouring himself another glass of wine, Nola felt a rush of relief at having finally found an explanation for the tensions around the table.

Guy scowled. 'You're right—it's not.' He picked up his glass. 'Doesn't stop you giving it, though. Which is one of the reasons why there's still so much to sort out.'

For perhaps a fraction of a second Pandora's beautiful face hardened, and then almost immediately she was smiling again.

'I know, darling. But at least we have one less thing to worry about now.' As Guy gazed at her blankly, she shook her head. 'Ram's guest. You *are* bringing Nola to the party, aren't you, Ramsay?'

There was a tiny suspended silence.

Nola froze. That aspect of the party hadn't even occurred to her. But obviously Ram would be going. Her heartbeat resonated in her throat as he turned towards her.

'Of course.'

Breath pummelled her lungs as he held her gaze, his cool, grey eyes silencing her confusion and shock.

'She's looking forward to it—aren't you, sweetheart?'

She gazed at him in silence, too stunned to reply. Over the last few days she had spent some of the most intense and demanding hours of her life with Ram. She had revealed more to him about herself than to any other person, and she had seen a side to him that few people knew existed.

But his parents' party was going to be big news, and although it was unlikely anyone would be interested in her on her own, as one half of a couple with Ram...

Her pulse fluttered.

She knew enough about his private life to know that it wasn't private at all, and that as soon she stepped out in public with him there would be a feeding frenzy—and that wasn't what she wanted at all.

Or was it?

Suddenly she was fighting her own heartbeat. Definitely she didn't want the feeding frenzy part, but she would be lying if she said that she didn't want the chance to walk into a room on his arm. And not just because he was so heart-stoppingly handsome and sexy.

She liked him.

A lot.

And the more she got to know him the more she liked him.

Looking up, she met his gaze, and nodded slowly. 'Yes, I'm really excited.'

Pandora clapped her hands together. 'Wonderful,' she purred. 'In that case I must give you the number of my stylist...'

After lunch, they returned to Stanmore.

Ram worked while Nola sat watching the boats in the harbour. After a light supper he excused himself, claiming work again, and she went upstairs to shower and get ready for bed.

Standing beneath the warm water, she closed her eyes and let her mind drift.

The drive home had been quiet—supper too. But then both of them had a lot to think about. Introducing her to his parents had probably been about as a big deal for Ram as meeting them had been for her.

Turning off the shower, she wrapped a towel around herself. And then, of course, there was the party. Her heart began to thump loudly inside her chest. Was that why he'd been so quiet? Was he regretting letting himself be chivvied into taking her as his guest?

But as she walked back into the bedroom that question went unanswered, for there, sitting on her bed, was Ram.

She stopped, eyes widening with surprise. 'I thought you were going to do some work?'

Glancing past her, he shrugged. 'I was worried about you. You seemed...' He hesitated, frowning. 'Distracted.'

There was an edge to his voice that she couldn't quite pinpoint.

'I'm just tired.'

His eyes on hers were dark and filled with intent. 'That's all? Just tired?'

For a moment she considered leaving it there. It had been a long day, but for the first time they seemed to be edging towards a calm she was reluctant to disturb. Although if she didn't tell him what she was really thinking, what would that achieve? Okay, it might just be one night in their lives, but if it was bothering her...bothering him...

She took a deep breath. 'I just want you to know that you don't have to take me to the party,' she said quickly.

His eyes narrowed. 'I know I don't. But I want to.' He studied her face. 'Is that really what this is about? What *I* want. Or is it about what *you* want?'

Nola looked at him uncertainly. 'What do you mean?'

He cleared his throat. 'Are you saying you don't want to go with me?'

She shook her head. 'No, but you only— I mean, your mother—'

He interrupted her, his voice suddenly blazing with an emotion she didn't recognise.

'Let me get one thing clear, Nola. *I want you to be there*

with me. And my mother has got nothing to do with that decision.'

She nodded—for what else could she do? She could hardly demand proof. And she wanted to believe him. Of course she did. Besides, if they were going to work even at the simplest level, wasn't it time to move on? To put all the doubt and suspicion and drama behind them and start to trust one another?

Drawing in a deep breath, she lifted her chin and looked into his eyes.

'Thank you for telling me that,' she said simply. 'And thank you for taking me to lunch. It was lovely.' Remembering the strange tension around the table, those odd pointed remarks, she hesitated. 'What about you? Did you enjoy yourself?'

Ram stared at her in silence. Her question was simple enough but it stunned him, for he couldn't remember anyone ever asking him that before.

'I suppose,' he said finally. 'Although they were a little tense. But there's a lot going on—I mean, with the party coming up—'

She nodded slowly. 'Thirty years together is an amazing achievement.'

'Yes, it is.'

He watched her bite her lip, glance up, try to speak, then look away. Finally she said quietly, 'I get that it's why you wanted me to meet them.'

His heart seemed to still in his chest. 'You do?'

She nodded. 'You wanted me to understand why you want us to marry. And I do understand. I know you want what they have.'

Her blue eyes were fixed on his face, and he stared back at her, his breath vibrating inside his chest.

You want what they have...

He tried to nod his head, tried to smile, to do what his mother had always required of him.

But he couldn't. Not anymore. Not with Nola.

Slowly he shook his head. 'Actually, what they have is why I've always been so *against* marriage.'

He watched her eyes widen with incomprehension, and it made him feel cruel—shattering her illusions, betraying his mother's confidences. But he was so tired of lying and feeling angry. His chest tightened. Nola deserved more than lies, more than his anger—she deserved the truth.

He cleared his throat. 'You see, Guy has a mistress.'

Confusion and shock spread out from her pupils like shock waves across a sea.

There was a thick, pulsing silence.

'But he can't have—' Nola bit her lip, stopped, tried again. 'Does your mother know?'

As she watched him nod slowly the room seemed to swim in front of her eyes.

There was another, shorter silence.

'I'm so sorry, Ram,' she whispered at last. 'That must have been such a shock.'

He stared past her, his eyes narrowing as though he was weighing something up.

'Yes, it was,' he said quietly. 'The first time it happened.'

The first time?

'I—I don't understand,' she said slowly. 'Isn't this the first time?'

His mouth twisted. 'Sadly not. That honour went to an actress called Francesca. Not that I knew or cared that she was an actress.' An ache of misery was spreading inside him. 'I was only six. To me, she was just some woman in my mother's bed.'

Nola flinched. *Six!* Still just a child.

Watching her reaction, Ram smiled stiffly. 'Guy told me it would upset my mother if I said anything. So I didn't.'

He was speaking precisely, owning each word in a way that made her feel sick.

'I thought if I kept quiet, then it would stop,' he continued. 'And it did with Francesca. Only then there was Tessa, and then Carrie. I stopped learning their names after that. It was the only way I could face my mother.'

'But you weren't responsible!' Nola stared up him, her eyes and her throat burning. 'You hadn't done anything.'

His skin was tight over his cheekbones.

'You're wrong. It *was* my fault. All of it.'

She shook her head. Her heart felt as if it was about to burst. 'You were a little boy. Your father should never have put you in that position.'

He was looking past her, his eyes dull with pain. 'You don't understand. *I'm* the reason they had to marry.'

She shivered. 'What do you mean?'

'My mother got pregnant with me when she was sixteen. In those days girls like her didn't do so well on their own.'

Nola blinked. She had imagined many reasons for what had made him the man he was, but nothing like this. No wonder he was so confused—and confusing—when it came to relationships.

'But that's not *your* fault,' she said quietly. 'I know it must have been hard for both of them. But just because Guy became a father too young, it doesn't mean you're responsible for his affairs.'

He shook his head, his mouth twisting into a smile that had nothing to do with laughter or happiness.

'Guy's not my father. My biological father, I mean.'

She stared at him in silence, too shocked to speak, the words in her mouth bunching into silent knots.

He looked away. 'My mother was staying with a friend and they heard about a party. A real party, on the wrong side of town, with drink and boys and no supervision. That's where she met my father. They were drunk and careless and they had sex.'

'Who is he?' she whispered. 'Your real father?'

Ram shrugged. 'Does it matter? When he found out she was pregnant he didn't want anything to do with her—or me.'

His eyes were suddenly dark and hostile, as though challenging her to contradict him.

She swallowed. 'So how did she meet Guy?'

He breathed out unsteadily.

'My grandparents knew his family socially. His father had made some bad investments. Money was tight, and Guy's never been that interested in working for a living, so when Grandfather offered him money to marry my mother he accepted.'

Nola didn't even try to hide her shock.

'That's awful. Your poor mother. But why did she agree to it?'

Ram's face was bleak. 'Because my grandfather told her he'd cut her off, disown her, cast her out if she didn't.'

A muscle pulsed in his cheek.

'She couldn't face that, didn't think she could survive without all this, so she gave in. Guy got a generous lifetime monthly allowance, my mother preserved her reputation and her lifestyle and my grandparents were able to keep their dirty linen private.'

The misery in his voice almost overwhelmed her.

She took a breath, counted to ten. 'How did you find out?'

'My mother told me.' This time his smile seemed to slice through her skin like a mezzaluna. 'We were arguing, and I compared her unfavourably to my grandparents. I hurt her, so I guess she thought it was time I knew the truth.'

Nola could feel her body shaking. How could his mother have done that? It had been needlessly cruel. She had to swallow hard against the tears building in her throat before she could speak.

'How old were you?'

He shrugged. 'Eleven...twelve, something like that.'

Her eyes held his as she struggled to think of something positive to say. 'But you get on with Guy?'

He shrugged. 'When I was a child he more or less ignored me. Now I'm older I just avoid him. After my grandfather died he made a big scene about needing more money, so I give him an allowance and in return he has to be devoted to my mother—in public, at least. And discreet about his affairs. Or he's supposed to be.'

Nola looked up into his face. There was nothing she could say to that.

'What about your real father?' she asked carefully. 'Do you have any contact with him?'

His eyes hardened. 'I know who he is, and since he knows who my mother is, he must know who *I* am, and how to find me. But he hasn't, so I guess he's even less interested in me than Guy.'

His face was expressionless but the desolation in his voice made her fists clench.

'It's his loss,' she said fiercely.

He gave a small, tight smile.

'Are you taking my side, Ms Mason?'

His words burned like a flame. Was she?

For months there had been an ocean between them. Then, for the last few days, she'd been fighting to keep him at a distance. Fighting to keep her independence. Fighting the simmering sexual tension between them. Her mouth twisted. In fact just fighting him.

Only now the fight had drained out of her, and instead she wanted nothing more than to wrap her arms around him, ease the desperate ache in his voice and that terrible tension in his body. Her breath seemed to swell in her throat as she reached out and tentatively touched his hand. For a moment he stared at her hand in silence, then finally he reached out and pulled her against him.

Burying her face against his body, she let out a shuddering breath. Being here in his arms felt so good, so right. If only she could stay this way for ever. But this wasn't about her, it was about Ram—*his* pain and his anger, his past. A past that still haunted him. A past she was determined to exorcise now.

Lifting her head, she looked up into his face. 'Your mother was so young. Too young. And she was scared and hurt and desperate. People don't always do the right thing when they're desperate. But they can do the wrong thing for the right reasons.'

Their eyes met, and they both knew she wasn't just talking about his mother.

Breathing out shakily, he shook his head. 'I've been struggling to figure that out for nearly twenty years. It's taken you less than half an hour.'

She smiled a little. 'It's all those in-flight magazines I read.'

Mouth twisting, he clasped her face, his thumbs gently stroking her cheeks.

'I'm sorry for what I did. Lying to you, dragging you off to the rainforest like that. It was completely out of order.'

Ram was apologising.

Her throat ached. She could hardly breathe.

'We both behaved badly,' she said shakily. 'And we both thought the worst of each other. But I'm glad you did what you did, otherwise we might never have got this far.'

Her gaze fastened on his face.

'But now we're here, and I think it's about time we

started figuring things out. If we're going to make it work, I mean.'

The words were out of her mouth before she even understood what it was she wanted to say. What it was she really wanted. Her heart began to beat fiercely as his grey eyes searched her face.

'Make what work?'

It wasn't too late. There was still time to backtrack. Ram couldn't read minds, and she'd said nothing damning or definitive. But she didn't want to backtrack—for wasn't that their problem in a nutshell? Both of them looking back to the past, and in so doing threatening to ruin the future—their child's future? 'Our marriage,' she said after a moment.

'Are you asking me to marry you?'

He looked tense, shaken, nothing like the cool, sophisticated Ramsay Walker who could stop meetings with a raised eyebrow. It scared her a little, seeing him so uncertain. But it made her feel stronger, more determined to tell him how she felt—and maybe, just maybe, get him to do the same.

She hesitated. 'Yes, I am.'

He had confided in her, and she knew what each and every word had cost him. Knew too why he was so conflicted, so determined to do his duty as a father even as he pushed away any hint of love or commitment.

'Is this what's changed your mind?' he asked slowly.

She bit her lip. 'Yes, but also it was that night we spent in your office—I've tried not to think about it, but I can't stop myself. It was so different…so incredible. I've never felt like that with anyone, and I wanted to tell you that. I wanted to stay, but I was too scared—scared of how you'd made me feel.'

'I felt the same,' he said hoarsely.

She felt a sudden twinge of panic. 'But it was a long time ago. Maybe we don't feel that way anymore.'

His grey eyes locked onto hers.

'We do feel it, Nola. We've felt it and fought it.'

The heat in his voice made blood surge through her body.

'But I don't want to fight you anymore. In fact fighting is the opposite of what I want to do with you.'

She held her breath as he stared down into her eyes. Chaos was building inside her.

'What is it you want to do?' she whispered.

His gaze moved from her face down to the slight V of her cleavage.

'This...'

Holding her gaze, he reached out and slowly unwrapped the towel from around her body. As it dropped to the floor she heard his sharp intake of breath.

She swallowed, her imagination stirring.

His mouth was so close to hers—those beautiful curving lips that had the power to unleash a blissful torment of heat and oblivion. For a moment she couldn't speak. All she could think about was how badly she wanted to kiss him, and how badly she wanted him to kiss her back.

And then her breath lurched in her throat as, lowering his hand, he began stroking her breast in a way that made her quiver inside.

'I want you, Nola,' he said softly.

'For ever?' She couldn't help asking.

His gaze held hers, then his hands dipped lower to caress her stomach and her thighs and the curve of her bottom.

'For the rest of my life.'

She pressed her hands against his chest, feeling his heart beneath her fingertips, and then she was pushing him backwards onto the bed, and he was pulling her onto his lap so that she was straddling him.

Fingers trembling, she undid the button of his jeans, tugging at the zipper, freeing him. His ragged breathing abruptly broke the silence as she ran her hand gently up the length of him and guided him inside her.

He groaned, his body trembling. Leaning forward, she found his mouth and kissed him desperately. And then his hands were tightening on her thighs, and she was lifting her hips, heat swamping her as he shuddered inside her, pulling her damp, shaking body against his.

But it wasn't just desire that was rocking her body—it was shock. For mere sex, no matter how incredible, could not make you want to hold a person for ever.

Only love could make you feel that way.

It was like a dam breaking inside her, but even as she acknowledged the truth she knew it was not a truth she was ready to share with Ram. Or one he was ready to hear. But wrapped in his arms, with his heart beating in time with hers, it didn't seem to matter. For right now this was enough.

CHAPTER NINE

THE NEXT MORNING Ram woke early, to a sky of the palest blue and yellow.

Next to him Nola lay curled on her side, her arm draped across his chest. For a moment he lay listening to her soft, even breathing, his body and his brain struggling to adjust to this entirely new sensation of intimacy.

Waking beside a woman was something he'd never done before. In the past, even the thought of it would have made his blood run cold.

But being here with Nola felt good.

Better than good, he thought, breathing in sharply as she shifted against him in her sleep.

After last night there could be no doubt that they still wanted one another. They had made love slowly, taking their time, holding back and letting the pleasure build. And, unlike that first time in his office, there had been tenderness as well as passion.

Forehead creasing, he stared out of the window. But last night had not just been about sex. Exploring the lush new curves of her body had eased an ache that was more than physical.

He froze as Nola stirred beside him, curling closer, and suddenly the touch of her naked body was too great a test for his self-control. Gritting his teeth against the instant rush of need clamouring inside him, he gently lifted her arm and slid across the bed, making his way to the shower.

Turning the temperature to cool, he winced as the water hit his body.

For years he'd never so much as hinted at his parents' unhappiness to anyone. Even imagining the pity in someone's eyes had been enough to ensure his silence. But last night—and he still wasn't quite sure why or how—he'd ended up telling Nola every sordid little detail about his life. Not just his mother's miserable marriage of necessity, but Guy's serial affairs too.

The words had just tumbled out.

Only Nola hadn't pitied him. Instead she had helped him to face his past. More than that, she'd finally agreed to build a future with him.

Tipping back his head, he closed his eyes, remembering how she'd asked him to marry her. His mouth curved. Of course she had—and wasn't that as much of an attraction as her glorious body? The way she kept him guessing, and her stubborn determination to do things her way and at her pace.

Switching off the water, he smoothed his dark hair back against the clean lines of his skull. It ought to drive him crazy, yet it only seemed to intensify his desire for her. And now that Nola had finally come round to his point of view he was determined that nothing would get in their way.

Whatever it took, they were going to get married—and as soon as possible.

'I need to drop by the office later, so I was wondering if you'd like to go into town?'

They had just finished breakfast and Ram was flicking through some paperwork.

Looking over at him, Nola frowned. 'Is there a problem?'

He shook his head. 'I just need to show my face—otherwise there might be a mutiny.'

'I doubt that. Your staff love you.'

He laughed. '*Love* might be pushing it a little. They respect me—'

'Yes, and respect is a kind of love,' she said slowly. 'Like duty and faith. Love isn't just all about passion and romance—it's about commitment and consideration, and sacrifice too.'

He leaned back in his chair. 'Then I take it back. I must be very loved. So must you.'

She felt her skin grow hot. Of course he wasn't talking about their relationship but his staff, and probably her friendship with Anna. Aware, though, of his sudden focus, she grasped helplessly towards his earlier remark.

'When are you thinking of going into the office, then?'

'Whenever suits you.'

'In that case, maybe I'll stay here. It's not as if I really need anything.'

He was silent a moment, and then he said quietly, 'Apart from a dress?'

A dress?

She stared at him. 'Oh, yes, of course—for the party.'

His gaze rested on her face. 'Are you having second thoughts?'

His tone was relaxed, but there was an intensity in his grey eyes that made her heart beat faster.

'About the party?'

'About agreeing to marry me?'

Looking up, she shook her head. 'No. Are you?'

Gently he reached over and, smoothing her hair back from her face, he gave her one of those sweet, extraordinary smiles that could light up a room.

'If I could walk outside and find a registrar and a couple of witnesses, you'd be making an honest man out of me right this second!'

She burst out laughing. 'I thought the bride was supposed to be the pushy one?'

His face grew serious. 'I don't want to push you into anything, Nola. Not anymore. I just want you to give me a chance—to give us a chance.'

Heart bumping into her ribs, she nodded. 'I want that too.' Taking a quick breath, she smiled at him. 'So what happens next?'

There was a fraction of a pause.

'I suppose we make it official,' he said casually. 'How do you feel about announcing our engagement at the party?'

Her pulse darted forward. *Engagement?*

But of course logically their getting engaged was the next step.

Only up until yesterday marrying Ram had been more of a hypothetical option than a solid, nuts and bolts reality. And now he wanted to announce their engagement in three days.

Three days!

Ram watched with narrowed eyes as Nola bit her lip. Taking her to the party was a statement of sorts, but announcing their engagement there would escalate and consolidate their relationship in the most public way possible. Clearly Nola thought so too, for he could see the conflict in her eyes. Only instead of making him question his actions, her doubt and confusion only made him more determined than ever to make it happen.

But he'd learnt his lesson, and he wasn't about to make demands or start backing her into a corner.

'It does make sense,' she said finally.

And it did—but that didn't stop the feeling of dread rising up inside her. For how was everyone going to react to the news? Her heart gave a shiver. She might have finally come to terms with the idea of marrying Ram, but this was a reminder that their marriage was going to be conducted in public, with not only friends and family having an opinion but the media too.

'What is it?'

The unexpected gentleness of his voice caught her off guard, and quickly she looked away—for how could she explain her fears to him? Ram didn't know what it felt like to be hurt and humiliated in public, to have his failures held up and examined.

A lump filled her throat as she remembered the first time her father had let her down in front of other people. She'd been on a school trip, and he'd promised to collect her in his new car. She had been so convinced that he would pick her up, adamant that he wouldn't forget her. In the end one of the mothers had taken pity on her and driven her home, but of course the next day at school everyone had known.

She clenched her fists. And then there was what had happened with Connor. It had been bad enough splitting up with him. To do so under the microscope of her colleagues' curiosity and judgement had been excruciating.

Even thinking about it made her feel sick to her stomach.

She took a breath. 'It's just...once we tell everyone it won't be just the two of us anymore.'

'Yes—but, like I said, if we go to the party together then they'll know about us anyway.' He frowned. 'I'm confused—I thought you *wanted* to get married.'

'I do. But what if our marriage doesn't work?' The words were spilling out of her—hot, panicky, unstoppable. 'What happens then? Have you thought about that? Have you any idea what that will feel like—?'

She broke off as Ram reached out and covered her hands with his.

'Slow down, sweetheart. At this point I'm still trying

to get you down the aisle. So right now I'm not thinking about the end of our marriage.'

Gently, he uncurled her fingers.

'Is this about your father?' he said quietly.

She shook her head, then nodded. 'Sort of. Him and Connor. He was my last boyfriend. We worked together. He told a couple of people in the office some stuff about us, and then it all got out of hand.'

'What stuff? And what do you mean by "out of hand"?'

She couldn't meet his eyes. 'Some of my colleagues went to the pub after work. Connor had been drinking, and he told them—well, he told them things about us. You know...what we'd done together, private things. The next day everyone was talking about me. It was so embarrassing. Even my boss knew. People I thought were my friends stopped talking to me, I was overlooked for a promotion, and then Connor dumped me.'

'Then, quite frankly, he was an idiot,' Ram said bluntly. Cupping her chin in his hand, he forced her face up to his. 'Correction. He's an idiot and a coward, and if ever I meet him I'll tell him so—shortly after I've punched him.'

She couldn't stop herself from smiling. 'You don't need to worry about me. I can fight my own battles.'

His gaze rested on her face, and he gripped her hand so tightly she could almost feel the energy and strength passing from his body into hers.

'Not anymore. You're with me now, Nola. Your battles are my battles. And, engaged or not, nothing anyone says or does is going to change that fact, so if you don't want to say anything, then we won't.'

Nola stared at him in silence. She knew how badly he wanted to get married, but he was offering to put his needs and feelings behind hers. Neither her father nor Connor had been willing to do that.

She couldn't speak—not just because his words had

taken her by surprise, but because she was terrified she would tell him that she loved him.

Finally, she shook her head. 'I do want to announce it. But I think I should ring my mum and Anna first. I want them to know before anyone else.'

He dropped a kiss on her mouth. 'Good idea. Why don't you call them now? And then you'd better come into town with me after all, so you can choose a dress.'

It was the afternoon of the party.

Slipping her feet into a pair of beautiful dark red court shoes, Nola breathed out softly. She could hardly believe that in the next few hours she would be standing beside Ram as his fiancée. Just days ago they had been like two boxers, circling one another in the ring. But all that had changed since they'd made peace with their pasts, and she had never felt happier.

Or more satisfied.

Her face grew hot. It was crazy, but they just couldn't seem to keep their hands off one another. Even when they weren't making love they couldn't stop touching—his hand on her hip, her fingers brushing against his face. And on the odd occasion when she forced Ram to do some work he'd stay close to her, using his laptop and making phone calls from the bed while she slept.

In fact this was probably the first time they'd been apart for days, and she was missing him so badly that it felt like an actual physical ache.

Her breath felt blunt and heavy in her throat. It was an ache that was compounded by the knowledge that, even though she loved him, Ram would never love her. She lifted her chin. But he did *need* her, and he felt responsible for her and the baby—and hadn't she told him that duty was a kind of love?

But she couldn't think about that now. There were other

more pressing matters to consider and, heart pounding, she turned to face the full-length mirror. She stared almost dazedly at her reflection. It was the first time she had seen herself since having her hair and make-up done, and the transformation was astonishing. With her dark hair swept to one side, her shimmering smoky eye make-up and bright red lips, she looked poised and glamorous—not at all like the anxious young woman she was feeling inside.

Which was lucky, she thought, picking up her clutch bag with a rush of nervous excitement, because soon she would be facing Sydney's A-listers as Ram's bride-to-be.

Downstairs, Ram was flicking resignedly through the pages of a magazine. If Nola was anything like Pandora he was going to be in for a long wait. Or maybe he wasn't! Already Nola had surprised him, by being sweetly excited by the party, whereas Pandora was just too much of a perfectionist to truly enjoy *any* public appearance. She saw only the flaws, however tiny or trifling. And of course that led inevitably to the reasons for those flaws.

His mouth tightened. Or rather *the* reason.

There was a movement behind him and, turning round, he felt his heartbeat stumble.

Nola was standing at the top of the stairs, wearing a beautiful pleated yellow silk dress that seemed to both cling and flow. It perfectly complemented her gleaming dark hair and crimson lips and, watching her walk towards him, he felt his breath catch fire as she stopped in front of him. She met his gaze, her blue eyes nervous, yet resolute.

'You look like sunlight in that dress,' he said softly and, reaching out he pulled her towards him. 'You're beautiful, Nola. Truly.'

'You look pretty damn spectacular too,' she said huskily.

The classic black dinner jacket fitted his muscular frame perfectly, and although all the male guests at the party would be similarly dressed, she knew that beside Ram they would look ordinary. His beauty and charisma would ensure that.

He glanced down at himself, then up to her face, his grey gaze dark and mocking. 'I doubt anyone's going to be looking at me.'

She shivered. 'Hopefully they won't be looking at me either.'

'They can look. But they can't touch.'

His arm tightened around her waist and she saw that his eyes were no longer mocking but intent and alert. Tipping her chin up, he cupped her face in his hand.

'You're mine. And I want everyone to know that. After tonight, they will.'

She felt her heart slip sideways, like a boat breaking free from its moorings. But of course he was just getting into the mood for the evening ahead, and it was her cue to do the same.

'I'll remind you of that later, when we're dancing and I'm trampling on your toes,' she said lightly. 'You'll be begging other men to take me off your hands.'

His face shifted, the corners of his mouth curving upwards, and his arms held her close against him.

'And what will you be begging *me* to do?'

Their eyes met, and she felt her face grow warm. She hadn't begged yet, but she hadn't been far off it. Remembering how frantic she had felt last night, how desperate she had been for his touch, the frenzy of release, she swallowed.

'We shouldn't—'

He nodded. 'I know. I just wish we could fast-forward tonight.'

She could hear the longing in his voice. 'So do I. I wish it was just the two of us.'

'It will be.' He frowned. 'I know you're nervous. But I'll

be there with you, and if for some reason I'm not—well, I thought this might help. I hope you like it.'

He lifted her hand and Nola stared mutely as he slid a beautiful sapphire ring onto her finger.

A sweet, shimmering lightness began to spread through her body. 'It—It's a ring,' she stammered.

His eyes glittered. 'You sound surprised. What were you expecting?'

'Nothing. I wasn't expecting anything.'

'We're getting engaged tonight, sweetheart. There has to be a ring.'

She nodded, some of her happiness fading. He was right: there did have to be a ring.

'Of course,' she said quickly. 'And it's lovely. Really...'

'Good.' Pulling out his phone, he glanced down at the screen and grimaced. 'In that case, I guess we should be going.'

Bypassing the queue of limousines and sports cars in the drive, Ram used the service entrance to reach the house. As they walked hand in hand towards the two huge marquees on the lawn Nola shivered. There were so many guests—several hundred at least.

'Do your parents really know this many people?' she asked, gazing nervously across the lawn.

He shrugged. 'Socially, yes. Personally, I doubt they could tell you much more than their names and which clubs they belong to.'

He turned as a waiter passed by with a tray of champagne and grabbed two glasses.

'I'm not drinking.'

'I know. But just hold it—otherwise somebody will wonder why.'

He smiled down at her and she nodded dumbly. He was

so aware, so in control of everything. In that respect this evening was no different for him than any other.

If only she could let him know how different it was for *her*.

But, much as she longed to tell him that she loved him, she knew it wasn't the right time. For there was a tension about him, a remoteness, as though he was holding himself apart. It was the same tension she'd felt at lunch that day with his parents. And of course it was understandable. This was a big moment for him too.

The party passed in a blur of lights and faces. She knew nobody, but it seemed that everybody knew Ram, and so wanted to know her too. Clutching her glass of champagne, she smiled and chatted with one glamorous couple after another as Ram stood by her side, looking cool and absurdly handsome in his tuxedo as he talked in French to a tall, elderly grey-haired man who turned out to be the Canadian Ambassador.

Later, ignoring her protests, he led her onto the dance floor and, holding her against his body, he circled her between the other couples.

'Are you having fun?' he said softly into her ear.

She nodded. 'Yes. I thought people might be a bit stiff and starchy. But everyone's been really friendly.'

His eyes glittered like molten silver beneath the soft lights. 'They like you.'

She shook her head. 'They're curious about me. It's *you* they like.'

'And what about you? Do *you* like me?'

Around them the music and the laughter seemed to fade, as though someone had turned down the volume, and the urge to tell him her true feelings welled up inside her again. But she bit it down.

She smiled. 'Yes, I like you.'

'And you still want to marry me?' He met her gaze, his

grey eyes oddly serious. 'It's not too late to change your mind...'

She shook her head. 'I want to marry you.'

'Then maybe now is a good time to tell everyone that.' Glancing round, he frowned. 'We need my parents here, though. Let's go and look for them.'

His hand was warm and firm around hers as he pulled her through the dancing couples and onto the lawn, but after ten minutes of looking they still hadn't found Guy and Pandora.

Nodding curtly at the security guards, he led her into the main house.

'My mother probably wanted to change her shoes or something. I'll go and find them.'

His eyes were fixed on her face and, seeing the hesitancy there, she felt her heart tumble inside her chest.

Taking his hands in hers, she gave them a squeeze. 'Why don't I come with you? We can tell them together.'

There was a brief silence as he stared away across the empty hallway. Then his mouth twisted, and he shook his head. 'It's probably better if I go on my own.'

She nodded. 'Okay. I'll wait here.'

He kissed her gently on the lips. 'I won't be long.'

Walking swiftly through the house, Ram felt his heart start to pound.

He could hardly believe he'd managed to get this far. Bringing Nola to the party had felt like a huge step but this—this was something almost beyond his comprehension, beyond any expectations he'd had up until now.

It hardly seemed possible, but by the end of the night he would be officially engaged to Nola. Finally, with her help, he had managed to bury his past, and now he had a future he'd never imagined, with a wife and a baby—

Abruptly, his feet stilled on the thick carpet and his

thoughts skidded forward, slamming into the side of his head with a sickening thud.

His heartbeat froze. Beneath the throb of music and laughter, he could hear raised voices. Somewhere in the house a man and woman were arguing loudly.

It was Guy and his mother.

His heart began beating again and, with the blood chilling in his veins, he walked towards the doorway to his mother's room. The voices grew louder and more unrestrained as he got closer.

And then he heard his mother laugh.

Only it wasn't a happy sound.

'You just can't help yourself, can you? Couldn't you have a little self-control? Just for one night?'

'Maybe you should have a little *less*, darling. It's a party—not a military tattoo.'

Ram winced. Guy sounded belligerent. And drunk.

For a moment he hesitated. There had been so many of these arguments during his life. Surely it wouldn't matter if he walked away from this one? But as his mother started to cry he braced his shoulders and walked into the bedroom.

'Oh, here's the cavalry.' Turning, Guy squinted across the room at him. 'Don't start, Ram. You don't pay me enough to take part in that gala performance downstairs.'

'But I pay you enough to treat my mother with respect,' he said coolly. 'However, if you don't think you can manage to do that, maybe I'll just have to cut back your allowance. No point in paying for something I'm not actually getting.'

For a moment Guy held his gaze defiantly, but then finally he shrugged and looked away. 'Fine. But if you think I'm going to deal with her in this state—'

'I'll deal with my mother.' Ram forced himself to stay calm. 'Why don't you go and enjoy the party? Eat some food...have a soft drink. Oh, and Guy? I meant what I said about treating my mother with respect.'

Grumbling, still avoiding Ram's eyes, Guy stumbled from the room.

Heart aching, Ram stared across the room to where his mother sat crying on the bed. Crossing the room, he crouched down in front of her and stroked her hair away from her face.

'Don't worry about him. He's been drinking, that's all. And he's had to get up before noon to make a couple of phone calls so he's probably exhausted.'

She tried to smile through her tears. 'That must be it.'

'It is. Now, here. Take this.' Reaching into his pocket, Ram pulled out a handkerchief and held it out to her. 'It's clean. I promise.'

Taking the handkerchief, Pandora wiped her eyes carefully. 'I just wanted it to be perfect, Ramsay. For one night.'

'And it is. Everyone's having a wonderful time.'

She shook her head, pressing her hand against his. '*You're* not. You'll say you are, but I know you're not.'

Ram swallowed. Whenever his mother and Guy argued there was a pattern. She would get angry, then cry, and then she would redo her make-up and carry on as if nothing had happened. But tonight was different, for he could never remember her talking about him or his feelings.

He looked at her uncertainly. 'You're right—normally. But it's different tonight. I really am enjoying myself.'

His mother smiled.

'That's because of Nola. *She's* the difference and you're different with her. Happier.' She squeezed his hand. 'I was happy like that when I found out I was pregnant with you. I know it sounds crazy, but when that line turned blue I just sat and looked at it, and those few hours when it was just you and me were the happiest of my life. I knew then that you'd be handsome and smart and strong.'

A tear rolled down her cheek.

'I just wish I'd been stronger.'

Ram dragged a hand through his hair. He felt her pain like a weight. 'You *were* strong, Mother.'

Shaking her head, she let the tears fall. 'I should never have married Guy. I should have had the courage to stand up to your grandfather. I should have waited for someone who wanted me and loved me for who I was.'

Looking up into Ram's eyes, she twisted her lips.

'But I was scared to give all this up. So I settled for a man who was paid to marry me and a marriage that's made me feel trapped and humiliated for thirty years.'

She bit her lip.

'I'm sorry, darling, for acting so selfishly, and for blaming you.'

Ram couldn't breathe.

His mother was apologising.

For so long he'd been so angry with her. Never to her face, because despite everything—the hysterics, the way she lashed out at him when she was upset—he loved her desperately. Instead he'd deliberately, repeatedly, and publicly scorned the very idea of becoming a husband and a father.

And he'd done that to punish her. For giving him a 'father' like Guy, for making choices that had taken away *his* choices, even though she'd been little more than a child herself.

'Don't,' he whispered. 'It wasn't your fault.'

'It was. It *is*.' Reaching out, Pandora gently stroked his face. 'And I can't change the past. But I don't want you to repeat my mistakes. Promise me, Ramsay, that you won't do what Guy and I did. Relationships can't be forced. There has to be love.'

'I know.'

He spoke mechanically, but inside he felt hollow, for

he knew his mother was right. Relationships couldn't be forced—and yet wasn't that exactly what he'd done to Nola? Right from the start he'd been intent on having his own way—overriding her at every turn, kidnapping her at the airport, pressuring her to get married.

He'd even 'persuaded' her into announcing their engagement tonight, despite knowing that she was nervous about taking that step.

His breath felt like lead in his throat. Whatever he might like to believe, the facts were undeniable. Nola wasn't marrying him through choice or love. Just like his mother, for her it would be a marriage of convenience. A marriage of duty.

Gazing into his mother's tear-stained face, he made up his mind.

He'd never wanted anything more than to give his child a secure home, a future, a name. But he couldn't marry Nola.

Now all he needed to do was find her and tell her that as soon as possible.

Glancing up, Nola saw Ram striding down the stairs towards her. Her heart gave a lurch. He didn't look as if news of his engagement had been joyfully received.

Standing up, she walked towards him—but before she had a chance to speak Ram was by her side, grabbing her hand, towing her after him, his grip on her hand mirroring the vice of confusion and fear squeezing her heart.

'What did they say?' she managed as he wrenched open the door, standing to one side to let her pass through it.

'Nothing,' he said curtly. 'I didn't tell them.'

She gazed at him in confusion.

'So what are we doing?'

'There's been a change of plan. We're leaving now!'

Five minutes later they were heading down the drive towards the main road. Cars were still arriving at the house, but even though Ram must have noticed them, he said nothing.

Several times she was on the verge of asking him to stop the car and tell her what had happened. But, glancing at his set, still profile, she knew that he was either incapable of telling her or unwilling. All she could do was watch and wait.

She was so busy watching him that she didn't even notice when they drove past Stanmore. In fact it wasn't until he stopped the car in front of a large Art Deco–style house that she finally became aware of anything other than the terrible rigidity of his body.

He had switched off the engine and was out of the car and striding round to her door, yanking it open before she even had a chance to take off her seatbelt.

'This way!'

Taking her hand, he led her to the front door, unlocking and opening it in one swift movement. Inside the house, Nola watched confusedly as he marched from room to room, flicking on lights.

'What is this place?' she said finally.

'It's a property I bought a couple of years ago as an investment. I lived here when Stanmore was being renovated.'

'Oh, right...' It was all she could manage.

Maybe this was some kind of bolthole? She flinched as he yanked the curtains across the windows. If so, he must have a good reason for coming here now. But as she stared over at him anxiously she had no idea what that reason might be. All she knew was that she wanted to put her arms around him and hold him tight. Only, he looked so brittle, so taut, she feared he might shatter into a thousand pieces if she so much as touched him.

But she couldn't just stand here and pretend that everything was all right when it so clearly wasn't.

'Are you okay?' she asked hesitantly.

'Yes. I'm fine.'

He smiled—the kind of smile she would use when sharing a lift with a stranger.

'I'm sure you're tired. Why don't I show you to your bedroom?'

'But don't you want to talk?'

Watching his expression shift, she shivered. It was like watching water turn to ice.

'No, not really.'

'But what happened? Why did we leave the party?' She bit her lip. 'Why didn't you tell them about the engagement?'

He stared at her impatiently, then fixed his eyes on a point somewhere past her head.

'I'm not having this conversation now. It's late. You're pregnant—'

'And you're upset!' She stared at him in exasperation. 'Not only that, you're shutting me out.'

His eyes narrowed. 'Shutting you out? You sound like you're in a soap opera.'

She blinked, shocked not so much by his words but by the sneer in his voice.

'Maybe that's because you've behaving like a character in a soap opera. Dragging me from the party. Refusing to talk to me.'

'And what exactly do you think talking about it will achieve?'

'I don't know.' Her breath felt tight inside her chest. 'But I don't think ignoring whatever it is can be the solution.'

He gave a short, bitter laugh. 'You've changed your tune. Not so long ago you managed to ignore me for three months without much problem.'

Nola felt her whole body tighten with shock and pain. Then, almost in the same moment, she knew he was lashing out at her because he was upset, and even though his words hurt her she cared more about *his* pain than her own.

'And I was wrong.'

'So maybe in three months I'll think I was wrong about this. But somehow I don't think so.'

She gritted her teeth. 'So that's it? You just want me to shut up and go to bed?'

His face hardened. 'No, what I want is for you to stop nagging me, like the wife you've clearly never wanted to be.'

'I *do* want to be your wife.' The injustice of his words felt like a slap. 'And I'm not nagging. I'm trying to have a conversation.'

He shook his head. 'This isn't a conversation. It's an interrogation.'

'Then *talk* to me.'

His jaw tightened. 'Fine. I was going to wait until the morning, but if you can't or won't wait, we'll do it now.'

'Do what?'

'Break up. Call it off.' His voice was colder and harder than his gaze. 'Whatever one does to end an engagement.'

Watching the colour drain from her face, he felt sick. But knowing that he could hurt her so easily only made him more determined to finish it there and then—for what was the alternative? That she spent the next thirty years trapped with him in a loveless marriage?

A marriage that would force their child to endure the same dark legacy as him.

No, that wasn't going to happen. His child deserved more than to be a witness to his parents' unhappy marriage. And Nola deserved more than him.

Across the room Nola took a breath, tried to focus, to make sense of what Ram had just said.

'I don't understand,' she said finally.

But then, staring at him, she did—for the man who had held her in his arms and made love to her so tenderly had been replaced by a stranger with blank, hostile eyes.

'You want to end our engagement? But you were going to announce it tonight...'

He shrugged. 'And now I'm not.'

But I love you, she thought, her heart banging against her ribcage as though it was trying to speak for itself. Only it was clear that Ram had no use for her love, for any kind of love.

'Why?' she whispered. 'Why are you doing this?'

'I've changed my mind. All this—us, marriage, becoming a father—it's not what I want.'

'But you said that children need to know where they come from. That they need to belong.' His words tasted like ash in her mouth.

His gaze locked onto hers. 'Don't look so surprised, Nola. You said yourself I'm not cut out to be a hands-on daddy. And you're right. I'm not. What was it you said? No father is better than a bad father. Well, you were right. You'll do a far better job on your own than with me messing up your life and our child's life. But you don't need to worry. I fully intend to take care of you and the baby financially.'

Nola stared at him in silence.

He was talking in the same voice he used for board meetings. In fact he might just as easily have been discussing an upcoming software project instead of his child.

Her heart was beating too fast. Misery and anger were tangling inside her chest.

'Is that what you think matters?' she asked, reining in her temper.

He sighed. 'Try not to let sentiment get in the way of

reason. Everything that baby needs is going to cost money so, yes, I think it *does* matter.'

'Not everything,' she said stubbornly. 'Children need love, consistency, patience and guidance, and all those are free.'

His mouth curled. 'Tell that to a divorce lawyer.'

Reaching into his pocket, he pulled out his car keys.

'There's no point in discussing this now. You can stay here, and I'll call my lawyers in the morning. I'll get them to draw up the paperwork and they can transfer this house into your name tomorrow.'

'What?' She stared at him, struggling to breathe.

'I'll work out a draft financial settlement at the same time. As soon as that's finalised we can put all this behind us and get back to our lives.'

Her skin felt cold, but she was burning up inside.

So was that it? Everything she had been through, that *they* had been through, had been for this? For him to pay her off. Just like her father had done with his ostentatious but impersonal presents.

Anger pounded through her. And, just like those presents, giving her this house and an allowance were for *his* benefit, not hers. He was offering them as a means to assuage his conscience and rectify the mistake he clearly believed he'd made by getting her pregnant.

'I don't want your house or your money,' she said stiffly.

He frowned. 'Please don't waste my time, or yours, making meaningless remarks like that. You're going to need—'

She shook her head. 'No, you don't get to offer me money. Aside from my salary, I've never asked for or expected any money from you, and nothing's changed.'

His eyes narrowed. 'Give it time.'

She felt sick—a sickness that was worse than anything she'd felt in those early months of pregnancy. For that nausea had been caused by the child growing inside her, a child she loved without question, even when she felt scared and alone.

Now, though, she felt sick at her own stupidity.

Ignoring all her instincts, she had let herself have hope, let herself trust him. Not just trust him—but love him too.

And here was the proof that she'd been wrong all along.

Ram was just like her father, for when it came to sacrificing himself for his family he couldn't do it.

He was weak and selfish and he was not fit to be a father to her child.

Wide-eyed, suddenly breathless with anger, Nola stepped forward, her fingers curling into fists.

'Get out! You can keep your stupid financial settlements and your paperwork. As of this moment I never want to see or speak to you again, Ramsay Walker. Now, get out!'

He stared at her in silence, then, tossing the house keys onto one of the tables, he turned and walked swiftly across the room.

The door slammed and moments later she heard his car start, the engine roaring in the silence of the night and then swiftly fading away until the only sound was her ragged breathing.

It was then that she realised she was still wearing his ring. Unclenching her fingers, she gazed down at the sapphire, thinking how beautiful it was, and yet how sad.

And then her legs seemed to give way beneath her and, sliding down against the wall, she began to sob.

CHAPTER TEN

FINALLY IT WAS time to stop crying.

Forcing herself to stand up, Nola walked into the kitchen and splashed her face with cold water. Her mascara had run, and she wiped it carefully away with her fingertips. But as she tried to steady her breathing she knew it would be a long time—and take a lot more than water—to wash away Ram's words or that look on his face.

Her chest tightened, and suddenly the floor seemed to be moving. She gripped the edge of the sink.

Ram giving up like that had been so shocking—brutal, and cruel.

Like a bomb exploding.

And she still didn't really understand what had happened to make him change his mind—not just about the engagement but about everything. For her, cocooned in her newly realised love, it had begun to feel as though finally there was a future for them.

She felt anger scrape over her skin.

But what use was love to a man like Ram?

A man who measured his feelings in monthly maintenance payments?

Steadying herself, she lifted her shoulders. She wasn't going to fall apart. For what had she really lost?

Even before she'd thrown him out she had felt as though the Ram she loved had already left. He'd been so remote, so cold, so ruthless. Changing his mind, her life, her future and their child's future without batting an eyelid, then offering her money as some kind of consolation prize.

Her throat tightened, and suddenly she was on the verge of tears again.

And now he was gone.

And she knew that she would never see him again.

Somewhere in the house a clock struck two, and she felt suddenly so tired and drained that standing was no longer an option. There were several sofas in the living room, but she knew that if she sat down she would never get up again, and lying on a sofa in a party dress seemed like the worst kind of defeat. If she was going to sleep, she was going to do it in a bed.

Slipping off her shoes, she walked wearily upstairs. There was no shortage of bedrooms—she counted at least seven—but as she opened one door after another she began to feel like Goldilocks. Each room was beautiful, but the beds were all too huge, too empty for just her on her own.

Except that she wasn't on her own, she thought defiantly, stroking the curve of her stomach with her hand. Nor was she going to lie there worrying about the future. Her mother had more or less brought her up on her own and, unlike her mother, *she* was financially independent. So, with or without Ram, she was going to survive this *and* flourish.

Getting undressed seemed like too much of an effort, though, and, stifling a yawn, she crawled onto the next bed and slid beneath the duvet.

She didn't remember falling asleep, but when she opened her eyes she felt sure that she must have dozed off only for a couple of minutes. But one glance at the clock on the bedside table told her that she had been asleep for two hours.

Her skin felt tight from all the crying, and her head was pounding—probably from all the crying too. Feeling a sudden terrible thirst, she sat up and wriggled out from under the duvet.

The house was silent and still, but she had left some of the lights on during her search for a bedroom. Squinting against the brightness, she made her way towards the stairs. It was dark in the living room, but her head was still so muddied with sleep that it was only as she began to grope for a light switch that she remembered she had also left the lights on downstairs.

So why were they off now?

In the time it took for her heart to start beating again she had already imagined several nightmare crazed intruder scenarios—and then something, or someone, moved in the darkness and her whole body seemed to turn to lead.

'It's okay...it's just me.'

A lamp flared in the corner of the room, but she didn't need it to know that it was Ram sitting in one of the armchairs. She would recognise that voice anywhere—even in darkness. And even had he lost his voice she would still have known him, for she had traced the pure, straight line of his jaw with her fingers. Touched those firm, curving lips with her mouth.

She felt a sudden sharp stab of desire, remembering the way his body had moved against hers. Remembering too how much she'd loved him. How much she still loved him. But with loving came feelings, and she wasn't going to let herself feel anything for this man anymore, or give him yet another chance to hurt her.

'How did you get in?' she asked stiffly.

'I have a spare key.'

Her heart began to race with anger, for his words had reminded her of the promise he'd made only a few hours ago. Not to love her and his child, but to take care of them financially, provide a fitting house and lifestyle.

Glancing round, she spotted the keys he'd left behind earlier, and with hands that shook slightly she picked them up.

'Here, you can have these too.' She tossed them to him. 'Since I'm not planning on staying here I won't be needing them. In fact…' She paused, tugging at the ring on her finger. 'I won't be needing this either.'

'Nola, please—don't do that.' He struggled to his feet, his mouth twisting.

'Don't do *what*, Ramsay?' She stared at him, a cloud of disbelief and anger swirling inside her. 'Why are you even here? I told you I never wanted to see you again.'

'I know. But you also said that ignoring this wasn't the solution.'

His voice was hoarse, not at all like his usual smooth drawl, but she was too strung out to notice the difference.

'Well, I was wrong. Like I was wrong to give you a chance. And wrong to think that you'd changed, that you could change.' Meeting his gaze, she said quickly, 'I know I've made a lot of mistakes, but I'm not about to repeat them by wasting any more of my time on you, so I'd like you to leave now.'

He sucked in a breath, but didn't move. 'I can't do that. I know you're angry, but I'm not leaving until you've listened to me.'

Her eyes widened, the pulse jerking in her throat. She didn't want to listen to anything he had to say, but she could tell by the set of his shoulders that he had meant what he said. He was just going to stand there and wait—stand there and wait for her to grow tired of fighting him and give in. Just as she always did, she thought angrily.

Blood was beating in her ears.

Taking a step backwards, she folded her arms protectively around her waist and looked at him coldly. 'Then say whatever it is and then I want you to leave.'

Ram stared at her in silence.

Her face was pale and shadowed. She was still wearing her dress from last night, and he knew that she must have slept in it, for it was impossibly crumpled now. But he didn't think she had ever looked more beautiful, or desirable, or determined.

Or that he had ever loved her more.

He stood frozen, his body still with shock. But inside the truth tugged him down and held him fast, like an anchor digging into the seabed.

He loved her.

He hadn't planned to. Or wanted to. But he knew unquestioningly that it was true.

And, crazy though it sounded, he knew it was the reason he'd broken up with her.

He'd told himself—told her—that he had never wanted to marry or have children. That he wasn't a good bet. That he would only ruin everything. And all of that had been true.

But it wasn't the whole truth.

He loved her, and in loving her he couldn't force her into a marriage of convenience. For, even though she had agreed to be his wife, he knew that she didn't love him. And he'd seen with his own eyes the damage and misery that kind of relationship could cause. He only had to look at his mother or look in the mirror for proof.

No, he didn't wanted to trap her—only he couldn't bear a life without Nola, a life without his child.

But how he could salvage this?

He took a deep breath. 'I know I've messed up. And I know you don't have any reason to listen to me, let alone forgive me, but I want a second chance. I want us to try again.'

For a moment she couldn't understand what he was saying, for it made no sense. Only a couple of hours ago he had said that he wanted to break up with her, to go back to his old life, and yet now he was here, asking her for a second chance.

But even as her brain raged against the inconsistency of his words her heart was responding to the desperation in his voice.

Only she couldn't do this again. Couldn't start to believe, to hope.

Ignoring the ache in her chest, she shook her head. '*You* gave up on *me*. And on our baby. Or have you forgotten that you were supposed to announce our engagement last night—?' She broke off, her voice catching in her throat as pain split her in two.

He took a step towards her, and for the first time it occurred to her that he looked as desperate as he sounded. There were shadows under his eyes and he was trembling all over.

'I haven't forgotten, and I'm sorry—'

'You're *sorry*!'

She shook her head. Did he really think that saying sorry was somehow going to make everything right again? If so, she had been right to throw him out.

'Well, don't be—I'm not. You know what? I'm *glad* you broke it off, because there's something wrong with you. Something that means that every time we get to a place of calm and understanding you have to smash it all to pieces. And I can't—I don't want to live like that.'

'I know, and I don't want to live like that either.'

He sounded so wretched. But why should she care? In fact she wasn't going to care, she told herself.

Only it was so hard, for despite her righteous anger she still loved him. But thankfully he would never know that.

'Then it's lucky for both of us that we don't have to,' she said quickly. 'As soon as I can get a flight back to Scotland I'm going home.'

She watched as he took a deep breath, and the pain in his eyes tugged at an ache inside her, so that suddenly she could hardly bear looking at his stricken face.

'But this is your home...'

She shook her head. 'It's *not* my home. It's a pay-off. A way for you to make yourself feel better. I don't want it.'

Ram stared at her in silence. The blood was roaring in his ears.

He was losing her. He was losing her.

The words echoed inside his head and he could hardly speak through the grief rising up in his throat. 'But I want you. And I want to marry you.'

Her heart began to beat faster. It was so tempting to give in, for she knew that right now he believed what he was saying. But now was just a moment in time: it wouldn't last for ever. And she was done with living in the moment.

Slowly she shook her head. 'Only because you can't have me. I don't know *what* you want, Ram. But I do know that you can't just break up with me and then two hours later come and tell me that you want me back and expect everything to be okay again. Maybe if this was a film we could kiss, and then the credits would roll, and everyone in the cinema would go home happy. But we're *not* in a film. This is real life, and it doesn't work like that.'

Tears filled her eyes.

'You hurt me, Ram...' she whispered.

'*I know.*'

The pain in his voice shocked her.

'I wish I could go back and change what I did and what I said. I panicked. When I went to find my mother she told me not to make the same mistake that she had. That relationships can't be forced. That they need love. That's why I couldn't go through with it.'

She nodded. 'Because you don't love me—I know,' she said dully.

'No!' He let out a ragged breath. 'I broke up with you because I *do* love you, Nola, and I didn't want to trap you in a marriage that you didn't want. That you never wanted.'

He took a step towards her, his hands gripping her arms, his eyes glittering not with tears but with passion.

'I *love* you, and that's why I want to marry you. Not out of duty, or because I want the baby to have my name. But I know you don't love me, and I've hurt you so much already. Only I couldn't just walk away. I tried, but I couldn't do it. That's why I came back—'

He stopped. There were tears in her eyes.

Only she was smiling.

'You love me? *You love me?*'

He stared at her uncertainly, his eyes burning, wishing there was another way to tell her that—to make her believe. But even before he'd started to nod she was pressing her hand against her mouth, as though that would somehow stop the tears spilling from her eyes.

'You're so smart, Ram. Easily the smartest person I've ever met. But you're also the stupidest. *Why* do think I agreed to marry you?'

'I don't know...' he whispered.

'Because I love you, of course.'

Gazing up into his face, Nola felt her heart almost stop beating as she saw that he too was crying.

'Why would you ever love me?'

His voice broke apart and she felt the crack inside her deepen as his mouth twisted in pain.

'How could you love me? After everything I've said and done? After how I've behaved?'

'I don't know.' She bit her lip. 'I didn't want to. And it scares me that I do. But I can't help it. I love you.' Her mouth trembled. 'I love you and I still want to marry you.'

His hands tightened around her arms, his eyes searching her face. 'Are you sure? I don't want to trap you. I don't want to be that kind of man—that kind of husband, that kind of father.'

Her heart began to beat faster. 'You're not. Not anymore. I don't think you ever were.'

Breathing out unsteadily, he pulled her close, smoothing the tears away from her face. 'Your parents married because it was the next step,' he said slowly. 'My mother married Guy out of desperation. They didn't think about what they were doing…it just happened. But we're different. We've fought to be together, and our marriage is going to work just fine.'

She breathed out shakily. 'How do you know?'

His eyes softened. 'Because you know me,' he said simply. 'You know everything about me—the good and the bad. And you still love me.'

Her lip trembled. 'Yes, I do.'

'It scares me, you knowing me like that.' He grimaced. 'But I trust you, and I love you, and I always will.'

Gently, he uncurled her arms from around her body, and as one they stepped towards each other.

Burying her face against his chest, Nola sighed with relief as Ram pulled her close.

'I love you, Nola.'

She lifted her head. 'I love you too.'

For several minutes they held each other in silence, neither wanting to let go of the other, to let go of what they had come so close to losing.

Finally Ram shifted backwards. 'Do you think it's too late to tell my mother?'

Tracing the curve of his mouth with her fingers, she laughed. 'I think it might be better for us to get some sleep first. Besides, what's a couple of hours when we have the rest of our lives together?'

'The rest of our lives together…' He repeated it softly, and then laying one hand across the swell of her stomach, he pulled her closer still, so that he and Nola and the baby were all connected. 'That's a hell of a future,' he whispered, kissing her gently on the forehead.

Looking up into his handsome face, Nola felt her heart swell with happiness. All the hardness and anger had gone and there was only hope and love in his grey eyes.

'Although, from where I'm standing, the present looks pretty damn good too.'

She bit her lip, her mouth curling up at the corners. 'I think it would look even better lying down.'

'My thoughts exactly,' he murmured, and with his heart beating with love and joy he scooped her up into his arms and carried her towards the stairs.

EPILOGUE

STEPPING UNDER THE shower head, Nola switched on the water and closed her eyes. If she was lucky, she might actually get to wash her hair today. Yesterday Evie, who was four months old today, had woken just as she'd stepped under the water. Not that she really minded. Her tiny daughter was the best thing in her life. The joint best thing, she amended silently.

Tipping her face up to meet the hot spray, she smiled as she thought back to the day of Evie's arrival. Ram had not only turned into a hands-on daddy, he'd practically taken over the entire labour ward.

It had been a small and rare reminder of the old work-hard, play-hard Ram, for nowadays she and Evie were the focus of his passion and devotion. He still loved his job, and the launch had been the most successful in the company's history—but he was happiest when he was at home.

And she was happy too. How could she not be?

She had a handsome, loving husband, a job working with her best friend, and a baby she adored.

Evie was beautiful, a perfect blend of both her parents. She'd inherited her pale skin and loose dark curls from Nola, but she had her father's grey eyes—a fact which, endearingly, Ram pointed out to everyone.

Her skin prickled as the fragrant warm air around her seemed to shift sideways, and then she gasped, her stomach tightening as two warm hands slid around her waist.

'Hi!'

Ram kissed her softly on the neck and, breathing out unsteadily, she leaned back against his warm naked body.

'Hey! That was quick.'

'I haven't done anything yet.'

The teasing note in his voice matched the light, almost tormenting touch of his fingers as they drifted casually over her flat stomach. Turning, she nipped him on the arm, softening it to a kiss as he pulled her closer.

'I meant the interview. I thought you were seeing that super-important woman from the news network?'

Tugging her round to face him, he looked down into her eyes, his mouth curving upwards into one of those sexy smiles she knew would always take her breath away.

'I talked really fast. Besides, I have two far more important women right here!'

'And in about half an hour you'll have three.' She pulled away slightly and smiled up at him. 'Pandora rang. She went shopping yesterday, and she wants to drop off a few things for Evie.'

Ram groaned. 'I presume she went shopping overseas? There can't be anything left in Australia for her to buy.'

Since the night of her anniversary party Pandora had been working hard to rebuild her relationship with her son, and Nola knew that, despite joking about her shopping habits, Ram was touched by his mother's efforts to make amends. She had separated from Guy, and now that they were no longer forced to live together the two of them had begun to enjoy each other's company as friends.

Nola laughed. 'You can talk. Every time you go out of the door you come back with something for me or Evie.'

'She deserves it for being so adorable,' Ram said softly as she glanced down at the beautiful diamond ring he'd given her when Evie was born. 'And you deserve it for giving me such a beautiful daughter.'

And for giving him a life, and a future filled with love.

Gently he ran his hand over her stomach. 'I miss your bump. I feel like I'd just got used to it, and then she was here. Not that I'm complaining.' His eyes softened. 'I can't imagine my life without her *or* you.'

Nola felt a pang of guilt. She knew how much he regretted not being there for the early stages of her pregnancy, for they had no secrets from one another now. That was one of the lessons they'd learnt from their past—to be open with one another.

'I miss it too. But there'll be other bumps.'

'Is that what you want?'

His face had gentled, and she loved him for it, because now everything was about what they *both* wanted.

'It is. It all happened so quickly last time.'

She hesitated, and then, leaning closer, ran her hand slowly over his stomach, her heart stumbling against her ribs as his skin twitched beneath her fingers.

His eyes narrowed, and a curl of heat rose up inside her as he pulled her against his smooth golden body.

'I'm happy to go slowly. On one condition.'

The roughness in his voice made her blood tingle.

'And what's that,' she asked softly.

'That we start right now.'

And, tipping her mouth up to his, he kissed her hungrily.

* * * * *

JOIN THE MILLS & BOON BOOKCLUB

* **FREE** delivery direct to your door
* **EXCLUSIVE** offers every month
* **EXCITING** rewards programme

50% OFF YOUR FIRST PARCEL

Join today at
Millsandboon.co.uk/Bookclub

MILLS & BOON
MODERN
Power and Passion

Prepare to be swept off your feet by sophisticated, sexy and seductive heroes, in some of the world's most glamourous and romantic locations, where power and passion collide.

ght Modern stories published every month, find them all at:

millsandboon.co.uk/Modern

LET'S TALK
Romance

For exclusive extracts, competitions
and special offers, find us online:

- facebook.com/millsandboon
- @MillsandBoon
- @MillsandBoonUK

Get in touch on 01413 063232

For all the latest titles coming soon, visit
millsandboon.co.uk/nextmonth

WANT EVEN MORE
ROMANCE?
SUBSCRIBE AND SAVE TODAY!

'Mills & Boon books, the perfect way to escape for an hour or so.'

MISS W. DYER

'Excellent service, promptly delivered and very good subscription choices.'

MISS A. PEARSON

'You get fantastic special offers and the chance to get books before they hit the shops.'

MRS V. HALL

Visit millsandboon.co.uk/Subscribe and save on brand new books.

MILLS & BOON

THE HEART OF ROMANCE

A ROMANCE FOR EVERY READER

MODERN

Prepare to be swept off your feet by sophisticated, sexy and seductive heroes, in some of the world's most glamourous and romantic locations, where power and passion collide.

HISTORICAL

Escape with historical heroes from time gone by. Whether your passion is for wicked Regency Rakes, muscled Vikings or rugged Highlanders, awaken the romance of the past.

MEDICAL

Set your pulse racing with dedicated, delectable doctors in the high-pressure world of medicine, where emotions run high and passion, comfort and love are the best medicine.

True Love

Celebrate true love with tender stories of heartfelt romance, from the rush of falling in love to the joy a new baby can bring, and a focus on the emotional heart of a relationship.

Desire

Indulge in secrets and scandal, intense drama and plenty of sizzling hot action with powerful and passionate heroes who have it all: wealth, status, good looks…everything but the right woman.

HEROES

Experience all the excitement of a gripping thriller, with an intense romance at its heart. Resourceful, true-to-life women and strong, fearless men face danger and desire - a killer combination!

To see which titles are coming soon, please visit

millsandboon.co.uk/nextmonth